Barbara Roddam trained as a s[...] BBC and after raising her family [...] a producer. She has studied at [...] Astrology and enjoys researchin[...] mythology and New Age philosophy.

Hilary Boyd trained as a nurse at Great Ormond Street Hospital, then as a marriage guidance counsellor and became a writer in her thirties. She has published six non-fiction books and wrote a weekly mind/body/spirit column for the *Express* newspaper. Her first novel, *Thursdays in the Park*, was published by Quercus in 2011 and her second, *Tangled Lives*, in 2012.

This is the first book they have written together.

Solstice

Barbara Roddam

Hilary Boyd

unbound

This edition first published in 2013

Unbound
4–7 Manchester Street, Marylebone, London, W1U 2AE
www.unbound.co.uk

Text design and typesetting by Palindrome
Cover design by Mark Ecob

A CIP record for this book
is available from the British Library

ISBN 978-1-908717-80-1

Printed in England by Clays Ltd, Bungay, Suffolk

Prologue

10,500 BC: Atlantis

Jude watched in despair as the black waters crept closer and closer to the small patch of dry land where the Seven were huddled. The gale force winds tore at his cloak and threatened to hurl them all into the raging seas. Jagged bolts of lightning briefly illuminated the drowning city of Atlantis before they were plunged once more into darkness. They were looking to him for guidance, for protection. But he knew no one could save them now.

This was all his fault. His foolish infatuation for Lilith, the High Priestess, and his misplaced loyalty to his ruthless half-brother, Brandon, had wrecked the vital ceremony to stabilise the earth and triggered this mayhem. The planet was in terrible danger.

Lilith must have known what he was thinking. She raised her voice against the roar of the tempest.

'There's still hope! We can't save ourselves, or Atlantis, but we did enough at the ceremony to protect the earth . . . for now.'

'But how long will it last?' Jude shook his head. 'The portal won't hold for ever.'

'We will come back. We must complete the ceremony.'

Lilith raised her arms as if to defy the destructive elements crashing around them. She addressed each of the six upturned faces.

'Swear that you will return to complete our sacred task, however many lifetimes it may take.'

One by one they responded.

'So be it.'

'But how shall we ever find each other again?' Maya, the keeper of the crystal, shouted above the howling wind.

Lilith smiled, serene in her authority.

'Trust that I shall find you . . . when the time is right.'

◉◉

Now, after countless lifetimes, they have one last chance to save the world.

It's 2012 – and they're back.

Part I

1

21 June 2012: Summer solstice, Stonehenge

The image came out of nowhere, startling and intense. One minute she was shivering in the cold half-light of the foggy June dawn, the next she was surrounded by dazzling light.

Rhiannon closed her eyes against the blinding rays and heard a voice in her head shouting *Don't . . . don't touch her!* The scream left her trembling with shock, reaching out blindly for support. Her hand met stone, solid and rough to the touch. This calmed her. Slowly, reluctantly, she opened her eyes.

The vast stone pillars of Stonehenge loomed dark and threatening against the feeble light struggling over the horizon. What had just happened? Other solstice watchers stood nearby, gazing in silence towards where the sun should be, their efforts hampered by the sinister yellow fog swirling around them. She looked at their still faces, but there was no sign they'd heard or seen anything strange.

Rhiannon breathed deeply, willing her racing heartbeat to return to normal. There had to be a rational explanation. She didn't believe in visions or the supernatural, horoscopes were for losers. She liked hard facts – that's what made her a good documentary-maker. Maybe research for her current film was getting to her: signs and portents, ancient wisdom, the Mayan calendar that ended on the next winter solstice, 21 December 2012, the ever-increasing fires and floods, earthquakes, volcanoes, hurricanes . . . this fog. The more she found out, the more she felt that time was running out for the world. Something catastrophic was about to happen.

She closed her eyes and for a moment the image flared again as if imprinted on her retina: seven figures standing in a circle, columns of white crystal shimmering in the light of a brilliant sun. One figure moved to the centre of the circle, raising her arms towards the light. Rhiannon tensed. Again, she heard herself pleading *Don't touch her, no, don't . . . !* And gasped in fright as a hand clutched her arm.

She spun round. There seemed to be no dawn. If anything it was getting darker in the fog. There was no sign of the seven figures, only a man who stepped back quickly when he saw her eyes flash with anger.

'Sorry . . . sorry. I didn't mean to frighten you. You seem upset, is something wrong?'

Rhiannon was torn between embarrassment and the need for human contact.

'I thought I saw people standing over there,' she said, pointing to the deserted area in the centre of the stone circle.

The man shrugged. 'Not surprising in this fog . . . it makes everything seem surreal.'

'No, I heard a scream. I definitely heard a scream.'

'That was you.' The man was grinning. 'People think they see things here, fog or no fog – all part of the Stonehenge experience.'

'Me? I screamed?' Had she? She shook herself. The man's attitude rankled. 'You think I'm being hysterical, don't you? Just a woman thing.'

'I didn't say that, but now you mention it . . .' The man grinned again and despite herself she smiled back. Even in the eerie light she could see that this was a very attractive man; older than her, maybe late thirties, tall with a thin, tanned face, shoulder-length dark hair and eyes that would probably be fierce if they weren't smiling.

He turned to go. 'Well, if you're OK . . .'

'I'm fine . . . thanks.'

'No problem, Rhiannon.'

She stared after him, amazed. 'Wait . . . you called me Rhiannon! How the hell do you know my name?'

The man looked nonplussed. 'Did I? Um . . . not sure.' He

4

held his hand out. 'By the way, I'm Michael. Michael Wolf.'

Not usually lost for words, she briefly clasped his outstretched hand, then watched as he turned away to join a small group nearby. She saw him murmur into the ear of the tall woman beside him, catching a glimpse of a proud, beautiful face and the glitter of jewels, before the woman strode off into the murk, linking her arm possessively through Michael's as she went. Rhiannon took one last look around the stone circle, now only partly visible as the fog grew denser. Nothing happened here, nothing at all, she told herself. But she was unable to control a shiver of unease. Time to go home.

2

'Can I come back?' Michael asked Lily as they drew level with the car. Lily hesitated, her piercing blue eyes flitting quickly from Michael to the stooped older man with them.

'No,' she answered, turning away. Michael, shocked at her bluntness, was about to remonstrate, but he caught Gabe's level gaze.

'Bye then,' he muttered moodily, then loped off towards his bike, a beat-up Ducati, red and black and dangerous-looking, which was propped at the edge of the visitors' car park. He found himself searching for the girl called Rhiannon in the crowd making their way home.

'You know you can't.' Gabe waited for Lily to start the car. He felt her bristle, the bracelets on her arm rattling ominously.

She started the engine and they eased out into the stream of cars making their way to the exit.

'I'm not jealous, but you know Michael's not for you.' Gabe held his hands in front of him rubbing one against the other, like the scraping of parchment.

Lily wasn't listening, she was watching Michael's figure as he disappeared into the mist, using all her concentration to tune into his thoughts. For a moment there was nothing, then she saw her in her mind's eye, as clear as if she were standing in front of her. The girl. The one Michael had been talking to at the Henge. *It's her*, she thought. *I knew it!*

'This is our last chance,' Gabe was saying. 'It's too important to mess up.'

'You think I don't know that?' Lily exploded beside him. 'You really think I'd risk the same thing happening with Michael as happened with Jude? You should give me more credit after all these interminable lifetimes together.' Her bracelets shook angrily.

'I do,' Gabe's voice was weary; this was not a new argument. 'But if Jude had not been in love with you, he'd never have done what he did and the world wouldn't be in this mess.'

There was silence for a minute, while each of them replayed for the millionth time the long-ago sequence of events which had led them to this place, this time, this life. Lily raised a hand to sweep her long dark hair from her face, and Gabe, glancing across, saw tears glinting in the light from the oncoming cars.

'If Michael got involved . . .' Gabe's tone was apologetic.

'Michael's not Jude,' Lily snapped, then her expression softened when she saw the anxiety on Gabe's face.

'I think we made a mistake bringing Michael here,' she continued in a softer tone. 'I thought it might trigger memories for him but it's obviously too dangerous. And then the girl turning up . . .'

'What girl?' Gabe turned towards her.

'Didn't you see her? Rhiannon was there. They even spoke to each other.'

'But that's good, isn't it?'

Lily shook her head impatiently.

'Good that the seven of us are getting close again. But she's not ready yet. And we may have put her in danger. If someone was watching . . .'

Gabe nodded slowly.

'You think he's back, don't you?'

'I'm sure of it. How else can you explain what's happening to the world. These aren't just natural disasters. There's a pattern emerging, one we've seen before. It's Atlantis all over again.'

Rhiannon sat motionless behind the wheel of her car. The car park had long since emptied, but she was upset and didn't yet trust herself to face the road.

To calm herself, she began to set the satnav on the dashboard. Practical tasks always calmed her. But she found nothing helped when she was woken, alone in her flat in the Archway, by the strange and unsettling visions that had haunted her sleep recently. At times she thought she must be going mad. This morning was another example – something she couldn't explain, but which at the same time felt intensely familiar to her.

And what was she doing here anyway? She should have been well on the way to London by now but accidents and diversions caused by the fog had forced her off the main roads and the satnav had led her closer and closer to Stonehenge. And then the thought had just popped into her mind: *Watch the sun rise on the summer solstice. It's important.*

But she hadn't seen it after all. The weird weather had ruined the magical moment. So much for intuition.

She leaned forward and stared at her reflection in the rear-view mirror. Her reflection stared solemnly back, her blue eyes huge in her pale finely boned face. As she looked, another face seemed to float across her reflection. The hair was long and loose, not her short, feathery cut, but the same shade of chestnut brown, and the girl's features slid neatly to fit over Rhiannon's, like a superimposed blueprint. Rhiannon started and looked around her, but the car was eerily silent. *I am going mad*, she thought, and quickly turned back to the satnav. She set it three or four times for her friend Lauren's flat in Peckham – she'd promised to pick Lauren up and take her into work on her way back – but the screen kept breaking up, crackling and fuzzing like a TV on the blink. She glanced out of the window and was suddenly aware of the howling of the wind. It had begun to pour with rain. She looked back at the half-shadowed circle of stones and shuddered.

'Pull yourself together,' she told herself firmly, hearing echoes of her tough Welsh foster-mother. She clicked on the CD player, turning it up full volume, forcing herself to sing along: 'Love hurts, love scars . . .'

As she drew out of the car park, her mobile rang.

'How's it going?' her friend asked sleepily. 'Just checking you're picking me up later.'

'Lauren . . . hi. God, I'm glad to hear you.'

'What's up? You sound freaked.'

'Nothing . . . just the satnav's kaput and there's a storm brewing. It's spooky here.'

'Where are you?'

'Stonehenge. I'm just . . .'

The phone suddenly crackled and went dead as an impressive bolt of lightning lit up the sky, accompanied a second later, directly overhead, by the menacing growl of thunder. Rhiannon hurled the useless mobile onto the seat next to her and drove off in what she hoped was the right direction, suddenly desperate to be away from the shadow of the stones.

3

Aunt Val's cottage, Marbury, Wiltshire

Michael got lost in the fog on the way home to his aunt's house. He was also distracted by his unrequited desire for Lily, and his strange meeting with Rhiannon. How had he known her name? Who was she?

Michael had been at Aunt Val's for three weeks now. His world had been turned on its head since the panic attacks. It was the terrible fear that he was dying, repeated over and over so that in the end, even though ragged and desperate for sleep, he hardly dared close his eyes.

It was the screams that had tipped him. Screams that accompanied the years looking down a lens at the most horrible moments inflicted on humankind, war zones from Bosnia to Rwanda to Afghanistan, Iraq – it didn't matter where.

'How do you do it?' was the sharp response to his photographs. They expected Michael to save them, all those tortured subjects, not just record them in their agonies. But up to six months ago he hadn't heard the screams, had never contemplated saving anyone. To him the image was the thing, the record, the moment in history. He'd always thought that if he'd had too much imagination he would have been useless, like a surgeon taking out a human heart to mend; the enormity would have paralysed him from doing his job.

Then things changed. He heard the screams. Even safe in his foreigner's hotel room, the screaming went on, like a tape on an endless loop. Nothing he did blotted out the agony. And the panic attacks began. He might be driving, eating, fiddling with his state-of-the-art Nikon camera, and his whole body would begin to shake, heart pounding, with a horrifying fear that felt as if it could only end in death. Three months lying on a holiday beach hadn't worked. It was only in the last weeks, under the tender care of his batty aunt – his father's older sister – that the fear had begun to fade a little. He screeched onto the gravel, his bike's headlights swung across Aunt Val's cottage, lighting up her pale, anxious face in the downstairs window. As soon as she saw him she wrenched the door open against the storm.

'Gracious, where have you been? I was worried sick with you driving in that dreadful fog,' she yelled, bustling him into the tiny, low-ceilinged cottage. 'Look at the state of you!' she shook her head at her nephew, who stood dripping on the flagstones, his bike leathers drenched, his dark hair wild from his helmet.

'I got lost, you couldn't see a hand in front of your face,' Michael grinned. 'Then the rain got rid of the fog, but what a storm . . . maybe those dodgy Stonehenge druids pissed off the gods.'

'Don't be ridiculous,' Aunt Val declared from the depths of her Christian soul. 'Now get that . . . that whatever you call it off at once, you'll catch your death.' She prodded the sodden leather disapprovingly.

By the time Michael had changed out of his wet clothes, Aunt Val had set toast and tea by the glowing fire.

'Shall I make you an egg?'

Michael shook his head, 'No thanks, this is great. Lily sent her regards,' he said, munching into a thick slice of buttery toast.

'Humph,' Aunt Val fixed her nephew with a disapproving stare. 'I wish I'd never introduced you. She's as mad as a snake you know.'

Michael thought this rich coming from Aunt Val, but said nothing.

'All this New Age poppycock. I don't know how she had the nerve to lecture the WI on "group awareness" and women having to band together to be strong. The WI invented that.'

Michael laughed. 'You said you liked her.'

'I do like her.' Aunt Val pushed the toast plate closer to

Michael's foot. 'I would say we were friends. But I've discovered over my long life that you can have friends you don't necessarily agree with. It's the spirit that's important. Lily has a good spirit.'

'Yes . . . Yes, she does. And Gabe?' Michael was still smarting from the look Gabe had given him.

'Gabe too . . .' Aunt Val paused, her weather-beaten old face thoughtful. 'But he seems a bit downtrodden to me. A bit worn out.'

Michael gazed into the fire, the food and the warmth making him sleepy – he'd been up at two thirty that morning. Whether he actually dozed off he wasn't sure, but suddenly there, in the flames, was the girl, Rhiannon. Only her shadow, but he knew for absolute certainty it was her. And he knew she was in danger, surrounded by rising water. He leapt up.

'I've got to go out,' he told his startled aunt.

'Now? In this? Are you mad? Michael . . .'

But before she could say another word, Michael had grabbed his helmet and was gone.

4

Lily and Gabe's farmhouse, Wiltshire

Gabe and Lily ran, crouching from the downpour, to the door of their farmhouse. As she struggled with the key, Gabe heard the howl of his dog, Atlas, coming from the stable. He hurried over, the rain drenching his thick wool jacket, his jeans, his walking boots, and found the husky cowering behind a bale of straw, his blue eyes wide with terror.

'It's only a storm boy,' he leaned down and rubbed the frightened animal's back. 'It's not like you to be scared of a bit of rain.' He tried to sound reassuring, but he too felt the tension. It wasn't fear, Gabe had been around too long to know fear in the common sense, but this was no ordinary storm.

The kitchen of the farmhouse was warm and welcoming, but Lily pushed through to her workroom. Even in the half-light it contained a powerful, serene energy that lit the room, emanating from hundreds of crystals. Crystals of all colours, shapes and sizes, some representing animals or birds, others wand-like, smooth or rough-hewn, rose, aquamarine, jet-black, pale as glass, all beautiful in their own way. They lay on shelves up and down the walls, on long, low tables, on wooden stands, carefully placed by Lily to create the energy force she needed. The single spare wall was dedicated to charts which followed the rising and setting of the sun and the moon, astrological computations and images from the Tarot.

A round table of smooth, honey-coloured oak stood alone. At the centre was engraved a gold six-pointed star, a small circular groove at each point. A smooth, water-polished seer stone shrouded in green velvet sat at the mid-point of the star and next to it a worn leather pouch. The room felt tranquil,

13

womb-like, but at the same time arcane and mysterious. Clients who came for readings were awed by it, sensing that the forces of both dark and light could be summoned in a trice.

Lily quickly went to light one of the fat ivory candles dotted about the room. The wick would not catch as match after match burnt down to her fingertips. She mouthed something silently and the candle caught. From that she lit ten more, needing the warmth of their flame.

Taking a deep breath, she sat down at the oak table, brushed her dark hair over her shoulders and unveiled the seer stone. Opening the leather pouch, she shook out six small sapphires into the palm of her hand and placed them carefully in the grooves at the star's points. Lily flexed her fingers for a moment, shook her hands away from her body, then passed them over the smooth surface of the stone without touching it. Immediately it seemed to come to life, dominating the other energy in the room.

Almost at once a faint image formed. Rhiannon, buffeted about in her car in rising water. As Lily watched, Gabe burst into her workroom.

'The dog's going berserk out there. What's up Lily?'

Lily turned briefly, her expression grim. 'This storm is manufactured – there's a presence, I felt it when I couldn't light the candles.'

She beckoned Gabe over, 'Look . . .'

Gabe leaned over her shoulder, close to the seer stone.

'This is *his* work – Rhiannon's in danger. I've tried to draw her to safety, but it's not working. I was afraid this would happen.' She looked up at Gabe, her blue eyes, an almost direct match to his own, flashing with anger. 'We have to help her.'

'But if it's him . . . the storm I mean, then . . .'

'We haven't got time for that now,' Lily snapped. 'Get her, Gabe, go now.'

Gabe rubbed his parchment hands wearily over his face.

'Now!' Lily shouted. 'Go . . . now. If we lose her the whole thing's over.'

14

Gabe came to life. Straightening up, he hurried from the room. Lily heard the car door slam and the sound of the old blue Volvo revving up against the howling of the wind and rain.

5

A narrow country road not far from Stonehenge

Rhiannon hunched over the wheel, desperately trying to make out the road ahead. Rain pounded the windscreen, the wipers useless against the huge volume of water. And the water now seemed to rain black, staining the windscreen as if mud were pouring from the heavens. She was ashamed to admit she was scared.

It's only rain. She tried to laugh at herself, glad at least the fog had dispersed. *It'll stop in a second.* As if in response, the black rain slackened off. Suddenly the way ahead looked clearer. The satnav sprang back into life and Rhiannon breathed a sigh of relief. Amazingly she was still on track.

She put her foot down hard towards the M4 and civilisation, anxious to get away from these narrow, high-banked country roads as quickly as possible. Not far now, not far, she whispered, then almost jumped out of her skin as a jagged fork of lightning streaked from above and hit a tree a few yards ahead of her, followed immediately by a deafening explosion of thunder.

For a second the landscape was lit up by an eerie violet glow, then the sky darkened as if it was night and she could see nothing at all. But she could hear the tree cracking and toppling into the lane in front of her. She stamped on the brakes and the car skidded to a halt among the branches blocking her way.

Her hands were shaking, her heart pounding. *Calm down, calm down,* she told herself. *There's bound to be another way round.* Although the car was shrouded in the eerie daytime darkness, she inched slowly backwards along the lane until she found a turning. This, too, was narrow with a high bank to her right and, judging by the gleam caught in her headlights, a river to her left.

Rhiannon clutched the wheel like a lifeline as she crept

forward. But as her heartbeat began to return to normal, the headlights fell on something that almost stopped her breath. The road was visibly moving, buckling and cracking in front of her. She slammed on the brakes, narrowly missing the huge fountain of water which shot upwards into the sky through a crater in the tarmac.

She felt dizzy. Air, she needed air. As she opened the window the full force of the storm hit her. But in the noisy darkness she heard voices carried on the wind. They seemed to be calling to her, Rhiannon: 'There's no escape . . . no escape . . . we're doomed . . . the others are lost . . . it's too late, we can't get out.'

She turned the key in the ignition; the engine was dead.

Panicking and breathless with fear, she wrenched at the door and half fell into a foot of swirling, freezing water. The shock brought her to her senses. She struggled back into the car and leaned on the horn. It seemed ridiculous to think that anyone might hear in that pitch-black maelstrom, but hope forced her to believe. Surely it was not meant to end this way.

Please . . . please . . . help me, save me. She prayed silently to a god she didn't believe in, and suddenly felt the car begin to slide slowly, inexorably forward, carried by the torrents of water exploding from beneath the earth. The car bumped against the high bank on one side, then veered dangerously towards the river. She gripped the steering wheel in vain. Where was the daylight? Was this the end of the world?

Then as the car picked up speed, tossed around like a fragile boat shooting the rapids, there ahead of her, piercing the blackness, were headlights. She felt a surge of hope. But the next moment the river broke its banks and a wild tide of water swept her violently into the path of the other car. The impact hurled her Polo against the bank, but this time it jammed fast into the wet mud. Rhiannon pushed frantically at the door but it wouldn't budge. As she struggled she realised with horror that her trainers were sloshing in inches of freezing water. Holding her hand to the door, she felt the water seeping silently through.

She was trapped.

6

The other side of the bridge, downstream from Rhiannon

Michael rode recklessly down the winding road towards the bridge. One thought dominated his mind: save Rhiannon. Buffeted by the gusting wind and driving rain, it took all his strength to keep the heavy motorcycle on course, but he knew she was close now. He concentrated on reaching her with his thoughts. *Hold on, Rhiannon. Just hold on. I'll find you.*

As he reached the bridge the powerful beam of the Ducati's headlight showed the bridge juddering and swaying alarmingly. There was a gap at the far end where some of the planks had already been swept away. The road beyond was under fast-moving water.

He heard a car horn in the distance and saw the flicker of headlights. *Found her!* Then the lights went out.

Michael peered into the murky darkness. The bridge looked close to collapse. Could he make it across in time? Only one way to find out. Backing up a hundred yards, he revved the bike and hurtled at full speed towards the bridge.

Rhiannon sat in the turbulent darkness. The other headlights had vanished. She fumbled on the seat for her mobile. No signal. *Ironic that my greatest fear has always been death by drowning,* she thought, as she gazed at the feeble light from the mobile's screen.

She felt oddly calm as she considered her options: drown in the car, drown out of the car. Well, action was better than sitting in rising water waiting for death. Perhaps she could get through the window and climb the bank to higher ground. But suddenly the car was moving, oddly against the direction of the current.

Peering out, hardly able to believe her eyes, she saw a shadowy figure pushing the car free from the bank. The door opened, and a hand reached in, palm outstretched.

'Rhiannon . . . take my hand.'

She hardly had time to wonder how this unknown rescuer knew her name. She just grasped the hand with all her strength and found herself out of the car, waist deep in water. Shaking with shock she turned to her rescuer. All she could make out was a tall figure. He seemed old, though how could he be old, given the incredible strength he'd just shown?

She felt herself being lifted and placed halfway up the bank. Her trainers scrabbled to get a hold on the slippery, muddy ground and she pulled herself onto a small ledge. Balancing precariously, she turned and reached down to grab her rescuer's hand and pull him up.

As their hands met, the lightning flashed in a spectacular light show. White light, inky darkness, white light, back to black. For a brief moment Rhiannon looked into calm, bright blue eyes that smiled up at her without fear. She felt his hand slipping away from her and glanced down. There was a mark on his wrist. One part of her mind recognised it, but every ounce of energy was taken up trying to save him.

As his hand slipped from her grasp she heard him call to her, 'Rhiannon . . . remember . . .', but the rest was lost as he fell back into the swirling water and was swept away. Rhiannon gasped with horror. She clung desperately to the sodden bank, searching the water in vain for any sign that he might have survived, suddenly overwhelmed by a shattering sense of loss.

Michael hit the bridge at 60 mph. The tyres slipped then gripped again as he headed towards the yawning gap at the far side. Then he was airborne, flying over the fast moving flood waters towards the high bank on the far side of the road. The bike hit the bank with a bone shaking jolt and started to slide backwards. Frantically, Michael gunned the engine. If he lost momentum now he'd end up in the river. But the Ducati roared in response carrying him up the steep bank and onto level ground. When he reached the spot where he thought he'd seen the headlights, he threw the bike to the ground and went to the edge, peering anxiously down the drop into the darkness below.

Rhiannon had not moved from the ledge. She was shaking and chilled to the bone. The rain was not as hard as it had been and a murky daylight was beginning to slowly return. She knew she should do something, but a strange lethargy had hold of her. When she heard her name being called, she did not reply.

'Rhiannon, Rhiannon, are you there?'

A man's voice, insistent, but not the same as her rescuer's.

She roused herself. 'Here, I'm here . . .'

She looked up and saw a hand reaching down towards her, the arm clad in black leather.

'Grab my hand.'

Rhiannon shrank back against the bank; she felt paralysed.

'I can't move . . . I can't.'

She heard the figure above her snort. Was he laughing at her?

'It's only a few feet.'

He *was* laughing at her. Rhiannon wished more than anything that she could skip to the top like a mountain goat but her limbs literally wouldn't budge. The voice changed, he sounded concerned, 'Stay there, I'm coming down.'

The voice hadn't been familiar, but Michael Wolf's face was. He slithered to a stop beside her, quickly clamped her arms firmly to her side and propelled her up the last few feet of the bank.

'Thanks.' Rhiannon knew that she sounded grudging but she was exhausted, desperately worried about the man who had rescued her and, absurdly, embarrassed to be seen like this by Michael Wolf.

'There's someone down there . . . our cars collided in the flood. He pulled me out, but then he was swept away.' She was furious with herself as she realised she was crying. 'We have to find him.' She didn't mention that he had somehow known her name.

Michael looked puzzled.

20

'There's only one car down there. A red one.'

'That's mine,' Rhiannon snapped. 'The other one must have been swept away too, with this old man . . . it was incredible the way he lifted the car free of the bank.'

Michael said nothing.

'You don't believe me.' She was furious, but she could see the story sounded strange.

'Well, there's no sign of him now.'

'Just take me to the nearest police station. I'll deal with this myself.' Rhiannon wanted to hit him, but she still needed his help to get out of this nightmare place.

'Tell you what, come back to my aunt's place and get dried off. We can ring the police from there.'

Rhiannon hated being told what to do, but was too tired to resist. She climbed wearily onto the back of his bike and couldn't stop herself leaning against him as they roared off into the strengthening daylight.

Crowe Corporation, west London

'What the hell's going on, Gutman?'

The overweight, pasty-faced young man sitting in front of a bank of computer screens swivelled awkwardly in his chair to see who was invading his lab.

'Yo, Xan, my man! Check it out!' He gestured towards the middle screen which was playing an endless loop of the eruption in the road and subsequent flood at Stonehenge.

'Awesome!'

The man called Xan remained silent and it gradually dawned on Gutman that perhaps all was not well. Thoughtfully, he bit into a doughnut, adding crumbs and icing sugar to the debris surrounding his chair. Xan moved closer and watched the scene unfolding at Stonehenge with silent concentration.

'Well, OK,' began Gutman. 'I know it's a bit off target but . . .'

Xan turned so suddenly that Gutman jumped, spilling coffee over his *Matrix* T-shirt. *Christ, the man's scary. Why hadn't he noticed it before?*

21

'The boss wants to see you, now.' Xan gestured to two security guards who stood either side of him as Gutman levered himself from his chair. Hardly anyone got to see the boss in person. Ever the optimist, Gutman decided it couldn't have anything to do with Stonehenge. Could it?

7

Aunt Val's cottage, Marbury, Wiltshire

Rhiannon was shaking by the time they arrived at Aunt Val's cottage. Soaked through, she shivered uncontrollably as Michael's aunt sprang into action.

'Take those wet things off before you catch your death,' she said for the second time that morning, cocking her head to one side as she noted the comparison between her tiny, bird-like figure and Rhiannon's long legs. She pushed Rhiannon gently in the direction of the bathroom. 'I think you'd better borrow some of Michael's clothes, but I'll get a blanket for now.' A moment later Aunt Val opened the bathroom door and handed in a heavy wool tartan rug, which Rhiannon wrapped tightly round her shoulders. When she came out, Michael was pacing the hallway, his mobile clutched to his ear.

'I don't know what ridiculous drama Michael has dragged you into,' Aunt Val frowned down at Rhiannon as she huddled in the armchair by the fire, 'but he really can be most impetuous at times. This is the second time this morning he's come home soaking wet and in a tizz, and it's not yet nine.' She waved the poker towards Michael in a gesture of frustration before bending to riddle the coals and heap new ones on the glowing fire.

Despite the disapproving tone, Rhiannon could detect in Aunt Val's tone her enormous love for her nephew.

'It wasn't his fault,' Rhiannon hastened to explain. 'In fact he rescued me. I might have died from exposure if he hadn't ridden up at that moment. It's freezing out there. How can it be June?' The shivering was less violent now, heat from the flames making her cold skin tingle. She could hear Michael on his mobile: 'Yes . . . No . . . not even further down? The water looked pretty dangerous.' There was silence for a moment. Rhiannon held her breath. 'So it was just the red Polo . . . no . . . no, I understand, nowhere for it to go . . . Well, yes, it must have been frightening for her . . . well let me know if you find anything . . . no I don't suppose so. I'll tell her. Thanks for your help. Yes . . . bye.'

Michael came in from the hallway.

'Didn't they find him?' Rhiannon wasn't sure what she was dreading most, to hear they had found the old man dead, or to hear that they hadn't found him at all.

'Um . . . no. They found your car. No sign of anyone else.' He seemed awkward, passing his phone from one hand to another, looking intently at Rhiannon.

'What? He can't just have disappeared into thin air.'

'Michael, get some of your clothes and give them to Rhiannon,' Aunt Val interrupted, poking her head round the kitchen door. 'Hurry up, she can't sit in that rug forever.' They heard the sound of plates and the kettle beginning to hum. 'And get dry yourself,' Aunt Val added from the kitchen.

Michael didn't move. 'This man, where was he exactly?'

'I can't believe you didn't see him,' she exploded. 'He was right there, in the water. I tried to hold on to him, but the water was too strong and he was pulled away. You must have seen him.'

Michael shook his head. 'It was so dark . . . maybe . . . it must have been frightening for you . . .' He turned to put his mobile on the mantelpiece.

Rhiannon recognised the phrase from the phone conversation. Springing up, she grabbed his arm, spinning him round to face her.

'You all think I'm mad don't you? You think I've imagined the whole thing?'

Michael raised his eyebrows in what she saw as an impossibly patronising gesture.

'I can't believe this.' She wanted to shout and beat her hands on his chest, anything to wipe that smug expression from his face, but she took a deep breath and began to explain slowly and precisely: 'Our cars collided in the water. I was trapped, the door

24

wouldn't open, but he pulled me out somehow – I don't know how because he was old and frail-looking – and pushed me up the bank. He saved my life.' She searched Michael's face.

'I know what you think you saw,' he began tentatively, 'but . . . well . . . at Stonehenge you were . . . sort of wound up . . . the scream, remember? You thought you'd seen something that you hadn't. The rescue services didn't find anything.' Rhiannon stared at him in disbelief.

'I've been there . . .' Michael was saying. 'I've been under such pressure that I began to . . . you know, see things that weren't real.'

'Just because *you're* losing your mind doesn't mean I am,' Rhiannon shot back. But being reminded of her Stonehenge experience had shaken her confidence.

Aunt Val came into the room carrying a tray with tea, crumpets, home-made jam and a plate of shortbread.

'Haven't you changed yet Michael?' she looked from one to the other and was bewildered by the sudden tension between them.

Michael shrugged. 'Just going,' he growled, and left the room.

Rhiannon felt guilty. Michael may be arrogant, but he had also rescued her. She might have died. She smiled apologetically at his aunt.

'It's all been a bit unnerving,' she said.

Aunt Val looked at her closely. 'Never be bullied by men dear,' she told her. 'They're problem-solvers, it's what they do, but it doesn't mean you have to go along with everything they say.'

The old lady's sympathy made her want to cry. She felt so confused by the morning's events. Suddenly nothing was what it seemed. She felt the tears pricking behind her eyes, but she was damned if she would show weakness in front of Michael.

'I'll be all right. I just need to get home,' she said.

Aunt Val looked sceptical, but patted her arm. 'You really should stay a while, you'd be very welcome,' she said. 'You look as if you need a good rest. But if you want to go, Michael can run you to the station in my car. You don't have to go on that horrid bike.'

The journey to the station was frosty. Rhiannon said nothing, awkward in the loose jeans and jumper that Michael had lent her, and pretended to be absorbed in texting Lauren to say she was sorry she wouldn't be able to make it. She just wanted to be left alone to think things out.

'You never know, once the weather improves they might find something,' Michael looked anxiously sideways at Rhiannon as he drove, baffled as to why he had offended her. 'Give me your number in case I hear something.'

The last thing Rhiannon wanted was more communication from this irritating man. But she was dressed in his clothes. She didn't have much choice.

8

Brandon Crowe's office, west London

Gutman squirmed uneasily in his chair. He'd been sitting there feeling like a schoolboy in detention for what seemed like hours while the boss scrutinised the satellite pictures on the bank of computer screens. He glanced hopefully towards Xan, leaning arms folded against the door, but Xan's cold, green eyes stared right through him.

What was their problem? He was the best technician they had; no one had his flair, his expertise. Sure, they paid well, but others might pay better for what he'd learnt at the Crowe Corporation.

Slowly Brandon Crowe turned to face him. Gutman looked at his arrogant, handsome face and felt a spurt of anger. He didn't have to put up with this. He began to stand up.

'Going somewhere?'

Gutman quailed at the menace in the silky voice. He'd heard the rumours about Brandon Crowe's mysterious rise to power, the ruthless takeovers, the multimedia corporation that influenced governments at a global level, but the public face had always been affable, charming. The private face chilled him to the bone. He subsided back into his seat and stared at the floor.

'I thought not. I have just one question.'

Gutman tried his best to look willing and able to answer.

'What is the one place, the only place, on this planet that I told you to keep well away from?'

Oh shit, thought Gutman. *Stonehenge.*

'Well?'

'I know what you're thinking, Mr Crowe,' Gutman knew he was gabbling but couldn't stop. 'Solar flares can be unpredictable, even with crystal technology. We'd locked on to the target, the

BBC TV centre at Cardiff, but . . .' His voice trailed away as Brandon shook his head.

'Not good enough, Gutman. You ignored the prime directive – stay away from Stonehenge. We'll have to let you go.'

Gutman suppressed a sigh of relief. He'd like nothing better than to leave right now, and knowing what he did he could sell his services to the highest bidder.

'OK, Mr Crowe.' Gutman rose unsteadily to his feet.

'And Gutman, remember our confidentiality agreement.'

'Of course, Mr Crowe. My lips are sealed.'

'How right you are.' Brandon glanced towards Xan who nodded impassively.

'Xan will take care of you.' Brandon turned back towards the screens, ignoring Gutman's outstretched hand, and Xan ushered him out towards the waiting security guards.

As the door closed behind him, Brandon replayed the Stonehenge sequence then froze one frame with a grunt of satisfaction. The image was grainy, obscured by drifting fog, but there she was. Lilith. She just couldn't stay away, and Gabriel probably wasn't far behind. It was almost amusing the way they refused to give up. Still, he had underestimated them once before and that had been a costly mistake. Brandon made a mental note to increase the surveillance around Stonehenge.

Lily and Gabe's farmhouse, Silbury, Wiltshire

Lily had not moved from the seer stone since Gabe left. The images came and went in the flickering candlelight. Nothing was completely clear; shadows, shapes, atmosphere, the crystal revealing vibrations rather than physical certainty. But occasionally a sharp image emerged from the shadows, and Lily knew this was the result of a strong emotional surge between the people she had conjured up.

Rhiannon was safe, but Lily couldn't relax. She knew beyond a shadow of doubt who was behind the sudden tempest. But why a storm? And how was Rhiannon involved? Was she the target? Lily had long since ceased to believe in coincidence.

But then, she realised, she was also too quick to believe only in evil forces at work. There were also forces for good; perhaps Rhiannon had been drawn there for a reason that would help their cause. Her plan had been to keep Rhiannon safe under the radar until Michael was ready to draw her out. Now she'd have to work with what she'd been given.

Suddenly in the crystal the clearest of images shone from the darkness. Rhiannon with Michael, both sodden, the girl leaning exhausted against Michael's back as he sliced the Ducati through the waning storm. For a moment Lily experienced a frisson of pure, uncomplicated jealousy. She didn't fight it – it was just the way it was, and, as Gabe so self-righteously told her, the way it should be.

As she watched, the scene changed. The two figures were in front of a fire now, and she sensed tension between them. More than tension – outright hostility. Just like the past, Lily thought, those two always at each other's throats. She sighed. *At least they've met*, she comforted herself, and one piece of this eternal jigsaw is in place. But despite the thought, she felt almost overwhelmed at the task ahead of her.

Lily heard Atlas bark excitedly in the kitchen, his feet scrabbling on the tiles, and Gabe's soft voice greeting his dog. The rain had stopped, the wind only battered weakly at the windows. She got up stiffly. Gabe was sitting slumped on a kitchen chair. She was shocked at his appearance: his face had lost all colour, his clothes were damp and bedraggled, his expression blankly numb.

'It went well, didn't it?' Lily asked.

Gabe attempted a smile. 'Oh, great, yes.'

'Meaning?'

'Meaning I'm too old for these heroics.'

'Rubbish,' Lily retorted. 'You have your strength when you need it. You did what you had to. And they've met, Michael and Rhiannon. It's not the way we planned it but it's a start.'

Gabe waved his hand dismissively. 'Well, I'm telling you, I'm tired. There's going to come a time . . .' He wiped his hands across his face in the familiar gesture.

'I know they don't exactly look like soulmates yet . . .' she went on, ignoring Gabe.

'No,' Gabe whispered, 'not like us. Not the way *we* were, Lilith.'

The words seemed to trigger something in Gabe. He stood up, pushing back his shoulders, straightening his spine, and for a moment the years fell away and once again he was a prince among men – powerful, handsome, able to achieve anything for the woman he loved. Lily watched and rose to face him, their bodies almost touching.

'No one,' she declared softly, meeting his gaze, 'no one will *ever* be the way we were.' And very gently she reached up and kissed his lips as if he were once again her young handsome lover.

'I'm tired too, Gabe.' She leaned briefly against his chest. 'That's why we have to make it work this time. Then we'll be free . . . we can do it. We must.'

9

10,500 BC: Atlantis

'Make way for the High Priest of Atlantis!'

The Captain of the Guard stared aggressively at the crowds milling around the entrance to the Citadel. The bystanders fell back but not quickly enough for the Captain.

'Get back! Out of the way! Fucking peasants!' he bellowed, forcing his heavily armoured horse into the centre of the crowd. Women scooped up their children and ran, frantic to escape the trampling hooves; a few men stood their ground, voices raised in angry protest.

One of the guards glanced back nervously towards the tall figure of the High Priest, riding in the centre of the procession.

'Erik! Are you crazy? He'll hear you.'

'Let him,' snapped the Captain. 'I'm not the only one thinks he gone soft. Did you hear what he did the . . .'

Whatever he was going to say was cut short by a high-pitched scream. A small boy, running to avoid the rearing horses, had tripped and was desperately trying to crawl to safety. Before the guards had time to react, the High Priest spurred his horse forward and lifted the terrified boy to his feet.

'Explain yourself, Captain.'

'My Lord Gabriel,' began the Captain. 'I was merely clearing the way and . . .' his voice faltered under the ironic gaze of the High Priest's piercing blue eyes.

'Captain, you seem to have forgotten that we are here to serve the people, not to terrorise them.'

'Yes, my lord,' muttered the Captain, 'I mean, no, my lord.'

The expression on Gabriel's handsome face suddenly hardened and his eyes grew cold.

'Return at once to the barracks. I shall see you after the council meeting.'

The Captain flashed a look of pure hatred at Gabriel. 'Yes, my lord,' he hissed through gritted teeth and wheeled his horse away from the procession.

The young man who'd been riding with Gabriel moved up to join him.

'You've made an enemy there, my lord.'

Gabriel nodded. 'He already was an enemy, Michael. I could read his thoughts as easily as I can read yours.'

Anxiety flashed across Michael's sensitive face but Gabriel didn't notice, he seemed to be thinking aloud.

'There's danger in the air, somewhere close at hand . . .'

Gabriel realised Michael was staring at him, open-mouthed. 'Don't worry boy, your secrets are safe with me!'

'But, my lord, you spoke of danger.'

Gabriel shrugged, 'I was probably looking ahead to the council meeting. And Lilith. She favours one candidate, I another.' He smiled ruefully, 'Wish me luck.'

Michael grinned sympathetically. 'If you're up against the High Priestess, you'll need more than luck!'

Chamber of the High Priestess, Atlantis

Lilith, High Priestess of the Moon, flung open the window of the tower room and looked down on the city. Distant shouts, angry voices had disturbed her meditations but all seemed peaceful now. Even from a great height she could pick out Gabriel, head and shoulders above his companions, leading the procession into the courtyard. A smile of satisfaction curved her lips. She had always been destined as consort of the High Priest but she couldn't have chosen better. Her match in every way, her soulmate. Her eyes travelled along the procession. There was Michael riding with Thomas, another of the young novices, and further back, Rhiannon and Maya, rival candidates for Keeper of the Crystal, but the figure she sought was not there. So, Jude had not yet returned.

Putting the thought aside, Lilith breathed slowly and deeply, *soothed by the beauty of the city below her. Sunlight glinted on the blue waters of the canals winding in labyrinthine patterns from the seven gates of the city through cultivated fields and gardens of iridescent green, encircling the shimmering white marble of the buildings that led towards the Citadel. The breathtaking design of the city was acknowledged by all, but few remembered its significance. Thousands of years had passed since the ancestors created Atlantis in the image of Gaia, a microcosm of Mother Earth, with seven gates representing the seven centres of power that linked the energy grid of the planet.*

Long ago her predecessors had learned to harness the power of the sun and the moon using the sacred crystal, the Heartstone. Control of the energy source had given Atlantis mastery of the earth. But maintaining that power depended on integrity and trust, the eternal alliance between followers of sun and moon. As High Priestess, she served the moon as Gabriel, the High Priest, served the sun. Each needed the other, neither held absolute power; a delicate balance but essential for the safety of the planet. She trusted Gabriel completely but something troubling flickered at the edges of her consciousness: did Gabriel trust her? Or rather, did she trust herself?

Impatiently Lilith crossed the room and sat in front of a polished obsidian mirror, studying her reflection dispassionately. Was she afraid that her beauty was fading, her power and authority on the wane? The image reflected in the dark glass reassured her. If anything she was even more beautiful and regal than when she first became High Priestess twenty years ago. So why had she allowed herself to be flattered by the open admiration of Jude, a mere boy compared with Gabriel? And was she supporting Rhiannon because the girl reminded her of her younger self and if she became Keeper of the Crystal she could never become the next High Priestess? Lilith acknowledged, if only to herself, that she was not ready to relinquish her throne, now or ever.

A hand lightly touched her shoulder and Lilith swung round, startled. She hadn't heard Gabriel come into the room.

'Ready for battle, my lady?' Gabriel smiled provocatively down at her and raised her to her feet.

'I'm always ready, as you know well, my lord.' Her reminiscent smile reflected the passion that always lay beneath the surface of even their most formal encounters and the cloud of self-doubt suddenly lifted. She could handle Jude; nothing could threaten her relationship with Gabriel. Perhaps he was right and Maya was the better candidate but she wasn't going to give in too easily. She was, after all, High Priestess of Atlantis.

10

Council chamber, Atlantis

'Wait! Before we vote, there's a matter of great importance I must put before the council.'

Eight heads turned in astonishment as the Supreme Commander, head of the military forces, rose to his feet. It was unprecedented for anyone to interrupt at this stage of the proceedings. Lilith had spoken first, supporting Rhiannon, and Gabriel had just completed his speech in favour of Maya. The stunned silence was broken by Gabriel.

'Go ahead, Commander. Tell us what is so important.'

The Commander, a powerfully built veteran of countless campaigns, looked around the table as if he was reviewing his troops. The Council of Nine represented the ruling powers of Atlantis. Only one other woman, thought Lilith ruefully, and she, the Priestess of the Healing Arts, was close to retirement. All the others were men – the masters of alchemy and magic, architecture, astronomy, and the secular members representing the merchants and townspeople. It hadn't always been that way. Lilith straightened in her seat, sensing trouble.

'My lord, my lady, members of the council,' began the Commander. 'We are all agreed that the guardianship of the crystal is crucial to the safety and prosperity of Atlantis – because the Heartstone controls the energy source that powers the whole of Atlantis and the world. However, the keeper of the crystal is an ancient office and I speak for many when I say that we feel it has little relevance today. Times have changed and we must change with them. I propose that the guardianship of the crystal should no longer be vested in one person and that person a young girl. Nor should control of the crystal lie solely with the priesthood. Such an important device should be guarded by those with the strength to protect it.'

Gabriel glanced around the table. Many looked shocked but one or two nodded thoughtfully. Gabriel felt Lilith stir beside him, her fury almost tangible. Willing her to stay calm, he rose to his feet and looked steadily at the Commander. After a long moment the Commander's eyes fell and he sat down abruptly.

'An interesting point, Commander, but I must remind you that the role of guardian is not merely ceremonial. The crystal is immensely powerful and reflects the qualities of the person holding it. Therefore she must be a pure channel of energy. Obviously it must be used for good. Put to evil purposes, ultimately that will rebound and destroy us all.'

The Commander leaned forward angrily. 'And are you saying only a woman, a girl, can do this? We all know the energy comes from the sun. You are High Priest of the Sun, our leader – why do you allow women to control our energy?'

Gabriel turned courteously towards Lilith, relieved to see how calm she looked as she rose gracefully to her feet.

'Commander!'

The battled-scarred soldier turned unwillingly towards her, unable to ignore the tone of command.

'Yes, Commander, it's true that our energy source, Selenios-3, comes from the sun. It's equally true that the moon holds that energy. Otherwise it would be scattered and lost throughout the universe. Without the sun there would be no energy, without the moon we would not be able to access it.'

The Commander stirred in his seat and Lilith paused, inviting him with a gesture to speak. His mouth opened then shut abruptly as he threw himself back in his seat, shielding his eyes from her gaze. The sleek and prosperous merchant sitting beside him whispered urgently in his ear, but the Commander brushed him aside. To Lilith's astonishment, she could see that he was holding his thumb between his fingers in the ancient charm against witches. Could he really believe that the source of her power was dark magic?

Careful not to let her amusement show, Lilith continued, 'I cannot reveal the secrets of the priesthood but I can tell you that our ancestors recognised the equal importance of the sun and the moon, or men and women in practical terms, and our rituals reflect that. The power of the crystal lies in the perfect balance between the masculine and the feminine – take either of those elements away and the power is lost. Together we are invincible.'

The council members nodded their agreement and the Commander knew he'd lost any chance of convincing them otherwise. Lilith looked towards Gabriel and continued, 'Gabriel and I have dedicated our lives to celebrating and protecting that union and you may be sure that between us we have the strength to continue doing so.'

'I was not questioning your commitment . . . or ability . . .' The Commander faltered to a stop, seemingly unable to remember what he wanted to say.

'And I value your unquestioned loyalty – to Atlantis and to me.' There was only the merest hint of mockery in Lilith's voice. 'And now, perhaps, we can return to business.'

Council room antechamber, Atlantis

Maya poured water from the onyx jug into two crystal glasses and offered one to Rhiannon. The room they were sitting in offered every comfort but neither of them could relax. The council had been sitting for far longer than expected and Maya sensed conflict, anxiety. Despite her training she found it difficult to control her thoughts and remain calm. She had always felt destined to be Keeper of the Crystal but Rhiannon was her friend and had been since childhood. How important was it to her? Hard to tell with Rhiannon.

Rhiannon accepted the glass with an abstracted smile. She felt detached from the whole affair and wondered why she had allowed her name to be put forward. Well, of course she knew why. Lilith had nominated her and you didn't say no to the High Priestess. The feeling of detachment intensified as she looked at her friend. Maya would make the perfect guardian. She even looked the part – angelically fair, serene. Rhiannon knew her own dark looks were equally admired but nobody would call her serene. Energy fizzled and crackled around her.

She suddenly knew very clearly that she did not want this

37

appointment, prestigious though it was. Her whole life had been mapped out for her – more than anything she wanted to be free. She became aware that Maya was looking anxiously at her and with an effort wrenched her thoughts back to the present.

'Don't worry Maya. I'm sure you'll get it.'

'I wasn't thinking about me. I was thinking about you . . . you looked so far away.'

'I wish I was.' Rhiannon rose swiftly to her feet as if she was about to put her words into action just as an attendant opened the door leading into the council chamber. He looked from one to the other then beckoned to Maya.

Maya stood and looked uncertainly at Rhiannon, whose sudden smile transformed her face.

'See, I knew it was you. Don't keep them waiting.'

As Maya hugged her, Rhiannon pushed her gently towards the door and watched her disappear into the council chamber. Rhiannon's smile slowly faded. 'Well, that's Maya's life sorted,' she thought, 'but what the hell am I going to do now?'

Citadel courtyard, Atlantis

'Why are they taking so long?' Michael paced impatiently back and forth across the sunlit courtyard. Tom looked up from his comfortable position squatting on his heels in the shadow cast by the high stone walls.

'What's the hurry? Have you got to be somewhere?'

Michael joined him in the shade.

'You know I haven't! No . . . it's just . . . something doesn't feel right. I can't explain it.'

'Then don't worry about it!' Tom was rarely troubled by doubts. If trouble came to him, he'd deal with it, but saw no point in looking for it.

Suddenly the doors to the Citadel were thrown open and Maya appeared on the steps flanked by Gabriel and Lilith.

'She's got it!' Tom leapt excitedly to his feet and turned to Michael. 'That's a hundred marks you owe me . . . What?' He stopped at the look on Michael's face. 'Aren't you pleased for her?'

'Of course I am, but Rhiannon... Well, she might be disappointed.'

Tom shook his head, exasperated. 'Not her! Look, does she seem disappointed?'

They could just see Rhiannon among the council members and attendants and sure enough she was smiling radiantly. Abruptly the Commander broke away from the group, bowed curtly to Gabriel and Lilith and strode purposefully towards his escort. Tom and Michael stood opened mouthed at this breach of protocol as the Commander and his men rode swiftly away.

Gabriel drew Lilith to one side and spoke quietly in her ear.

'You're right. We have to take this challenge seriously. He seems determined to test our authority.'

'He's only the spokesman,' Lilith replied. 'There's someone else behind him, egging him on, but I can't see clearly yet ...' She shook her head in frustration, 'No, too many shadows. What does it mean Gabriel? I have a bad feeling about this.'

Outskirts of the city, Atlantis

The Captain of the Guard galloped into the courtyard of an impressive house on the outskirts of the city and leapt from his horse. Still fuming from his encounter with Gabriel earlier in the day, he scowled at the stable boy who came running to take his horse, and ran up the steps to the main doors. A fighting man himself, he was nevertheless a little wary of the man who stood there silently waiting for him. Xan was named for his Chinese ancestors and his dark Asiatic looks contrasted oddly with his Atlantean eyes of purest green.

Drawing a deep breath, the Captain delivered his message.

'I have important news from the Commander for Lord Brandon. It's imperative I speak with him immediately. It's about the crystal.'

11

Gleaming black, the rectangular slab of building rose out of the hinterland leading to Heathrow airport. From the outside there was no break in the glass, just a smooth, perfect sheet of blackness stretching the length and breadth of the seven floors.

In the penthouse a tall figure, motionless against the window, looked out across London. This was Brandon Crowe's habitual position. Lean and tanned, his body honed from hours of tennis, he looked ten years younger than his fifty years. The office was sparsely furnished with a large, black wooden desk holding a featureless bank of computers. The only other furniture consisted of three black-leather, wide-armed sofas, positioned round a low, teak coffee table, facing the panoramic view. On the one wall not made of glass were a series of black and silver demi-globes, each showing a different section of the world in miniature, including latitudes and longitudes and the phases of the moon. Nothing in the room suggested anything personal about the owner; there were no paintings, no photos, no books, no plants.

In the outer office, Christina looked dispiritedly at the long list of things she had to do, or, according to her boss, should have done yesterday.

'Hurry up with that coffee,' she hissed at her junior, who was slowly and carefully wiping the nozzle of the milk frother on the espresso machine as if she had all the time in the world. The girl, a thin, irritatingly timid temp, jumped.

'Coffee . . . Mr Crowe . . . This century would be just splendid.' Christina hated the sound of her own sarcasm, but the tension in the office this morning was wearing her down.

The temp, gripping the tray, made her way slowly towards

the double doors leading to Brandon Crowe's office, two cappuccinos rattling nervously in their saucers.

'Mind the double doors – they swing inwards,' Christina added, wondering if it would have been less stressful to do it herself.

◎◎

The door had closed on the temp and the coffee was cooling on the teak table as Brandon reached for his mobile and punched in a number. As it connected an echo of the ring tone sounded from behind him.

The man to whom the phone belonged was standing silently by the door. He held his mobile up, and without smiling, clicked it off.

'For Christ's sake Xan, do you have to creep up on me all the time?' Brandon threw his phone down again. 'Where have you been?'

Xan seemed unrepentant, but then he never wasted emotion. If Brandon was handsome, Xan was beautiful. Every inch of his tall frame was refined to the most perfect proportions. His thick black hair, which hung just above his shoulders, his honey-coloured skin and the epicanthal fold of his upper eyelid came direct from his Chinese mother; his strong nose and long limbs from his Scottish father. His eyes were his alone. Sea-green and intense, they brought his androgynous beauty to life. But it was the essence of him that drew the eye. He seemed utterly separate from the rest of the world, as if he lived in his own perfect space. He was untouchable. And even his boss treated him with a wary respect.

'I've been working on the problem at Stonehenge, checking data from the L590, but the interface was down and I had to wait for Arun to fix it,' Xan said quietly, moving towards the big screens. Brandon followed in silence as his henchman began to open files on the central screen. He did not ask for more details, he employed Xan to take care of the technology.

'And?' Brandon became impatient as the younger man continued to input data, his fingers speeding over the keyboard in a baffling sequence.

41

'It is weak. You were right, which is to our advantage. But there seems to be a strange block, like a negative force field isolating it. We don't have a problem drawing the energy down, but as soon as it hits Stonehenge the flow's interrupted, broken up. It's not converting, so we can't store it. It's almost as if we're being denied access.' Xan frowned. He was not used to failure.

'The crystal technology still needs work. Once that's sorted I'm sure the energy will convert.' He tried to sound more confident than he was. Arun had told him only that morning that he was running out of ideas. Work on the crystal replica had ground to a halt.

Brandon had moved away from the screen and was once more standing looking out across London. He had gone very still.

'I've suddenly realised what the problem is here. And who's responsible.' Brandon swung round, glaring at him with a face suddenly dark with rage. 'The bastard's used Stonehenge to protect the portal.'

Seldom unnerved, Xan was shocked by the hatred in his boss's eyes.

'I should have known,' Brandon fumed. 'It's so bloody obvious. It's his territory.' He looked at Xan. 'There's only one man who can solve our problem . . .' there was a pause. 'And he'd rather die first,' Brandon added grimly.

'That's not usually the case,' the younger man attempted a smile.

But his boss's look was contemptuous. 'Don't be glib about things you don't understand.'

'Who is he?' Xan was intrigued. He had never seen this reaction from Mr Brandon Crowe before. The international tycoon, friend to the world's ruling elite, seemed almost apprehensive.

'Last time we met, his name was Jude.'

12

Temple precincts, Atlantis

'Jude's back!' Tom jumped down from his vantage point high on the city walls and joined Michael at the doors to the temple.

'He's just ridden in through the main gate. Now, perhaps, we'll find out what's going on.'

'What do you mean, going on?' asked a voice behind them. Michael spun round and blushed like a schoolboy at the sight of Rhiannon standing there. Tom smiled sympathetically at his friend. Rhiannon always had this effect on him. As Michael seemed unable to speak, Tom jumped in.

'You tell us, Rhiannon. You're the one who's always talking about secrets and conspiracies, and you're closer to the inner circle than we are.'

For once, Rhiannon didn't rise to the bait, her expression serious.

'All I know is that Lilith and Gabriel are worried about something and the security around the crystal has been doubled. I hardly see Maya these days.'

Michael pulled himself together. 'Sorry it wasn't you,' he said. 'You would have been great . . .'

'No, I wouldn't,' Rhiannon cut in, sharply. 'You know nothing about me if you think I wanted to be Keeper of the Crystal. In fact, I don't want . . .' She stopped mid-sentence as she caught sight of Jude entering a side door of the temple apartments. Michael followed her gaze.

'No chance there . . . You're wasting your time if you think he has eyes for anyone but the High Priestess,' he teased.

Rhiannon shot him a fiery look.

'Well, he wouldn't be the only one then,' she retorted, and gathering her robes around her swept off in the direction Jude had taken.

Michael turned to Tom in frustration.

'Now what did I do?'

Tom shrugged. They'd had this conversation before.

'You know what she's like – hates to be told what to do, what to think. Now that Maya is Keeper of the Crystal, there's a good chance our Rhiannon may be the next High Priestess. And you know what that means . . .'

Michael answered unwillingly, 'She thinks that I might be the next High Priest and she hates the idea. But it could just as easily be you, Tom.'

'No way. I'm going to work for Jude.'

Now it was Michael's turn to smile. Another conversation they'd had before.

'Yeah, yeah. Jude the Magician, Jude the Master of Energy. He who controls the tides, the winds, the rain. Is there anything the man can't do?'

An uncomfortable silence fell. Finally Michael spoke again.

'And of course he's irresistible to women, even Rhiannon can't keep her eyes off him. I know Tom, I know I can't compete with Jude – yet.'

Gabriel's chambers, Atlantis

Jude found Gabriel hunched over a complex astrological chart.

'Well?' the High Priest looked questioningly at the younger man.

'It's as we thought. There is a problem. I tested all seven portals and in each one there is disruption, a variation of the energy flow. The conversion and storage is going ahead as usual, but the flow itself is intermittent, quite seriously in some places. As if someone has tapped in and is trying to control it.'

Gabriel stared straight ahead, not answering, apparently lost in thought.

'I didn't do anything . . . I didn't know what to do.'

'No . . . no . . . That's right, we have to wait. We have to know for certain who is responsible for this before we act.'

'Could it be a problem at source, not man-made? Could the moon be out of alignment or something and the Selenios-3 blocked?'

Gabriel shook his head.

'I wish that were true, it would be simpler to deal with. No, this is definitely a man-made problem . . . And it's someone close to home.'

As Jude left, Gabriel called after him, 'Tell no one what you've found. We will all meet at the temple at noon.'

The main square, Atlantis

Brandon dismissed his guards and strode across the square, ignoring the obsequious greetings from passers-by. He planned to waylay his half-brother as if by chance and wanted no witnesses to the meeting. He stopped in the shade of a tall flowering tree and idly twisted the intricate golden ring on his index finger. Where the hell had Jude got to? He'd been seen leaving the temple precinct ten minutes ago. Brandon hated waiting, and rarely had to, but this was important. When he'd left the priesthood, against the advice and the wishes of the elders, he knew he'd prove them wrong. And he had. All the skills they had taught him hadn't been wasted. And now the biggest prize of all was almost within his grasp, but for that he needed Jude's help.

He looked up and suddenly Jude was there. How did he do that? Suddenly appear and disappear at will? Brandon felt the familiar rush of affection and irritation – they shared their father's height and aquamarine eyes, but that was all. His father's second wife, Jude's mother, had been of African descent, and Jude's golden skin was a constant reminder of his own mother's sadness and humiliation. With cold deliberation Brandon dismissed memories of the past and focused on business. As Jude swiftly passed him, Brandon grabbed his arm and swung him around.

'Where are you off to in such a hurry?'

'Nowhere . . .' Jude found himself reddening in an effort to hide the burning secret he couldn't even share with his beloved brother.

'I haven't seen you for weeks and I need to talk to you.' Brandon didn't seem to notice Jude's embarrassment.

'Can it wait?'

Brandon gave him a quizzical look. 'No it can't. I need your help now.' His steely tone brooked no argument, and under normal circumstances Jude wouldn't have hesitated. He waited to see what his brother had to say.

'I'm planning something huge.' Brandon's voice had sunk to a whisper as he gazed across the crowded square. 'It'll make Atlantis the greatest power in the world, and make us rich beyond your wildest dreams.'

Brandon put his arm across his brother's broad shoulder, but Jude's blood ran cold. In a flash he knew, beyond a shadow of a doubt, who was responsible for disrupting the energy.

'Well,' Brandon whispered, 'don't you want to know what it is?' Taking Jude's stunned silence for assent, Brandon continued.

'We knew the old guard wouldn't listen to us; too locked in the old ways, outdated traditions. The power of the crystal is being wasted so we've been developing our own. And it works! We've already managed to tap into Selenios-3.'

'No!' Jude exploded, gripping his brother's arm as if he hoped somehow to physically stop Brandon from making such a terrible mistake. 'Don't you understand how dangerous this is? It's a wild violent force that could destroy us if the balance of control is tampered with. You must be mad if you think you can harness something so dangerous on your own.'

Brandon laughed. 'Hey, little brother, don't panic. That's where you come in. There are problems right now, but once we have the last final piece of information our crystal will do everything the Heartstone can do and more.'

'You don't understand,' Jude said desperately. 'You can't just programme another crystal to do what the Heartstone does. Only the chosen guardians can control it, and they have to work together, bringing the seven rays together in harmony . . .'

Brandon interrupted, angrily. 'Harmony and balance, blah, blah! All that's leading to is stagnation. We need sun energy to drive us forward. The power of the moon is negative energy. It's holding us back.' His voice rose with passion. 'Do you want to see Atlantis weaken and die just because the High Priestess – a mere woman when all's said and done – thinks she knows what's best for us?'

Jude stared. 'That's insane. Don't you see the effects your

46

tampering is already having on the world?'

But Brandon wasn't interested in debate. 'So we've had a few earthquakes, a flood or two. That's why I need your help. You're friendly with the new keeper, that Maya girl, so it will be easy for you to get into the inner sanctum. I need to know . . .'

'No! Don't tell me any more.'

'No?' Brandon stared at Jude in disbelief. He was so used to his brother doing everything he asked, he'd never thought Jude would refuse. 'What do you mean, "no", little brother?'

'I won't help you,' Jude spoke quietly, but his determination, never before pitted against Brandon's will, was unquestionable.

'You're scared,' Brandon resorted to an old trick. 'You always were a coward, even when you were a boy.'

'I'm scared, yes,' Jude admitted. 'But it's you I'm scared of. You've lost your reason and I fear for you and the rest of us if you get your way.'

Abruptly Jude turned on his heel and strode away. Without his help, Brandon's plan was sure to fail. Should he warn the others? But that would mean betraying his brother. Surely the High Priest could handle the situation without knowing about Brandon's involvement. As his thoughts went round and round in circles, he suddenly became aware of someone watching him. Looking up, he met Rhiannon's smiling eyes. Overcome with anxiety and guilt he nodded curtly to her and walked swiftly on, leaving her looking after him in bewilderment.

13

The taxi hooted impatiently as Michael opened the door of the cottage.

'Two minutes, OK!'

The driver nodded and Michael turned back to Aunt Val who was smiling bravely but couldn't hide the anxiety in her eyes.

'Are you sure you're fit enough . . .' she began.

'I'm fine,' Michael interrupted firmly. 'Staying here has made all the difference. Now I'm ready to go back to work. I have to,' he added in a different tone.

'That's what I'm worried about. This compulsion that's driving you into danger again and again.' She stopped, on the verge of tears.

Michael hugged her close.

'I promise you, I'm OK. I'll be back in less than a month. If anyone . . .' he paused, looking slightly self-conscious. 'If anyone calls, just tell them when I'll be back.'

'Who's going to call?' asked his aunt briskly. 'Hardly anyone knows you're here except . . .' Her faded blue eyes twinkled mischievously. 'You're thinking of that girl, Rhiannon, aren't you?'

Michael didn't reply, just hugged her again and walked quickly to the waiting taxi.

12 July 2012: Rhiannon's flat, Archway, north London

Since she'd returned from Stonehenge three weeks ago, Rhiannon had hardly slept. Every night she had flopped exhausted into bed, but then tossed and turned under the duvet as the events on the solstice tormented her tired brain in a series of semi-dreams, which seemed horribly real. Tonight she lay fretful and exhausted, moonlight streaming through the window directly onto her troubled face, too tired even to get up and close the curtains. A silver glow bathed the room in an eerie daylight as disjointed images from her dreams flickered back and forth across her mind.

There was Michael again, and the feel of his soaking leathers beneath her hands; looming shapes of a stone circle, faces lit by the rising sun; a brilliant crystal hanging round the neck of a tall, dark-haired woman; water rising in the darkness; the piercing blue eyes of her rescuer.

Try as she might to make light of the storm as merely a wrong place, wrong time situation, she couldn't get the image of the old man out of her mind. Why hadn't he looked frightened as he was swept away? He'd gazed at her as if he was concerned for *her*, but why wasn't he concerned for his own safety? And in her dreams she knew him too. She stood beside him in the same circle of people, within the same glittering white crystal columns she remembered from Stonehenge. She felt young and overwhelmed as the circle filled with an intense energy which crackled with tension. This man, her rescuer, was no longer old and frail, but a towering, exalted presence who dazzled her senses. But even he couldn't save her from the terror that was about to assail them all.

She sat up shaking. The dreams had seemed so real, as if she were living them, hardly dreams at all. Yanking the duvet from her sweating body, she tried to make sense of what she had seen. But as her heartbeat returned to something approaching normal, she told herself firmly that the strange images were no more than the consequence of an overwrought mind. What niggled her waking self was that the police had not believed her. Nor that arrogant arse, Michael. OK, he hadn't seen the car or the old man – it was pitch black for god's sake – but how dare he question her sanity? And another thing: she'd finally got round to posting the borrowed clothes back to him so she wouldn't have to speak to him and he hadn't even had the courtesy to ring her. She grimaced in the dark, realising how unreasonable she was being.

In the end she risked her friend's wrath and rang Lauren. It was five in the morning, but Rhiannon needed a reality check.

'Is this about the old man again?' Lauren seemed resigned to the same conversation she'd had repeatedly with her friend over the previous days and weeks.

'Lauren, I owe him my life. I would have drowned for sure if he hadn't pushed me up the bank. But where is he? Why haven't the police found him or his car?'

'He must have climbed out further downstream. But it's good news isn't it . . . that he hasn't been found?'

'I suppose . . .' Rhiannon wanted this to be true. 'But you should have seen it, Lauren, the water was raging, waist high and freezing. I watched as he was swept under. No one could've survived that. And anyway, what about the car? Surely the police should have found the car.'

'Only if he or the car were so damaged he couldn't drive away. That's why I'm saying he must have just gotten out somehow and gone home.' Lauren, always so reassuringly level-headed, paused in her comforting scenario. 'People and their cars don't just disappear, Rhi,' she added.

'No, you're right.' Rhiannon began to believe in a normal world again.

'Any news from the cute man with the spare trousers yet?' she heard a teasing note in her friend's question.

'If you mean that smug, patronising idiot who claims to have rescued me when I had been already rescued, then no, I haven't heard from him, thank God,' Rhiannon retorted.

'Hmm,' Lauren chuckled. 'I haven't heard you so passionate about a man since the dreadful Tyler from Media Connections.'

Rhiannon groaned. 'Yeah, yeah, have your laugh. I don't give a toss if you believe me. I can't stand the man.'

She heard Lauren yawn.

'Listen, sorry for waking you.'

'It's OK. You need to talk about it. It must have been

terrifying. But don't forget, it'd take more than a storm to flatten the redoubtable Rhiannon Davies.'

Rhiannon was just about to hang up, then she remembered.

'The mark on his wrist . . .'

'What mark?' the question was reluctant; Lauren didn't sound as if she wanted to know.

'The old man . . . he had a mark on his wrist that was identical to the one on mine. It's a sort of white circle enclosing a crescent, like a moon in the centre. I've just remembered.'

'You have a mark on your wrist?' Lauren was awake again. 'I've never noticed.'

'It's a birthmark. I wear my watch over it. It's tiny. But the old man's was the same . . . exactly the same. I saw it as I held on to him, Lauren. Bigger, but the same. I saw it.'

This was obviously a step too far for her tired friend.

'Rhi, it's late. Can we talk about this tomorrow?'

'You don't believe me do you?'

'Of course I believe you . . . it's just I'm too tired to work out what it means.'

'OK, sorry . . . sorry . . . Night.' If her friend found it hard to believe the mark, Rhiannon knew she certainly wouldn't believe the fact that her rescuer had called her name. Had she imagined it? *It's those bloody stones*, she thought as she put the phone down. She had always been a forthright person, efficient, in control, someone whom others trusted. Now, suddenly, she was being treated like a deluded fantasist. Even by Lauren, her best friend. Angrily, she leapt out of bed and dragged the curtains tight across the window, almost as if she were blaming the moon for all her problems. And in the darkness she finally slept.

14

10,500 BC: Hills above Atlantis

Rhiannon lay back against the soft turf and closed her eyes. The sun was warm on her face and the rich scents of summer surrounded her – wild thyme and sage, pine resin from the trees fringing the hill, the highest point on the island. How peaceful it was here, only the sound of bees droning among the flowers and the gentle bubbling of the water springing up from the rocks nearby. Perhaps she could be happy here.

Her fingers strayed to the small tattoo on the inside of her left wrist and traced the circular outline of the sun and the crescent of the moon. The symbol of harmony and union. But not for her.

Rhiannon sat up abruptly. The symbol of the priesthood meant only servitude to her. She looked down on the city of Atlantis, glistening in the sunlight, and on to the turquoise waters of the ocean beyond. Why was she destined to remain here? She wanted to travel like Tom and Michael . . . like Jude. Why did they have the freedom denied to her? She glanced over at Maya who was kneeling beside the spring collecting water in a crystal phial. Despite herself she smiled. Lucky Maya. She was happy to come here and collect the pure water to cleanse the crystals in her care.

As if reading her thoughts, Maya sat back on her heels and looked searchingly at her.

'What's wrong? You've been in a black mood for days. Has something happened?'

Maya's wolfhound, lying companionably by Rhiannon's side, growled softly as her fingers tightened in his rough fur. Rhiannon released her hold and patted his huge head apologetically as he wandered off to sit beside his mistress. Rhiannon looked into her friend's sympathetic blue eyes – she knew she could trust Maya but could she trust her with this? Oh, what the hell. She had to tell somebody.

'Something did happen,' she began slowly.

Maya looked at her encouragingly.

'I found out who my father is.'

'What!' Maya rocked back on her heels. 'I thought you were going to tell me something about . . .'

She stopped abruptly and gathered her thoughts.

'Your father? I thought he was a distant cousin of Lord Gabriel's. That's why Gabriel and Lilith adopted you when you were a baby, after your parents died.'

Rhiannon was shaking her head.

'My mother was a Celtic princess and she met my father when he was travelling in the Western Isles over twenty years ago. He came back to Atlantis without her but brought me with him.'

Maya stared at her in bewilderment.

'He brought you with him? So he's not dead? Who is he then?'

Rhiannon sighed.

'My father is the High Priest of Atlantis, Lord Gabriel himself.'

'Are you sure?' Maya blurted out, 'I mean, how did you find out? Does Lilith know?'

'Oh, she knows. Which could explain a lot about her attitude to me – like I'm a rival or something. And in answer to your other question, I did do some studying you know. It was all there in the crystal archives.'

'Rhiannon!' Maya was scandalised. 'We're not supposed to touch them let alone read them!'

Rhiannon shrugged. 'Why not? Why should only the hierarchy see them – it's our history too. In fact, it really is my history.'

'So now what? How do you feel?'

'I don't know what to feel. I've found my father but he's never acknowledged me.'

'Well, that could have been difficult.' Maya was scrupulously fair. 'It must have been just before he married Lilith and became High Priest. And he's always treated you like a daughter.'

'Yes, I suppose I should be grateful I wasn't left on a hillside to die.'

Maya could see how upset Rhiannon really was and crouched down beside her, holding her close.

'And,' continued Rhiannon, her voice slightly muffled, 'my mother just let me go, a tiny baby . . .'

'We don't know why she did that,' Maya said gently. 'There could be all sorts of reasons. It doesn't mean she didn't love you.'

'Love! They didn't need me and I certainly don't need them. Anyway, we'd better get going.'

She gently disentangled herself from Maya's arms.

'But Rhiannon,' Maya's eyes were troubled. 'What are you going to do? Are you going to say anything?'

'What's to say? All I really want to do is get as far away from here as possible.'

Maya looked so worried that Rhiannon relented.

'Don't worry. I'm not going anywhere yet. And when I've made my plans you'll be the first to know.'

Maya followed Rhiannon down the path towards the tree where their horses were tethered. A crack had appeared in her ordered, harmonious world and she felt as if the ground was shifting beneath her feet. A shiver ran through her and for a moment all she could see was separation and loss.

15

Woods above the city of Atlantis

'Race you back to the Citadel!'

Rhiannon threw the challenge over her shoulder then turned in the saddle to check Maya's reaction. Maya looked at Rhiannon's powerful chestnut, then patted her docile grey's head. No contest there, but she was pleased that Rhiannon's high spirits were returning.

'You're on! And the last one back cleans all the crystals.'

Rhiannon smiled affectionately at her friend and took off down the bridle path leading through the woods. Maya followed and managed to keep her in sight as the path twisted and turned through the trees, but she was already far behind when she saw Rhiannon's horse veer violently to the left, whinnying and snorting in fear. As Maya watched in horror, the horse reared as Rhiannon struggled to control him then she was catapulted through the air, falling heavily to the ground.

White with anxiety, Maya spurred her horse forward but before she got there she heard pounding hooves coming from the opposite direction and a rider, travelling fast, skidded to a halt when he saw the scene before him. Maya recognised Jude's gleaming back stallion and felt mingled relief and dismay. Relief that Jude would know what to do, dismay that he'd see Rhiannon like this – Maya was well aware of her friend's infatuation.

Jude leapt from his horse and knelt beside Rhiannon, running his hands expertly over her motionless body, then carefully placing his cloak beneath her head. Maya pulled up beside him as her wolfhound disappeared into the undergrowth, growling ferociously.

'She's only stunned. Nothing seems to be broken.'

Jude smiled up at Maya who felt her heart skip a beat. He really had a devastating smile. She slid to the ground as her dog reappeared with a huge snake dangling limply from his jaws. He dropped the dead snake at Maya's feet and Jude prodded it with his sword.

'It must have spooked her horse. You don't normally see them at this time of year.'

'Yes,' Maya agreed. 'She's a very good horsewoman,' she added loyally.

'I'm sure she is. You stay with her while I check her horse.'

Maya knelt by Rhiannon and looked at her anxiously. Her face was very pale but she was breathing normally and as Maya watched, her eyes opened and she struggled to sit up.

'Maya, what happened? Where's my horse?'

'A snake spooked him. Don't worry, Jude's gone to find him.'

'Jude? Oh no!'

'Ssh, he's coming back.'

Jude walked slowly towards then, leading Rhiannon's horse which was limping badly.

'Thank you,' said Rhiannon formally and leaning heavily on Maya she tried to stand only to grimace with pain.

Jude sprang to her side.

'Don't put any weight on it. You've probably just sprained it.'

Rhiannon bit her lip in frustration.

'And my horse is lame too!'

Jude smiled down at her.

'I'll take you home.'

He picked her up as if she weighed no more than a feather and lifted her onto her horse. Maya suppressed a smile and looked to see how Rhiannon was taking this display of masculine authority, but the only sign of emotion she could see was a faint blush.

'Maya, can you lead her horse back? I'll take care of Rhiannon.'

'Of course,' Maya agreed and watched as Jude leapt up behind Rhiannon and rode off. Lucky Rhiannon, she thought, as she followed slowly behind.

Rhiannon wasn't sure if she was feeling lucky or not. She was riding on a magnificent black stallion encircled by the strong arms of the man of her dreams, but what must he be thinking of her, *falling off her horse like that.*

Jude was wrestling with his own thoughts. Why hadn't he noticed her before? Sure, he knew who she was – they'd exchanged a few words now and then, but it was as if he'd never really seen her before. She was beautiful. He looked at her slim form sitting so upright in front of him and a strand of her silky chestnut hair brushed across his cheek. He tightened his hold on the reins and Rhiannon relaxed slightly against him. To his surprise he could feel his heart beating loudly in his chest and he was sure he could hear her heart beating in unison.

At that moment, she turned to speak to him and they smiled into each other's eyes with total recognition.

'Tell me,' Rhiannon began as Jude said, 'Rhiannon, why . . .' then they both broke off in confusion.

Rhiannon took a deep breath.

'I was only going to ask you to tell me about your travels. There's nothing I want to do more than see the world.'

'Really? But surely you're training to be a Priestess of the Moon. That's a great honour – to be one of the chosen.'

'That's exactly what's wrong with it,' Rhiannon burst out passionately. 'I was chosen. It was not my choice.'

'And choice is important to you. I understand, though usually we choose the priesthood as much as it chooses us.'

'Your brother walked away from it.'

Rhiannon felt Jude's sharp intake of breath and wondered if she'd gone too far. No one knew exactly why Brandon had left the priesthood. There had been some malicious rumours but she knew that Jude was very loyal to his brother.

To her relief, Jude laughed.

'You should talk to Brandon about it some time. It's true he found the priesthood a bit claustrophobic, but he cares deeply about Atlantis.'

She must have looked worried because Jude touched her hand reassuringly and the smile was back in his voice.

'Now tell me more about these plans of yours. Where do you want to go to first?'

57

Relieved that she hadn't offended him, Rhiannon started telling him about her secret ambitions and found him a sympathetic audience. Far too soon the gates of the Citadel were before them.

Citadel courtyard, Atlantis

'Michael, look who's just ridden in!'

Tom pulled Michael to his vantage point on the battlements and they looked down to see Jude and Rhiannon riding through the gates, followed at a distance by Maya. Michael's face dropped and Tom put his arm round his shoulders in ready sympathy.

Gabriel had seen them too and smiled at the handsome couple they made.

'Perhaps they'll make a match of it yet,' he remarked to Lilith.

'Who?' she asked absently.

Gabriel nodded over to where Jude was helping Rhiannon down from his horse.

'Rhiannon and . . . Jude!' Lilith was incredulous. *'Never. Michael will be her consort.'*

Gabriel looked at her quizzically.

'You couldn't blame her for preferring a man to a boy.'

Lilith just shook her head and turned to see Rhiannon and Jude deep in conversation. She gazed intently at Jude and as if drawn by a magnet he turned towards her. Rhiannon put her hand on his arm and he smiled briefly at her then walked briskly away, following Lilith into the Citadel. Rhiannon looked after him, a hurt expression on her face, and her eyes briefly met Gabriel's before she too turned and limped away.

16

3 August 2012: Heathrow Airport arrivals hall

Michael blinked as the flashlights popped and dozens of voices demanded his attention.

'Michael! Michael, over here! Mr Wolf, just a word!'

Now he knew what it felt like to be on the other side of the camera. The sling on his left arm was slowing him down but he hitched his bag over his good shoulder and sidestepped the cameras and microphones with a nod and a smile.

He'd almost reached the exit when a stunning Chinese girl stepped firmly in his path.

'That's no way to treat an old friend,' she said with a challenging smile. 'And all publicity's good publicity, right?'

'Shuang, hi! I can't stop.'

'Mi – chael . . .' she drew the syllables out and looked deep into his eyes. 'Not even for me?'

Michael returned the smile. He remembered too well the persuasive power of those disturbing green eyes.

'I'm sorry, Shuang. No press, no interviews.'

She saw he meant it and changed tack.

'Well, how about a drink later? We have a lot to catch up on.'

'Not this time. I already have a date this evening.'

Shuang pouted then declared dramatically, 'You've thrown me over for another woman!'

Michael, thinking of Aunt Val waiting anxiously at home, nodded.

'Got it in one!'

Glastonbury at dawn, Somerset, 8 August 2012
The summer dawn was cool and still as Lily and Gabe made their

way to the top of Glastonbury Tor. Together they watched the sun light up the hillside and gazed in awe at the panoramic landscape revealed below them. This was their still point, where the veil between the worlds was thinnest and they both felt the strong pull of the universe. Both also remembered the temple that had once stood there, with the twelve columns and the intricate mosaic floor depicting the signs of the zodiac. Gabe leaned gratefully against the square tower that now stood in the temple's place.

'Maybe if we stay here long enough we'll be whisked aloft.'

Lily laughed at his fanciful notion. 'We haven't finished Gabe. But this time . . . I don't know, it feels right this time.'

The smile faded from Gabe's face. 'All I know for sure is that this is our last chance. You've seen the charts. 21 December 2012. The power focusing on Stonehenge will blast the earth apart unless we can reactivate the crystal and seal the portal.'

'And we will.' Lily refused to acknowledge the possibility of failure. 'We've already found Michael and Rhiannon.'

'Yes, but that was weeks ago. Michael seems to have disappeared off the face of the earth.'

'He'll be back.'

Gabe wasn't sure if she was trying to convince him or herself. 'And the other three?'

'Jude can be found. He's near, I can feel him, but he's masking. He's avoiding us.'

Gabe laughed. 'You can't blame the man.'

'What do you mean?' Lily was immediately defensive, as she always was when Jude's name was mentioned.

'I'm just saying we set ourselves a mammoth task all those lifetimes ago. And we've tried so many times before to set the ceremony up and never really got close. Perhaps Jude just can't be bothered any more.'

Lily turned her face towards the light morning breeze that was building on the deserted Tor. 'You mean *you* can't.'

Gabe sighed. 'I didn't say that. But yes, if you're asking me, perhaps I am tired of it all. Perhaps it's just too difficult.' He began to crack the husky's leather lead rhythmically against the tower wall. Atlas was away across the other side of the hill, running down the numerous scents on offer.

Lily drew herself up to her full height and swung round to face her husband. 'You think I'm not tired?' she demanded, her Atlantean blue eyes flashing. 'You think I enjoy this struggle each lifetime? Of course I don't. But what we feel is irrelevant.'

Now her voice dropped and her words were clear and slow and very intense in the silence. 'Gabe, this is our responsibility, ours alone. I know we were acting for the best but our failure to complete the seventh level left Stonehenge vulnerable.'

Gabe nodded wearily, 'And Atlantis disappeared beneath the waves for ever.'

Lily grabbed his arms, pinned them to his side. 'The same thing's happening again. Can't you see? The signs of separation are everywhere, the total dominance of a masculine force field. Gabe . . . Gabe . . . You can't give up on me now.'

Gabe shook her off. He had heard this so many times before. 'I know, I know.'

Looking around for the dog, Gabe began to move off down the steps that led towards the town.

'You say Jude is close, but how close? He's managed to evade us for centuries. Why should this time be any different? And the other two? Where are they?'

For a moment they plodded in single file, in silence, then Gabe stopped and turned, repentant, taking Lily's resistant hand in his. 'I'm sorry. Of course I'll do everything I can to help you. Of course I will.'

Despite Gabe's reassurance, Lily still felt the whole weight of responsibility on her own shoulders. Perhaps because she had been to blame in the first place, by not seeing how Jude's passion for her could cloud the purity of his actions. Perhaps what was driving her was her own need to atone for that one fatal mistake.

It was a little before seven as Gabe and Lily entered Glastonbury. The streets were mostly deserted at this hour. Only a few dazed

61

young hippies lay slumped around the base of the nineteenth-century market cross in the town centre as if they had spent the night there.

Gabe and Lily made for a small café they knew to be open. There was a wooden table outside on the pavement and they sat in silence in the sunshine, sipping their tea. Atlas lay quietly at Gabe's feet. Neither felt they belonged in this cosy, colourful market town. Their home was elsewhere, beyond the confines of this earthly universe. If only they could return there.

Suddenly Atlas shot up and began to bark. They saw Aunt Val making her way along the narrow pavement. Atlas bounded up to her and began licking her hand.

'Hey, boy,' Aunt Val stroked the husky's pale coat.

She looked round for Lily.

The women embraced, a full, warm hug. 'What are you two doing out so early?'

Gabe shuffled his feet. 'Oh, you know . . . such a lovely day.' He didn't want to explain why they had come to the Tor at dawn.

Aunt Val thought she detected a sadness about her two friends. 'Why don't you come over to me for lunch today? It's just me and Michael, so it won't be very exciting, but we could have something in the garden.' She looked expectantly from one to the other.

'Thanks,' Lily touched the old lady's arm. 'That's very kind, but we've got things we should do at home.'

Aunt Val shook her finger at them. 'It's only lunch. We've all got to eat.'

The others laughed, but Aunt Val's face quickly fell.

'I'm worried about Michael. Since he got back from North Africa he's looked like death warmed up.'

She turned to Lily. 'He says he keeps seeing visions, but he won't say what of. He's not sleeping, I can hear him treading up and down all night. I don't know what to do.'

'Send him to me,' Lily replied immediately. 'I can treat him, Val. Tell him to come whenever he likes. You have my number.'

'How will you do it?' Aunt Val had lived too long not to ask questions.

Lily laughed. 'Don't worry, I shan't turn him into a druid. Light hypnosis is much more effective.'

Aunt Val shook her head. 'To be honest that boy needs something to believe in, I'm almost prepared to concede to the pre-Christian mob.'

'I have to hand it to you,' Gabe chuckled as Aunt Val hurried off down the high street. 'You never miss an opportunity.'

'You said it Gabe, we haven't much time. Maybe this time I can awaken Michael's memories fully.'

'But can't you do anything to speed things up? We've only got a few months left.'

'I know what I'm doing,' Lily snapped. 'You know as well as I do that Michael has to remember his destiny. He has to know without a shadow of a doubt who he is and what he has to do. I can't just tell him. It doesn't work that way.'

'I know, I know,' said Gabe soothingly. 'He's not ready yet, but when?'

'Soon,' Lily said firmly. 'And I can sense the other two, Tom and Maya. They're far away, on the other side of the world, but something,' she paused momentarily, 'something will happen to alert them.'

'So why do you look worried?'

Lily didn't reply.

17

It was dark when Tom reached the deserted cliff edge, determined to catch the very first rays of the rising sun. Rafaella had insisted he go, she said it was important, though Tom couldn't see why. But he didn't feel he had a choice; there was something spookily powerful about his new friend.

Just as the first bright fingers of light pierced the horizon, he heard someone behind him. Turning, he saw a girl coming quickly down the slope towards him. The golden light caught in her long fair hair, which floated around her like a veil. Tom, not given to fanciful notions, thought she looked like an angel.

She hesitated as she drew close, then veered off to sit at a short distance from him, curling her long legs gracefully under her as she sank onto the dry headland grass. It was as if she hadn't seen him, but Tom was not put off.

He pointed towards the mountain in the distance, lit up by the first rays of golden light.

'Did you know, there's a legend that Mount Warning is made entirely of quartz, so it's a crystal mountain.'

The girl turned to look. There was an intensity in her gaze, as if she were searching for something on the horizon.

'I'm told the light hits the mountain, which transmits the energy to Uluru, which in turn amplifies it and sends it on to all the earth chakras,' Tom went on, parroting what Rafaella had told him, but with a smile on his lips.

For a moment the girl stared at him, then she laughed softly.

'And you don't believe a word of it?'

Tom shrugged. 'Hey, I'm an open-minded kinda guy. But there's a way of talking here in Byron that's real strange.' He paused, 'I'm Tom Page by the way.' He held his hand out across the space.

'Maya,' she took his hand and smiled, her eyes, as piercingly blue as his own, lighting up her beautiful face. 'I know what you mean about Byron. Everyone's a New Age guru.'

'Have you been here long?' Tom moved closer, still not entirely convinced that this stunning girl was real.

Maya shook her head. 'A few weeks. I'm going back to England in a few days. I was on a dig near Alice – I'm an archaeologist.'

'Is England your home?'

She shook her head again. 'Not really; I have family there, my father's in Oxford, but I'm not sure where my home is. I travel all the time, round and round the globe. You?'

'Same. I'm from Arizona, but I haven't been home for months. I've been monitoring ocean currents off the north coast, but we had to close the operation down after the last cyclone. I stopped off here on my way to London and a new job.'

'I wouldn't have thought there were too many ocean currents in London.'

Tom laughed. 'The job spec's sorta weird. The head honcho seems intent on saving the planet, but then doesn't give a toss about global warming. It's all about energy supply. I don't have a clue what he wants from me.'

Maya didn't answer, but put her head on one side and frowned at him for a moment. She found herself drawn to this man, not just because of his blond good looks and dazzling smile, there was something else.

'Do I know you from somewhere? I feel I do, but . . .'

'That should be my line,' Tom said.

Their laughter was interrupted by a high-pitched barking. They both jerked round and saw a large white husky bounding across the headland towards them.

Maya smiled. 'That's the dog I saw on the beach yesterday,' she said, 'I've always wanted one like that.'

But Tom tensed, 'He doesn't look too friendly to me . . . get up . . . quick.'

He went to pull Maya to her feet, but she shook him off, laughing.

'Don't be daft, it's a she, and she's gorgeous.' She held her hands out to the approaching dog, then caught sight of a tall stocky figure, running behind the husky.

'That's Erik, her owner.'

Suddenly the golden light seemed to dim and the cliff shuddered beneath them. It felt like an earth tremor and after the cyclones and floods further up the coast, no one knew what was going to happen next. He turned to Maya who was finally scrambling to her feet, white with shock. She grabbed Tom's arm.

'We have to get out of here. Erik . . . he's the Captain of the Guard. He's come for the crystal.'

Tom looked into her eyes. Where was she? But as he stared, he felt as if he too was being sucked into another world, and it was strangely familiar. He stepped in front of Maya as the man's figure leapt down towards them, pulsating red in the fierce, bright sunlight. The dog reached them first and stood four-square, snarling up at them.

'Go Maya, run . . . now!' Tom pushed Maya away from the growling dog, but it was too late.

'Hold her, Tikani,' Tom heard the man roar.

The dog tried unsuccessfully to dart around Tom's legs to get at the girl. Busy with the dog, Tom didn't see Erik coming until the side of the man's large hand slashed down like a weapon on Tom's neck.

'Out of the way, boy. It's not you I want.'

Tom, reeling from the blow, threw himself at Erik, trying to wrestle him to the ground. But Erik shook him off effortlessly, a flicker of curiosity, almost amusement in his eyes. Sprawled at Erik's feet, Tom felt himself being lifted bodily off the ground, arms pinned to his side like a plank of wood. Erik shook his head dismissively, 'I warned you.' Heaving Tom high above his head he hurled him towards the edge of the cliff as if Tom's tall, muscled frame weighed no more than a feather.

66

Arms and legs flailing helplessly, Tom flew through the air and landed painfully with his body hanging over the sheer drop to the sea beneath. He scrabbled desperately to pull himself up, dimly aware of Maya's frantic voice shouting his name. A shadow fell across him and he looked up to see Erik staring down.

'You must have known I'd never give up,' Erik grinned maliciously, obviously enjoying the moment before stamping viciously on Tom's left hand. Tom grunted with pain and swung his other hand over to grab Erik's foot. Erik stepped back and aimed one final kick which sent Tom reeling backwards, disappearing from sight over the edge of the cliff.

Erik turned to Maya, who flinched at the hatred in his eyes. She couldn't run, the dog blocked her every move, its fierce, ice-blue gaze locked onto Maya's face, a low growl rumbling in its throat.

'You know why I'm here,' Erik stated calmly. 'The crystal, Maya. Where is it?'

The dog's hackles began to rise and she growled again.

'Do it, Tikani,' he whispered, snapping his fingers at the dog.

Maya stood rigid with shock. As if in a nightmare, she watched the dog bare her teeth in a ferocious snarl as she prepared to launch herself. Tikani leapt, but, amazingly, not at Maya. Instead she crashed the full weight of her body at her owner's chest. Erik staggered backwards in surprise, his angry commands turning to fear as the dog drove him relentlessly towards the cliff edge, biting and snapping at his legs. Dangerously close to the edge, Erik tried desperately to get away. His eyes met Maya's for one agonising second, then the dog renewed her frenzied attack and Erik stepped backwards into space. Maya heard a despairing scream, followed by the heavy thud of a body hitting the cliff side. Then silence.

Maya fell to her knees, stunned. She couldn't comprehend what had just happened. Who was that man, what did he mean about the crystal? She became aware of the dog nuzzling her face, licking away her tears. Maya hugged the dog to her. Terrified at what she might see, she leaned over the edge of the cliff, then jerked back in shock as Tom's blond head almost hit hers, a resolute grin on his tanned, handsome face as he clambered towards safety.

They both stood and looked down at Erik's body, lying absolutely still on a ledge only feet from the treacherous rocks.

'Is he dead?' Maya whispered, shaking.

'Only one way to find out,' Tom stated softly.

'No . . . no . . . please . . .' Maya clung to Tom's arm as she realised he was going back down. 'We should ring the emergency services. If he's not dead, he'll kill you Tom.'

Tom searched Maya's face. 'Why? Why should a perfect stranger want to kill me?' He shrugged off her hand. 'I don't know what happened just now, but I can't just leave him there. If he's badly injured every second counts.'

Maya took a shaky breath. 'You'll never be able to get him up alone. Be sensible . . . please.'

But Tom had already gone, shinning down the cliff as if he were walking along a pavement.

'Call triple 0,' he shouted as he went. Within minutes he had reached the prone body. Maya watched him shake the man, feel his pulse, talk to him. He looked up to Maya and made a thumbs-up sign.

'He's alive,' he called, and Maya didn't know whether to be relieved or not. She didn't understand, any more than Tom, what had just happened. But she knew that Erik, or some part of Erik, was her deadly enemy. She saw him slowly pulling Erik into a sitting position, his back cradled against Tom's chest.

Tom watched Erik open his eyes and look around.

'Where . . . what happened?'

There was no sign of the hatred and aggression in his eyes as he stared, baffled, at Tom.

'You fell,' Tom gestured towards the cliff top.

'Fell? How?'

'Not sure, pal . . . stay still, rescue's on its way. I think you've broken your leg.'

Erik looked down at his left leg, the thigh bone twisted outwards at an odd angle.

'Thanks . . . thanks, mate.' Erik looked up and Tom saw the man's eyes suddenly unfocused and losing consciousness.

'Wake up Erik . . . wake up, stay with me,' he voice was loud and urgent, and a second later Erik's eyes snapped open. Tom recoiled. This was the other man again, the one who'd tried to kill him.

'Don't think you've won,' Erik hissed through clenched teeth. 'You and your bastard friends.'

'Stay still,' Tom answered as calmly as he could, 'help's on its way.'

Erik's breathing became more laboured.

'I will have the crystal . . . I've been sent. Brandon . . . always gets what he wants . . .'

The man's eyes shut slowly, veiling his strange hatred.

Tom could hear sirens in the distance. Feeling helpless, he touched Erik's shoulder.

'Hold on, you've got to hold on.'

Erik's eyes fluttered open again. He looked confused.

'What happened to me?' he asked again, and now he seemed just an ordinary guy, his gaze soft and bewildered, no memories of other lives.

Tom and Maya stood bemused on the cliff as the ambulance drove off with Erik. It was already baking hot, sun glancing off the clear turquoise water that stretched to the horizon. The husky had hovered at Maya's feet, reluctant to go in the ambulance with her owner, despite his painful pleas.

'Do you understand what that was all about? You seemed to know him,' Tom asked Maya.

Maya shook her head. 'I did know him . . . but it was as if I was in a dream . . . nightmare rather . . . I wasn't me . . . well it was, but . . .' she looked up helplessly at Tom. 'I can't explain.'

Tom shrugged, smiled. 'I sorta know what you mean . . . but best not to tell the cops about him being the Captain of the Guard. They might lock *you* up, not him.'

She smiled weakly. 'Will he remember anything?'

'I don't know, doubt it somehow. Stick to the story that he got too close to the edge and fell, or we'll never be allowed to leave for London.'

Maya couldn't really take in what he was saying. Erik's attack was the stuff of nightmares, yet her own part in the drama, where she had recognised him as the Captain of the Guard and known why he wanted the crystal, had been totally real. She felt her legs give way suddenly and sank onto the rough headland grass.

'Are you staying in Byron alone?' Tom asked anxiously. She realised she had known Tom for barely three hours, yet he seemed like the oldest friend she had in the world.

She nodded. She was booked into a small bed and breakfast in the town.

'I don't think you should be by yourself,' Tom was saying. 'You can stay with me. Then we'll go and talk to Rafaella. She's the genuine article. If anyone can shed light on the evil captain, it'll be her.'

18

Gabe finished off the astrological chart he had drawn for Michael Wolf and leaned back in his chair, flexing his aching shoulders. It had been hard work, not like in the past when his effortless mastery of the stars, the movement of energy and the mysteries of alchemy was unsurpassed. Michael had been his star pupil back then, destined to succeed him when his training was complete.

He glanced at the chart and sighed. The challenges facing Michael precisely mirrored the task that faced them all. Michael's Aries sun directly opposed his Libra moon. The masculine versus the feminine, individuality versus partnership.

His fingers traced the aspects between the planets. Chiron, signifying karma carried forward from previous lifetimes, sat right next to the sun – Michael, the wounded warrior. Still, Michael's journey in this lifetime was more encouraging; he was following the path of the seeker, his quest the search for meaning, for higher knowledge. Lily would need great delicacy to unlock Michael's memories but the potential was there.

'Anything I should know before Michael gets here?' Gabe looked round to see Lily standing behind him. How had she remained so beautiful, so vibrant while he felt his life force ebbing away? She was wearing a delicate silk robe in shades of amethyst and turquoise and the crystals on her fingers and around her neck reflected rainbow prisms around the room. Her familiar perfume, tantalising and elusive . . . Gabe shook his head ruefully. She would have to be careful not to distract Michael from recognising his true soulmate.

'I know, I know,' she said impatiently, answering his unspoken criticism, 'but the attraction that Michael feels is part of the process. It's an attraction to what I was then, back in Atlantis, not what I am now.'

Gabe handed her the chart. She studied it briefly then laid her hand gently on his shoulder. 'Rhiannon's the one who will heal his heart, as he will heal hers. If all goes well they will take our place and we shall have peace at last.'

There was a moment of companionable silence broken by the sound of a motorbike approaching the house. 'There he is now,' said Lily, and for a moment she looked anxious. 'So much depends on this.'

Gabe stood up and raised her hand to his lips. 'And you will succeed,' he said confidently. 'Go and work your magic.'

Lily watched Michael dismount and wrench his helmet off. For a moment he stood, as if lost, gazing vacantly towards the barn. The morning sun played on his face, lighting up his strong features, still tanned from the weeks in the sun, but his normally luminous eyes were dull and empty. Lily smiled to herself and allowed a frisson of desire for this handsome man to come and go. Inappropriate, she knew it was, but a woman could dream.

'Hi . . .' He came towards her and bent to the kiss she laid on his cheek.

'I thought you might not come.' Lily led Michael into the kitchen.

'Aunt Val threatened to cut me off without a penny if I didn't,' he gave her a wan smile. 'I haven't slept for a week.'

Lily pushed ineffectively at the piles of papers and books that covered the kitchen table to clear a space. 'Sit. I'll get you some tea.'

She filled the kettle and put it on the Rayburn. Trying to tune in to the man behind her, she suddenly realised what was bothering him.

'The young soldier survived,' she said quietly. 'They managed to get him to a doctor, but he would have died if you hadn't gone back for him.'

Michael's face was white beneath his tan.

'How do you know that? It wasn't in the papers.'

Lily turned to meet his suspicious gaze.

'You were in a convoy with the rebel troops. A mortar shell landed a few yards away and the truck in front drove off so fast that the boy in the back fell off and landed on his head. They drove off without him. You forced your driver to stop, ran back and picked up the boy. That's when you got the shrapnel wound to your arm. You got the boy into the car and took him to the next village.'

Michael stared at her in shock. All this was true but how could she possibly know?

Lily answered his unspoken question.

'I saw it happen. I've told you this because I want you to trust what I'm about to tell you. I know you are troubled by something buried deep in your memory. You can't rest until you find out what it is.'

'There's something I have to do,' Michael mumbled, almost to himself. 'People's lives depend on it and I can't remember.'

'I can help you remember,' Lily said softly. 'If you trust me, I can help you.'

Lily settled Michael in the deep armchair in her workroom.

'What are you going to do to me?' Michael joked, but he looked apprehensive.

'I want to put you into a state of deep relaxation.' Lily sat beside him, out of his eyeline.

'Sort of "you're getting sleepy" stuff?' He fidgeted, pulling the cushion behind his head deeper into his neck.

'Exactly. But none of what is about to happen can happen if you don't want it to.'

'That sounds sinister . . .' Lily could tell that Michael barely had the energy to speak and she was worried he might fall asleep.

'Close your eyes and focus on your breath. In, out, deep, slow breaths.' For a while she watched as he battled to relax, then gradually she sensed his muscles begin to loosen, his breathing deepen. 'Now imagine a bright white light filling your head. See this light and watch as it flows down through your body, taking with it a warmth that brings peace . . .'

It took less than ten minutes after Lily began to count in descending order before she deemed Michael ready. She carefully pressed the record button on the machine beside her.

'Go back in time, you have your camera . . . what do you see?'

She saw Michael twitch, his whole body became tense and alert, but his eyes remained closed. His voice was no more than a whisper.

'She's just sitting there, it's as if she's dead, but it's her child who's dead. In her lap, so still.'

'What are you doing?'

'I'm taking a photograph, a lot of photographs . . . click, click, click. Putting my camera almost in her face and she doesn't move, not a muscle. Just sits there cross-legged on the ground with her child in her lap. She's not even covered it, and it might be sleeping but I know it's not.'

'Can you do anything for her?'

Michael shook his head vigorously. 'There's nothing, except money, I can give her money, and I do, but there are hundreds like her all around. The living dead. The bomb went off outside a school.' Tears began to trickle down Michael's face, but he did nothing to wipe them away.

'Go back again. Further, much further back. You don't have a camera now . . . this is another life. What do you see?'

There is silence for a moment, as if Michael is watching something. 'It's dark, dusty and very, very hot. I can't breathe. I'm hiding under a pile of sacks and I can't breathe.' His breathing becomes laboured and shallow, his hands rise to his face as if to move the sacks.

'Do you know why you're hiding?'

'Yes . . . I'm with my big brother. The soldiers are torching the village. If they find us they'll kill us.'

'Where are you?'

74

'Spain, I'm Basque. My brother holds my hand under the sacks, he's as frightened as me. I can hear the soldiers coming. We're in an outhouse . . . they'll find us . . . I know they'll find us . . .'

Lily watched for a minute or two as his breathing came and went in agonising gasps, then suddenly his face softened and he relaxed. That life was over. She let him rest, then she spoke again.

'Now, Michael, go even further back. This time there's a temple. You are part of a group that has a purpose in the temple, seven of you, in a circle . . . Can you see that?'

The look on Michael's face was puzzled. 'No . . . no I can't see a temple. I'm in a garden. It's very beautiful . . . the flowers are strong colours, like you get in the Med, but this garden is lush and green, very peaceful. There is a fountain in the centre with a ledge running round it. It's in the shape of a . . . it looks like a crescent moon and a sun intertwined. I am sitting on the edge.'

'Go on.'

'I'm excited. There's a girl, she's tall, dark-haired . . . beautiful. She and I have been chosen. It's a great honour. At least I think so. I'm not sure what she's thinking.'

'Do you recognise her?' Lily had to contain her own, present-day excitement.

Michael laughed. 'Of course . . . it's Rhiannon.'

'And what have you and Rhiannon been chosen for?'

'We're disciples to the High Priest and Priestess of Atlantis. We are to be trained up, to be part of their small group.'

'Do you see me, Michael?' Lily found herself holding her breath.

Without hesitation Michael whispered, 'You're the High Priestess.'

Lily's breath softly released and she switched off the tape. Slowly she brought him out of the hypnotic trance. When he opened his eyes she noticed they were no longer dulled with pain, but curiously at peace.

'So . . . what did I say?' Michael tried to pull himself upright in the chair, but seemed to have no strength and flopped back on the cushions.

'What do you remember?'

'Umm . . .' he sighed. 'Not much. Sort of jumbled images . . . no, I can't say for sure. Was I rambling?'

Lily laughed. 'All over the place. But I've taped it. Take it home and listen to what you said. Do you feel all right?'

Michael still looked bewildered. 'I feel weak, a bit light-headed. But good . . . calmer I think.' He looked directly at Lily. 'What have you done to me?'

'Listen to the tape and ring me,' she told him, and would say no more. She was exhausted herself, but she knew that there had been a vital breakthrough and another step forward in her complex plan.

'Promise me you'll listen to the tape,' she said, handing it to Michael as he got up to go. 'It's important.'

Michael gave her a quizzical glance. 'Important for what?'

Lily didn't answer him, but her eyes bore into his, intense and passionate. He felt she was almost compelling him to do as she asked, and for a moment he had the curious sensation that he belonged to her. He wondered if she were a bit mad. But then all these New Age people were touched weren't they?

'OK, OK, keep your hair on.' He pulled on his leather jacket and stuffed the tape into his pocket.

'He was there, in Atlantis!' Lily found Gabe in the barn, mending the leg of one of the kitchen chairs.

Gabe stopped what he was doing, placing the chair carefully right-side up on the dirt floor.

'At the temple?'

'In the temple garden. He saw Rhiannon, he knew it was her.' Lily clapped her hands. 'I recognised it, the flowers, the stone fountain. Gabe he was there and he saw her. He saw me too.'

Gabe smiled slowly. 'Well done.' He paused and Lily knew

what he was thinking. It was important, but such a small step. 'And he'll listen to the tape?'

Lily nodded emphatically. 'Oh he'll listen. I made sure of that. He won't know why he is listening, beyond curiosity of course, but he'll listen all right.'

19

Rhiannon forced her way through the crowds at Tottenham Court Road tube station and emerged breathless onto the busy street. She hated being underground and the tubes seemed more nightmarish than ever with disgruntled hordes of tourists searching for something to do as the unpredictable weather forced yet another Olympic event to be rescheduled. Now the rain had stopped and the air was warm but curiously thin as if the oxygen was being sucked out of it and little gusts of wind blew swirls of litter around her ankles.

Desperate to get away from the crowds, she cut through a series of narrow alleyways leading to her office in Berwick Street. Today she was on a mission. She had spent the previous evening assembling the footage she'd shot for her documentary. It was very disturbing. She'd been commissioned to make a trite, half-hour trawl through the recent spate of strange phenomena that had hit the headlines – sort of *X Files* lite – but her material was anything but trite. She was determined to persuade Sharon, her boss, to take it seriously and find her more money to expand it.

The alleyway was curiously deserted and Rhiannon's heart sank when she saw a dishevelled figure appear at the far end. It looked like an old woman, one of the persistent lucky white-heather sellers who haunted the area. Rhiannon picked up speed but the old woman grabbed her arm as she passed and forced her to stop.

'Lucky heather, dearie. Bring you a handsome young lover. Only three pounds.'

Dark brown eyes set in a wrinkled, whiskery face twinkled up at her then narrowed in surprise.

'Though I'm thinking it'll be more than luck you'll be needing.'

Rhiannon sighed. Here came the spiel – cross my palm with silver. But the old woman said nothing as she grabbed Rhiannon's hand and scanned her palm. Rhiannon tried to pull her hand away but the woman held on tight, tracing the lines and humming to herself. Finally she released Rhiannon's hand and looked sadly into her eyes.

'So many lives. So many heartaches. But hold on, be brave, it's coming to an end.'

Then, as Rhiannon stared at her in bewilderment, she scrabbled at the grubby layers of scarves around her neck, tugged sharply, and detached a small silver disc from the necklace she was wearing.

'Take it, dearie. You need it more than I do.'

She pushed the disc into Rhiannon's unresisting hand and Rhiannon looked at it – a circle surrounding a crescent moon. Rhiannon's heart lurched. It reminded her of the mark on her wrist and something else too, something she couldn't remember.

'What does this mean . . .' she began, but the woman had gone. The alleyway was deserted and there was no sign she'd ever been there. *Maybe I am going mad*, Rhiannon thought, then pulled herself together. She wasn't going mad, something was going on and she was going to sort it. With the light of battle in her eyes, she strode on to tackle Sharon.

The black door of the office stuck, as usual, as Rhiannon was buzzed in, and she had to heft her shoulder to it. She climbed the four flights of narrow, rickety stairs at breakneck speed, past the chilly toilet with the shelf of dirty mugs and stained, blue linoleum, to the top floor. The offices of Stargate Productions were, like the rest of the building, pokey and dark. Two desks were crammed together in the centre of the room, each with a massive VDU, while around the edges of the room were shelves full of CDs, DVDs, books and magazines, an ancient poster of Arnie Schwarzenegger in *Pumping Iron*, and another of *Darfur Now*.

Sharon had perched her ageing, fleshy bottom, always dressed in tight black trousers, on the edge of Rhiannon's desk, while she talked to Philip, the third member of their team. Philip's title was Assistant Producer and Production Manager, but in reality he was Sharon's yes-man. As Rhiannon walked in, Philip leapt to his feet and turned up the volume on the TV news station playing in the background.

'Oh my God. Look at that!'

Rhiannon and Sharon turned to see a news report from the Olympic velodrome. A freak hurricane had appeared out of nowhere, removed the gigantic roof and dropped it several miles away in the middle of the equestrian park.

'Wow.' Philip seemed almost to be enjoying the devastation. 'What are the chances of that happening?'

Rhiannon waved the disc at her boss.

'That's why we've got to expand the scope of the documentary. Too many things like that have happened recently.'

Sharon looked at her watch and sighed. 'You're exaggerating. It's a bit unusual, I grant you, but nobody got hurt.'

'Apart from five dead, forty-three injured and two horses,' Philip chipped in, his eyes on the TV screen.

'Well, get on with it.' Sharon, impatient, grabbed the disc from Rhiannon's hand and shoved it into the nearest computer.

The footage played with no comment from anyone. When the disc stopped Rhiannon glanced at Philip. 'Wow,' he mouthed.

'OK . . .' Sharon sat pinching her full lips between her carmine-painted fingers. 'I admit, if all this is real then it's powerful stuff.' She shot Rhiannon a sceptical look. 'But I've never got the significance of the Mayan calendar. The Mayan's were . . . ?'

'Everyone says something a bit different, but basically it was an ancient civilisation that extended from southern Mexico to Honduras, sort of Central America. Their calendar, which is hideously complicated, ends 21 December 2012.'

'So what's it got to do with frogs falling from the sky, cows with six legs and ocean dead zones?' Philip piped up – he could never resist being glib.

'Maybe nothing, but some people think that the end of the calendar predicts the end of the world. Others think it may mean the day the poles reverse.' She shrugged. 'I don't know what to believe, and it's only part of the debate. But you'd be amazed at how seriously some very intelligent people take all this.'

Sharon sighed. 'You're in way too deep, sugar. The grotesque stuff's fab, the genetic mutations, the frogs, I love 'em. And obviously the floods and earthquakes and tsunamis. But the rest, the fish problem, the bee population being wiped out, the toxic food and the low sperm count, is straying into environmental territory, and that's not the commission. As for the Mayan calendar, that's New Age bollocks and I don't believe a word of it.' She snorted. 'Christ, you'd think people had enough to do without inventing bloody pole reversal.' She got up and threw Rhiannon's papers on the desk. 'Anyway, what would happen if the poles *did* reverse?'

'Literally, the earth's magnetic field changes. North becomes south and vice versa. But this isn't just New Age bollocks, as you call it, even NASA says the earth's magnetic force is weakening, which some think precedes a pole reversal.'

'I reckon they make it up as they go along,' Philip offered, casting his eyes heavenwards for Sharon's benefit.

Rhiannon ignored him. 'And if the poles do reverse, it might trigger all sorts of horrors, from volcanoes to earthquakes, hurricanes, tsunamis, the works. It could also affect electronic equipment and satellites and increase radiation.'

'So basically it's good night, Charlie.' Sharon seemed unmoved by the earth's impending doom.

'Or nothing could happen,' Rhiannon added.

'Exactly. Which is much more likely,' Her boss wagged her finger. 'Stop complicating the issue. Our audience is the half-wit wanting a few scary sound bites with his takeaway kebab, not a complicated geophysics lecture. Remember, it's the Crowe Channel.' Sharon pushed her glasses up into her coarse, dyed-black fringe.

'Brandon Crowe's channel may be crass, but he never stops

trumpeting his high-minded eco-cred,' Rhiannon protested. 'Why can't we make a full-on doc which tackles all the issues – you can see I've found such amazing stuff. And it's not been done. We get told to recycle our 4x4s and eat more vegetables, but this is way beyond all that. Nature seems to have lost control. Maybe the Mayans are right and we are out of time. People need to know what's really going on.'

As Rhiannon stared at Sharon's complacent, uncomprehending face, something thudded against the grimy office window. Rhiannon turned to see a small bird lying motionless on the windowsill and, as she watched, more and more tumbled out of the blood-red sky like giant black hailstones hurtling to the ground. Rhiannon grabbed Sharon's arm and dragged her to the window.

'You can't say this is normal. Look at the colour of the sky. Look at the ground. It's covered in dead birds!'

Sharon pulled away from her.

'Calm down, Rhiannon. It's probably the aftermath of the hurricane.'

Rhiannon felt her temper rising.

'You just don't get it, do you?' she shouted. 'Why can't you see what's happening?'

Rhiannon paused, frightened by her own words. 'Crowe's money could be the only thing between us and doomsday.'

'He's certainly putting shedloads of cash into researching new energy sources,' Philip pointed out. 'It's on his website.'

'Whatever . . .' Sharon made off briskly towards her office, leaving a trail of musky perfume in her wake. 'Just get on with the commission Rhiannon, that's what's paying your wages. It's the Crowe way or the highway. Make up your mind.'

As the door slammed Philip smirked. 'She doesn't mean it.'

'Yes, she does,' Rhiannon said tiredly. Although she'd known this would be the outcome, she was still deflated.

'Well, she does,' Philip amended, 'but she'd never really fire you.'

'Yes, she would,' Rhiannon said. She texted Lauren: 'Coffee?'

She received an immediate response and, grabbing her coat, clattered down the narrow Dickensian stairs to the street, leaving Philip to wonder what he could do to make Rhiannon like him a bit more.

◎◎

'She didn't hear a word I said,' Rhiannon handed Lauren her regular latte and they went to sit in the window of the coffee shop.

Lauren shrugged. 'What did you expect from Our Shazzer? Never one to favour integrity over hard cash, eh?'

'She's probably right.' Rhiannon remembered the six months she'd been through last year, trying to find a job. The awards she'd won meant nothing. A man passed the coffee-shop window and her heart lurched. She was sure it was Michael, but he disappeared quickly into the Old Compton Street crowd.

'Did you ever hear from the police?' Lauren was asking.

'The police?' Rhiannon wasn't listening.

'About the old man?'

'Oh . . . no . . . no I didn't.' She shook herself. 'I'm sure you were right, he must have climbed out further down the road.'

'Odd though,' her friend commented. 'No one seeing him . . .'

'Everything's odd at the moment,' Rhiannon muttered, as much to herself as to Lauren.

'Anyway, I've had an idea,' Lauren shook her fringe out of her large brown eyes. 'You remember Sam?' Rhiannon nodded. Sam was one of the many men who had almost died for love of Lauren, silently pining for her huge brown eyes and her almost naïve integrity. 'He works for Brandon Crowe now, in IT. Apparently Crowe's just about to announce a massive international grant scheme for original ideas on alternative energy sources.'

'Yeah, Philip mentioned it this morning.'

'Well, there's a press conference in a couple of weeks. You should go and heckle him, get him to notice you, then ask for more money.'

Rhiannon laughed. 'You make it sound so simple.'

'Well, couldn't it be?'

'The great Brandon Crowe isn't going to listen to me though, is he? It doesn't work like that.'

Lauren raised her eyebrows. 'Most people listen to you, Rhi,' she said, with touching faith.

It was Rhiannon's turn to look sceptical. 'I've heard weird things about that place. They say it's like Fort Knox and you can't get in without permission from God. What have they got to hide I'd like to know.'

Lauren laughed. 'You love a good conspiracy theory don't you. Sam assures me it's just some sort of extreme weather research.'

'When did you say this press conference was?' As Rhiannon spoke her phone buzzed.

'Probably Shazzer ringing to fire you,' Lauren joked, but Rhiannon shook her head. She didn't recognise the number.

'Hello?' she answered cautiously.

'Rhiannon, it's Michael. Michael Wolf. I was just . . .'

'Are you stalking me?' she demanded. Lauren looked at her expectantly and Rhiannon found she was blushing. 'It's just I thought I saw you half an hour ago through a window.'

'No . . . no, of course not. I was just wondering if we could meet. I have something I'd like to talk to you about.'

Rhiannon got up, away from her friend's knowing smile, and went to stand out of earshot. 'What do you want to talk about?'

'It's hard to explain over the phone . . . could we meet?'

His tone was subdued, almost pleading, and Rhiannon hesitated. Did she really want to get involved in this man's problems? Automatically she reached into her coat pocket for a coin. Heads or tails. Let the fates decide. Her fingers closed on a small metal circle and brought out the silver disc the old woman had given her.

'Rhiannon? Are you still there?'

'Yeah . . .' Rhiannon took one last look at the silver disc and reached a decision. 'I can't today . . . tomorrow evening I could . . . OK, see you there.'

'So, how was Mr Darcy?' Lauren teased.

'Michael Wolf is no Mr Darcy.'

Lauren's eyes widened.

'Your Michael is Michael Wolf? *The* Michael Wolf?'

Rhiannon shrugged. 'So?'

'Rhiannon!' Lauren bounced in her chair with excitement. 'Michael Wolf, the war photographer. He's gorgeous. All tall, dark and brooding. He was on the news the other day. You know, those amazing photos he sent back from Somalia. The ones in Mogadishu with the kids?'

She stared at her friend in exasperation. 'Don't you watch the news any more?'

'Oh . . . of course.' Rhiannon looked thoughtful. 'That's why I knew his face. I thought I'd met him before but . . . Yes, of course, that's all it is.'

'All what is?'

'Nothing. Anyway, he wants to meet me.'

'Wow. I'll go if you don't want him.'

Rhiannon smiled. 'I definitely don't want him. But I'm going to meet him tomorrow. He says he's got something to tell me.'

20

Tom's car rattled over the chain and plank bridge spanning the creek. The water was very high, almost to the level of the bridge – flash floods they said – but then freakish weather was becoming the norm these days.

Tom's friend Rafaella had finally returned from a retreat and had issued an invitation to tea. Maya couldn't shake the horrifying events on the headland from her mind and was hoping Rafaella could help.

'Do you think Erik really believes he blacked out?' she asked for the fiftieth time.

'Well, the cops believe him, which is all that matters,' Tom shook his head. 'Maybe it's never happened before . . . whatever it was that *did* happen.'

'It's never happened to me before,' Maya said quietly.

They drove past a small community of wooden houses with tin roofs, a giant tepee and a brightly painted school bus. Two young children played under a canopy stretched from the side of the bus and a woman pegged out washing on a line. They all turned and waved as they passed. Then the road narrowed before suddenly opening out in front of a small wooden house that looked as if it was growing out of the rainforest landscape.

As they pulled up, a woman walked down the steps from the open veranda. She was tall and slim with waist-length hair of purest silver, her sea-green dress flowing around her as she walked gracefully towards the car.

For a moment the three stood silently in the burning afternoon sun. Maya, normally reserved with strangers, felt instantly at ease as she looked into eyes as blue as her own, but infinitely wiser. As with Tom earlier, she felt an instant flicker of recognition, though she knew she'd never met Rafaella before. Rafaella smiled back at her.

⊚⊚

Tom and Maya settled on the cushions on the balcony while Rafaella went to make tea.

'She's cool, no?' Tom whispered.

Maya nodded, 'How do you know her?'

'My mother . . . they met in India back in the sixties when they were all hippies searching for the meaning of life. Ma says she's got magic powers.'

The both laughed, then stopped, embarrassed, as Rafaella glided into the room carrying a tray. A small tabby cat walked delicately up the wooden steps, paused as she took in the assembled company, then stretched out across Maya's feet, gazing up at her with unblinking green eyes.

'You're honoured. Magoo doesn't usually bond,' Rafaella commented as she handed Tom and Maya their tea.

There was silence on the veranda. Despite the warmth of the sun, Maya shivered. Rafaella seemed lost in thought, her head slightly turned as if she was listening to voices no one else could hear. A glittering blue ring on her left hand caught the light and again Maya felt a tug of recognition.

Suddenly Rafaella turned to her.

'You know who he is, the man on the cliff.' It wasn't a question.

Maya could feel Tom's eyes on her.

'I . . . I did . . . at the time . . .'

Rafaella nodded, waited.

'And what he wanted.'

Maya shook her head. 'He said he'd come for the crystal, but I don't know where it is,' she found herself saying, catching Tom's puzzled gaze.

'It's not time,' Rafaella closed her eyes, 'no . . . no, you don't know yet, nobody knows . . .'

Maya felt her heart begin to pound in her chest.

'Why is it so important? Why was Erik prepared to kill me for it?' Suddenly she found herself going in and out of what seemed like two worlds. One moment she could actually see the crystal, glimmering, multifaceted, sparking prisms of light clear and pure as spring water as it sat in the palm of her hand. Then a moment later she was back on the purple cushion, Magoo purring at her feet.

Rafaella sighed. 'I can't tell you. But soon you will have to know, Maya.'

Tom laughed, an uncomfortable sound which he immediately tried to suppress. Rafaella looked at him sympathetically.

'This seems absurd to you . . . unreal, right?'

Tom looked sheepish and shrugged.

'It felt like a dream to me,' Maya said.

'What happened on the cliff wasn't a dream. That bastard wanted us both dead for sure,' he muttered.

Rafaella sat up and clasped her hands round her knees. Her eyes were burning with intensity.

'It may look like some sort of altered reality, but you're right, Tom, it *is* real, very real. I can't explain, but you have to understand that you're in great danger. You both, even you Tom, remembered something from another life when Erik attacked, however vague and shadowy the knowledge seems. And the remembering has opened up a channel. It's put you on the radar of certain people. They may be able to see you now. Erik is only a foot soldier in a much bigger game – but these people have much to lose.'

'Wait a minute,' Tom stood up and began pacing the bleached wood of the veranda. He threw his hands up, '*See* us? Look, I'm happy to have an open mind about stuff, but now you're scaring me. What do you mean danger? Who are "these people"?'

Tom and Maya stared at their host. Rafaella took a handful of silvery hair and wrapped it slowly round her fingers. She was miles away, listening again to those other voices. She did not answer Tom, but they saw her blue eyes sparkle with unshed tears.

Holding out her hand towards Maya, she offered her the blue ring.

88

'Take it, please.'

Maya tentatively took the ring. It seemed heavy and very cold. Without prompting she gazed into its brilliant sapphire depths. The sounds around her, birds, insects, the breeze gently stirring the trees, faded and all she could hear was the sea breaking on a distant shore. Maya felt as if she was being physically drawn into the deep azure glow. Now she was climbing a steep pathway leading from a beach up into a beautiful tropical garden. She looked around, delighted, realising that she was finally home.

Images came thick and fast, she was with people whose faces she recognised, knew well . . . Rafaella was there, and Tom. But although the images were disjointed and made little sense to her, one thing was clear: Maya knew she had a valuable purpose among this group. She had to guard the crystal, the Heartstone, protect it against a violent enemy. She felt danger all around her.

Rafaella, keeping a close watch on Maya's reactions, reached and took the ring back, laying her hand on the girl's forehead. Maya's eyes fluttered open, she had tears on her face as she looked up in alarm.

'It hasn't worked . . . the ceremony . . . how will I keep the Heartstone safe in all this mayhem . . . help me . . . please help me . . . I know we're going to die.'

'You're back now. You're safe.' The frightening images of chaos and destruction began to break up at the sound of Rafaella's voice.

'That was Atlantis, Maya,' Rafaella said quietly, glancing at Tom as she spoke. She waited for the two young people to react. 'What you were seeing was Atlantis before it was destroyed. Erik . . . both of you . . . myself . . . we were all there, it was our home.'

Maya brushed her hand across her eyes, her mind was reeling. Everything she'd seen felt true but her logical mind was resistant.

'Atlantis? How can that be? I saw Tom in the temple – and you.'

Tom had gone pale beneath his tan. Maya stared at him.

'What . . . was I talking out loud? What did I say?'

◎◎

89

Suddenly Rafaella rose to her feet, her startling eyes veiled and distant.

'I can't tell you any more.'

'Hey, you can't leave it there,' Tom protested. 'Maya was talking about a crystal, about us all in a group. What group? What's this stuff about Atlantis? That's only a legend isn't it? Please, tell us what you mean.'

Rafaella took Maya's hand, reached out for Tom's. For a moment she held them tightly, her eyes closed.

'Take great care,' she whispered. 'Don't forget you pose a threat to these people. They are very powerful and can hurt you. But you and the others are more powerful by far if you stand together. Go to London. That is where you're both meant to be, where you will find them. And take note of everything that happens to you . . . anything odd, out of place . . . be aware.'

She hugged each of them close.

'I have to go now. I won't be back before you leave, Tom.'

She gathered up a cream cloth bag and walked down the steps and slowly off along the track that led deeper into the rainforest, the sun flashing in the folds of her green dress as she disappeared from sight.

'Where's she going?' Maya asked, taken aback and feeling suddenly bereft.

'She has a wooden shack up the hill. I think she meditates or something,' Tom answered vaguely, staring after his host. Then he shook himself. 'Weird . . . weird, weird, weird.'

'Do you believe her? About Atlantis? About the danger?' Maya asked.

'I can't help believing her. But I don't have a clue what she's talking about.'

Maya shivered, remembering the hatred in Erik's eyes.

'It frightens me.'

Tom raked his fingers through his thick blond hair. 'Me too Maya . . . me too.'

21

It had begun to rain hard by the time Rhiannon left the office to meet Michael. They said this was the wettest summer since records began. She had been distracted all afternoon, annoyed that she had agreed to the drink. What she resented most was that he made her heart beat faster. He was sitting expectantly in the corner of the wine bar in Poland Street. The place was empty except for three damp, dispirited-looking Italian tourists, a boy and two girls, who were slumped over empty coffee cups, gazing at the rain.

Michael rose and moved to kiss Rhiannon on the cheek, but thought better of it and held out his hand. She smiled briefly.

'Thanks for coming. Horrible night.' He was startled at how beautiful she was, the rain glistening on her pale skin and chestnut hair, her tall elegance so feminine, yet at odds with her almost brutal black jeans and leather jacket.

Rhiannon nodded. 'Do you want a drink?'

'I'll get them,' Michael said hastily.

'No, I asked first,' Rhiannon insisted, and looked questioningly at him.

Michael saw the familiar irritation in Rhiannon's eyes and backed off. 'OK . . . Peroni please.'

The beers sat on the table between them, and Michael knew he had to begin. There would be no small-talk with this woman. He dreaded her reaction to what he was about to say.

'Listen,' he cleared his throat, sounding nervous, even to himself. 'This is going to sound so totally odd. I don't understand it either, I don't really know what it means . . . but I had to tell you.'

'Well, get on with it then,' Rhiannon seemed to find everything he said irritating, but he pushed on.

'I had a session with Lily . . . you remember Lily? At Stonehenge?'

Rhiannon shook her head, then had an image of a tall, imposing woman with the extraordinary crystal around her neck, whom Michael had been so taken with.

'You didn't meet but . . .'

'No, I do remember her,' Rhiannon interrupted.

'Well, she does hypnosis . . . it's for panic attacks.' Michael looked sheepish, hating to seem weak in front of this powerful woman. But his confession seemed to soften Rhiannon's impatience.

'You have them?'

He nodded. 'I'm a war photographer. I saw stuff . . . anyway, what Lily does is take you back and make you see things in a light which doesn't frighten you. At least that's what I think she does. It's all new to me, and I don't go in for this type of mumbo-jumbo, but, well Aunt Val is worried and I went for her I suppose.'

Yeah, sure, Rhiannon thought, remembering the beautiful older woman and the hold she seemed to have over Michael that morning.

'What's this got to do with me?'

'I wasn't awake, but I sort of was . . . and Lily guided me back to past times in my existence. Well, to past lives I suppose.' He saw Rhiannon's lip curl in amusement. 'I told you this was weird,' he apologised, 'but hear me out.'

Rhiannon just stared at him.

'I saw things I've never seen before, where I was present, where it was me, in my life, and I was living it. It was the strangest thing ever. Then, the last life I came to, I was in this beautiful garden – it was hundreds, maybe thousands of years ago. I've seen places like that in Spain . . . Tunisia.' He paused, seeing that finally he had his companion's attention. 'And this is why I want to tell you . . . you were there, Rhiannon. You and I were in this garden together.'

Rhiannon began to laugh. 'Well, that really is the lamest chat-up line in history. Sorry to be mean, but I think these panic attacks have affected your mind. You were dreaming Michael, just dreaming.' She sounded harsher than she intended, but she was frightened. She too had seen things she couldn't understand recently. And even if they hadn't included gardens and Michael, they had still been too powerful for comfort.

Michael sighed, frustrated. 'I knew this is how you'd react. I don't blame you – I sound mental. But Rhiannon, it was so in-credibly real. I knew you, in that other life. I'm convinced of it.'

Rhiannon got up. She couldn't stay with this man who disturbed her so, who seemed to want to lead her down some path she had absolutely no intention of following.

'Please . . . please don't go.' Rhiannon was out of the door and striding down the wet street, Michael in hot pursuit.

As they got to the corner, Rhiannon crashed into a youth running in the opposite direction.

'Mind where the fuck you're going,' the figure snarled at Rhiannon, pushing her hard in the chest, and Rhiannon realised with a shock that it was a girl. The force made her slip and fall against the half-lit plate-glass window of a betting shop. Shocked too, and without thinking, Michael grabbed the girl's wet sleeve and held her.

'For Christ's sake,' he exploded. 'Apologise to the lady.'

But another girl, small and wiry and also dressed like a boy, leapt onto Michael's back and wrapped her arms round his neck, clinging on like a malevolent monkey. Michael prised away the fingers that were trying to choke him, wincing with pain as the stitches tore in his injured arm, but as he shook her off the first girl suddenly kicked his feet from under him, sending him sprawling into the sodden gutter, his head catching the gleaming bumper of a Lexus as he fell.

As the two feral girls leered down at him, he watched, dazed, as Rhiannon, upright now and behind his attackers, lunged her right foot in an effortless high karate arc at the shoulders of the girl who had attacked her. It was smooth and unhurried, seemingly without the intention of violence, yet the girl dropped like a stone, her face white with shock. Her companion, frightened now, swung round to face Rhiannon, who just raised her eyebrows, then slowly lifted her open right hand, fingers together and solid, to the level of her shoulder, her eyes never leaving the girl's terrified face.

'OK, OK . . . fuck it . . .' the girl glanced briefly at her mate, still prone on the pavement, then, obviously thinking better of rescuing her, raced off down the street like a greyhound out of a trap.

Rhiannon offered a hand to Michael and hauled him out of the gutter.

'Fuck it indeed. Where did you learn that?'

'Girls ain't what they used to be.'

'You can say that again,' Michael muttered sulkily, feeling humiliated at being attacked by a girl and then defended by one.

'Are you OK?'

'Of course I am,' he snapped, suddenly sick of trying to communicate with this prickly woman. 'Anyway, sorry I wasted your time. I was just telling you what I saw.'

' "Dreamed" don't you mean?' Rhiannon countered, turning away towards the Tube station.

'Whatever . . . but just explain one thing before you go,' Michael called after her. 'How come you and I've got the exact same mark on our wrists?'

Rhiannon stopped dead in her tracks.

'Mark? What do you mean, mark?'

'I don't know where mine came from – it was a birthmark.' Michael pulled back his sleeve and held his wrist towards her. There, lit up by the street lamp, was a replica of the small circle containing the crescent shape she kept hidden under her watch strap. 'I saw it,' he was saying.

'When, when did you see it?' She never took her watch off. Never showed it to anyone. She thought back to the night of the flood, but no, the watch was waterproof, she had not taken it off.

'Not in this life,' Michael sighed, unwilling to say more

94

because he didn't understand himself how he knew. He just did. 'It is the same, exactly the same as mine.' He waited, hoping she might relent and move the face of the large watch she wore to confirm what he said. Although he knew it was there, just as he knew he breathed.

Rhiannon stared at him.

'This is ludicrous. Stop it, just bloody stop it.' Beneath the angry words, Michael could hear the tears. He tried to put his arm round her shoulders, but she shook him off fiercely and he finally lost his temper.

'I'm outta here. You can kick the rest of the female population of London into the gutter if you like, but leave me alone. Christ, I've never met anyone so fucking hostile in my whole life.' And with that Michael turned on his heel and strode off into the night.

The tears fell freely down Rhiannon's cold cheeks. She wanted to call after Michael's retreating figure; she wanted to feel his arms round her, to be held, to be safe for once in her life . . . to say she was sorry. Yes, she could defend herself physically against any angry, streetwise yob, but mentally she was scared and tired of endlessly protecting herself from the increasing city violence. Most of all she wanted what Michael had said to go away. She fingered the small mark beneath her watch face. It was the same. Not just the same as Michael's but the same as the old man's, the one who had saved her from drowning on the road from Stonehenge. She was as familiar with it as she was with her own face. But why them? Why the three of them? She was certain Michael wouldn't contact her again. If she wanted to find out more, she knew it would have to be her who made the first move.

22

Christina stood with a clipboard to the side of the main desk in the lobby of the Crowe Corporation building, looking on nervously as the hordes began to push and shove through the heavy doors in an untidy stream. Checks were being made on the journalists and photographers presenting their credentials at reception and the lobby and the massive glass-ceilinged conference room to the left were being policed by hundreds of security guards, all wearing the Crowe logo on their black uniforms. Lifts and stairs to the upper floors had been sealed and cameras swept every inch of the glassed-in space on a continuous trawl.

Despite this, Christina was anxious. Mr Crowe was the most paranoid man she'd ever met – she wasn't sure why. Every single visitor, phone call, email or paper document had to be logged, scrutinised and secured against outside interference.

'We have become the ultimate consumers . . .' as Brandon spoke he ran his eyes over the rows of faces in front of him. He was unfazed: to him this was a game, a manipulation, an act to flush out any competition to his own purpose. He knew he could charm them, convince them of anything he chose and his body buzzed with the adrenaline of the trick. He calculated there must be upwards of three hundred people in the light, high-ceilinged atrium, all crouched over their electronic pads, or pencils poised, or tensed behind their lenses, their faces almost innocent in their expectation.

'We've lost touch with our survival. To most of us now the planet is just a commodity, like a shop we can rob to get yet more things. A form of replacement happiness. We don't have any respect for what this earth does for us . . . for free if we let it.'

Rhiannon had placed herself on the last chair at the end of the back row. She hated being trapped in a crowd and this crowd seemed dangerous in its eagerness to be near the great Brandon Crowe. She eyed the solid ring of guards against the room's perimeter with amazement. *What did Mr Crowe, an 'eco-philanthropist', have to hide*, she wondered. A man came and stood behind her left shoulder. For some reason his presence unsettled her, but she chose not to look up.

'*Earth Rescue* is for anyone, anyone who has an idea that might change the way we see energy in the future. We're stuck in the dark ages, still limiting ourselves to nuclear power and fossil fuels. Wind and solar power won't do it alone, we have to be more creative, find a way to get the planet to do what it does best: renew and progress. Remember, it does this for free if we stop plundering and destroying its resources.' Brandon knew they'd heard the gist a million times before, and most of them didn't give a toss. These people had come to hear about the money. And to see the man who was promising thirty million in grants. 'So show me what you're made of. Let me hear the off-the-wall ideas your family and friends tease you about. Tell me how you see the energy of the future, how you might harness the wind from a hurricane, turn sea shells into domestic fuel. You give me your ideas, I'll give you my money. Together we'll save Planet Earth.'

Thunderous applause and the blinding flash of hundreds of cameras greeted this final charm offensive. Brandon wasn't sure whether they were applauding his ideas or his cash – money did funny things to people. He glanced to the back of the room and caught Xan's eye. As usual, his henchman was unmoved by the proceedings, and Brandon could tell his thoughts were far away from this cattle market, no doubt concentrated still on the blocked connection at Stonehenge. Rage at Jude's power once more gripped Brandon, but his iron discipline allowed nothing but urbane charm to show on his handsome face.

'We'll take questions now.' Christina stepped onto the podium beside her boss, looking for all the world like a headmistress at school assembly in her neat navy suit and polished court shoes. 'If you stand you will be heard more easily.'

Rhiannon's thoughts drifted as a burly journalist rose to his feet and began to question Crowe on the government's role in the grant scheme. There was something not right about all this, Rhiannon decided, but she couldn't put her finger on it. She raised her hand to get the attention of the woman with the clipboard.

'You . . . the girl at the back . . .' Six or seven questions later, Christina eventually acknowledged Rhiannon.

As she got up to speak, she bumped into the man standing so close by her chair. Turning to apologise, she confronted the gaze from two astonishingly cold, green eyes. The owner neither spoke nor smiled, merely glided backwards out of her way.

'Rhiannon Davies, Stargate Productions.' Rhiannon took a deep breath, reminding herself that she needed this man on board if she was to get more money for her film. 'Mr Crowe, I am making a documentary for your channel about the strange phenomena happening in the world . . .'

She's a beauty, Brandon thought, *although she's trying hard to disguise it under all that black.* Brandon was something of a connoisseur of women. Not in an intimate way, he had no interest in intimacy beyond the fleeting sexual connection, but he prized beauty almost separately from the person to whom it belonged. He smiled, encouraging her to continue.

'You talk about us ruining the planet, but do our actions really account for such terrible storms and earthquakes, the strange mutations, dead zones in the sea? It's as if the world is coming to an end.'

Rhiannon heard the sniggers fill the silence and knew that she had sounded like a naïve child. But the effect of her words on the millionaire was immediate. He took an involuntary step backwards, his face rigid with shock, then stared at her for what seemed like an age, in total silence, as if he'd seen a ghost. People in the rows in front of her were beginning to turn and look to see who had sparked this reaction.

Rhiannon felt herself blushing under the intensity of his stare. She went over the words she had used to see if she had insulted him in any way, but it was the most innocuous of questions, really designed to get his attention so she could collar him later, no more than that. She heard a cough behind her and turned to see the cold green eyes again. This time, she thought, taking a keener interest in her.

'It's too big a question for now, Miss Davies,' Brandon finally found his tongue. 'Perhaps you'd like to stay at the end and we could discuss your film in greater depth.'

To the assembled press his smile appeared as urbanely charming as before, but Brandon felt it fixed like a plaster to his face. It was all he could do not to walk out. He'd been so carried away by her beauty it had taken him a moment to recognise her. But she was definitely one of Them. He hadn't taken the sighting of Lilith as a serious threat but now another of the Seven had appeared right in front of him. This had to be more than coincidence. Brandon was anxious in a way that had become totally unfamiliar to him, but as his thoughts cleared he sensed that the girl was not yet aware of her role. She might even be useful to him.

'Next question . . . Yes, you in the second row with the red T-shirt . . .' Christina's words were muffled in his head, but he knew he had to pull himself together and finish with this rabble before he could give time and thought to the implications of Rhiannon's appearance.

Rhiannon steeled herself. Her instinct was to run because, ridiculously in that room full of people, she felt threatened. Not just by the strangeness of Crowe's stare but because of his creepy, cold-eyed henchman, who refused to leave her side. But Rhiannon was not a quitter, and she held herself firmly in check until the last photographer had filed from the room. Brandon stepped down off the podium and came towards her across the polished wood parquet, hand outstretched.

'Delighted to meet you Miss Davies.'

'And you Mr Crowe,' Rhiannon responded automatically, barely suppressing a shudder as he grasped her hand. *What's the matter with me*, she asked herself. She felt almost light-headed in this man's presence, but she couldn't understand why. Instinct made her look back over her shoulder, but the henchman had vanished.

'Obviously this isn't a good time for an in-depth discussion,' Brandon purred, 'much as I'd like to spend time with you on my favourite subject. But there is someone, an extreme weather expert, who might be helpful in explaining some of the scientific side of the current phenomenon. His name is Jude.'

'Great . . . Uh, thank you . . .' Rhiannon got out her pad and pen, dropping her bag between her feet.

'I don't have his contact details I'm afraid. You'll have to find them out for yourself.'

As the heavy glass doors swung shut behind her and she felt the summer sun on her face, Rhiannon decided she had got Brandon Crowe wrong. Too much coffee and too many nights disturbed by vivid, almost living dreams were making her fanciful, she thought. He was charming, and helpful. She was annoyed she hadn't asked him for any money, but at least they'd met, and she would definitely check out this Jude character.

'Bug her phone. I've put her on to Jude and I need to know when she makes contact.'

Brandon paced the penthouse office, not looking at Xan.

'Who is she?' Xan felt he was owed an explanation. He'd never seen his boss so jumpy.

For a moment Brandon seemed to hesitate.

'She is one of the Seven. Her, the man, Jude . . . and five more. Don't you remember anything I tell you?'

Brandon felt his temper rising and forced himself to be calm.

Xan didn't share his total recall of the past.

'Xan, I told you about Atlantis and the ceremony. These are the seven people who were trying to stop me getting my hands on the energy source, S-3, back then. I thought they'd given up lifetimes ago, but that girl . . . she's definitely one of the group.'

'But surely they're not as powerful as us?'

Brandon glowered, 'Separately, no. They have no power as individuals. But together? Together they are trouble. If they *are* back, they could screw our entire project.' He paused, lost in thought.

Xan wasn't sure what all the fuss was about. The girl had looked harmless enough.

'Do you want her followed?'

Brandon shook his head. 'Not yet. But if she makes any arrangement to meet up with Jude, then let me know at once. Jude has made sure that I can't find him but he might lower his guard for the girl.'

Xan nodded and made to leave.

'And Xan . . . don't hurt her,' he heard his boss say. 'We need her alive . . . we need them all alive. For now.'

23

Jude travelled across the rain-slicked surface of the cliff with effortless ease. Despite being a tall, powerfully built man, his movement was elegant, with a poise that was almost balletic. Half way up the cliff, his boots slipping on the precarious jibs that passed for footholds, he came to a narrow horn of rock that jutted from the wall above him. Left of the overhang was a wide gully, probably six feet across. He paused, eyeing the handholds on the far side in the dim dawn light. For a moment he let go of his foothold and balanced in a dead hang from the buttress, the muscles of his back standing proud through his thin navy jacket, his only contact with the rock through the fingertips of his right hand. Then very gently he began to swing his body across the cliff face, back and forth, back and forth, gathering momentum with each swing until suddenly he let go, his length suspended in mid-air for seconds before his left hand grabbed an insubstantial edge of rock on the gully's opposite face. Regaining his balance almost immediately and barely stopping to draw breath, he moved on across the rock wall until he found what he was looking for. A narrow, deep cleft which lay directly over a geological fault in the earth's crust.

Leaning into the wet cliff, he pressed the length of his body to the fissure, his head to the right, flush with the slippery rock wall. He listened. For a while all he could hear was the pounding of the sea beneath him and the cry of the swooping petrels. But as his body began to relax and become one with the rock, he started to feel, as much as hear, the quality and strength of the deep earth energy waves pulsating beneath the original access points, the portals where the earth's crust was thinnest.

He followed the ley lines linking the earth's chakras through Tibet, Nepal, Angkor Wat, Uluru, Machu Picchu, Sedona and back home to Stonehenge. Something was definitely up. Six of the portals were still sealed, as they had been for thousands of years now, and the energy flowed smoothly until it reached the seventh portal, Stonehenge. That's where the problem lay.

Stonehenge felt different. Always the weak link in the chain since Lilith's attempt to seal the seventh level had ended in disaster, that portal had always had the potential to explode if anyone were reckless enough to tamper with it. He had created Stonehenge all those years ago as a temporary measure to protect the portal until they could complete the ceremony. But would it hold? And for how long? He knew without doubt that someone was trying to break the seal and there was only one person it could be.

Shaking himself free from thoughts of the past, he began the precarious ascent to the top of the cliff as if he were walking the flat tarmac of the peninsula road. As he pulled himself over the lip of the cliff, he felt the vibration of his mobile through the zipped sleeve of his jacket.

'Yes?' he spoke absently, his mind miles from this deserted Scottish shore.

'Is that Jude?' the voice was polite, a little nervous he thought.

'It is.'

There was silence for a moment, then Rhiannon stammered, 'Um, I was given your name by Brandon Crowe . . .' When Jude didn't respond she ploughed on, 'I am doing a documentary about strange phenomena, you know, weather stuff, weird happenings, that have become more frequent . . .' she knew she was being inarticulate, but she couldn't seem to get her thoughts together while speaking to this man. Still he said nothing. 'And Mr Crowe suggested I get in touch with you.'

'Ah . . .'

Christ, she thought, he's not making this easy.

'And I wondered, seeing as much of what's going on is extreme weather, and you're the world expert, if I might come to Scotland and see you . . . talk it through.'

She waited. She could hear his breathing.

'No,' he said eventually, 'that won't be possible.' He spoke softly, but she heard the absolute refusal in his tone.

'But . . . it wouldn't be for long, just a few hours . . . if you're going away or something . . .'

'I'm sorry,' he spoke slowly, as if he were worried she couldn't understand, 'it won't be possible.'

Used as Rhiannon was to battering down doors to get the interviews she wanted, she had never come across such a blatant rejection. And before she had another chance to persuade him, the phone went dead.

Later, at home in his croft, Jude knelt in front of the grate, his strong hands carefully twisting twills of newspaper before covering them with kindling and finally the turf bricks he stored in a tin crate by the hearth. He worked automatically, his thoughts far from this mundane domestic scene.

So, brother of mine, he thought as he held a match to a twill and watched the blue-gold flame leap upwards. *Up to your old tricks again? I trusted you once and you lied to me, to all of us. But if you succeed, the disaster will be global this time. It won't be just Atlantis you destroy.*

He got up and in a sudden spurt of anger and frustration, aimed a vicious kick at the peat box with his heavy climbing boot, sending a single brick flying onto the mat. 'I can't do it,' he shouted to the empty room. 'I can't . . . not again. Please . . . Please . . .' he seemed to plead with an unseen presence. He stood still under the low ceiling, his eyes shut, his elegant body suddenly lifeless. 'Lilith . . .' it was no more than a whisper as his mind was dragged unwillingly back over thousands of years to relive yet again the fatal error he could never forgive himself for.

24

10,500 BC: Council Chamber, Atlantis

'Enough!' Gabriel's fist slammed down on the council table, scattering the charts and diagrams. Slowly his tense features softened.

'Sit down Tom, and . . . thank you. Good work.'

Tom sat down thankfully and glanced at Jude sitting beside him. Why hadn't Jude given the report himself, Gabriel wondered. It was mostly his work, his conclusions. Was this the best time to let the apprentice take centre stage?

Jude looked straight ahead, his expression guarded. Gabriel turned to Lilith.

'I think we are all agreed. It is beyond doubt that someone is tampering with Selenios-3 and has to be using a crystal as powerful as the Heartstone. Only that could cause such disruption to the weather patterns, the earthquakes, volcanic eruptions. Even the moon is beginning to move away from us.'

Lilith looked up, shocked. 'Who would do this? I can understand lust for power, but not at the expense of destroying us all. We have to stop them before it's too late.'

Jude stirred in his seat, but remained silent.

'Whoever it is has covered his tracks well,' continued Gabriel. 'We need a contingency plan, and there's only one thing I can think of.'

Lilith shook her head. 'It's too dangerous. If anything goes wrong, Atlantis will be completely destroyed.'

She turned to Jude, who met her eyes with difficulty. 'Surely you agree?'

Jude nodded slowly, then rose abruptly to his feet.

'If you will excuse me. There's one last possible solution.'

Gabriel watched Jude rush from the room with a sympathetic smile. Lilith always had that effect on him. Lilith merely shrugged *her shoulders, suppressing a small secret smile.*

'Perhaps you're right, Gabriel,' she said at last. 'We'll make the necessary preparations for the ceremony and pray we don't have to do it.'

Citadel courtyard, Atlantis

Jude erupted into the courtyard and stopped short. Where was everybody? The gatehouse was deserted, the stables empty. He ran to the main gate and in the distance he could see the guards riding at speed towards the market place. Surely Brandon wouldn't be so crazy as to take on the authority of the priesthood? He had to stop him, save him from himself.

Jude hurtled through the twisting streets, dimly aware of the shuttered shops and houses, far away shouts and screams, the acrid smell of smoke. Brandon had promised, *he kept telling himself,* he gave me his word. *As he drew nearer to the market place he could hear chanting: 'Brandon! Brandon!' He skidded to a halt at the edge of an excited, cheering crowd, all looking to a raised dais at the centre of the square. Armed troops surrounded the perimeter and the flags of Atlantis lay trampled in the dust, replaced by golden banners flaunting a blood-red sun in the centre.*

As Jude watched in horror he saw his brother step forward holding a huge fiery crystal that emitted a low humming sound.

'People of Atlantis!'

The crowd fell silent and concentrated on the charismatic figure on the dais.

'See what I have brought you!'

Brandon raised the crystal high and sparks of energy crackled around it.

'Freedom and power!'

The crowd surged forward, cheering wildly. Jude couldn't believe his eyes. Brandon had the Heartstone. Then his thoughts cleared – this wasn't the Heartstone, it was the replica Brandon had told him about. But replica or not, he could feel its power and the power it held over the crowd.

Brandon's deep voice rolled on hypnotically.

'Too long we have suffered the tyranny of the priesthood . . . too long we have surrendered our freedom to an unelected elite . . . now we shall take power into our own hands!'

Jude felt a hand on his arm and whirled round to see Rhiannon, her face half hidden by the hood of her cloak.

'We've got to warn Lord Gabriel,' she whispered, trying to pull him away, but Jude grabbed her by the shoulders and stared urgently into her eyes.

'You go, now! I have to try to stop him.'

'Or join him!' came another voice, accusingly. Michael stood behind them, glaring angrily at Jude, and Rhiannon turned on him.

'How dare you! Jude is as loyal as you or . . .'

Jude interrupted her impassioned defence.

'We haven't time for this. Michael, take Rhiannon to the Citadel. Tell them to make for the temple. I'll join you as soon as I can.'

Michael bit back the retort hovering on his lips and grabbed Rhiannon by the arm.

'Let me go.' She struggled to release herself. 'I'm staying with Jude.'

'No, Rhiannon,' Jude ordered. 'Go now!'

Reluctantly she followed Michael and Jude melted into the crowd, heading for the dais and his brother.

The market place, Atlantis

Brandon gazed out over the sea of faces chanting his name. This was going even better than he had hoped. The patient months he'd spent subverting the military had paid off brilliantly but even he couldn't believe the power of the crystal in his hands. The people were like sheep, he thought contemptuously. Just think what he could do once he got his hands on the real Heartstone.

As if in answer to his thoughts, the Captain of the Guard forced his way to his side.

'My lord,' he began breathlessly.

Brandon looked critically at the dishevelled figure. His face was scratched and bruised and he held a bloodied hand to a ragged

107

wound in his arm.

'Well, where is it?' Brandon demanded impatiently.

The Captain's eyes fell.

'She got away, my lord. That hellhound of hers kept us at bay and . . .'

'You let a dog stop you!' Brandon was incredulous. 'Captain, I want that crystal. Go and get it now if it's the last thing you do.'

The Captain stumbled away and Jude materialised in his place.

'Jude!' Brandon was startled. 'Where did you spring from?'

Jude seized his arm.

'We have to talk. You promised me you would never harm Atlantis. I trusted you.'

Brandon smiled patronisingly. 'I'm doing this for Atlantis. I thought you understood. You can help me Jude. Decide now – are you for me or against me?'

Council Chamber, Atlantis

Gabriel paced angrily, digesting the news Michael had given him.

'We have to get to the temple.' He turned to Lilith, 'And we need to do the Ceremony now.'

Lilith nodded. 'My preparations are complete. This isn't the time I would have chosen but . . .' she shrugged and looked around the group.

Maya sat on the floor cradling the lifeless body of her wolfhound while Tom murmured softly in her ear. Slowly she nodded her head.

'Maya and I are ready,' said Tom firmly as Rhiannon and Michael stepped forward in agreement.

'Where's Jude?' asked Lilith suddenly.

'You may well ask,' replied Michael. 'Last time we saw him he was with Brandon.'

'Michael!' Rhiannon hissed. 'If you say one more word, I shall never forgive you, ever.'

'We can't do the ceremony without Jude,' Lilith continued as if they hadn't spoken.

'Just as well I'm here then,' came Jude's voice from the doorway.

25

Gabe climbed the last few yards to the top of the ancient earthworks and stopped to get his breath back. Even in the fading light he could see for miles and he let his gaze roam from Avebury and on towards Stonehenge. If all went well in the next few months then he and Lily would be able to return home.

The sky was almost dark now, the stars brilliant pinpricks of light as they took their accustomed place in the heavens. Gabe felt the familiar ache in his heart. He had chosen this task, he knew he would never leave Lily, and yet . . . the stars were calling him home. Gabe shivered as the evening breeze ruffled the long blades of grass. All this could have been avoided, if only he'd seen what had really been going on.

He'd been wrong about the source of Jude's divided loyalties, Jude had been wrong to trust Brandon's solemn promise, and Lily . . . suddenly Gabe became aware of Atlas barking furiously. Now that his own powers were weakening he relied more and more on the dog's sensitivity. Something had changed. With a sudden sense of urgency he knew he had to get back to the farmhouse and to Lily.

Lily and Gabe's farmhouse, Wiltshire

Lily reached towards the polished crystal lying at the centre of the six-pointed star, then jerked back as if it had burned her. A shuddering sigh escaped her as the candles flickered and flared then gradually dimmed their radiance.

She lifted her head and gazed at the familiar surroundings. The fire burning in the grate, the light glinting on the sapphires placed so carefully around the seer stone. She had concentrated all her energies on finding Jude and suddenly he was there. She had found him.

Why he'd let his guard down, she couldn't tell, but finding him made her focus on the reality of the ceremony ahead. Because with Jude it could happen, it could really happen.

But with this knowledge came a much darker truth. Never before had she doubted her own position as High Priestess of the ceremony. Now, for the first time, she had to question it.

Gabe burst into the room and stopped short at the look of desolation on her face. In all their lifetimes together he had experienced a range of emotions that to him defined the woman he now knew as Lily, but never had he seen despair.

'What happened? What's wrong?'

Lily slowly looked up and her pain-filled eyes met his.

'I found Jude.'

'You found Jude? But that's great . . . Isn't it?'

'It's good, yes. But Gabe . . . Gabe it can't be me who leads the ceremony.'

Gabe stared at her. 'What are you talking about? You have to lead us, who else could do it?'

Lily shook her head. 'No. For centuries now I haven't been able to see beyond my own ego. I failed you all, including Jude. I failed you because I was vain, flattered by Jude's infatuation. I was responsible, but I did nothing to stop him, nothing to keep the situation under control. He's been blaming himself . . . and I've been blaming him.' She paused, 'Don't you see Gabe? My power is tainted. I can't do it.'

'Well, in that case,' Gabe replied, 'I am equally to blame. I knew how Jude felt about you.' He laughed. 'He wasn't exactly subtle. Anyway, doesn't a young priest always fancy the High Priestess? Look at Michael.'

Lily let that go.

'No, my mistake was not realising how much Jude hero-worshipped his half-brother. If he'd warned us . . .' Lily smiled sadly. 'Well, it's no good raking over it all again. But it's hardly surprising he wants nothing to do with us. I'm afraid he won't help us now.'

Gabe moved towards her. 'I think you're underestimating Jude. I trust him. I believe he'll do the right thing when we need him.'

Lily rose to stand beside him and looked up into his face. 'Whatever the rights and wrongs, I have to accept that our time, *my* time, is past. We need a new Priestess to take my place and that has to be Rhiannon.'

'I see the problem,' Gabe smiled quizzically. 'She's headstrong, passionate, wilful . . .'

'Won't listen to anyone else,' Lily interrupted.

Gabe nodded. 'Yes, funny that . . . she reminds me of someone . . .'

Lily shook her head impatiently. 'We'd have to train her and that's the last thing she'd consider. It's one thing to persuade her to join the group, entirely another to convince her that she could be the High Priestess. She'll never do it.'

Gabe put his arm around her shoulder. 'Yes she will. And Michael will help her.' He felt her stiffen.

'Gabe, we have to face the possibility of failure.'

'Come with me,' Gabe replied, taking her hand and leading her outside. The dark velvet sky shone with a million splinters of light. He placed his hands on her shoulder and turned her towards the most brilliant star in the heavens.

'That's home, Lily. When we've achieved what we set out to do then we can go home.'

Lily breathed out slowly. 'Home. Yes, you're right Gabe. We have to reach Rhiannon. You really think Michael can bring her here?'

Gabe nodded slowly. 'They are all moving towards us. You can feel it, I can feel it. Trust them, they will feel it too.'

26

Maya felt as if she was waking from a dream as she climbed into the taxi with Tom. Her tired, jet-lagged body shivered in the bracing early morning air. But worse was the distance that had sprung up between them.

They hardly knew each other, she reminded herself. The terrifying incident on the cliffs had thrown them together against an evil force that Maya had begun to believe was real. But now, the grey, sensible British light seemed to mock her, and she felt awkward in Tom's company. It was as if they both wanted to forget what had happened, forget Rafaella's warning. It all seemed slightly ridiculous.

As if catching her thoughts, Tom turned to her and grinned.

'What happened in Oz doesn't seem real now, does it?'

'I know what you mean. Do you think we should have stayed longer, tried to find out more?'

'I don't think there was more to find. They're all concentrating on . . . what did they call it? "Raising the consciousness of the planet", but that doesn't explain why we're in danger.'

'I know, I know. I'm sure there's a connection somewhere but I just can't see it. Still, Rafaella did tell us to come to London. But then what?'

Tom didn't reply. As the taxi slowed almost to a stop, the motorway narrowing into the tailback to central London, his eye was caught by the shiny glass blackness of the Crowe Corporation building, which rose like a beacon to the left of the M4. Twisting in his seat, he gazed back through the taxi window.

'That's it,' he said. 'Looks sinister doesn't it?'

As Maya looked she felt an inexplicable shudder go through her.

'It's just a building,' she snapped. This was London, she didn't want things to be weird any more, she didn't want to think about anything but her work, seeing her friends, normal stuff.

Tom looked across at her profile as she stared resolutely out at the dreary landscape of the airport road.

'OK . . . but we'll keep in touch won't we?' he asked.

They looked at each other and suddenly Maya didn't want to lose this new friend. She realised she felt deeply connected with him, even though they hadn't known each other long.

'Of course. I've got your mobile number.' She laughed, 'although I can always ring your "sinister" place of work and track you down.'

Tom shook his head, 'First impressions are not cosy. They probably shoot you for taking personal calls, so stick to my cell!'

Suddenly he was serious, laying his hand gently on her arm for a second.

'Maya . . . I know all that stuff in Byron seems like some dumb nightmare now, but please, take care, won't you.'

'I'll be fine, there aren't any cliffs in London,' she joked, because she didn't want to hear what Tom was saying.

27

'I'm not concerned about how the press conference went,' Brandon snapped pushing Christina's report back across the desk impatiently as he got up and walked over to his favourite position by the plate-glass window.

'I've told you, Jude is both the problem and the solution. Has the girl been in touch with him?'

'This morning. But he refused to see her.' Xan was angry. Jude, Jude, always bloody Jude, his boss was obsessed.

'That won't stop her,' Brandon chuckled.

'It didn't,' Xan confirmed, surprised at his boss's insight. 'She's just booked a train to Fort William, leaving tomorrow. She's going to doorstep him.'

'He won't turn her away,' Brandon stated quietly. He moved from the window and sat down again at his desk. Looking at Xan hard, he seemed to read his mind.

'You think you don't know about Jude, but you do.'

Xan shook his head in frustrated denial.

'I'm surprised. Last time you met was so memorable.'

Xan winced at the cold, almost sneering tone.

'The day Atlantis fell . . . you spearheaded the attack on the temple. It was your responsibility to disrupt the ceremony. And destroy the group.' Brandon's words, although softly spoken, seemed somehow to blame him.

There was silence in the penthouse office except for the distant ring of a phone in the outer office, quickly answered by Christina.

Xan found he was shaking; his body, normally held so firmly under control, was suddenly sweating and pumping with adrenaline. All he could see was a glittering knife thrown with

114

deadly accuracy straight for his eyes. And behind it a face, calm, focused, almost detached. Then nothing.

'That was Jude,' he heard Brandon's whisper. 'The man who killed you.'

For a moment Xan was unable to speak. But his rigid mental training forced his thoughts back to the present. Breathing slow and deep, he struggled to respond as if nothing had happened. He knew this was what Crowe expected of him.

'So we get to him through the girl?'

Brandon nodded approvingly.

'Follow her. Hear everything they say. He won't talk to us, but he will to her.' Brandon paused, 'But let me tell you, whatever they are up to, it won't be to our advantage. Count on that.'

'Do they know what we're doing with S-3?' Xan couldn't help asking.

'I told you, I don't know what they know, what they're up to. But remember Xan, these are not ordinary people. They're clever, focused and determined. They're Atlanteans. You may not fully understand what that means in this life, but never, *ever* underestimate them.'

'Even the girl?' Xan had not been particularly impressed with her at the press conference. She'd seemed nervy and arrogant. Although, she'd got the attention of his boss without much difficulty. He hated asking these questions, everything Crowe was saying was taking him out of his comfort zone. Brandon had told him what seemed to him a bit of a fairy tale when Xan had first joined the corporation. So he knew that his boss, and indeed himself, had been involved in the fall of Atlantis. And he understood about the crystal and S-3. But he had no memory of the place, no memory of the group of seven. In fact he wasn't sure what he really knew or didn't know any more.

'Jude will protect the girl at all costs,' Brandon smiled, a faraway look in his eye that his henchman failed to interpret. 'And that – luckily for us – is his Achilles heel.'

◎◎

Alone in his office Brandon accessed the hidden files detailing the progress of the crystal replica. He'd always assumed the Heartstone had been destroyed when Atlantis fell but if the group of seven had returned, if they were planning to complete the ceremony, they would need the crystal. So they must know it still existed and where to find it. So far, he had seen Lilith and Rhiannon. His sixth sense told him that his brother was nearby. And where Lilith was, Gabe was bound to be. No sight of the others yet. Well, what did he expect? Lilith would be using all her powers to shield them. Just because he couldn't see them, didn't mean they weren't there.

Brandon looked at the 3-D simulation revolving slowly on his screen. Only once had he held the original in his hands. This one looked the same, it had the potential to unleash the same unlimited power, but something was lacking. The central core remained unstable and split apart every time he activated the crystal. There was something he didn't know about the inner structure, something Jude had kept from him.

Brandon weighed up the pros and cons. As things stood, he was sure that in time he could make the replica fully operational. On the other hand, if the real crystal still existed, that would save him vast amounts of time and money. And if his adversaries *were* back again, one of them would lead him to the crystal. Then all he had to do was take it from them before they had a chance to use it. And, of course, persuade Jude to unlock Stonehenge. A very dangerous game, but Brandon enjoyed taking risks. The greater the risk, the greater the reward.

Brandon reset the password, closed down the computer and crossed to the massive plate-glass window. Outside the sun had set over the city and glittering lights stretched to the far horizon. All things considered, this was working out well. He'd enjoy crossing swords with Lilith again, as long as the odds were stacked in his favour. And they would be, once he had Jude on his side.

28

Now the girl was safely seated on the train, Xan made his way to her carriage and walked straight past her, studying her as he went, with no apparent concern at being recognised from the press conference. The seat he decided upon, three rows behind Rhiannon, was booked in another name from Rugby, but Xan wasn't worried about that either. He carried no luggage, not even a paper, book or computer, he didn't sleep, he just sat very still, seeming to sink into himself, almost as if he were not there at all.

Rhiannon didn't see Xan. She had quickly buried herself in her laptop, wanting to be word perfect in case her opportunity for asking questions was brief. From her research it seemed as if Jude had his finger firmly on the meteorological pulse, both nationally and internationally. If anyone could, he was the man to explain the possible causes of the recent freak weather patterns. Maybe he was aware of the flash flood near Stonehenge, where Rhiannon was convinced she nearly died. As she sat gazing out of the train window, her rescuer's face floated across the glass. Those calm blue eyes, the mark clear on his wrist as he was swept away. Absently she fingered her own mark beneath her watch and thought of Michael. There must be some rational explanation for him knowing about the mark, for having one himself. But why would he want to play such a game?

The trolley creaking its way down between the seats, catching bags, feet, children, as it went, interrupted her thoughts. Rhiannon ordered a black coffee, a Kit Kat and a bag of crisps; the sandwiches looked dodgy.

Suddenly she felt tired. Why was she doing this, getting up at the crack of dawn to travel the length and breadth of the country for a man who clearly had no intention of talking to her? The film didn't really need it – she had plenty of compelling footage – but she knew it wasn't just her obsessive love of a challenge that was drawing her north. No, there was something about the man himself that she couldn't begin to explain, even to herself.

The trolley stopped for Xan too. He didn't even bother to review the contents, just asked for a cup of hot water, into which he sank a tea bag he'd retrieved from his pocket. He allowed the bag to steep a long time before he drank, by which time the liquid was almost cold.

29

The mist was already coming in off the sea as Jude made his way back from the cliffs; he could feel the chilling moisture settling on his clothes and face. For the second time that week he'd been to the rock face to test the vibrations from the seven portals, and his suspicions were confirmed that the deep earth energy was experiencing serious disruption. Stepping off the tarmac onto the sea path leading to his croft, he thought he noticed the shape of a car through the mist, parked on the next bend, but he was cold and in need of the comfort of his peat fire and thought no more about it until he reached his door, and almost stumbled on a huddled figure crouched on the doorstep in the dark. Shocked, he stepped back as Rhiannon sprang to her feet.

Rhiannon had always believed it was best to come out fighting, and the half hour she'd just spent slowly freezing to the stone step in the gathering mist she'd used to work out her plan of attack. It would be along the lines of: 'Listen here, you can't send me away, . . . I only want an hour of your time, . . . I've come all this way, etc.' but before her numbed lips could form a single word, Jude said: 'You'd better come in.'

Small and simply furnished, the house was warm and seemed so peaceful to Rhiannon that for one mad second all she wanted to do was curl up on the deep sofa in front of the fire and go to sleep. Jude had his back to her as he bent to stoke the smouldering ashes, carefully arranging the peat bricks in a pyramid to get the best draw. She had barely seen his face yet.

Then he stood and turned, their eyes met, and Rhiannon felt a sickening lurch in her chest, followed by the deafening thump, thump of her heart.

Neither of them said a word, just stared at each other as if they had both seen a ghost. Jude was the first to recover.

'Please . . . sit, I'll get tea . . . Or whisky?'

Rhiannon nodded dumbly. What was the matter with her?

'Which?' Jude smiled, his beautiful eyes lighting up the powerful lines of his face. She wanted to touch him, to lay her head against his chest, to feel the essence of this man whom she had never met before in her life but seemed to know her like she knew herself.

'Uh . . . whisky, definitely,' she said, hearing the tremor in her voice and laughing to cover it.

While Jude was in the kitchen, Rhiannon tried to breathe normally. She had met hundreds of men who'd attracted her, but this was something else. This felt as if she was coming home, as if the electricity between them was based on a deep, ancient knowledge. She contemplated running, just getting up and leaving right now, before she had to face him again, but his footsteps sounded on the stone flagstones.

'Only one ice cube,' Jude remarked, placing the small tin tray he carried carefully on the coffee table. 'I forgot to fill it,' he smiled that smile again, looking curiously at Rhiannon as she slumped on the sofa, and Rhiannon couldn't do anything but stare back.

'I don't take ice,' she managed to say, and was surprised that her voice sounded pretty normal.

'Lucky really . . .' Jude laughed and poured half an inch of malt into each tumbler. He picked up the small water jug and hovered it above one of the glasses. Rhiannon shook her head. She never drank spirits – certainly never whisky. In fact she didn't even like it, but if there was ever a moment for Dutch courage, this was it, and the neater the better. She sipped the smooth, fiery liquid gratefully as Jude lowered himself into the armchair beside the fire.

There was silence, neither daring to look at the other, but the air was electric between them. Jude finally glanced across at Rhiannon's lowered head, the fire playing softly on her beautiful face, on the chestnut lights in her hair. He noticed the trembling in her hands as they held tightly to the glass, the awkward jigging of her foot, and just wanted to take her in his arms and stay her anxiety. She looked so fragile, more so, he thought, because of the contrast with her heavy, workmanlike clothes. He resisted all thoughts about why she had come, or what the implications might be. For now she was just a woman who, in the brief moment of knowing her, had stirred his closed-up heart.

' I'm sorry . . .' Rhiannon was speaking. 'Sorry to burst in on you like this. But I really needed to talk to you. I'll go as soon as I can . . .'

Jude laughed. 'You won't get far in this fog, except into a stone wall perhaps.'

There was panic in Rhiannon's glance. 'What do you mean?'

'I mean you'll have to stay the night.' As he said it, he felt himself begin to panic too. No one stepped over his threshold, either of his house or his heart, and here suddenly was a girl who threatened to do both.

'But –' she looked towards the window, but the darkness had a blank, opaque look to it. She knew he was right.

Outside, impervious to the chilly, damp fog curling round him, Xan drew back as he caught the girl's eyes flick towards the window, although he knew no one ever saw him unless he chose. Bored with the domestic scene, which seemed to be going nowhere, he moved off from the house and took his mobile out of his pocket. The display light shone eerily through the fog, but when he punched in Brandon's number, the connection failed. No surprise that there was no signal in this god-forsaken place. What was it Brandon wanted him to do exactly? Wasn't it enough that Jude and the girl had made contact? He badly wanted to get away from this dangerous man, who made even him, Xan, nervous.

To cover the awkward silence, Jude rose to fill their glasses. 'The good news is it gives you hours and hours to ask me anything you want,' he joked.

Rhiannon nodded vigorously, trying to marshal her thoughts, searching for her carefully prepared dossier in a brain loosened by whisky and this unnerving attraction for the man opposite her. As he refilled her glass she breathed in the warm, masculine smell of wool and peat. The world appeared to have shrunk. She hadn't forgotten about the global nightmare unfolding beyond the door, but right now it seemed as if nothing existed except the two of them, drawn together within the cocoon of firelight, whisky, and their unspoken, overwhelming desire.

'I'm making a film about the strange natural phenomena the world's been experiencing recently.' Rhiannon went into automatic pilot, using the words she'd spoken hundreds of times over recent months to explain her documentary. But as she spoke she began to relax. She knew her subject like the back of her hand and as passion for her work took over she found she couldn't stop talking, sensing for the first time that she might be truly understood.

'It can't just be global warming. If it was, then surely it would be a slow burn, things gradually getting worse, but these events are so violent and almost as if they had specific targets. The floods in Asia, the cyclones in Australia and the States, even the hurricane that finally put paid to the Olympics in London. They'll never recoup the billions that have been lost. It's as if a malign force has suddenly been unleashed on the world . . .' Rhiannon smiled apologetically, 'Almost like a vengeful god.'

Jude was silent for a moment. His thoughts were in turmoil. How much could he tell this girl? How much did he really know himself?

'What's your connection with Brandon Crowe?'

Rhiannon looked puzzled. 'Crowe? My film's being financed by his corporation, but I have no connection with him otherwise.'

'But he suggested you contact me?'

'He had a press conference to announce his fund for eco-schemes to save the planet. I went along to try and get more money out of him to expand my film.'

'And how did my name come up?'

Rhiannon sensed the atmosphere had changed with the mention of Brandon Crowe.

'I asked about extreme weather and he said you were the only man for the job. I knew about your work of course, but you keep yourself to yourself and my pathetic budget was limited to following actual events.'

Jude stood up, his back to the fire. 'Rhiannon . . .' It was the first time he had said her name, and she realised with surprise that he must have remembered it from her brief phone call. His eyes burned fiercely, his gaze was intent, but he said no more, he didn't even seem to see her.

'For instance, there was this flash flood . . .' she kept talking, not interested in Crowe, 'near Stonehenge . . . and I was nearly swept away. It came from nowhere, just exploded through the road. It may be nothing, but it's that sort of thing that seems to be happening everywhere.'

Jude nodded. He muttered something quietly, just a word, that Rhiannon thought was 'Brandon', but she wasn't sure. What did he know about Crowe, she wondered.

'Rhiannon,' Jude came over and sat beside her at the other end of the sofa. She took a deep breath as his closeness set her heart thudding again. 'We could go next door to my workroom and we could pore over charts, graphs, figures, simulated projections, and you might get what you came for . . . but you're right. Nothing in the predicted cycles of extreme weather events comes close to explaining what's happening at the moment. There's no precedent.' He shifted beside her, his strong hands clasped together, his fingers pressing tight against the backs of his hands.

'So can you explain it?'

Jude shrugged, turning to face her, his brilliant aquamarine eyes suddenly alight with laughter. 'Global meltdown? Umm . . . will a sentence do?'

Rhiannon laughed too, as much with joy at the shared moment as at anything he'd said. Then her face fell, 'It's not funny though. I'm scared by what I've seen.'

'So am I . . . and when you say it's as if there is a malign force, you're not far from the truth.' He hesitated. 'Weather manipulation is the new political weapon. People like, well, like Brandon Crowe for instance, can hold great power over world economy if they can manipulate the climate. You're right about what's happening in Australia and America. And the volcanic explosions in Iceland cost Europe billions. India has had to cancel its moon probe to search for a new source of energy because the deteriorating weather is destroying their economy. I'm not saying this is Crowe, of course, but . . . by the way, what were you doing at Stonehenge?'

Rhiannon felt the tension return. 'Watching the summer solstice with a bunch of hippies.'

'Did you know any of them?'

'The hippies? No . . . although one of them introduced himself.' She paused, 'But he wasn't really a hippy.' She remembered the odd moment when Michael spoke her name and wondered again how he could have known. 'He was with this woman who was full-on New Age though, all dramatic dark hair and flowing robe with a huge crystal round her neck. Michael told me her name was Lily and she does psychic readings or something.' Rhiannon looked at Jude, 'Why do you ask?'

'And this man, you've seen him since then?' Jude went on as if she hadn't spoken.

Rhiannon twisted on the sofa, drawing her long legs up underneath her, her old feistiness reasserting itself under his questioning.

'I have, as it happens, although I don't see it's any of your business.' For the first time since arriving at the house, she felt on edge, almost resenting being sucked in to this man's powerful aegis.

She doesn't know, Jude thought. *They're tracking her, but she doesn't know yet.*

Jude gazed at her as he tried to work out how much to tell

her. She would think him mad of course, but he didn't mind that.

Then the moment when he could speak was lost. Almost unconsciously he felt his hand reach out to touch the unbearable softness of her cheek, heard his own sharp intake of breath, found himself drawing her gently towards him until he held her trembling body against his own. For a moment this was enough – desire superseded by the overwhelming pleasure of their closeness in that magical, fire-lit world – then finally he bent his head to kiss her upturned face and all thought ceased.

Beyond the window Xan cursed softly. Nothing, he decided, would be served by standing watching this all night, so he disappeared down the lane to his car. He would be back when it was light.

Neither Jude nor Rhiannon knew how long they lay wrapped in each other's arms; time had stopped. But as the fire sank to no more than glowing ashes, the room began to lose its warmth.

'Stay there,' he whispered, stroking the soft spikes of brown hair back from her face.

'Don't be long,' she whispered back, her eyes tracing him as he moved towards the fire.

Jude bent close to the hearth, adding peat bricks to the embers. As the fire took hold he gazed into the flames, and as he stared, his body suddenly went rigid with shock. It was her, Lilith . . . her face, in the flames.

Jude reeled back on his haunches, shooting an involuntary glance at the recumbent figure of the girl he had been planning to make love to for the rest of time. The gaze she gave back was one of rending innocence. He cursed under his breath. All he wanted was to forget the past, forget about the destiny which had driven him through so many painful lifetimes. He could love this girl – they could be happy.

'Hurry up,' Rhiannon murmured, reaching out a hand towards him.

For a second he resisted, trying with all his will to blot out Lilith's image. But even in that second, part of him knew he couldn't do it. Every impulse of his being for as long as he could remember was set to atone for the mistake that had cost the world so dear.

'I think we'd better cool it,' Jude stood up abruptly, looking directly at Rhiannon, and dying inside as he registered the bewilderment, the disbelief, the shock that flashed across her features. She pulled herself up on the sofa cushions, wiping her hair back from her face until it stood up in almost comical peaks.

'Cool it? What does that mean? Why? Why should we cool it?' she said when she was able to speak. It was as if he had hit her.

Jude sighed, clinging on to the mantelpiece for support. 'Rhiannon . . .'

She was standing now, facing him across the table, the flames playing fiercely in her hurt, angry eyes.

'Don't "Rhiannon" me,' she shouted. 'Don't do this . . . don't . . .' turning away she fled the room for the cold, quiet darkness of the stone hallway.

How could he deny her? She knew he felt the same passion, the same compelling connection – she knew nothing about him, but she knew at least that. What had suddenly changed?

There was silence from the sitting room. Taking a deep breath she went back to collect her things. Fog or no fog, she couldn't stay in this house a minute longer. And if that meant she met her end against a stone wall, then so be it.

Jude hadn't moved from the fireside. His face looked blank, dead.

'You don't understand,' he said wearily. 'This is not only about us, there are wider implications.'

Rhiannon held her hand up, palm flat towards him as if to fend off any more hurt. 'Please . . . don't tell me . . . you've got a wife and fourteen kids down the road, you don't love her of course, but one of the children's dying from a crippling disease and you have to be there.'

She collected up the camera bag and her black down jacket, then realised she didn't have her boots on. Tears pressed behind her eyes as she bent under the sofa to retrieve them, but she was damned if she would give this bastard the satisfaction of seeing her cry.

'You can't drive in this fog,' Jude was pleading with her. 'Please Rhiannon, please don't go like this . . .'

She stared at him, 'And you care . . . why?'

She began to make for the door, but Jude grabbed her arm.

'Listen, go if you like, I can't keep you here . . . but . . .'

'That'd be right,' she snorted, pulling herself free. She felt as if she might burst if she didn't get out of there.

'But give me just ten minutes to explain something it's vital you know. Please . . . this is going to sound melodramatic, but it could affect your whole life.'

The urgency in his tone stopped her in her tracks.

'Please . . . sit down.' Jude gently guided her back to the sofa, and suddenly Rhiannon felt exhausted and unable to resist.

Jude sat next to her and for a moment was silent.

'What I'm going to say will sound very odd.'

Rhiannon watched his strong, square hands, weather-beaten and calloused from his climbing, twist in his lap, and couldn't help remembering the heart-stopping tenderness of his touch – now a world away.

'First . . . what happened between us was real.' He turned to look at her, but she wouldn't raise her eyes. 'I have never, in this lifetime, felt such –' He hesitated, then went on, 'Such desire . . . such love . . .'

She heard him take a long, deep breath, which seemed to hold a wealth of sadness. Suddenly the tears came, she could no longer hold them back.

'Then why . . .' she sobbed, burying her face in her hands, 'why can't we be together?'

127

Jude tried to take her in his arms but Rhiannon pulled back, unwilling to experience the pain all over again.

'Just get on with it. Tell me what's so life-threateningly important.'

'It's a strange tale, but please, hear me out.'

Rhiannon said nothing.

'Thousands of years ago, in Atlantis –'

She snorted with derision and tried to stand up, but Jude held lightly to her arm.

'Hear me out, please,' he repeated. 'We, you and I, lived in Atlantis. We are Atlanteans.' Jude paused and pulled the sleeve of his thick jumper up to reveal a mark on his wrist. 'That's why we have this mark. It's the symbol of the group we belonged to. There were seven of us and we were together at the fall of Atlantis.'

He felt Rhiannon stiffen beside him, and he knew then that she had an identical mark somewhere on her own wrist. But before he could go on with the story, Rhiannon cut him short, rose swiftly from the sofa and stood over him, her arms akimbo.

'OK, OK, I get it. You like to play with people. You take advantage of me. Fine, I'll survive.' Her voice was clipped and raw. 'But what I don't get is why you have to invent some pathetic, ridiculous fairy tale to get yourself off the hook.'

This time when she gathered up her stuff, Jude didn't try to stop her.

'I honestly don't think I've deserved you,' she added, almost to herself, as she opened the door on the dense, freezing fog.

Rhiannon was beyond even crying she was so angry. Anger gave her the energy to stride through the solid wall of fog to her car, it gave her the energy to unpack her case and put on every piece of clothing she had, it stopped her from being afraid. But once she was wrapped like a parcel and huddled, shivering, in the front seat waiting for daylight, the events of the past hours came back to torment her.

◉◉

Instinct sent Jude out into the night. In the hours since Rhiannon had left, he'd sat numb and hardly moving beside the dying fire, his thoughts in turmoil. Now, as he rounded the bend in the lifting fog, he froze, dropping to a crouch as he pressed his body against the stone wall. Beside Rhiannon's car in the darkness was a tall figure, standing stock still as he peered through the driver's window into the car's interior. Jude saw the figure raise his head, his face suddenly lit by a sudden shaft of moonlight. He would have known him anywhere, those cold-blooded, inhuman features etched on his brain over thousands of years as he'd watched his knife find its target.

Without thinking, Jude picked up a stone from the wall beside him and hurled it in the direction of the car. The figure jumped and looked around, then melted into the night. Jude moved silently towards the car. Rhiannon slept, her head nestled against the seat back, her face childlike and smeared with the heartbreaking evidence of many tears. Resisting his desire to gather her up and take her back to the safety of his home, Jude banged loudly on the window, then retreated to wait in the shadow of the wall. He couldn't speak to her again, he knew he wasn't strong enough, but he needed to know she was safe, far away from whatever evil purpose that figure intended. At least for now.

The banging shocked Rhiannon awake. Chilled to the bone, her mouth claggy from the whisky, her limbs cramped, her head aching, she blinked and stretched, her thoughts still mired in another powerful dream. What had woken her? She looked outside, noticing the fog had all but vanished, but it was dark and still. At least she could drive now, get away from here. She reached automatically for her mobile, longing to hear a friendly voice, then remembered from the night before that there was no signal. Firing the ignition, she took off along the single-track peninsula road, the reassuring sweep of headlights lighting up the road ahead. She drove fast, not giving herself time to think. And the thought she was avoiding was this: how come they all had the same mark? The old man, Michael, herself, now Jude. Could it possibly be coincidence?

Behind her, Jude sighed with relief and Xan tried unsuccessfully to start his rental car.

Later that morning Jude sat cross-legged on the edge of the cliffs and looked out to sea. Several hours of meditation had confirmed what he already knew but was reluctant to face. Rhiannon's appearance on his doorstep was no accident. He could no longer hide from his responsibilities. The time had come to take action. And if he was to have any sort of future, he had to confront the past.

30

Gabriel seized Jude's arm and helped him to a chair.

'I'm OK,' Jude protested. 'Just a few problems getting away from Brandon's men.'

The group surrounded him with eager questions, all except Michael who kept his distance.

'So,' concluded Jude, 'Brandon holds most of the city and we are trapped here with no way to the temple that I can think of.'

'There is one way,' said Gabriel slowly, 'though no one has used it for thousands of years.'

He walked to the far end of the chamber and delicately ran his fingers around a carving of the Tree of Life. The others watched hopefully. Nothing happened. Just as they were giving up hope, they heard a sharp click and the panel creaked open to reveal a dark passageway beyond.

'Why didn't I know about this?' Lilith sounded offended.

'Because you were never a master builder,' Gabriel replied briskly. 'They always build in a secret entrance. Come on, we have no time to waste.'

Leading the way he plunged into the passageway and the others followed in single file. The passage was hot and airless and Rhiannon fought down the feeling of claustrophobia that was threatening to overwhelm her. She paused, gasping for breath, but Jude grabbed her hand and led her onwards until they came to an abrupt halt at a solid wall of stone.

Gabriel held his hand to the wall and spoke a word of command. Silently a doorway opened up before them and they stepped through into the temple.

The light was dazzling after the darkness of the passage. Sunlight poured through a hexagonal skylight which refracted rainbow prisms over the graceful crystal columns that supported the roof.

'Seal the doorway the best you can,' Gabriel ordered as Lilith led the way to the centre of the temple. She looked reverently at the six-sided star engraved in the marble floor and positioned herself at the centre.

'You all understand what we have to do here to protect the earth's energy source from Brandon. I shall use the Heartstone to close each of the seven portals in turn. You must all hold the energy within the circle and no one must waver, even for a second, or I shall lose control of the crystal. If the energy escapes from the circle it will destroy everything in its path. It is imperative that we all trust each other absolutely.'

She looked searchingly around the circle and they all nodded their agreement. Then Maya unwrapped the Heartstone and handed it to her. When they were all in position on the six points of the star Lilith raised the Heartstone to the light.

'Remember to hold the circle, whatever happens.'

Lilith began to chant an incantation in an ancient language none of them recognised. The crystal columns around them appeared to recede until they were standing alone in a circle of light. The silence around them was profound.

Lilith turned to them each in turn, summoning their energy, charging the Heartstone and releasing it towards the portals. She moved through the levels – one, two, three. Rhiannon held her breath. Had she heard shouting outside? Despite herself she glanced at Jude. He'd heard something too and she could feel his concentration waver.

Hold the circle, she willed him. Hold the circle.

Four, five, now six portals were sealed. Only one remained, the portal representing the union of the sacred masculine and feminine. Lilith held the crystal aloft, summoning her remaining energy. Rhiannon watched spellbound as the energy flickered and crackled through Lilith's body and was absorbed into the Heartstone, then closed her eyes in shock as the doors to the temple burst open.

No, she prayed silently, and opened her eyes to see Xan and a troop of heavily armed guards racing towards them. Lilith seemed oblivious, holding the pulsating energy steady, as Xan drew a dagger from his belt and aimed for her heart. Rhiannon sensed Jude poised to move. 'No!' she screamed. 'Don't touch her!' but Jude had already pushed Lilith to one side, grabbed the dagger out of the air and hurled it straight back at Xan who dropped like a stone. The circle was broken.

Instantly everything went black. Bolts of energy ricocheted off the walls, gouging great holes in the crystal columns, then a huge ball of fire exploded through the roof and the pillars began to fall like dominoes.

Gabriel picked up Lilith in his arms and ran, picking his way through the devastation and dodging the falling debris. 'Follow me,' he shouted, 'there's nothing we can do now.' They raced across the undulating floor towards a gaping hole in the wall and stopped, aghast. Jets of steam and molten rock were exploding from the gaping earth and out to sea a wall of water fifty feet high was racing towards the island.

The graceful marble buildings were crumbling as the earth shook violently beneath them, and the screams of the trapped and dying were all but drowned by the howling wind. Cinders and burning ash fell around them as Jude led them towards higher ground, but they knew it was hopeless. The tsunami hit the island with devastating force and the city was overwhelmed in seconds.

Gabriel lifted Lilith onto a rock and reached down to help Rhiannon. For a moment their eyes met and Rhiannon felt a sharp pang of regret that she would never see him again. Tom and Maya huddled together with Michael, still hoping against hope that Gabriel and Lilith would know what to do. Jude stood to one side in despair. This was all his fault.

Lilith drew herself up to her full commanding height and held the Heartstone towards them, shouting to make herself heard above the storm.

'You must all swear to return and complete the ceremony other-wise the whole world will eventually be destroyed as Atlantis is now. However many lifetimes it may take, you must return. Swear it!'

133

One by one they swore on the crystal to return. Lilith bowed her head, murmuring 'So be it' and the crystal suddenly split apart into a thousand splinters of light, then vanished completely.

Maya gasped with shock then turned to Lilith. 'How shall we ever find each other again?'

Lilith looked down at the raging black waters which would soon engulf them but her face was serene.

'Trust that I shall find you all, when the time is right.'

Part II

31

15 October 2012: Lily and Gabe's farmhouse, Wiltshire

It was past midnight, but Gabe and Lily still sat on in front of the fire. Suddenly Atlas, sleeping at Gabe's feet, sprang up, running from the room and barking excitedly. Gabe raised his eyebrows at Lily. Neither of them had heard anything, but it was a ferocious night, the wind howling like a banshee round the farmhouse. Then through the wind they heard a frenzied pounding on the front door.

'Who'd be out on a night like this?' Gabe muttered, getting up stiffly from his armchair.

Lily said nothing, but she knew quite well who it was. She'd spent the last two hours drawing him away from his aunt's cottage.

'Where's Lily?' Michael demanded, pushing past as Gabe opened the door.

Gabe pointed silently to the sitting room.

Lily had risen and was standing in the doorway as Michael strode towards her and grabbed her arms.

'Lily, you've got to help me. Ever since that day you hypnotised me I can't stop thinking about Atlantis. It feels like I'm living two lives and that life is more real than this one. I think I'm going crazy.'

Lily took his arm and led him to a chair by the fire.

'Just relax, Michael, and tell me what you remember.'

Michael took a deep breath, gathering his thoughts.

'After I listened to the tape, I tried to talk to Rhiannon but she just laughed in my face. So I tried to forget about it but . . . I can't.'

Michael ran his hands through his thick dark hair, his eyes wild like a man possessed.

'Tell me,' Lily prompted.

'OK. I can remember the city and the temple . . . the daily rituals of the priesthood. I was studying alchemy, kinetic arts . . . Rhiannon was there, you and Gabe, and others I don't know now but I can see them clearly.'

Michael looked across at Lily, his eyes dark with pain.

'But most of all, I remember the destruction of Atlantis.'

'Do you remember why that happened?' asked Lily quietly.

'Oh yes. We had no choice. We knew we'd never be able to use Selenios-3 again but the ceremony was the only way we could stop Brandon.'

Lily heaved a sigh of relief – this was better than she'd hoped for.

'Then Jude broke the circle. He did it to protect you but you lost control of the crystal and then . . . that's when Atlantis was destroyed.'

Michael looked challengingly at Lily.

'Are these the words of a sane man?'

'Do you really think you're crazy?' Lily asked seriously.

Michael shrugged. 'If I'm not crazy, why am I remembering all this stuff?'

'Because you are here for a reason, Michael. What happened in those final moments?'

Michael closed his eyes, concentrating hard, then suddenly looked at Lily.

'You made us promise to return, all seven of us, and complete the ceremony. We all promised to return. Is that what this is all about?'

Lily nodded.

'And I'm not crazy?'

Lily laughed aloud. 'Most people would think you are, but they're not Atlanteans.'

'And I am . . . an Atlantean . . .' it wasn't quite a question.

'Of course.'

Michael stood up and paced around the room. It all felt so real but his rational side was struggling to take it all in.

'So,' he began tentatively, 'what happens next?'

'We have only a very small window of time left. When we failed to seal the seventh portal it left a weak spot in the underground energy grid. All the pressure is focused on that one point. Stonehenge was built to remedy the problem but it was only a temporary repair and Brandon's experiments have made things worse. It's like a pressure cooker about to explode.'

'How long have we got?'

'Until the winter solstice. On 21 December the sun will be aligned with the centre of the Milky Way for the first time in 26,000 years. This will provide the power we need to activate the crystal and finally seal Stonehenge. But if we don't get the balance of masculine and feminine energy exactly right we could blow the portal apart and the earth with it.'

Michael felt overwhelmed. 'So what am I supposed to do?'

Lily got up and went to sit down at the table in the centre of the room. She unveiled the crystal, placing the six stones from the green velvet bag on the points of the star scored into the table top.

'Come and look,' she beckoned Michael over.

He waited, fascinated, as the seer stone sprang to life. At first it was fuzzy, like the screen on a malfunctioning television, but as he watched, shapes began to emerge. As the image cleared he could see Rhiannon, as clearly as if she were on his Skype screen. She was slumped in the corner of a train seat, sobbing silently.

'What's happened? What's the matter with her?'

Lily sighed. 'That's a long story, but what you have to know is that Rhiannon is in great danger from Brandon's forces.'

Michael started, 'Brandon? The same one that I knew in Atlantis?'

She paused, making sure he was paying attention. 'The same. You realise this is Brandon Crowe, *the* Brandon Crowe of Crowe Corporation fame? He's become very powerful in this world – more so than he was even in Atlantis. If he is trying to reinstate S-3 as an energy source using the weak portal at Stonehenge, then the world is in trouble.'

Lily's voice shook with anger. 'He'll never be able to control it. Selenios-3 is much too volatile to let loose in a world which is so unbalanced. There's so much chaos and destruction – war, religious intolerance, centuries of female oppression, nature in revolt at the damage we've inflicted – my fault in a way . . . if the ceremony had worked . . .'

'But how does he know about Rhiannon?'

'She stumbled onto his radar with her documentary. He recognised her.'

'From Atlantis? That's ridiculous.'

Lily raised her eyebrows. 'Is it? You recognised her.'

Michael stood frozen in front of this strange woman. His heart was still pounding in his chest, his thoughts racing.

'But I still don't know what to do,' he said finally.

Lily smiled. 'You must find Rhiannon and convince her to join us. Then the rest will fall into place, I promise you.'

32

'You can't go out dressed like that!'

Rhiannon looked down at her scruffy jeans and T-shirt then back at her friend. *What's she talking about? I'm not going anywhere tonight.*

Lauren was almost hopping on the spot with impatience.

'Don't tell me you've forgotten. Rhi, you promised! Lucy's hen night!'

Vague memories were stirring now.

'Oh, is it tonight? You know, I'm not really in the mood.'

'I know,' Lauren snapped back, eyeing her friend through narrowed eyes. 'I know you'd rather sit here moping after whatshisname, the Scottish hunk, but it will do you good to get out. In fact, a few hours with the blushing bride and you'll be happy to be single.'

Rhiannon had to smile. Lucy had been planning her wedding since she was a toddler, all her ambitions directed towards married bliss with the man she loved. Rhiannon's heart constricted as Jude came unbidden to her mind. Sternly she dismissed him. She didn't need a man, now or ever.

Lauren had disappeared into Rhiannon's bedroom and came back holding up two dresses. 'Black or red, long or short?'

Rhiannon felt herself weakening. There was only one person she knew more stubborn than she was and that was Lauren. She put up only token resistance as Lauren dragged her into the bathroom and with a slick of lipstick, eyeliner and mascara transformed her into a supermodel. Rhiannon stared at her unfamiliar reflection critically – she hardly ever wore make-up.

'It's not frivolous to celebrate being a woman, and a gorgeous one at that!' Lauren silenced any further objections and dragged Rhiannon off to west London.

Lucy's flat, Shepherds Bush, west London

Rhiannon eased off her high heels and tucked her feet under her. The sofa was soft and deep and she sank back into it with relief. Around her Lucy and her friends sipped wine and chattered excitedly about the wedding and dresses and make-up and boyfriends and babies . . . Rhiannon sighed inwardly. What was wrong with her? Why couldn't she enter into the spirit of this celebration? *Because*, she answered herself, *she didn't believe a word of it. It was all a fairy tale. An illusion. And if you do find your soulmate he'll break your heart.*

And to top it all, Lucy had booked a tarot-card reader to tell them whether they were all going to share her good fortune. Rhiannon looked around for Lauren. She was ready to go and it seemed ages since Lauren had gone in for her tarot reading. Just then, Lauren came back into the room and beckoned to her. *Your turn*. Reluctantly, Rhiannon got to her feet and joined her.

'Well, what did she tell you?'

Lauren shrugged her shoulders. 'Nothing much.'

'Come on, you were in there for ages. I know, she told you Sam's got tired of waiting for you and found someone else!'

Rhiannon was only teasing but she stopped short when she saw the troubled look in her friend's eyes.

'No, no it was nothing like that but . . . well Sam did come into it. At least I think he did.'

'And,' Rhiannon prompted.

'Well, it sounded like he might be getting involved in something . . .' Lauren's voice trailed away and she looked anxiously at her friend.

'Like what?

'Oh, I don't know. Something to do with work.'

Rhiannon looked at her curiously. It wasn't like Lauren to get wound up, especially by a fortune-teller.

Lauren pulled herself together.

142

'I know, I know. I'm reading too much into it. And it could just have easily been about you. You're far more likely to stir up trouble than Sam! Anyway, she's waiting for you.'

'Come in Rhiannon, sit down. I'm Magdalena.'

The room was shadowy, lit only by dozens of candles, and Rhiannon could just make out a dark-haired woman sitting at a table by the doors leading out into the garden. *So far, so predictable; a little bit of scene setting.*

The voice was a soft Irish lilt but the gaze of the dark blue eyes was challenging.

'I'm not about to waste my time or yours so let's cut to the chase.'

Rhiannon sat down beside her, this was not what she'd been expecting.

'That's fine with me.'

'It's obvious you think this is a load of mumbo-jumbo.'

Slightly taken aback, Rhiannon started to explain that she was open to new experiences and – but Magdalena cut her short.

'You're a woman who needs hard evidence. OK, here's what you need to know.'

She picked up the cards lying in front of her.

'This pack of cards charts the journey of the soul from innocence to enlightenment. Along the way we have good experiences and bad and they shape the person we become. The cards can help point the way and reveal things we don't know, things hidden in the unconscious, things we are afraid to look at but need to know if we are to progress.'

Rhiannon swallowed hard. 'I don't see how they can do that.'

Magdalena's fierce eyes softened.

'I'll show you. Take the cards and shuffle them.'

Rhiannon took the pack of cards. They were larger than she had expected and she shuffled them clumsily.

'Now concentrate on whatever is important to you at the moment. Do you have a specific question?'

143

'No,' Rhiannon answered quickly. 'No, just things in general.'

Magdalena smiled as she took the cards and spread them face down on the table in a semi-circle.

'OK. Just things in general. Now I want you to choose ten cards. Keep your mind focused on what you want to know.'

Rhiannon's hand hovered over the cards. Outside she could hear music, reggae and drum and bass from competing neighbours. She closed her eyes and tried to concentrate. *Jude!* She was determined not to think about Jude but there they were in his croft by the fire . . . She sighed and allowed her hand to take a card, then another until ten were sitting face down beside her.

Magdalena gathered up the remaining cards and put them to one side. Then she shook out a black silk cloth and laid it on the table.

'Ready?'

Rhiannon nodded.

Magdalena took the first card and laid it in the centre of the cloth.

'The Eight of Cups. This is you, where you are at this moment.'

Rhiannon peered at the card. A sad young woman, darkness, a full moon shedding cold silver light. Rhiannon shivered and looked at Magdalena. *What does this mean?*

Magdalena tapped the card gently with a long silver fingernail.

'The suit of Cups represents feeling, like the water signs in astrology, and describes our emotional journey through life. The Eight of Cups is about giving up a treasured hope for the future. A time to face the truth, let go and walk away.'

Rhiannon stifled a gasp, then her rational mind took hold. Coincidence, or maybe Lauren had left slip something about Jude. She kept her expression neutral.

'And the next card?'

Magdalena turned over the second card and laid it across the first.

'The crossing card – the apparent cause of the situation.'

144

Rhiannon stared in bewilderment at the figure of a man hanging upside down, his head touching the ground.

Magdalena glanced at her. 'The Hanged Man. Sometimes known as the wounded healer. Someone who makes a voluntary sacrifice for the greater good. Perhaps someone you know?'

Rhiannon shook her head. This was too weird. She blocked out Jude's voice trying to tell her why they couldn't be together. She hardly noticed as Magdalena laid the third card above the other two.

'The crowning card – what's hanging over you. The Lovers.'

Rhiannon held her hand to her mouth to stifle a sob as she stared at the card. *What was this woman trying to do to her?*

Magdalena touched her arm gently. 'Listen, Rhiannon. The Lovers is about choice. Once that choice is made, everything changes. The ancients believed that our souls are split in two and we spend a lifetime looking for the missing other half so we can feel whole. But it's important to make the right choice, not to be blinded by passion.'

Rhiannon lifted her head and stared hard at Magdalena. 'I hope there's a solution at the end of all this.'

Magdalena turned over the fourth card and laid it beneath the other three.

'There's always an answer. Now the fourth card is the base of the matter – the underlying cause of your situation. Something you may not be aware of.'

Rhiannon looked at the card. A beautiful woman, a goddess perhaps, pouring water from a gold cup to a silver one.

'Temperance,' said Magdalena. 'She represents balance. In this card she is pouring water from a gold cup, representing the sun, into a silver cup, representing the moon. If you can integrate your heart and your mind you will be able to act correctly.'

Rhiannon was struggling to make sense of it.

'Is this something I need to learn?'

'It's a quality you already have. Allow it to come to the surface.'

Magdalena laid the fifth card to the left of the others.

'Past influences. The Wheel of Fortune.'

She glanced at Rhiannon. 'This tells me karma, fate, has a huge influence on your life. But remember, the wheel turns and when one cycle ends another begins.'

Rhiannon sat back in her chair feeling drained. She was feeling weighed down. Things felt out of control. She summoned up a weak smile.

'So things are definitely getting better!'

Magdalena smiled back. 'Let's see.'

She turned over the sixth card.

'The Knight of Wands, reversed.'

Rhiannon saw a young warrior riding a white horse. 'Who's he?'

'He represents an influence coming your way, maybe a real person. He's an idealist, searching for meaning, but he's lost his way. If he can heal himself, he can heal others.'

'That's all I need,' said Rhiannon grumpily. 'A knight in tarnished armour.'

Magdalena smiled to herself. *He's going to have his work cut out getting through to you!*

Rhiannon looked at the remaining cards.

'I'm still waiting for the good news.'

'The next card is about now and the near future. The Ten of Swords. Something is leaving your life, there's a difficult and painful separation but look,' she pointed to the card, 'the sun is rising in the background. Face the situation truthfully and there will be new beginning.'

'A new beginning without my soulmate?' Rhiannon couldn't help asking and was surprised by the irritation in Magdalena's eyes.

'I thought you understood. He's not the one you're destined to be with. There's someone else but your heart doesn't know it yet.'

Her fierce expression softened. 'You don't trust your heart, do you?'

Magdalena turned over the next card and looked at it thoughtfully.

146

'See, this one shows how other people see you.'

Rhiannon looked curiously at the Queen of Swords.

'That's how people see me?'

'Well, she's a queen, a strong woman, but the suit of swords corresponds to the astrological air signs which are masculine so she's not entirely at ease there. She's admired but perhaps a little isolated.'

At least you don't get hurt that way, Rhiannon muttered to herself.

Magdalena reached for the next card, then turned impulsively to Rhiannon.

'There's something strange about this. On the surface it all makes sense. It seems obvious you're trying to recover from an unhappy love affair but there's something else,' she tapped the Wheel of Fortune card, 'something karmic, all the references to the divine feminine . . .'

She realised Rhiannon was looking at her blankly and turned the card over.

'See, The Star. The feminine principle and the possibility of wholeness despite past disappointments.'

'But what does that mean for me?' asked Rhiannon impatiently.

'It means that there's hope.'

Rhiannon looked at the final card.

'So one more positive card to see me on my way?'

Magdalena turned the final card and they both stared in silence at the tower struck by lightning.

'Doesn't look good,' said Rhiannon gloomily.

'I agree it looks like the end of the world, but you can look at it positively. The tower is the only man-made structure in the whole tarot so could represent the defences we build around ourselves. If that no longer serves us, it must be destroyed to make way for a new order.'

'But it looks so . . . catastrophic.'

'Oh, it doesn't have to mean the end of the world as we know it . . .' Magdalena paused and looked at Rhiannon searchingly.

147

'But in your case, I think it might.'

Taxi en route to North London

'Rhi, I swear I didn't say a word about Jude.'

Rhiannon could see that Lauren was telling the truth, so how did Magdalena know so much?

'Anyway,' Lauren continued, 'it was only a tarot reading. It was meant to be fun. Surely you don't believe all that stuff.'

'No, of course not. Anyway, she was right about one thing. It's over with Jude and I'm moving on.'

Looking at her friend's drawn face, Lauren wasn't so sure.

33

Tom swivelled on his computer chair and stretched.

'Coffee?' he asked the man sitting over the partition on the next desk.

'Oh, please, yes,' groaned Sam. There was such a driven work ethic at the Crowe Corporation that all the employees stayed longer at their desks than was normal.

The canteen was not the average, scuzzy basement space with plastic cups and cutlery and smelling of cabbage and bleach. It was designed more like a first-class lounge in an airport, with comfortable sofas and chairs, and freshly cooked food and drinks on tap even in the middle of the night. No expense spared. Tom and Sam slouched, exhausted, over their white china mugs of coffee.

'Aren't you going home tonight?' Sam asked.

Tom shook his head. 'I have too much to do. Bit of a keen-bean syndrome going on at the moment I suppose. I want them to think I'm indispensable.'

Sam laughed. He was a small man, but solid and friendly, with floppy, shoulder-length brown hair and intelligent hazel eyes. Lauren, before she'd broken Sam's heart, described him as 'too nerdy to be cute', but Rhiannon liked him and thought them a perfect match. Lauren could be nerdy too.

'They won't . . . at least they'll never admit it. There's only one indispensable person around here and that's Brandon Crowe.'

'Have you met him?'

Sam looked shocked. 'Uh, no, of course not. I'm a minion. If I met him he would have to kill me.'

Tom grinned. 'Nor me. It's a good place to work though isn't it? I mean he's got the money to do what I want to do.'

Sam hesitated, obviously trying to decide something. Finally he looked round, making sure no one was in hearing distance, and leaned closer to Tom.

'I'm leaving next week. I can't tell you why exactly because I don't know. Just a feeling, but there's something wrong with this place. None of the work we do ever leads anywhere and some of our best ideas disappear without trace. And people too. There was a guy called Gutman on the third floor. Security escorted him off the premises a few weeks ago and nobody's heard from him since.'

Tom looked thoughtful. 'He worked on the third floor? Any idea what goes on there?' Sam shook his head.

'There's some totally secret project on the third floor that none of us is supposed to know about, but the word is it's to do with weather control. I'd love to get a look, but it's job suicide to even mention you know about it.'

Sam yawned. 'Anyway, enough of the conspiracy theories. This time next week I'll be in fair Helsinki setting up a new IT system for a Finnish energy company. Boring, but eye-wateringly well paid. It's only six months and it'll buy me time to work out my next career move.' He shrugged. 'But no reason why you shouldn't make use of the mighty Crowe dollar. What *are* you doing here?'

Tom pulled a face. 'Oceans are my thing. I've been looking at genetic changes in marine life, dead zones, water chemistry and thermal expansion, biodiversity – the usual stuff. I came here to work on the connection between changes in ocean currents and the earth's magnetic field. Some of the changes are so dramatic that there's a possibility that the North and South Poles may reverse completely, and all this freak weather is a contributory factor.'

Sam laughed. 'The end is nigh. Maybe the answer lies on the third floor. Anyway, I'm off. See ya tomorrow.'

'I guess,' Tom agreed, and made his way to the lift. But Sam had intrigued him, and instead of waiting for the lift he began to walk up the stairs to his desk on the fifth floor, deliberately passing the third floor. The door to the third floor was firmly bolted and padlocked from the stairwell, with a large yellow notice saying Keep Out – Danger.

As Tom opened the door to the fifth floor, he saw two men standing by the lift. He immediately recognised his boss, Mr Crowe, from photographs, and decided to go up and introduce himself. Why not? The man wasn't God. But as he stepped into the corridor, something made him catch his breath and flatten himself into the niche where the fire alarm sat, out of sight of the two men. He knew them. Both of them. Not from photos in the media, but really knew them from somewhere. His heart pounded in his chest. He was frightened of them, but why? What had Brandon Crowe ever done to him? The lift arrived and they stepped in, the doors closing silently behind them. Tom made his way to his desk, furious with himself. What was wrong with him? He'd just lost a perfect opportunity to bond with the boss and instead had shrunk out of sight like a pathetic wuss. But as he sat at his computer, trying to concentrate on the chart he was trying to finish, images kept swimming in front of his eyes like flashing lights. And in the images were faces, Crowe and his companion . . . Erik . . . the man on the Byron cliffs . . . harsh and aggressive, coming at Tom out of nowhere. Like a nightmare. He shook himself, thinking he had fallen asleep, but checking the computer clock, no time had passed.

Brandon's office, west London

'I don't get it.' Xan stared hard at his boss. 'Why are we still watching the girl? Nothing happened at the cottage. Nothing's happened since.'

Brandon looked up from his chair and smiled slowly. 'On the contrary. It confirmed that Rhiannon is definitely the key to our problem at Stonehenge. Why else would Lilith break cover to warn him off? Watch and wait, Xan, watch and wait, and Rhiannon will deliver Jude to us.'

151

Xan stifled an irritated sigh. The boss seemed to think the girl had some hold over this Jude character but none of it made sense to him.

'OK, we keep watching, but there's been no trace of him since he left Scotland. He's not an easy man to find.'

'Tell me something I don't know.' Brandon seemed oddly amused. 'That's why we need the girl. Of course she's being watched twenty-four-seven?'

'Of course.' Xan hoped this was indeed the case.

'Don't lose sight of her for a second. Put as many men on it as you need. And keep looking for Jude. He won't be far behind her.'

Xan nodded. 'What shall I do if she contacts anyone?'

'Nothing. Yet. Remember, there are seven in the group. Keep monitoring everyone the girl gets in touch with. I'll know if they're significant. Once they're all together, that's when they'll go after the crystal. And we'll be right behind.'

Xan frowned. 'You seem very sure, boss. But there's no proof the crystal actually exists.'

'It's out there somewhere, Xan. I can feel it. Now you do the job I've given you. Find Jude.'

Brandon waved his hand in dismissal. But as Xan left the office he heard Brandon murmuring, 'So, little brother, you've become chivalrous in your very old age. Rescuing young damsels eh? We'll see about that.'

Xan shuddered at the chilling laugh that followed these puzzling words. So this Jude fellow was his *brother*? *Whose side is Jude on then*? Xan wondered as the lift doors closed.

30 October 2012: Lily and Gabe's farmhouse, Wiltshire

'At last,' Lily announced, after a long session on her crystal. 'They're finally going to meet up.'

Gabe looked up from his book. 'That's good,' he smiled encouragingly at his wife.

Lily sat down hard on one of the wooden kitchen chairs.

'Yes . . . thank goodness . . . but we have to move things

on fast now. There's only seven weeks till the solstice. It's clear Brandon is on to us, and the more the others tune in to their past, the greater danger they'll be in from him. Tom and Maya have already had a run-in with the foot soldier in Australia. And I saw Tom clocking Brandon and Xan. He still doesn't understand, but Brandon will recognise him at once if he sets eyes on him. And Rhiannon – they are following her every move.' She took a deep breath. 'I'm frightened for them, Gabe. We have to get them together soon, keep them together; there's strength in numbers. Brandon can pick them off so easily if they're alone.'

'What do you have in mind?' Gabe asked. 'Will seven weeks be enough to train them and –' he paused, looking anxious.

'Find the crystal?' Lily shrugged. 'It'll have to be. Rhiannon, Tom and Maya should meet tomorrow night if all goes well . . .'

34

31 October 2012: Tulies wine bar, Soho, London

Rhiannon was already hunched at a corner table in the almost empty bar when Lauren arrived. Her friend's message had sounded both angry and upset and Lauren was worried.

As soon as Lauren had squeezed into the seat opposite, Rhiannon began.

'Sharon's an idiot, she doesn't believe me. I know I'm right but all she's thinking about is her precious revenue stream. She's fired me because I said Crowe might be causing global meltdown. The Mighty Crowe's cash is god for Shazzer.'

'Whoa . . . slow down. Crowe causing global meltdown?'

Rhiannon sighed deeply and explained what Jude had told her.

Lauren looked sceptical. 'He actually said that Crowe was responsible?' Lauren remarked gently.

'He pretty much implied it.'

'So you have no proof?'

'No . . .' her friend's voice was calmer now, the anger leaving her deflated and unsure. 'But he's powerful enough . . .' she rubbed her hands across her spiky chestnut hair. 'I know . . . I'm being mad aren't I. But something sinister is happening and I need to find out what.'

'Well, you have a chance to find out more about your pet villain. Sam is meeting me later for a drink and bringing another employee of the Crowe Corp, a blond all-American oceanographer called Tom. Come along, he could be cute.' She laughed, but Rhiannon just shrugged tiredly.

'I will . . . but not because he's cute.'

'Great, it might cheer you up. You seem very low, Rhi. It isn't that Michael fellow is it? Has he been stalking you again?'

The mention of Michael's name brought the spark back to Rhiannon's eye.

'Oh, him,' she spat scornfully. 'He rings me every hour on the hour, whining about I don't-know-what. He says he has to speak to me urgently, but it's just a ruse to bend my ear about us both living in Atlantis ten thousand years ago. The man's quite mad.'

That makes two of you, Lauren thought silently, but she dropped the subject.

35

Tom was nervous. He was confident that his charts were pretty incomprehensible to anyone but himself, but the stuff he was dragging from the net about Crowe would be easily identified to anyone checking his computer. He didn't know what monitoring processes the boss employed to keep track of his employees' activities. He felt a tap on his shoulder and froze.

'Are you coming or what?' Sam laughed. 'You're American, so I'll forgive you, but in the UK the pub is God, not Crowe. So shut that damned machine off and let's get out of here.'

Tom laughed, mostly from relief, and followed his new friend willingly from the building.

The White Horse, Soho, London

Rhiannon and Lauren made snatched conversation as they pushed and dived their way down Carnaby Street – heaving with the early evening rush – to the pub Sam had designated. An icy wind blew flurries of raindrops in their faces, and both were relieved to be inside in the noisy fug. Sam was on the lookout for them and waved from a closely guarded table by the window.

'Hi guys,' Rhiannon noticed his careful attention to Lauren and felt momentarily sorry for him. 'This is Tom Page,' Sam made the introductions, and Rhiannon felt a flush rising to her face. She knew him. And judging by the way he was staring at her, Tom knew her too. But from where?

'Corny line, but have we met before?' Tom asked slowly, as Rhiannon removed her coat and sat down on the tattered stool beside him.

Rhiannon shook her head. 'I . . . I don't know . . .' she saw Lauren watching her and knew her friend would be mis-interpreting the situation, probably assuming she was attracted to the American. 'Were you at the Crowe conference last month?' she asked, to give herself time.

'I wasn't here then; it can't be that.'

'Drinks? What'll you have Rhi?' Sam interrupted.

As Rhiannon gave her order, Tom couldn't take his eyes off the girl. She seemed so completely familiar to him, yet she didn't fit into any of the places in his life where he tried to imagine her.

'So you're making a documentary for my boss?'

Rhiannon, dropping for once her normal hostility on being questioned about her work, especially by a man, nodded.

'Well, I was, until today, when I got fired for saying the wrong thing.'

Tom raised his eyebrows, 'Whoa . . . bad luck. What did you say?'

She laughed. 'If I tell you, you'll think I'm nuts.'

'Try me.'

'I think Brandon Crowe is interfering with the world's weather patterns, especially in China, Japan and India, and I told my boss that I couldn't go ahead with the film as it was, without investigating the Crowe Corporation. There – now tell me I'm mad.' She thought they would do just that, but as she watched Tom shot Sam a knowing look.

'Why do you think this?' Sam asked.

Rhiannon looked from one to another. 'No real reason; except this man, a weather expert in Scotland seemed to implicate him.' She threw her hands in the air. 'No reason at all if I'm honest, just gut instinct.'

The two men looked uncomfortable, as if they were both independently making a decision.

'Come on guys, what do you know? It's clearly something, from the shifty way you keep staring at each other.'

Sam took a deep breath. 'We don't know much more than you, except that there's this totally secret stuff happening on

157

the third floor, which none of us is supposed to know about or question. We think it's about manipulating the weather, but why would they do that?'

'Of course!' Rhiannon leaned forward excitedly. 'Look at what's been happening: extreme monsoons in India destroying the harvest, floods in Pakistan, hurricanes in the US, earthquakes in China, the tsunami in Japan that took out the nuclear power stations . . . And the result is?'

She looked expectantly at her audience. They stared back blankly.

'Global economic meltdown.'

Sam nodded. 'Yeah, the last twelve months have been disastrous but what's the connection?'

'OK. They've all been investigating a new energy source on the moon. India and China sent probes in 2010 but they've had to cancel any further exploration because their economies are completely destabilised by all the natural disasters.'

Tom nodded. 'I get it. It's about energy.'

Sam shook his head. 'I don't follow. Surely no one would bring the earth to the brink of disaster so they've got a monopoly on an energy source that may or may not exist on the moon.'

'Why not?' Rhiannon said scornfully. 'It's the perfect cover: Mr Eco Warrior saving the planet. Nuclear energy's out after the earthquake in Japan, all the other energy sources fail, and who do we turn to?'

Lauren grabbed her arm. 'That's crazy, Rhi. All these disasters have got to be coincidence.'

Tom interrupted, 'Crowe's been setting up outposts in places like Nepal, Sedona and Stonehenge.'

'So what?' Lauren shrugged.

'Stonehenge?' Rhiannon held her breath.

'Energy portals,' Sam explained to Lauren. 'These are supposedly mystical energy points, along the ley lines that criss-cross the globe. Odd because you'd never imagine a man like Crowe would believe in that New Age stuff.'

'The sinister thing is, he's hiding it,' Tom added. 'It isn't on his website. I had to download Freenet and search the darknet to find it. There was a recent electrical storm at Stonehenge and that was attributed to Crowe.'

'I was there, at Stonehenge,' Rhiannon told them, feeling weak at the thought. 'I nearly died, the whole road exploded in front of me, flooding everything. I couldn't get out of the car. If this old man hadn't saved me . . . and Michael –' as she spoke she had a sudden clarity. The old man, Crowe, Michael, Jude, even this man sitting right next to her – they had a bond, some-how they were powerfully linked. *Was this what Michael had been trying to tell her?*

Tom seemed to sense what she was thinking. 'Was it co-incidence that you were there?'

Rhiannon took a deep breath. 'I just felt I had to go there. Oh, I don't know what to think any more. It's all too fantastical.'

'But to get back to Crowe,' Sam said firmly. 'Let's look at some of the possibilities. One, he's trying to find a new energy source. Two, this could be good for the world, or it could be just good for Brandon Crowe. Three, if he's already found a new source, maybe he's trying to destabilise the world with bad weather so that it'll be ripe for his own discovery – hence the suspicious third floor. But where does it come from? And does it enter the earth through the various energy portals? Which might explain his sudden and secretive interest in places like Stonehenge.'

'A new energy source would make him the most powerful man in the world,' Lauren spoke quietly, but there was fear in her voice.

'So what are we going to do about it?' Rhiannon demanded. 'We've got to find out what's happening on the third floor.'

Tom laughed. 'We'd never get past security. We'd be caught and exterminated!' Rhiannon turned impatiently to Sam. 'You're the IT expert . . .'

'Leave Sam alone,' Lauren snapped, 'I think we should all stay well away from Brandon Crowe.'

Rhiannon smiled. At last Lauren was showing some interest

in Sam, just when he was about to leave the country.

As they sat and discussed Crowe, Tom kept looking towards the pub door.

'Are you expecting someone?' Rhiannon finally asked.

'My friend Maya; we met in Australia . . .' He stopped, looking embarrassed, which Rhiannon took to mean they were an item.

Maya saw the group around the table, and Tom, before he saw her. He was deep in conversation with a dark intense girl wearing a black leather jacket and Maya felt a jolt of recognition. The girl looked up as if she could feel Maya's eyes on her and smiled tentatively as Tom jumped up to perform the introductions. Maya sat down feeling stunned – she knew this girl – and only slowly tuned into the conversation swirling around her. Tom was explaining their theories about Crowe and weather control: 'And Rhiannon met a weather expert who thinks Crowe is implicated in all this.' Rhiannon's face reddened. 'I'm not sure how reliable he is. He also told me that we first met in Atlantis thousands of years ago.' She looked around the table expecting the others to laugh. Sam and Lauren smiled, but Tom and Maya exchanged glances.

'Remember what Rafaella said,' began Maya. 'Well, I found something strange on my laptop.'

She clicked the folder marked 'Stonehenge' and swivelled the laptop round to face Tom.

'Look,' she pointed, suddenly feeling foolish. 'In the centre of the stone circle . . . the golden shapes . . . they weren't there when I took the photos . . . it's probably nothing.'

For a moment she watched their faces take in the images.

'When did you take these?'

Maya turned to the girl introduced as Rhiannon, slightly shocked by her staccato tone.

'A year ago. Why?'

'That's what I saw. When I was there at the summer solstice. Those shapes, glowing like that. I saw them too. Seven of them in a circle.' Rhiannon felt suddenly sick. She had to get out of

160

there, away from these people, who seemed to mean more to her than she wanted. Even the girl, Maya, was familiar in a way she found uncomfortable.

'I've got to go,' she got up abruptly, pushing rudely past Tom.

'Rhi,' Lauren looked alarmed.

'I'll call you,' Rhiannon muttered, and fled onto the street.

36

The streets of Soho, London

Xan was waiting for her. He began to follow her as she hurried, almost ran down Brewer Street, in the direction of Soho Square. It was still raining and there was a chill in the air, but neither Xan nor Rhiannon noticed.

The short cut across the square garden was closed after dark and she had to walk around the narrow pavement which skirted the gardens. The area was still packed, the queues for the various clubs already forming, the bouncers behind the ruby rope cordons wielding their power to send packing the eager clubbers. She waited by the public convenience booth on the north side of the square to cross the road. Xan was not far behind, but he was suddenly surrounded by a group of very drunk ghosts and witches and warlocks who tried to take him along with them. Xan broke free with contemptuous ease. He'd never understand this weird culture. Now Rhiannon was nowhere to be seen. Cursing loudly, Xan searched everywhere for her, but he quickly realised he would never find her in this crowd. He pulled out his mobile and rang the man whom he'd detailed to watch her house, and alerted him that Rhiannon was probably on her way home.

'Bastard, get off . . . what the fuck are you doing here? Leave me . . . leave me alone damn you.' Rhiannon beat her fists uselessly on Jude's chest, wanting to both kill him and embrace him at the same time. He had come out of nowhere.

'Please . . . Rhiannon, I must talk to you. I must explain.'

She felt his hand firmly on her arm, guiding her through the streets in the opposite direction from the way she had come. She tried to shake it off, but he was much stronger and even more determined than she.

'I don't want your poxy explanations. Just so as you can feel better about how you treated me. No way. Just bugger off and live with your guilt,' she shouted in his face. None of the passers-by paid any attention, probably assuming she was drunk.

But Jude was relentless, finally arriving at the last car parked in a small dead end off Wardour Street.

'Get in . . . please, just get in and let me talk.'

Rhiannon twisted in his grip, but part of her wanted to be with him, whatever the pain might be in what he had to tell her. She ducked her head into the front of the car and sat, trembling, as he got into the driver's seat.

'Well?' She stared straight ahead out of the windscreen at a dirty brick wall, not daring to look into those intense green eyes again.

Jude starting the car snapped her back to life.

'Where are you taking me?'

'We have to get out of here. You were being followed.'

Rhiannon snorted. 'Oh right. And I suppose the next thing you'll tell me is that my life is in danger from the evil forces of the moon.'

To her surprise and outrage, Jude chuckled softly, 'Not quite, but you're not far off.' Then he became serious again.

'I need to make you understand the seriousness of the threat to . . . yes, your life, Rhiannon.'

Rhiannon shivered at his tone and remained silent as they drove south to the Embankment. Jude parked the car in the line of cars underneath Hungerford Bridge. It was dark, almost womb-like in the shadow of the bridge, and loud with the trains pottering overhead to and from Charing Cross.

She wasn't sure what happened next. One moment she was wide awake and angry, the next she felt the touch of Jude's hand on her own and found herself slipping away, as if down a dark tunnel, though she could see the light at the other end coming up towards her as she fell. It was a very bright light which hurt her eyes, but she knew she had to look, to concentrate on what was in front of her.

Jude whispering flirtatiously to a tall, dark-haired woman Rhiannon knew to be Lilith the High Priestess; her hand laid firmly to the cool surface of a magnificent crystal; running, running through a tunnel, her heart pounding in terror; herself standing in a white-pillared temple with others, all gazing up at the radiant shaft of light shining down on the High Priestess. Jude's hand reaching out. A scream . . . her own voice . . . then blackness.

∞

'Did you see it all?' Jude's voice was soft in the darkness.

Rhiannon looked around, saw Jude, the car. 'Was I asleep?' She rubbed her wrist where the mark was. It was oddly painful.

Jude shook his head. 'I was showing you . . . Atlantis. I wanted you to see what happened last time, when my infatuation with the High Priestess had such disastrous consequences.'

Rhiannon forced a small laugh. 'Not Atlantis again,' she tried to sound sneering and cool.

'But you did recognise it, didn't you?' Jude asked, knowing the answer. 'You were there.'

Rhiannon remained silent.

'I was trying to explain to you what happened in the cottage . . . between us.' Jude reached over and took Rhiannon's limp, cold hand in his own warm one. 'Lilith, Lily as she is now, warned me. The ceremony is more important than us. I can't fall in love with the High Priestess again.'

This time Rhiannon did laugh. 'So I'm the High Priestess now am I? Christ, pull the other one.' She dragged herself upright in the car seat and confronted Jude. 'Listen, I don't know what you just did to me, hypnotised me or something, but what I saw must be just a vision. There's no reality in Atlantis. It isn't a real place, Jude.'

'OK, have it your way, but please listen. Whatever you believe, I promise you that the same forces that broke into the

164

temple in your vision have a modern counterpart. They are headed by Brandon Crowe of the Crowe Corporation, and they are following you. They, Brandon and his henchmen, wish you ill, they know that you are their link to me, Lilith and the Seven – of whom you are one.'

Rhiannon sighed, she felt almost too tired to speak. 'Please, I've heard enough. Just take me home.'

Jude reluctantly started the car.

As they drove through the streets, Rhiannon's brain teemed with images of past and present. She remembered Stonehenge, her crying out, and the photos on Maya's computer. She remembered the birthmarks they all seemed to share and the look in the old man's eyes as he was swept away in the flood. She shied away from the Scottish cottage, but she remembered the shock on Jude's face as he turned away from the peat fire that night.

'What am I supposed to do?' she whispered, as much to herself as to the man driving her.

'You must find Lily and Gabe,' Jude told her. 'As soon as possible.'

'And how do I do that?'

'Michael will help you. And Tom, Maya.'

As the car pulled up in her north London street, Rhiannon hardly had the energy to get out.

'Brandon will harm you if he can . . . please believe me.' Jude's voice was low and urgent.

As she moved to open the door she felt his hand rest firmly on hers. It was only for a second, but Rhiannon felt her heart would break for what could have been.

'If ever you need help, Rhiannon, just call me and I promise you, I will be there,' Jude whispered as she heaved her weary body from the car.

37

The White Horse, Soho, London

'Stop worrying, Lauren. Rhiannon can take care of herself,' Sam tried to reassure Lauren who hadn't taken her eyes off the door since Rhiannon rushed out.

'Yeah, Rhiannon's OK,' agreed Tom, wanting to get back to their conversation. 'Sam, you're leaving soon. If we *are* going to do something we haven't much time to come up with a plan.'

Lauren shook her head. 'You're both mad. You could get into serious trouble.'

Sam ignored her. 'There's something going on up there and I want to know what before I quit. Seriously, if what Rhiannon says is true and Crowe is interfering in world weather then we need to know and alert someone don't you think?'

'For sure,' Tom said. 'But I can't see how we could break into the third floor – it's tighter than Fort Knox.' He fell silent, then his face lit up. 'What about Crowe's office computer? It must all be stored on there as well. Crowe's a famous control freak.'

Sam frowned. 'They have massive security up there. The lift's the only way in . . .' He paused, thinking hard. 'There might be a way. And Crowe's away at that awards dinner on Friday evening.'

Tom took a deep breath, 'You reckon you'd be able to hack in?'

Sam nodded. 'Sure. I can do that. If you can find the stuff we need when I'm in.'

Lauren, who had been talking to Maya and only heard snippets of the conversation, began to gather her things. Surely Sam would never stoop to such a hare-brained scheme.

'I'm off,' she announced.

Sam looked at her questioningly.

'Can I treat you to dim sum? You'll miss me when I'm gone!'

For a second Lauren hesitated, then nodded. 'As long as you stop talking nonsense,' she muttered tartly as they said their goodbyes.

◎◎

Tom turned to Maya. What was wrong with Rhiannon? Why did she suddenly vanish?'

'No idea,' Maya replied, but somehow she knew that Rhiannon had been overwhelmed by what was happening to them all. 'She always was a drama queen,' she added, not quite knowing where that information came from. 'She's the person we had to meet, I'm sure of it. I saw her . . . when Rafaella took me back . . . in the temple. She's one of the people, the "others", that Rafaella spoke of.'

Tom nodded slowly. 'I know.'

'We have to talk to her again, about Crowe and what's going on there. You remember Rafaella said we had to watch for anything odd. Well, those photos on my computer were certainly odd. They must be a sign.'

Tom sighed. 'If only Rafaella had told us what this is really about. Perhaps Rhiannon knows more than we do.'

For what seemed like a long time, the two sat together, feeling the powerful bond their new-found awareness had created between them, and not wanting to be alone with their thoughts.

'I'm frightened,' Maya admitted. 'Everywhere I go I keep checking people out.' Even as she spoke she found herself watching the other drinkers warily. 'But it's pointless. Erik looked quite normal until he attacked us.'

Tom sighed. 'If we knew who the enemy was, we could do something, protect ourselves.'

'Do you think Crowe is involved?'

For a moment he hesitated. 'He's involved in something. I don't see how it ties up with Erik . . . the crystal you're supposed to have . . . Atlantis . . . but yes, yes I do.' He leant

167

closer to Maya. 'I saw him at work the other day, with this cold-eyed minder who's always at his side, and . . . I hate to admit this . . . but I was scared of them both.'

Maya nodded. 'You weren't serious about breaking into Crowe's computer were you? It's way too dangerous.'

Tom sighed. 'It's too dangerous not to, Maya.'

38

Michael had been standing outside Rhiannon's flat for nearly two hours. He had come to find her because she wouldn't answer his calls. At first he had kept ringing the bell, the top bell of three in a terraced house in Whitehall Park, every few minutes, as if he thought she was there, but refusing to answer. In fact he did not believe that, he was just bored and anxious, and it seemed like action.

By eleven he was badly in need of some hot food or drink and decided to leave his bike and walk down the hill, crossing Archway Road to the chippy on the far side by vaulting the central reservation and taking his life into his own hands on the busy road. He thought that if she came home while he was away, he would see her lights on.

The fish shop was empty so near closing time, the sweaty Cypriot manning the fryer standing, bored, with his hand on his hip, waiting for Michael to decide.

'Closed?' he asked and piled chips into the open paper cone when Michael shook his head.

Michael strolled slowly back to Rhiannon's road, munching the hot, salty chips with relish. *This is madness*, he thought, *I'm waiting for a girl to tell her that some ancient foe has it in for her, and possibly me too, because of some bizarre ceremony I still don't understand. I need a job.*

But as he turned the corner of the street, he saw a car draw up close to the flat. He stopped, watching to see who got out. At first the car just idled in the middle of the narrow road, the tail lights glowing brightly in the foggy darkness. Then he saw a tall, slim figure emerge from the front seat. It was definitely her.

Michael wondered who it was who'd dropped her home, but the car sped off before he had time to see.

Michael threw the remains of his chips in the gutter and ran the last yards to her door, catching her just as she fitted her key in the outside door.

'Rhiannon . . .'

Rhiannon spun round, her face filled with rage and misery, and for a moment he worried she might pull one of her karate moves on him.

'It's me, Michael . . . sorry, sorry if I frightened you.'

'Very likely,' she snapped, pushing ahead into the house and trying to shut the door in his face.

'Please . . . I have to talk to you,' Michael pleaded.

'You and the rest of the world seemingly,' Rhiannon said tiredly, quite unable to maintain her aggressive stance. She held the door open for Michael. 'I need to talk to you too,' she added, much to Michael's relief.

The flat was stark, functional and immaculately clean. There was barely any colour, just white walls, a plain, dark sofa sitting in the middle of the stripped-wood floor, a wide TV screen mounted on the far wall, a desk covered with computer equipment and neat piles of DVDs, and one poster – of a documentary Rhiannon had made. Michael thought that if he hadn't known different, he would have assumed it was a man's flat.

'Sit down. Do you want a drink?'

Michael shrugged. 'Tea?'

He sat on the sofa, his mug of tea on the floor at his feet, Rhiannon sat on her desk chair, empty-handed, and neither of them spoke. In the end it was Michael who gave way. 'You know why I'm here.'

Rhiannon nodded. 'Yes . . .'

Again there was long silence. Neither wanting to admit they were taking seriously the fanciful half-memories, visions and events they had recently been assailed by. Then Michael began to talk.

Rhiannon listened impassively until he had finished then she suddenly exploded into speech.

'So, let me see if I've got this right. We were part of an elite group living in Atlantis thousands of years ago. Atlantis ruled the world because we controlled an energy source called S-3 using a crystal called the Heartstone. We performed a ceremony to block access to S-3 for all time to stop a man, who happens to be Brandon Crowe in this lifetime, abusing its power.'

Michael nodded. 'I know it sounds crazy.'

Rhiannon steamed on, ignoring him. 'The ceremony failed at the last minute because some guy called Jude broke the circle to protect the High Priestess.' Her face contorted momentarily with pain, then she pulled herself together.

'And finally, in our dying moments, as Atlantis sank beneath the waves, we promised to return to complete the ceremony and save the world. Oh, and our deadline is 21 December and there's a good chance we'll blow up the entire planet anyway.'

Rhiannon paused for breath, trying to suppress the anger that was threatening to overwhelm her.

Michael looked at her anxiously, 'I know it's hard to believe.'

'Oh, I can believe it,' Rhiannon shouted. 'It's just so fucking unfair!'

'Unfair?' Michael looked confused and Rhiannon forced herself to calm down. 'It's not your fault. Forget I said that. Look, some of it makes sense to me. I do have some weird connection with you, and I met two people in the pub tonight, somehow I knew them too. And the old man who saved me at Stonehenge . . . the mark on his wrist . . . the weatherman's too . . .' Rhiannon paused. She couldn't bring herself to mention Jude's name, the strength of her connection to him. It felt so raw. She saw the sympathy in Michael's eyes and wondered what he knew, how he knew it. She forced herself to go on.

'Perhaps we did meet in a past life – I can just about hack the past-life concept. But all this Atlantis stuff? You obviously believe everything Lily has told you, but why should I take her word for it? I don't even know her. I need proof.'

Suddenly Rhiannon felt exhausted. Michael stood and looked down at her weary face.

'Then we'll get proof. Let's talk about it tomorrow. You look worn out.'

She opened the hall cupboard and handed him a rug and a spare pillow. As they said good night, for a moment they both saw the humour in their situation, and began to laugh.

'Are we mad?' she asked, suddenly feeling the pull of this man who had come all this way to protect her, and who, miraculously, seemed to understand her.

Michael looked suddenly serious. 'Mad, yes. But I know in my gut that we can't ignore what's happening to us. Lily said you were in danger, Rhiannon. We have to take that seriously until we are proved wrong.'

Outside the flat, Jude leant against his car and watched the light in Rhiannon's flat. He felt an insane stab of jealousy, knowing she was closeted with Michael, and knowing what Michael would eventually mean to her. *Hope you're satisfied, Lily,* he muttered into the darkness, *You've got what you wanted.* But he also felt a burgeoning excitement. This was it. This was the beginning of the end of his torment. They would do the ceremony perfectly this time and then he would finally be free. The full moon above the city seemed very close tonight. It shone down on the deserted street with a cold, silver radiance, as Jude tried to convince himself that his lingering regret for Rhiannon was only part of this lifetime's self. In the bigger scheme of things it was unimportant. He had to believe that.

A cigarette glowed from inside a parked car further down the street. Xan's man wasn't getting out of his car, no way in these almost sub-zero temperatures. Anyway, he could see all he wanted from here. He watched Rhiannon's light too, and also watched Jude watching it. He had no idea who any of them

172

were, but he knew he would meet a sticky end at the hands of his terrifying boss if he lost sight of the girl. He thought of his warm bed and his even warmer girlfriend and cursed.

39

1 November 2012: Crowe Corporation, west London

Tom and Sam met in the basement canteen, lurking in a corner away from the crowd.

'It's the password that worries me. I could probably hack in eventually, but it might take a long time, and that we don't have.' Sam twisted his empty sugar wrapper into a spiral between nervous fingers.

'We'll have to risk that. No one's going to tell us what it is,' Tom replied.

'And there's the access to the floor. You need a swipe card and only Brandon, Christina, probably Xan his right-hand man, and the security guys are authorised, unless you're invited.'

'Aren't you friends with Christina?'

Sam smiled. 'I'm not sure our friendship stretches to betraying Brandon. He's her sainted hero.'

'Worth a try?'

'Yeah, worth a try . . . I'm also friends with Darren Flint, the head of security. But Daz'd want cash, a lot of it, to help us; and even then . . .'

Tom's eyes widened. 'Don't go near him, Sam.' He shook his head in disbelief that he was even having this conversation. When he'd boasted to Maya that he'd been in scrapes before and survived, he didn't mean this kind of cloak-and-dagger stuff. He meant Arizona desert stuff. Rattlesnakes were beginning to look like a walk in the park compared to this.

Sam's phone rang.

'Oh, hi . . . yeah, sure, hold on.' Sam passed the phone to Tom.

'It's Rhiannon,' Tom heard. 'Can you get away for an hour

or two this afternoon? I need to talk to you.'

'OK . . . what's this about?'

'I'll tell you when I see you. Highgate Cemetery – say around three?' Her voice sounded tense.

'Fine. See you there.'

He handed the phone back to his friend. 'Where's Highgate Cemetery?'

40

Highgate Cemetery, north London

Maya waited nervously at the entrance to Highgate Cemetery. She couldn't shake off the feeling that danger was stalking her, and jumped like a scalded cat when a hand touched her arm.

'Tom! Don't creep up on me like that!'

'Sorry. Didn't mean to startle you.' As Maya's heartbeat gradually returned to normal, Tom looked around them.

'What is this place? It's beautiful, but all these dead people . . . like something from a horror movie.'

Maya smiled. 'Trust Rhiannon to pick a cemetery for a meeting. It's quiet though and usually deserted. Now all we have to do is find her. Did she tell you anything else?'

'Nope. All very mysterious, look for the third angel on the right stuff. Let's go.'

Rhiannon perched on a crumbling lichened gravestone watched over by a weeping marble angel. She had asked Michael to stay out of sight until the others arrived – she wanted to see how they reacted to each other. If they didn't know him perhaps the Atlantis part of his story wasn't true and . . . *Stop it*, she told herself sternly, *you're just looking for ways to keep Jude in your life*.

A brief shower of rain had stopped as abruptly as it had begun and a rare shaft of sunlight broke through the low-lying clouds. Raindrops on the overhanging branches glittered like tiny crystals as two figures appeared through the dense foliage. Rhiannon stood up as Maya came racing towards her, arms outstretched.

'Rhiannon! I knew it was you. I recognised you last night.'

176

Rhiannon hugged her then stood back to look at her friend. Yes, she knew this girl. Had known her forever. Despite everything her heart lifted.

'You haven't changed a bit.'

'You have,' Maya replied. 'Your hair's so short.'

Tom coughed apologetically. 'Sorry to interrupt this touching scene, but what are we doing here?'

Rhiannon suddenly remembered Michael.

'There's someone I want you meet.' Putting her fingers to her mouth, she blew a piercing whistle and Michael emerged from cover.

Tom and Maya stared in amazement and Rhiannon held her breath. Then as one they yelled 'Michael!' As Michael walked towards them he raised a quizzical eyebrow at Rhiannon. Now, perhaps, she would accept his story.

Rhiannon's heart turned over and the ground seemed to shift beneath her feet as they came together in a flurry of hugs and kisses and handshakes. The sunlight seemed to intensify and suddenly she could see them all as they were in Atlantis superimposed on their present-day selves. By the look on their faces, they could see it too. Silent communication passed between them: *We were together in Atlantis; now, finally, we are together again.*

Michael broke the spell. 'I don't know how much everybody knows, but are we all agreed that we are here for a purpose?'

They all nodded then Rhiannon spoke decisively.

'Tell them what Lily told you about S-3 and Brandon Crowe.'

As Michael retold his story, Rhiannon watched their faces and saw some of her own doubts reflected in theirs.

After a moment's silence Tom spoke. 'We know there's definitely something dodgy going on at Crowe. It's possible that he *is* trying to access S-3. But if he is, and we stop him, that's an energy source lost to the world.'

Rhiannon broke in eagerly, 'Yes, it's Crowe that's the problem, not S-3. Surely there's a safe way of using it.'

'Lily says –' began Michael but Rhiannon stopped him.

'Your precious Lily is talking about methods that worked, or rather didn't work, twelve thousand years ago. How do we know this ceremony is the solution?'

Unexpectedly, Maya answered. 'Because we can't control the energy, the way things are now. It would destroy us all.'

They looked at her in surprise.

'How do you know?' Tom asked.

Maya shrugged. 'I don't know. It just came to me.'

Rhiannon was getting impatient.

'We need to find out what Crowe is up to, then we can decide what to do.'

Tom smiled. 'Same old Rhiannon. After you left the pub, Sam and I decided to try to hack into Crowe's computer and look for files on weather control and energy. Maybe we can get some proof for you.'

Rhiannon brightened. 'Great. I'll come with you.'

'No, you won't,' said Michael calmly, ignoring the angry glint in her eye. 'Crowe knows you, it's too dangerous. Leave it to Tom and Sam.'

Rhiannon glowered at him but backed down.

'I still think it's too dangerous,' Maya said, 'and what about Sam? He's not one of us, is he? Why should he risk so much?'

'He's not from Atlantis,' Tom replied, 'but Crowe's antics have been bugging him for months. He wants to find out before he leaves. With a bit of luck we'll get the info we need tomorrow night and Sam will be safe in Helsinki by lunchtime.'

'And then what?' demanded Rhiannon.

'Then we all go to Lily's,' Michael answered. 'Now that *we* know who we are, it's easier for Crowe to tune into us she says. At Lily's we should be safe.'

'That's why we're meeting here,' added Rhiannon. 'I'm sure somebody's watching my flat. There's a creepy guy always parked across the road.'

The brief burst of sunshine faded and heavy grey clouds hung threateningly above them.

'I'd better get going,' said Tom, 'see how Sam's getting on.

Assuming all goes well, we'll meet at Maya's flat afterwards and take it from there.'

Maya shivered. 'Take care. And Tom . . . look for the file about the crystal.'

Tom looked at her in surprise. 'Brandon has a blueprint of the crystal? How do you know?'

Maya shook her head in frustration. 'I can't see it clearly. I just know it's all in there, all we need to know.'

She was shaking and Tom held her close for a moment.

'Please . . . please take care,' she said.

'I've survived worse than this.' He tried to sound brave and fearless, but Maya wasn't fooled.

41

Sam followed Christina out of the lift and dumped the heavy box of disks on her desk.

'Thanks, Sam,' Christina smiled indulgently, she'd always had a soft spot for Sam. 'You didn't have to come all this way. I could have managed.'

'I know you could, but it's my pleasure. And it's my last chance to see the famous corridors of power. You know, I've never even spoken to the boss.'

He looked hopefully round the office towards the double doors leading into Crowe's inner sanctum.

'Well, you're out of luck. He's out all afternoon then straight on to the Dorchester for the awards ceremony.'

'And he needs these disks for the conference tomorrow?'

Christine looked sharply at him.

'You're taking a great interest in Mr Crowe's movements all of a sudden.'

Sam gave her his most winning smile. 'Well, he is a legend. It's been a privilege to work for him. But you know what I'll miss most about the Crowe Corporation?'

She laughed, 'Well, me, obviously, you old schmoozer. Now, be off with you. You shouldn't be up here and I have a million and one things to do. It's my sister's fiftieth birthday party tonight and I'm organising it. I need to get off early.'

As she reached for her security card to summon the lift, her phone rang and she raised her eyebrows at Sam.

'I've got to get this, it's Himself. Keep in touch from Finland.'

Sam grabbed the card, 'Don't worry, I'll let myself out.' Christina picked up the phone as Sam used her card to swipe the lift pad and turned back to her desk.

'Yes, Mr Crowe . . . I'll deliver it myself . . .'

She barely looked up as Sam waved the card in front of her and gestured him to replace it on her desk. Sam moved out of her eyeline, put down the card, then slipped it into his pocket. Christina was now scribbling furiously and didn't look up as Sam sprinted to the lift and the doors closed behind him.

∞

Tom strolled into the office and found Sam bristling with impatience. 'Where've you been? We need to talk.'

Tom strolled over to Sam's desk and pretended to be engrossed in something on his screen. 'What's happening?'

Sam glanced around then slowly opened his hand to reveal Christina's security pass.

'How did you get that?' Tom hissed.

'It wasn't easy, but it's our way into you-know-where.'

'It's not biometric?' Tom asked and Sam shook his head.

'But our security tags are biometric.'

'Yes, but the security techies haven't reached the sixth floor. Too keen on sealing the third. It's being phased in next month. The lift is what's holding them up apparently. It's too old to accept the biometric technology without being modified. And even better news, they were replacing the security camera in the lift when I went down and I heard the man say there was a problem with the new computer feed. It seems Daz is going mental because there's only one camera on the penthouse floor, just outside the lift, that's working, and even that's not reliable. The engineer was well pissed off that Flint wanted them to work over the weekend.'

'We still have to get out of the lift,' Tom pointed out.

'Yeah, but maybe they won't be trusting what they see.'

Tom shook his head. This was madness. He was amazed that his friend seemed so unconcerned.

'Won't Christina cancel her card once she knows it's missing?' he asked.

'She won't have time. She's organising her sister's birthday party and Flint will keep her for hours if she says she's lost it. My guess is she'll wait till Monday and say it was stolen or something.'

'How will she get down in the lift then?'

'She'll use the fire exit I imagine. There's a keypad by the door to the stairs in case they're in danger of being fried, and she'll have the password.'

'Suppose she does tell Flint?'

Sam shrugged. 'Then we're fucked!'

42

Brandon's office was dimly lit from the city lights outside, although the rest of the penthouse was silent and dark. Tom held the torch so that Sam could work on the keyboard. For what seemed like hours he tapped away, long sequences of numbers, each leading deeper into the computer. Sam shot a distressed look at his friend.

'This is impossible without the password. It's such a complex system, I doubt I'll ever be able to break it this side of Christmas.'

Lily gasped as she watched the scene unfolding in the curved glass of her crystal. Fools, bloody fools, she whispered. What do they think they're doing, risking their lives like this?

Tom's heart sank. 'Keep trying . . . we have to keep trying.'

Lily hesitated only for a moment. She knew Brandon's password. It was so simple a child could guess it. 'Merkaba', the name of the Heartstone. It had been Brandon's burning desire to possess it for thousands of years, what else would he use? She closed her eyes and began to tune in to Tom's thought processes.

Tom suddenly found his gaze had lost its focus and a strange word was pushing to the front of his brain.

'Wait . . . merkar . . . merkarber . . . try this Sam: m-e-r-k-a-r-b-e-r.'

Sam glanced questioningly up at his friend, but did as he asked.

'No luck.'

'OK, try m-e-r-k-a-r-b-a.'

Sam hastily tapped in the letters. 'No, not working. Why this word? We're wasting time Tom.'

Tom didn't answer him. 'One more time. M-e-r-k-a-b-a.'

Sam punched in the new version impatiently. Then looked up triumphantly as the password screen was replaced by a slew of desktop files.

'We're in!' he almost shouted, his eyes shining with excitement. 'I can't believe you did that!'

Tom waved the memory stick and Sam hurriedly got up from the chair.

'Your turn now, I've got as far as I can.'

Because of Maya Tom knew exactly what he was looking for.

The minutes ticked by, but all was silent in the eerie penthouse except for the tap-tapping as Tom's fingers flew across the keyboard. Both men seemed to hold their breath.

'How's it going?' Sam hovered over Tom's shoulder, casting anxious glances towards the door.

Tom didn't reply.

Suddenly they both froze. The unmistakable sound of the lift, purring ominously towards the sixth floor, broke the silence.

'Fuck.' Tom barely took his eyes off the screen, but his typing became more frantic.

'What'll we do?' Sam's eyes darted around the sparsely furnished office.

'Just . . . just another . . .' he cast a pleading glance at his friend. He couldn't stop now.

The lift clunked its arrival at the penthouse floor and was followed by the sound of a heavy tread in the outer office. Sam and Tom flattened themselves on the floor behind the desk. Tom could feel the sweat trickling down his back and Sam's shallow, terrified breath on his face as they lay, almost touching in the narrow space. They both knew that the screen glow was piercing the room like a neon light and that if the guard saw this, they would be lost. Sam thought his heart would explode through his chest as the door to the office opened. There was a short laugh and both men knew that the guard had spotted them. It was over.

'Shut up you moron,' the voice rumbled with amusement. 'No I fucking won't . . . no, that's bollocks. It was a bet and I won fair and square. Pay up you shyster.' The voice laughed again. 'Yeah . . . same old, same old. Call me when you've got it. Yeah . . . and fuck you too.' They heard him chuckle as he put his phone back in the shirt pocket of his black Crowe Corporation uniform.

For a moment there was silence, just the swing of a torch beam flicked carelessly around the office, then boots squeaking on the wooden floor as the man strolled back to the lift.

Tom thought he wouldn't have the strength to get up. His whole body felt as if it had been assaulted. Sam grinned and began to take huge, desperate gulps of air.

'Thought it was Good Night Charlie for a moment there.'

Tom dragged himself upright and pulled up his friend.

'We're not done yet,' he whispered and began another frenzied attack on the keyboard.

Now both were feeling the aftershock of fear, Sam shivering with cold and Tom's hands shaking as he typed. He was looking for the file that contained the crystal image Maya had described, but without knowing the file name it was like looking for a needle in a haystack. The computer was massive, stuffed with potential files, all of which had to be checked. He couldn't afford to make a mistake. The sweat was pouring down his face by the time he found it. The file opened easily, exposing a 3-D image and pages of notation on the diagram. All the text was encrypted, but Tom wasn't concerned with that, he had expected it. His job had been to find the file.

They both watched the blue progress tab on the download screen creeping slowly towards completion. It was a massive file and it was taking forever. They both held their breath.

'Get on with it,' Sam muttered through clenched teeth.

Tom tapped impatiently on the desk with his index finger, as if this would hurry the process along. 'Two minutes remaining', the seconds clocked down, stalled, rose to five minutes, then fell again to forty seconds, seeming to pause for an eternity before finally announcing, 'File downloaded'.

Tom let out a long, trembling sigh.

'Let's go,' he hissed, snatching the memory stick from the

back of the computer and they both ran silently towards the lift.

Sam swiped Christina's card as the lift arrived. They waited for the lift to open. But nothing happened. He looked at Tom, frowned, swiped again. The doors still didn't open.

'What the fuck's happened?' Tom asked. He strained to detect any sound from below, but all he could hear was the pounding of his heart.

'Try it one more time,' he urged.

Sam swiped the card for the third time and his efforts were rewarded by the intense, ear-splitting, shriek of the alarm. Both men nearly jumped out of their skins.

'Fuck. Fuck, fuck, fuck,' Sam looked wildly towards the emergency stairs, but as they arrived at the heavy metal door at the end of the corridor they were confronted with the keypad.

'What the hell would happen if there was a fire?' Tom demanded.

'I guess intruders deserve to fry.'

Sam suddenly seemed unnaturally calm and Tom looked at him with awe.

'I've got an idea . . .' He dug his mobile from the back pocket of his jeans. There was a tense pause as the call connected.

'Daz it's me, Sam . . .'

'I'm upstairs and the fucking alarm has gone off. The lift won't work. Is there a problem?' He sounded confident and in charge as he shouted above the alarm.

'Well, how do I get out? No, the sixth.' There was a pause. 'I had a call from the boss. He needs some data right now which is only on his office computer. But the lift door won't open and this bloody noise is doing my head in.' Another pause, while Tom bit his lip and tried to breathe normally. 'Give me the code for the stairs can you? Or come up and get me. No, well I suppose you don't know for sure it's me, but who else dares to call you Daz, Mr Flint?' Suddenly the ear-splitting noise stopped, leaving their ears ringing.

Sam grinned as he held his mobile tight to his head. '21122012,' he repeated it and then punched the keypad beside

186

the emergency door. The stairwell was brightly lit and they almost fell down the first flight of concrete steps in their haste to be out of danger.

At the fifth floor, Sam paused. 'We'd better go through this way. Darren'll expect me to go back to my desk.'

'How will we explain my being here too?'

'With a bit of luck we won't have to.'

But a thickset man was waiting for them in the forbidding black Crowe uniform, two younger guards by his side, all packing handguns on their flanks. Sam went over to Flint.

'Hey, thanks for that. What happened?'

Flint shook his head, a brutal buzz-cut making his demeanour militaristic and menacing.

'What card did you use to access the sixth floor?' His tone was outwardly friendly, but Tom noted the cold, professional eye he cast on Sam and himself.

'This one . . .' Sam started fumbling in his trouser pockets while Flint looked patiently on. 'Bugger. I had it . . . it must be here somewhere . . .' He played the charade out a while longer, then innocently held his hands out, empty. 'Must have dropped it in my haste to get away from that bloody noise.'

Flint said nothing for a moment, his heavy body absolutely still. 'No one has a swipe for the penthouse except Mr Crowe, Christina and Xan,' he said evenly, still eye-balling Sam.

Sam grinned his most winning smile and shrugged. 'The boss got Christina to lend me hers, when he knew he couldn't access the files himself.'

Flint swung his gaze towards Tom. 'And you?'

Tom tried to smile too, but his face wouldn't move properly, it seemed frozen in a rictus of fear.

'I've been ill . . . I stayed late to work and then felt bad . . . I've been chucking up in the washroom for hours. I – I went to the stairs for some air and Sam here found me.' It sounded so lame, but he thought his pallor might be a clincher. Under Flint's cold stare he began to shake in earnest and fell back into a nearby chair.

Sam looked concerned.

'I'd better take you home, mate. You look fucking terrible. Must've been the dodgy biryani at lunch. I did warn you.' He winked at Flint, but the guard didn't wink back.

'The smart-card codes change at midnight,' he said coldly. 'That's why the alarm went off.'

'Oh . . . right . . . sorry . . . Christina didn't warn me.' Sam began to haul Tom upright. 'I'm going to get this fella home before he throws up on someone's computer.'

But Flint barred their way. 'Not so fast. We have to write up a report about the alarm, and we can't do that till you've found that card. Mr Crowe'll want chapter and verse, so perhaps you'd accompany me to the sixth floor so we can sort this out.' It wasn't a question. He flicked his eye at his subordinate, who stood to attention rather too close to Sam.

'No, no, I understand,' Sam agreed hastily. Both of them knew that once Sam went on this journey, there would be no coming back. 'But can I just email the boss first with the info he wanted? You know he doesn't like being kept waiting.' Sam felt like a condemned man, his brilliant mind flitting from one escape plan to another in seconds.

Tom could see Flint was conflicted. He was clearly suspicious of them both, but also terrified of his boss's wrath.

'Mr Crowe is at an awards dinner. How come he wants information now?'

Sam shrugged. 'Ours not to reason why.' He turned to Tom, 'Why don't you go home?' But Tom, even though he had the memory stick with the vital file safe in his pocket, was not going to run out on his friend while that goon had him in his sights.

'I can't go anywhere yet,' he muttered, feigning nausea again.

Flint didn't budge, just crossed his arms across his solid chest and nodded to his henchman, who stood silent guard over Sam as he opened up his screen.

'When did Christina give you the card exactly?' Flint interrupted Sam's pretence at emailing Brandon Crowe, his voice heavy with suspicion. Sam thought it best to say nothing, and stared fixedly at the screen.

All of a sudden Tom lurched upright. 'Oh god, fuck . . . I think I'm going to . . . oh fuck,' he collapsed on the grey office carpet tiles.

The guards, distracted, gathered round him, and Sam made for the exit. When Flint looked up, Sam was gone.

'Fuck . . . fuck him . . . Get after him. Go go go!' He screamed at his juniors, and all three leapt towards the door to the stairs. Tom got up quickly and ran to the lift which took him swiftly to the ground floor. As the doors swung open, Sam's figure shot through the emergency exit and the two ran for their lives, slamming through the glass doors of the Crowe Corporation and startling the guards idling by the desk, but not in time for them to stop them.

43

The cool night air hit Tom and Sam like a welcome blast of freedom. The alarm was screaming again from the black glass building behind them and they heard the heavy stamping of boots and shouting at their back. But Michael was waiting at the far edge of the car park in Maya's car, chewing his finger nails off at the time the two were taking. As soon as he saw them he screeched up beside them, barely stopping to make sure they were safely on board before swerving off at high speed towards the M4, revving the engine as if it was his bike – and wishing it were. Sam and Tom were bundled together, all arms and legs, on the back seat.

For a moment there was a stunned silence in the car.

'Blimey,' Sam's previous confidence drained suddenly away.

'Christ, man, you were awesome in there,' Tom smacked his friend hard on the back in appreciation. He filled Michael in about what had happened. 'If it wasn't for this guy, we'd both be dead by now I reckon. That Flint's mean as shit, he'd take no prisoners.'

'At least we got the stuff we needed,' Sam muttered modestly. 'Let me know what you find out when you've broken the encryption.'

'It's encrypted?' Michael asked.

'Yeah, but we'd expected that. Very Crowe,' Tom said.

'Drop me at the turning to the airport can you,' Sam shot an anxious glance out of the back window. 'Terminal One.'

'But it'll be closed at this time of night,' Tom pointed out.

'I'll be OK. It's already after two. Anyway, I'm not risking missing that 7 a.m. plane.'

'Listen, thanks,' Tom told his friend. 'We could've got killed in there, and you didn't need to take that risk.'

Sam just shook his head. 'I want to know as much as you do. Keep in touch.' He leapt out of the car as Michael pulled to a stop on the hard shoulder, grabbing the bag he'd left in the boot before disappearing up the grass verge and out of sight.

'I'll miss him,' Tom said. 'He's an amazing guy.'

Michael said nothing, driving west along the M4 and back towards London and Maya's flat.

Crowe Corporation, security office, west London

Brandon, still immaculate in a sharply tailored dinner jacket and black tie despite the hour, stood rigid with fury in front of Darren Flint and his two muscle boys.

'How? How exactly did this man calmly stroll into my office, access my computer, then walk out of this building, right in front of your bloody useless noses, and you don't have a fucking clue where he is now?'

Flint had obviously decided to tough it out, because he thrust his considerable chest out and crossed his arms in silent defiance at his boss's attack.

'What the fuck do we have security cameras for? Why wasn't he picked up at once?' He glared at Flint. 'Who the fuck is he anyway? Do you know him?'

'It was Sam Lane, Mr Crowe, sir. He's an employee. How was I to know he was lying? He's a good guy, Sam. He's worked here for years.'

Brandon snorted with rage. 'A "good guy"? Yeah right. How the fuck can he be a good guy when he's infiltrated my computer and stolen my goddamn files? He's a bloody thief.'

'What was he after, sir? Was it industrial espionage?' Flint made the mistake of asking, and received a terrifying tirade in response.

'So who was this other man? The one you say was with Lane? Was he part of it?' Xan, who had been standing behind Crowe and watching the proceedings, interrupted calmly.

Flint glared at Xan. They'd never hit it off and Flint knew Xan

191

would be enjoying the roasting he was getting.

'It would seem so, sir,' Flint pointedly addressed his remarks to his boss. 'He's one of the scientists on the fifth floor. New boy, American, name of Tom Page. I thought he was ill . . .'

Neither Brandon nor Xan had heard of Tom.

'Show us the CCTV from the sixth floor,' Brandon barked.

Flint had anticipated this and had his laptop at the ready.

For a minute Xan and his boss peered at the grainy images of Tom and Sam coming in via the lift and, later, trying desperately to get out.

'Can you sharpen it?' Brandon asked.

Flint swivelled the laptop to face himself. The framed image of Tom's upturned face zoomed larger, frozen for a moment as Flint upped the pixel resolution.

'It's not going to get much better than this.'

Brandon stared at the image. Xan stared too.

'I've seen him somewhere before . . .' Xan stopped and looked at his boss.

'Right. Get lost you useless specimens. Let me know the second you find that thieving little bastard.' Brandon motioned Xan towards the door. 'We need to talk. NOW.'

Brandon's office, West London

'You saw his face. You recognised him too.' Brandon confronted his henchman.

Xan looked confused. 'Maybe in the canteen?'

Brandon shook his head. 'No. I know him, and so do you.'

Xan saw the troubled look on his boss's face and didn't dare speak.

'It's Tom all right. He did some odd jobs for me, before he was hijacked by the other side. I'd recognise that pretty boy anywhere.'

'The other side?' Xan didn't understand.

'He's one of them. The Seven.' Brandon's face was grim.

'And Lane too?' Xan asked.

His boss shook his head. 'No, not Lane. I don't know what

his role in this is. But Tom is one of the Seven.'

For a while he paced the floor, his face twisting in thought.

'So Tom is here, and Lilith, Rhiannon . . . and Jude. I was right. The group are re-forming.' He chuckled grimly. 'They want to know what I'm up to!'

He sat down in his desk chair.

'Things are moving fast. I need to know where they're going, what they're doing. How much they know. Find them for god's sake, just find them.'

He got up and turned his back on Xan. 'And don't forget, don't harm a hair on their heads. We need them alive if they're going to help us with the crystal.'

Maya's flat, Fitzrovia

Tom plugged the memory stick into Maya's computer.

'Look at that.'

Rhiannon, Michael and Maya all watched as Tom trawled through the encrypted file.

'Gobbledegook.'

'Will Lily be able to read it?' Tom asked, having complete faith in Lily's powers.

'Maybe,' Michael looked doubtful. 'Not sure it's her thing, technology.'

There was a dispirited silence.

'We have to move fast,' Tom's voice was urgent. 'They may have tracked us here already.'

'I know who can help,' Maya said softly. She reached for her mobile. 'He never sleeps,' she added mysteriously.

'Dad? It's Maya.'

Xan's car, approaching Maya's flat

'I'm checking the flat in Bloomsbury . . . Yeah, the blonde girl Rhiannon met the other night lives there. They might go there to meet up.' His boss fumed silently on the other end of the phone. 'I'll call you as soon as I find them,' Xan said, with as much confidence as he could muster.

The flat was silent and in darkness when he arrived outside. He got out of the car and beckoned to his henchman, Gary, who was ahead of him.

'Any luck?'

Gary, overweight and pasty from too much surveillance work and junk food, shook his head tiredly.

'I've been here for the last hour and there's been no one in or out. And Kayden's round the back and he says there's no action there either. But the bike's gone.'

Xan spun round and gazed at the spot by the pavement he'd last seen Michael's bike.

Without replying he whipped out his iPhone and punched in some letters. In a moment he was watching the small red dot moving swiftly over the map on the screen.

'Tell Kayden to get round here, NOW.'

44

Maya's father's house, Jericho, Oxford

Maya clung on for dear life as Michael gunned his bike down the M40. It was nearly 4 a.m. as they neared Oxford and it had begun to drizzle with a cold rain. Maya had not had time to think about seeing her father for the first time in so many years, but as they neared his house she felt her stomach flutter in anticipation. She realised she still cared for him, however hard she had tried not to. He loved her in his own peculiar way, even if he couldn't show it. She knew that, and she loved him. When she'd called him earlier he had sounded so pleased to hear from her, even though it was the middle of the night.

'Is it down here?' Michael twisted round, pointing to a turning off Walton Street. Maya hesitated. She'd only been there once and that was over ten years ago.

'No, next one I think.'

The street was silent and empty. Michael left the bike in the mews beside the house. Her father's place was part of a terrace of five old red-brick cottages which gave directly on to the pavement, built originally to house the workers at St John's College. Maya glanced anxiously at Michael before banging the brass knocker. But Michael was checking the street for signs of anything suspicious. He was sure that someone like Brandon Crowe would not leave Tom and Sam's theft unpunished, but he had no idea how extensive Crowe's manpower or intelligence was, and if they themselves would have been tracked to Oxford.

'Come, come in.'

Stephen, Maya's father, was in his pyjamas and an ancient brown wool dressing gown as he beckoned them inside the narrow hallway and through to the back of the house.

195

'Hi, Dad.'

Stephen gave her a tentative peck on the cheek. Michael thought he looked quite mad, his grey hair standing out in long, wild strands around his thin face, his eyes burning with intensity as he gazed at his daughter.

The room, part kitchen, part sitting room, part workroom, was chaotic and dimly lit. Not a surface was clear of papers and books. A modern, obviously new PC sat pride of place on the table, surrounded by stained cups with traces of mouldering coffee, scrunched up wrappers from assorted chocolate bars and a pile of apple cores. Open boxes crammed with more junk lined the walls, one of them topped by a black cat who observed the intruders with a bored and supercilious eye.

'Beatrice,' Stephen pointed to the cat, then looked around vaguely for somewhere his guests could sit. There was nowhere, so he gave up and lifted his hands in bewilderment.

Maya was shocked at how much older her father looked. And so thin. But he hadn't changed otherwise. He was still the same distracted character, but she found she no longer expected anything from him.

'Well, this is a surprise . . . coffee?' Stephen muttered awkwardly.

Knowing it was useless to embark on a family reunion after so long, Maya got straight to the point.

'No, thanks. Dad I know this is weird, but we have an important document we need to read, and it's encrypted.'

Stephen flashed a shy smile at them both. 'Well, you've come to the right man.'

She handed him the memory stick and without another word he plumped down on his battered leather desk chair, reached for his reading glasses, and plugged the stick into the back of his computer. For a while he peered at the cipher on the screen.

'Hmm . . . this is an interesting one all right. Let's see . . . hmm . . . no . . . no, that won't work . . .'

Stephen muttered on as he tapped the keys, while Michael and Maya stood tense and impatient at his shoulder.

'Who is responsible for this?' he looked up at his daughter.

'A man called Brandon Crowe. The Crowe Corporation. It's . . .'

'Oh, I know the Crowe Corporation,' Stephen raised his eyebrows. 'Well, he's certainly employed one clever bastard on this one.'

'Can you crack it?' Michael asked, trying to keep the impatience out of his voice.

For a moment Stephen didn't answer, just concentrated on the document on the screen.

'Never been one that fooled me yet,' he assured them softly.

Maya couldn't watch any longer. She wandered off, looking around at her father's possessions, seeing if there was anything familiar, something that would remind her that he was really her dad. But there was nothing but the impersonal clutter of his work.

The street outside Stephen's house

Xan parked the car on the corner of Walton Street and waited, watching the row of houses. He could see the bike in the mews and he immediately resorted to his smartphone to work out which house they were visiting. Google told him that Professor Stephen Shields, who lived at number 4, was the world expert in encryption. He seemed the most obvious target. They must be here to decode the file they had stolen. Or perhaps they were on the trail of the crystal. He would find out. He nudged his sleeping muscle boy, Kayden, who was alert in an instant, his heavy frame overpowering the space inside the car.

Xan pointed silently to number 4 and they both got out of the car.

Stephen's workroom, Oxford

'Gotcha!' Stephen was typing furiously now. 'Thought you'd fool me with that old trick you bastard,' he whispered to the screen. Turning triumphant to Michael and Maya he showed them the document.

197

'There, you can read it now.'

Michael nodded, but after a few moments he shrugged. 'This might as well still be encrypted as far as I'm concerned. I don't understand a word of it.'

Stephen scanned the text briefly.

'Not surprising . . . I haven't seen anything quite like this before. It's the blueprint for an energy converter, but it's off the scale; way more sophisticated than the one we're working on here.'

'So what does it mean?'

Stephen shrugged and kept scrolling through the pages, gazing long and hard at the complex diagrams.

'Ah . . . my God. Can it be Selenios-3 they're talking about?'

Michael seized on that. 'S-3 . . . so Lily was right.'

Stephen looked up at Michael, his face suddenly suspicious.

'What do you know about Selenios-3?'

'Dad, it's hard to explain right now and we don't have much time. But how is Crowe accessing it?' Maya said.

'It looks as if they're using some powerful crystal technology. But S-3 is energy carried by solar winds and stored on the moon. You'd have to go to the moon to get it. That's why China and India are sending probes up there – or trying to – and the US has a massive programme for something similar.'

'But if he could somehow bring it from the moon?' Maya asked.

'Selenios-3 is the most volatile substance in the known universe. If he's messing with that then we really are in serious trouble.' Stephen began to store the decoded document back onto the memory stick.

As they waited for this process to finish, the silence was loaded with his words.

'Maya,' Stephen looked hard at his daughter, then accusingly at Michael. 'I don't know what you two are getting into, but it's highly, highly dangerous to meddle with this. And if Crowe is doing so, he won't appreciate you trying to stop him. Go to the authorities, expose him. You have enough proof on this disk.

198

But don't think you can solve this yourselves.'

'I know what you're saying, Dad, but it's more complicated than it looks, and I don't know if you'd understand. I'm not sure even I understand.'

'Try me,' Stephen insisted. But as he spoke there was a frenzied pounding on the door.

Maya jumped.

'Don't answer it,' Michael hissed. He looked wildly around. 'Is there a way out the back?'

Stephen was about to protest, but he saw the genuine fear in his daughter's eyes. He hurried over to the French window out to the garden, threw it open and handed Michael a key.

'This unlocks the garage. It leads directly on to the mews at the side of the house.'

Michael grabbed it gratefully and pushed Maya out into the overgrown plot.

'Maya,' Stephen raised his hand in farewell, and Maya paused for a moment to look back at her father.

'I'll ring,' she promised, before stumbling after Michael through the weeds.

As they reached the garage door, Michael turned.

'Whatever you do, don't let them in. Call the police,' he shouted urgently to the figure framed by the light from the open window.

☺☺

The door burst open as Stephen was giving his address to the police.

'What do you want?' he demanded of Xan, his countenance showing a total absence of fear.

Xan didn't answer, just pushed Stephen back inside his house, Kayden close behind.

Kayden immediately grabbed the professor and slammed him down in the desk chair, his large paws clamped firmly on Stephen's shoulders. He swung the chair round to face Xan.

Xan had given the house a quick search.

199

'Where are they?'

'Where are who?' Stephen asked mildly.

Infuriated, Xan smashed his hand across the professor's gaunt cheek.

'The man and the girl. Where are they and what were they doing here?'

Stephen, dazed, said nothing. A nod from Xan brought Kayden's fist thumping square into his solar plexus. Stephen doubled up and gasped for breath, but Kayden pulled him upright in the chair, ready for the next onslaught.

Xan took Stephen by the chin in a pincer-like grasp, his cold green eyes only inches from the professor's. Stephen noted the look of detached cruelty in the man's eyes and knew he wouldn't rest until he had destroyed him. But oddly Stephen found he didn't care. He had lived his life outside the normal gamut of emotions, surrounded by the dispassionate discipline of numbers, but there was, and always had been, one thing in his life he cared about: Maya. He hadn't understood how to show his love. He had barely understood that love was what it was. But seeing her again, knowing she was under threat, he only wanted to protect her. His own life was meaningless to him.

'I don't know what you're talking about,' he gasped stubbornly.

Another nod from his boss and Kayden flicked open a small knife. For a moment he paused, as if considering his options, then slowly drew the razor-sharp point along Stephen's cheek, bringing it to rest on the outer corner of his right eye where a tiny drop of blood formed. Stephen could not help flinching.

'He will use it, please believe me,' Xan spoke softly.

'Do what you have to do,' the professor looked him square in the eye and Xan could not help but be impressed by the old man's courage. Impressed and daunted. There was no point in killing him and he clearly wasn't going to talk voluntarily. What was his connection to the man and the girl that made him so unafraid?

He looked at his watch and calculated it was only seven

minutes since they had entered the house. The tracking device on the bike gave them a certain amount of leeway to follow them. Maybe he was wasting his time here.

Kayden was watching his boss, his normally dull eyes alight with his drug of choice: violence. He flicked the knife across the professor's eyes, the edge grazing the professor's eyelashes, and looked questioningly at Xan.

'Boss?'

Disappointingly, Xan shook his head.

'Let's go.'

Oxford ring road leading to the A40

'Michael, stop! We've got to stop!'

The bike skidded to a halt and Michael turned to see Maya already dialling 999. He waited impatiently as she reported a violent break in, pleading with them to get there urgently.

'Maya, we've got to get going. Now!'

'We can't leave Dad like this. Those thugs might hurt him.'

Michael knew Maya was right, but he was torn. If they got hold of Maya, that could be even worse. He hoped Stephen could look after himself. He was no fool.

'He won't let them in. The police'll be there in a minute. Your father has nothing that they want, whereas we do. It's us they're after. Maya . . .' he almost shouted at the girl, thanking his lucky stars that this was not Rhiannon. If it had been, she would have been taking on Crowe's thugs single-handed by now.

With one more look behind her, Maya reluctantly conceded and pulled on her helmet. Michael accelerated away fast into the grey dawn.

Xan stood by his car and dialled his boss's number with some trepidation.

45

'You need to turn left at Swindon.' Tom pored over the map, wishing that Maya's ancient Ford was equipped with satnav. 'It should be in the direction of Winterbourne Bassett.'

Rhiannon said nothing. She'd hardly spoken since they took off in the early hours from Bloomsbury. Tom had tried to engage her in conversation, but she had remained stonily silent.

'What's bothering you?' Tom finally dared to ask, watching the girl's rigid jaw and fists clenched white on the steering wheel.

Rhiannon flashed him an angry look.

'You have to ask?' she snapped.

'You mean all this . . . this stuff.' Tom was at a loss for words to describe what was happening to them. 'I guess it's pretty overwhelming, right?'

'I'm not "overwhelmed", thank you. I'm bloody angry.'

Tom raised his eyebrows but said nothing. He saw Rhiannon take a long breath.

'It's always the same. The men take over, patronise us, boss us around, leave us out. I could have gone to the Crowe building and helped out. I could have gone to Oxford. But no . . . I just get to drive to sodding Lily's house and wait like a good little woman.'

'It's not like that.'

Rhiannon glared at him. 'Oh, it's not? Explain why not?'

Tom didn't bother. He knew this wasn't about being left out of the action.

'I've fought all my life to be independent, and now I'm being forced into a group where the men seem to make all the decisions. You're all playing with me.'

Rhiannon's breath was more like a sob and Tom waited silently for her rant to finish.

'Playing with me as if I'm some rag doll you can manipulate with ludicrous fairy stories.'

'Who's done that?' Tom asked, surprised.

For a moment there was no response.

'Michael . . . Jude . . .' she almost choked as she spoke his name.

'Jude?'

'Yes, fucking Jude,' she whispered.

'Tell me . . .'

Rhiannon looked resolutely ahead at the empty dawn road as she spoke.

'We had something. We both knew it. In Scotland, when I went to interview him. I've never felt like that about anyone . . . and I know he felt the same. Then that bloody Lily intervened and ruined it all.'

Tom didn't really understand but dared not interrupt.

'And now I'm expected to ignore the man who feels to me like my one-time soulmate for some literally unbelievable bollocks about Atlantis and High Priestesses and crystals and the end of the world.'

She turned a fierce look at her companion.

'Are you surprised I'm angry?'

Tom shook his head. He hadn't realised she felt so strongly about the mysterious Jude.

'This is the real world, Tom. Why can't we have each other?'

'Don't you believe in Atlantis?'

Rhiannon groaned. 'I don't know what I fucking believe in. I don't care; I don't fucking care about anything any more. Everyone can go to hell in a fucking handbasket for all I give a damn.'

Tom glanced sideways and saw a tear trickle down Rhiannon's cheek, brushed angrily away.

'Turn next left,' he advised, and there was silence in the car once more.

Tom and Rhiannon were nervous as they drew up to the old stone farmhouse, but neither of them spoke. It was Atlas that broke the tension, bouncing out of the doorway where he had been dozing to greet them like long-lost friends.

'Hey boy,' Tom bent down and rubbed the husky's thick pelt, enjoying the uncomplicated pleasure he had missed so much since leaving the four dogs on his Arizona ranch.

Gabe's tall frame bent through the front door into the early morning light. For a moment they all stood awkwardly, seeing each other for the first time, yet also aware of the powerful, half-remembered past they shared.

'Welcome.' Gabe held his hands out first to Tom and then to Rhiannon, who found herself paralysed with awe. This was the High Priest. This was Gabriel. At first she didn't notice the stooped shoulders, the ageing skin – all she saw was the dazzling figure of might and authority, revered throughout Atlantis. But as she looked into his eyes, she immediately recognised them from a more recent time. These were the blue eyes that had gazed so calmly up at her as he was swept away in the darkness and torrential rain. No wonder he hadn't been afraid.

'Come in, come in,' Gabe was ushering them through the narrow stone hallway into the kitchen.

'Are the others here yet?' Tom asked.

Gabe shook his head.

'They should be,' Rhiannon muttered anxiously, glancing up at the large kitchen clock mounted on the wall above the fridge. 'It's gone seven. I hope nothing went wrong.'

'They'll be here in the next five minutes,' Gabe reassured her as he put the kettle on the Rayburn.

Tom looked sideways at Gabe, wondering if he had intuited this or whether he had hard information. But as promised, before the kettle had a chance to boil, they heard the heavy spluttering of the bike's engine as it pulled into the yard.

Rhiannon leapt up, then paused, unsure if she should go and greet them. She felt instantly angry with herself for being cowed by Gabe's presence, and strode purposefully to the door accompanied by a barking Atlas.

'How did it go?' Rhiannon addressed Michael, who grinned as he pulled his helmet off.

'Great, we got it.' He reached into his leathers and pulled out the small memory stick, waving it in the air.

Rhiannon noticed that Maya wasn't smiling. She looked pale and worried.

'Michael's driving shaken you up?' she joked, but Maya's eyes filled with tears.

'Maya?' she was immediately contrite and put her hand out to the girl.

Maya gently shook her off, grabbing the length of blonde hair released from the helmet and twisting it into a business-like knot at her neck as she walked past her friend without a word. Rhiannon looked at Michael.

'It's her dad. Crowe's heavies must have followed us to Oxford. She's worried they'll have hurt him. He's not answering his mobile.'

Rhiannon was shocked. 'You left him?'

'We had to,' Michael was immediately defensive. 'They weren't interested in him. And I didn't fancy Maya's chances if they got their hands on her.'

'Still,' Rhiannon fumed that she hadn't been there. She'd never have left a defenceless old man in the hands of those thugs. She'd seen that cold-eyed henchman at the conference. He was capable of anything.

Michael was worried about Stephen too, but he wasn't interested in being torn off a strip by Rhiannon. He stalked ahead of her into the house and joined the others in the kitchen. Gabe was putting out mugs and a carton of milk on the cluttered table.

As they sat awkwardly round the table, each with a mug of tea, a strange hush fell. They glanced towards Gabe, but he had his head cocked, as if he was listening for something. Then into the silence, as if from nowhere, strode Lilith. She looked magnificent, regal in flowing purple robes, her dark hair loose around her shoulders, silver bracelets covering her wrists and a crystal hanging on a heavy silver chain around her neck which glinted as she moved, spinning prisms of bright rainbow light around the shadowy farmhouse kitchen. Maya and Tom gasped. Rhiannon found herself bowing her head.

For a moment Lilith just stood there, aware of the power she still held over her one-time followers. She knew she had an uphill task ahead of her and she would need their compliance.

'Welcome to you all,' she began, moving to the head of the table and glancing from face to face. She saw Maya's sadness and knew why. She noted Rhiannon's reluctant awe and Michael's irritation with her. Tom, she saw, seemed the most at ease.

'Maya, your father is all right.'

She wouldn't lie to the girl, but she was reluctant to tell Maya the extent of his injuries.

'So they didn't hurt him?' Maya asked, her face lighting up with relief.

'He stood up to their threats; he's a brave man.'

'Brave? Why, what did they do?' Maya's expression clouded.

'He's all right,' Lily said firmly. Then she cast an angry look around the group.

'But he might not have been. What do you think you were doing, taking the law into your own hands and risking everything . . . *everything*?'

They were shocked at her anger.

'Do you have any idea who you're dealing with?' Lily's voice rose. 'Brandon Crowe is one of the most single-minded, ruthless opponents on this planet. You could all have been killed.'

Nobody dared speak.

'And if you had been killed, if any one of you had died, all this,' she threw her hands around the assembled group 'would have been over for ever.'

'How do you know about it?' Tom managed to ask.

Lily raised her eyebrows imperiously, waited for a moment.

'Who do you think gave you the password, Tom?'

Tom looked confused, shook his head.

'Just popped into your head did it?' She saw Gabe give her a warning frown, but she was furious at their stupidity.

'All seven of us are needed to complete the ceremony Brandon interrupted in Atlantis. ALL SEVEN.'

There was silence.

Eventually Michael picked up the memory stick and held it out to Lily.

'We wanted to know what he was up to at Crowe Corp. We thought it wasn't such a big deal, with Tom and Sam working there. It's all on here. Maya's father says it *is* about Selenios-3, as you thought.'

Lily found curiosity replacing her anger. She took the stick and held it out to Gabe.

'Let's see what we've got,' Gabe muttered, heading for his office.

46

Gabe's office, the farmhouse, Wiltshire

Gabe scrolled slowly through the information on the decoded file. Lily stood behind him, along with Rhiannon and Tom. The others hung back. Michael knew there was no way he could understand the complex calculations and 3-D models on the screen. Maya was still worrying about her father, and every few minutes surreptitiously re-dialled his number. But the phone went to answerphone each time.

Gabe looked up from the screen at Lily.

'He can't have the real crystal. This is a blueprint for an imitation.' He shook his head. 'And he's definitely aiming to use it to reinstate S-3 as an energy source; you can see,' he pointed to the screen, 'these are details for a converter; it's extremely sophisticated, he's obviously got the best brains.'

'Could it work, the fake crystal?' Tom asked, then immediately wished he hadn't. Lily's eyes bore into him.

'Any attempt to access Selenios-3 that doesn't involve the Heartstone crystal will destroy the world,' she said curtly. 'It will literally blow it apart.'

'And Crowe doesn't realise this?' Rhiannon asked.

Gabe glanced up at her. 'His ego blinds him. Always did.'

For a moment there was silence in the room. Rhiannon's head was spinning. She liked a challenge and she was finding this ridiculous other world into which she'd been dragged was certainly intriguing, if she put her normally super-rational mind on hold.

'So where is the real crystal?' she asked Lily, but the woman seemed miles away. It was Gabe who answered.

'Lily had no choice. Atlantis was minutes from total destruction –'

208

'I dematerialised the stone,' Lily interrupted her husband. 'It was all I could do. Even in that chaos, there was a chance it would fall into the wrong hands. It was the last thing I was able to do before we were all lost.' Rhiannon could see pain flit across the High Priestess's face, and was unwillingly dragged back to memories of that terrifying moment. She took a deep breath and glanced around at the others. Tom had his head down, Michael was staring at her with blank eyes.

'So, when you say "dematerialised", does that mean it's no longer . . . a whole crystal?' Tom was struggling.

Lily looked at Maya, who was still intent on her mobile phone.

'No . . . The crystal is a life force. It cannot be destroyed. All I did was free it from the Atlantis imprint. It will have re-formed . . . Somewhere.'

Rhiannon raised her eyebrows. *Well, that narrows it down,* she thought, but wisely said nothing.

'It will have been drawn to one of the major energy portals. A place of safety,' Gabe told the group. 'And there it will have re-formed.'

Tom sighed. 'Which are?' He was feeling suddenly hopeless. This task seemed so vast, so complex, so global. For a moment he wished himself safely back in Arizona, under the harsh, brilliant light of the desert, where things appeared so simple.

'Egypt, Tibet, Nepal, Angkor Wat, Uluru, Machu Picchu, Sedona,' Lily intoned.

'But those places are massive,' Tom said. 'How will we ever find a small crystal if we don't know where to look?'

'I think we can rule out the monuments,' Gabe said with authority. 'They were created well after the fall of Atlantis to help hold the planet in balance.'

Lily nodded. 'The Pyramids represent science, Angkor Wat – spirituality. And Stonehenge, of course, celebrates the union of the sacred feminine with the masculine.' *Jude's eternal quest to put right his fatal mistake,* she thought sadly.

'I think,' Gabe continued, 'the crystal will be hidden somewhere remote, a high-energy spot linked to the earth grid by ley lines.'

Tom and Michael exchanged baffled glances. *Could be anywhere.*

Lily was looking intently at Maya again, who finally seemed to notice and glanced up from her mobile. Her gaze was far away.

'Maya was Keeper of the Crystal. She will know.'

Maya's eyes focused. 'Me?' Tom could see panic in her eyes. 'I haven't the first idea where the crystal is.'

'How could she know?' Rhiannon asked.

'Your work has taken you to those places, the energy portals,' Lily stated, ignoring Rhiannon.

Maya nodded uncertainly. 'Most of them,' she said, dazed, 'not all.'

Lily took a long, slow breath. 'Were you drawn to any particular one? Did you feel any special affinity to one place?'

Maya still looked confused, anxious.

'No . . . well, I suppose I felt drawn to them all . . . but nowhere that stood out.' She threw her hands up and looked beseechingly round the group of friends. 'If this is down to me, then I can't do it, I don't know where the crystal is. How could I possibly know? I hadn't even heard of it till a few weeks ago.'

They all saw the tears start in her eyes.

Michael put his arm round Maya's slim shoulders. She's no more than a girl, he thought, and was suddenly angry with Lily for putting such pressure on her.

Gabe got up from the desk.

'Please, let's take a break. I'm sure everyone is exhausted.'

Gabe stirred the soup bubbling on the hob. After all they'd been through, they needed food and rest. Then they could work out how to find the crystal. Atlas nudged his leg, hoping for a titbit, and Gabe patted his head affectionately.

The others sat silently round the table. Lily had disappeared.

'Why isn't Jude here?' Tom whispered to Michael.

Michael pulled a face. 'No idea. Lily says he's one of the Seven, but he's Brandon's brother too. How does she know he's trustworthy?'

'Yeah, blood's thicker etc.,' Tom agreed, then caught

Rhiannon's flashing eyes from the other side of the kitchen table.

'I trust Jude absolutely,' she hissed.

'With all due respect,' Tom said, 'you're a tad conflicted here.'

Rhiannon looked furious now. She was breathing fast. 'I'm telling you, Jude can be trusted.'

'Like at the ceremony in Atlantis?' Michael chimed in.

'For fuck's sake,' Rhiannon exploded. 'That was twelve thousand years ago now. Give the guy a break. He knows what he did: he's paid for it ever since.'

Michael began to laugh. 'Christ, listen to us. We really have come a long way! A couple of months ago we hadn't even heard of Atlantis, except in fairy stories, and now we're talking like fully paid-up members of Atlantis's ruling elite.'

Tom and Maya laughed too, but Rhiannon's face was stony.

'Laugh if you like, but none of you know Jude. Lily would hardly go to all these lengths to get the ceremony set up again if she didn't trust him to be there.'

But Michael and Tom didn't reply. They didn't want to point out, again, that it was Lily's trust of Jude all those centuries ago that had caused this mess in the first place.

Rhiannon got up.

'Bollocks to this,' she muttered as she strode out of the kitchen.

Atlas followed her, and they heard the front door slammed angrily, then there was silence.

Tom helped Gabe lay the table. A large spelt loaf was placed in the centre which Michael began to slice. Lily was called from her room, and the five settled down to their meal.

'Where's Rhiannon?' Lily asked as she sat down.

Michael shrugged.

'We had an argument about Jude. She stomped off.'

Lily raised her eyebrows.

'We were questioning his loyalty,' Tom explained, 'seeing as he's Brandon's brother.'

Lily looked at Gabe.

'Do *you* trust him?' Michael asked Lily directly, having seen the look that passed between husband and wife.

'I have to,' she said simply.

'I trust him,' Gabe stated firmly. 'He was foolish back then, but he was always a man of integrity, a man who believed passionately in the true path.'

'Will Brandon try to get to him?' Michael asked.

'Brandon Crowe will do anything to get what he wants,' Lily's voice was low, but they could all hear the conviction.

'We should tell Rhiannon food's ready,' Maya spoke into the silence.

Gabe nodded and rose to his feet.

'I'll go,' Michael said. He was feeling guilty about the row and wanted to speak to Rhiannon first.

Michael walked out into the watery November sunshine. There was relief in being outside, on his own and away from the group. So much tension. It was hard to bear. He looked around Gabe and Lily's garden. There was a large vegetable patch on the left of the house, immaculately kept, the neat rows of half-grown leeks, deep-purple cabbage leaves and frilly carrot tops reassuring somehow.

'Rhiannon . . . Rhiannon . . .'

There was no reply, just the peaceful sounds of the country. He wondered where Atlas was. He walked to the right towards the barn. Gabe's carpentry hobby took up most of the cool, dusty space. There was a pitted and scarred wooden work table with a vice at one end. On the wall an impressive array of tools, orderly like the vegetable patch. And piles of various sizes, colours and types of wood. The floor was covered in sawdust.

No sign of Rhiannon.

Where the hell was the woman? Michael sighed impatiently and turned on his heel to head back to the house. As he crossed the yard, he thought he heard a muffled yelp. Curiously he looked

212

around but could see nothing. 'Atlas,' he called softly. 'Atlas, where are you boy?'

As he glanced towards the gate, he stiffened in shock. There was a bright splash of red on the gatepost and drops of blood leading towards the road. Michael's heart lurched. Something bad had happened here. Atlas had followed Rhiannon from the house. Where were they?

He opened the gate and crossed the heavy stone spanning the stream that ran alongside the garden. The road was deserted in both directions. Then, faintly, he heard again that soft, piteous yelp. He dropped to his knees by the stream and peered under the stone bridge. Wedged in the small space, his body twisted and soaking wet, was Atlas.

It was clear the husky was barely breathing.

Michael lay on his front and reached in, laying his hand gently on his head. At Michael's touch, Atlas twitched convulsively, his blue eyes rolling back in his head.

'It's OK, boy, it's OK, we'll get you out.' As Michael withdrew his hand, he saw his fingers were covered in blood. He sprang to his feet and rushed back to the farmhouse.

Within seconds they were all by the stream.

'I don't know if his back is broken,' Michael said. 'We'll have to be really careful getting him out.'

Gabe was lying on the ground talking softly as he stroked his dog, a gentle stream of love. Michael joined him and together they began to ease Atlas out from under the stone. Atlas made no sound now. His eyes were shut, his heavy body limp between them.

Gabe gathered him up, and sitting cross-legged on the damp ground cradled him in his arms, still firmly stroking his dog's thick, pale fur in an attempt to revive him. Lily stood close by, her eyes shut, her right hand clenched tight around the crystal hanging from her neck.

Everyone was frozen in horror. Michael had an unwelcome impulse to take a photograph and realised that the scene reminded him of the woman he had recorded in Indonesia, after a primary school had been bombed, who had cradled her dead child in her lap in just the same way. The image would haunt him forever.

'Where's Rhiannon?' Maya suddenly whispered to Michael, and there was dread in her voice.

Michael didn't have time to answer before Lily's head whipped round, her eyes suddenly wide with rage.

'They were here. *They* did this to Atlas.'

'They? You mean Brandon Crowe?' Michael asked.

He saw Gabe nod, his face full of pain. His hands were still now.

'But . . . why would they do something so horrible?' Maya thought sadly of Tikani, the dog from the cliffs in Byron Bay, who had looked so similar to Atlas.

'He was trying to protect Rhiannon. They've taken her, haven't they?' Maya's voice was hesitant, but she knew in her heart she was right.

Lily didn't bother to reply. She knew Rhiannon was already far away.

47

'We've got her . . . in the boot . . . no, she's OK . . . bloody tough cookie though, she put up quite a fight . . . no, I said, she's OK, just a bit bruised . . . yeah, yeah . . . of course . . . she's not going to be there for long and there's enough air.' Xan made a face at Kayden, shook his head as he held his phone away from his ear. 'Got the message, boss. It's all set up.'

Xan cut the connection and glared at the screen.

'Don't harm her . . . make sure she's comfortable . . . blah blah. Christ, this isn't a Caribbean cruise she's on.'

'Kidnapping's not a comfort thing, I s'pose,' Kayden stated laconically, which made Xan smile.

'You suppose right, Kay.'

'Should I check on her?'

Xan glared at his muscle boy. 'Here? Not such a hot idea with the world and his fucking wife nosing past the car boot. Be a bit hard to explain.'

Kayden shrugged. 'Just askin'.'

'We'll pull off the motorway at the next exit and find a quiet road. But she's no shrinking violet. She'd survive worse than this.'

Xan sent Kayden for some coffees and got back in the car. There was no sound, no movement from the boot, the thumping and moaning had stopped a while back, and Xan was concerned, even with his fighting talk, that she might be short of oxygen or something. He wasn't a kidnapper – he didn't know the finer points. And Kayden had hit her quite hard to shut her up.

She could hardly breathe. A shooting pain ran from the shoulder she was lying on down to her hands bound behind her back. Her long legs were cramped up tight to her chest and she had a thumping pain in her temple where Kayden had smashed his fist into her head. But the worst thing was the claustrophobia. Rhiannon had never liked enclosed spaces, and when she'd come round from the blow and realised where she was, she had felt the panic bubbling up through her body until she wanted to scream. But she couldn't scream; she had silver duct tape across her mouth, and she was sure she would suffocate because of it. So she kicked and thrashed in the dark, rank space, totally out of control, moaning in pain and fear. But part of her knew this was pointless and making things worse, so with a supreme effort she began to deep-breathe. *You can't panic if you're breathing deeply,* she remembered from somewhere. And it worked. Long, slow breaths through her nose, her heartbeat gradually returning to near normal.

They're taking me somewhere for a purpose, she told herself, *if they were going to kill me they would have done so by now. This is Brandon Crowe. Lily will see, they will come and find me . . .*

So when Xan stopped the car, she did nothing, hoping they had reached their destination. Now they were on the move again, and she knew she had to wait, bide her time.

Images kept flashing across her dazed brain. Kicking that brute in the shins when he grabbed her from behind, Atlas growling like a wild animal as he went for his arm . . . the brute kicking the dog so hard he just fell like a stone . . . the cold-eyed henchman she recognised from the conference just watching, waiting patiently, as if he were in a supermarket queue. Then the brute kicking and kicking Atlas – while still holding her pinned to his chest, her feet off the ground like a rag-doll – with such brutality, and such terrifying enjoyment, until poor Atlas was wedged under the stone . . . then nothing until she woke up in the boot of the car. What did Crowe intend to gain by kidnapping her? One thing she knew beyond a shadow of doubt, neither of these men would hesitate for even a second if they were ordered to kill her. She had to hope Brandon needed her alive. She tried to get her breathing under control again. She needed water, her mouth was dry as a bone. A sob rose in her throat. *Don't cry, don't bloody cry, you moron*, she berated herself silently, knowing that crying might choke her to death behind the suffocating duct tape.

A quiet lane between Newbury and the M4

The light was dazzling as the boot lifted. Rhiannon blinked and tried to turn away.

'She's still alive,' she heard the brute declare in a tone that showed a perfunctory curiosity.

Then the cold-eyed one appeared silhouetted against the blue sky. He leaned in until his head was only inches from her own. He said nothing, just stared at her. She flinched from the blank detachment in his sea-green eyes. There was no emotion there, just a calculated observation.

Xan took a deep breath and nodded to Kayden, who slammed the boot shut again. Rhiannon felt the panic rising. *No . . . no . . . don't leave me here . . . nooooo . . .*

This time the tears came unbidden. *In out, in out*, she intoned silently, desperately, until she felt her heart rate begin to slow again.

She heard the two talking beside the car.

'It's about an hour and a half from here,' the cold-eyed one said.

'Then what, boss?'

'Then we keep her safe and wait for further instructions.'

'How long will that be?'

There was a pause.

'None of your fucking business.'

In truth, Xan didn't know what the plan was. Crowe had instructed him to kidnap Rhiannon and find somewhere to hold her. But what the boss planned for her was as much a mystery to Xan as it was to Rhiannon herself.

48

Maya leant against the side of the house, hidden from the others, and cried. She cried for Atlas and for Rhiannon. She cried for her father. How had it come to this? A month ago she was wandering peacefully from dig to dig, criss-crossing the globe at her own pace. Yes, she was rootless. Yes, she was questioning her life. But it was a normal life, contained and relatively safe. Now it was as if her very DNA had been exploded; she no longer knew herself. She felt raw, vulnerable and afraid, always looking over her shoulder, never at peace for a second. For the millionth time she reached for her mobile and punched in her father's number.

'Maya?'

She felt a massive surge of happiness at the sound of his voice, weak though it was.

'Dad? Dad! Oh, thank God, you answered at last. I've been so worried about you. What happened? How are you?'

She heard her father take a long breath.

'I'll survive,' he said quietly. 'I'm more concerned about you. How in hell's name did you get yourself involved with these monsters?'

Maya tried to control her tears of relief.

'Dad, it's such a long story. I told you before, I don't really understand it myself.'

'Not good enough,' her father told her. 'These men are killers. I'm only alive because it wasn't me they wanted . . . it was you and your friend.'

Maya sighed.

'I know . . . we know. But it's something I have to do, Dad.

218

I'm just so sorry I involved you and you got hurt. Are you OK, really? What did they do to you?'

'It doesn't matter. But please . . . please go to the police. Maya listen to me . . . I know I've been a useless father to you, but I love you very much . . .' There was an awkward pause, and Maya knew that if he'd been standing there in front of her he wouldn't have been able to say those words.

'I know, Dad, and I love you too. I will take care, I promise.'

'And go to the police?'

'If that's the best thing to do,' she hedged.

She heard her father sigh with frustration.

'You always were wilful. Well, remember what I said . . . and keep in touch. I couldn't bear to lose you again.'

Lily's room, Wiltshire

Lily passed her hands over the crystal globe for the third time. Michael stood behind her and watched indistinct shapes, shadows, lights flashing around the sphere.

'Can you see her?'

Lily didn't answer, intent on her task. She watched for another long moment, narrowed her eyes.

'I can see her . . . or at least I know it's Rhiannon. She's in the dark . . . I can't tell where.' She looked up at Michael, her face a mask of anxiety.

'But she's OK . . .'

Lily shook her head. 'Her aura is still strong, she hasn't been hurt badly. But she's frightened . . . thirsty.'

'Christ, Lily. What can we do? Why is he doing this?'

'If he was going to kill her, he would have done it already. They want her as a bargaining tool.'

'Bargaining for what? The crystal?'

'Maybe.'

'You can't see where she is? What location?'

Lily shook her head again. 'I think she's still in the car . . . she seems to be moving. But I can't pin her down.'

Michael began pacing the room in angry frustration.

219

'We can't just leave her and hope for the best,' he snapped.

'I didn't suggest we did,' Lily said coldly.

'Well, what *do* you suggest? Shouldn't we go to the police?'

Lily thought for a moment, her hands resting uselessly on either side of the crystal.

'What do we tell them? That we're absolutely sure – although there's no evidence – that the great philanthropist, Brandon Crowe, has, for reasons that might sound a little bizarre and involve the long-lost city of Atlantis, kidnapped our friend?'

Michael couldn't answer that.

'If Brandon has taken Rhiannon to blackmail me, to reveal the whereabouts of the crystal . . .' Lily went on.

'Then he'll be in touch, right?'

Lily nodded. But something was bothering her.

'This doesn't feel right. It makes sense, but it doesn't feel right. I'm missing something.'

Michael tried to control his impatience. He hated this inaction. There must be something they could do.

Lily saw clearly that he was about to blow.

'Where are the others?'

'Gabe and Tom are burying Atlas. I haven't seen Maya.' Michael banged his fist against the wall, making the nearest crystals jump on the shelf.

'I can't just hang about in the hope she'll walk through the door. I'm going out on the bike.'

Lily knew this was pointless, but said nothing.

'Don't go alone,' she warned. 'Take Tom.' Although she was sure Brandon was currently occupied with a plan that didn't threaten either of them.

Lily listened to the bike roar out of the drive then went to find Maya. She knew she couldn't be distracted by the immediate circumstances – however dire. There was work to be done.

Maya was still crouched against the side of the house. She felt numb, no longer able even to cry. Lily helped her up.

'Come with me,' she said firmly, guiding Maya to her room. She didn't have time to indulge Maya's misery. She knew the cause, and the solution.

'Sit down.' She guided the girl to the deep armchair and wrapped her in the soft wool rug from the window seat. Then she busied herself lighting a number of candles around the darkening room. Maya was silent, she seemed almost in a trance, but Lily did nothing to dispel this. A deep silence descended on the room.

After a few minutes of deliberation, Lily picked up a smooth oval crystal, around five centimetres wide and a deep golden brown in colour, from one of the shelves. She handed it to Maya. The girl's hand closed over the crystal. She looked up at Lily as she ran her fingers across the stone's surface and without prompting said immediately: 'Smokey quartz palmstone,' she paused, giving her a faint smile. 'A good antidote for stress.'

Lily didn't bother to hide her surprise. So Maya was more in tune with her Atlantis knowledge than she thought. Without another word, Lily selected another stone and handed it to Maya. For a moment Maya looked at the rough, cloudy crystal. The pale blue-green of the stone was shot through with translucent silver. She gently traced the outline of the crystal.

'Aquamarine, the stone of courage,' she said firmly. 'Clarity of thought. Strength to deal with difficult situations and release the past.' Maya found she was talking with a confidence she hadn't known she possessed. Certainly her work at archaeological sites had made her familiar with a range of ancient artefacts from Iron Age flints to Roman pots, but never crystals. She handed the stone back to Lily, who replaced it with another. This one was milky and smooth. Maya held it up to the candlelight and watched rainbow prisms shoot across the pale translucent surface.

'Moonstone.' She held the crystal against her heart for a moment. This was her stone, the stone of women, of intuition, of spiritual awareness. In that second she was back in Atlantis. Round her neck was a moonstone pendant which her beloved father had given her. She took a deep breath and looked at Lily.

'I know all this,' she said simply.

Lily did not reply. She held one more stone out to the girl.

'Hold this one, Maya.'

Maya took the rough, transparent crystal. One end drew to a three-sided point, and on one of the three sides was engraved a triangular-shaped mark. She knew this represented the trinity of the physical, emotional and mental aspects of being.

'You remember?' Lily asked quietly.

For a moment the girl sat staring at the stone. Then instinctively she closed her eyes and held the marked side of the crystal to the centre of her forehead – her third eye.

'Record Keeper,' she whispered. She began to relax, emptying her mind of the jumble of tormenting thoughts triggered by the last forty-eight hours.

Lily watched her. This was the crystal that she hoped would activate Maya's cellular memory. It was the stone that the girl had used in Atlantis for meditation. The one that had helped tune her in to the power and wisdom of the Heartstone crystal. She was relieved Maya had recognised it.

For a while the womb-like space was silent, neither woman moving or speaking. Then Maya opened her eyes. She looked calm, her eyes shining. But as soon as she saw Lily her gaze clouded.

'Why can't you see where Rhiannon is?' she asked. 'Does this mean she's . . . dead?'

Lily shook her head.

'I can see her, and she's very much alive. I just can't pinpoint where she is.'

Maya looked as if she didn't believe her.

'Maya, if Rhiannon is dead then this project is over. I wouldn't be helping you raise your consciousness and find the crystal if I knew Rhiannon was dead.'

'But I haven't found the crystal,' Maya objected.

'You will,' Lily assured her. 'You will.'

◎◎

It was only much later that night, when they had buried Atlas in the orchard and everyone had fallen into a sad, exhausted sleep, that Lily realised what had been bothering her. Jude. Where was Jude in all this?

49

Show flat, Imperial Wharf, London

Rhiannon's surge of pure joy at being released from the dark, airless tomb of the boot was short-lived. The underground car park was empty of cars, but dusty and piled high with grey concrete slabs on pallets covered with tight plastic. Rhiannon had summoned up images of all the lightless basements, echoing warehouses and creepy stone dungeons where fictitious characters in fiction had been held prisoner. There would be chains on the dank walls and water dripping; crumbling, dangerous masonry; darkness and the stink of urine; rats and worse. The deserted car park, clearly still a building site, was shaping up nicely.

Kayden had scooped Rhiannon out of the boot in one easy swing of his huge arms, as if she were an overnight bag. He didn't bother to stand her up – which was just as well because her legs were seized with cramp – just hefted her tall body into the lift, which shot upwards, sickeningly fast.

Instead of a basement dungeon, the lift doors opened onto a luxurious – and in Rhiannon's opinion, utterly tasteless – penthouse apartment. Kayden threw her down on a white leather sofa facing the astonishing river view, which, as she later discovered, looked south towards Battersea. The floors were pale, polished wood, the light fittings of dangling turquoise glass looked as if they came straight out of eighties Hollywood, the coffee table was a gleaming cube of see-through perspex. Prints of the river at night lined the walls and the room opened out into a state-of the-art kitchen, clearly never designed to be sullied with actual food. Her head rested on a soft cream cushion.

She lay for a moment, dazed. For a ridiculous moment she wondered if this was Brandon Crowe's home, then dismissed the idea immediately. This was a show apartment – unlived in, soulless. The two men went over to the sliding glass window to confer. The cold-eyed one, that the thug had called Xan, was giving his henchman a bunch of keys and a long list of instructions. Rhiannon caught snippets as his voice rose in irritation.

'No . . . boss's orders are that she's to be treated well. She's our prisoner, yes, and priority number one is making sure she doesn't get away, but she is not, repeat NOT, to be abused in any way. Got it, Kayden?' The man tapped his forehead with his index finger, 'Got it, have you?'

Rhiannon saw Kayden shrug. 'Yeah, yeah. Got it. Keep your wig on.'

The other man paused only for a second, then lunged at his employee, grabbing him round the collar and pressing his face close until their noses were almost touching. They were the same height, although Kayden was at least twice the width in muscle.

'Fucking Neanderthal, mind your fucking manners.' Then his voice fell, his words dropping cold as ice into the room. 'Do not cross me, Kayden. Believe me, you will regret it.'

Rhiannon saw Kayden's face change and was pleased to see a flash of fear cross the thug's lumpen features. He shook the other man off sulkily.

Xan walked over to where Rhiannon was lying and looked her in the eye. Rhiannon stared back at him defiantly. He bent towards her and reached for the pocket of her black jeans. Rhiannon flinched. She felt his hand feeling each pocket in turn, flipping her over until he located her mobile phone in the back pocket. He held the phone up for her to see.

'Boss's orders,' he told her, his expression blank. 'Get that tape off and untie her,' he barked over his shoulder as he made for the lift. 'I'll be back in a couple of hours.'

Kayden seemed nervous as he approached Rhiannon.

'Gotta take the tape off.' He hesitated. 'If you fucking scream there's not a living soul'll hear you.'

Rhiannon tensed for the pain as he ripped the duct tape from her mouth. She didn't mind, it was pure heaven to be able to

225

breathe normally again. And speak.

She waited for him to untie her, then gratefully sat up, rubbing her wrists where the rope had bitten into her flesh. Her shoulder was agony, she could hardly move it.

'I need a drink,' she demanded, realising her mouth was dry as dust. She was confident the thug wasn't allowed to harm her. Yet.

Kayden moved through to the kitchen and looked around, baffled by the lack of knobs on the white, shiny surfaces of the cupboards and draws.

'Don't fuckin' know how this works,' he muttered, pulling hard on a door.

Rhiannon got up tentatively. Her legs were weak and stiff. Kayden spun round when he heard her moving, clearly unsure how he should deal with her.

'Don't try anything funny,' he snapped. 'Everything's locked, you can't get out.'

'I need the bathroom,' she said.

He went with her to the gleaming grey-marble bathroom.

Rhiannon waited. Kayden waited.

'You can't watch,' she stated.

Kayden looked around the empty, windowless room. But he stood his ground.

'You ain't shutting this door,' he said.

'You ain't watching me,' she replied stonily.

The thug examined the lock, shook his head. Then grabbed the seemingly solid door in both his huge fists and pulled it clean off its hinges, waving it at Rhiannon as if it were a piece of paper. Rhiannon winced.

'Fucking cowboys,' he said.

Round one to the thug, she thought grimly.

He turned his back on her and stood four-square, filling the doorway. Rhiannon looked nervously at his bulk, but decided she had no choice.

50

Lily and Gabe's farmhouse, Wiltshire

Gabe turned towards the west, watching the fiery sun sink slowly towards the horizon. *Sunset – the hour of power.* Gabe shook his head sadly. No, too much had happened. The years weighed heavily on his heart; so many lifetimes, so many failures.

Hoping against hope, Gabe raised his hands high above his head, reached towards the dying sun and brought his cupped hands slowly towards his heart. Nothing.

Suddenly the blood-red light strengthened and pulsed between his hands. Gabe stood transfixed, feeling the energy flow and spread through his body. He bowed his head in prayer and gratitude. At last. This was the sign he'd been waiting for.

Tom climbed wearily off the bike, thankful to be in one piece. Michael had taken them halfway to London in an increasingly frantic search for Rhiannon. He'd forced Michael to stop while he made some phone calls from a service station, but afterwards he'd wished he hadn't. When he'd finally got some sense out of his flatmate, it seemed clear that Brandon's men had wasted no time tracking him down. They'd torn his room apart and left his flatmate a gibbering wreck. Worse still, Sam wasn't answering his phone. Tom could only hope he was safe in Finland by now. What on earth had they got themselves into?

Michael wheeled the bike into the barn and as they turned towards the farmhouse they glimpsed a shadowy figure in the orchard, standing motionless in the gathering dusk. As one, they turned towards him. It looked like Gabe but . . . something felt different. The atmosphere felt charged with an energy they couldn't quite recognise. Their footsteps felt unnaturally loud, the quiet sounds of evening suddenly magnified. The bare branches of the trees shook and shivered though the air was still. They came to an uncertain halt and Gabe turned slowly towards them. Without thinking they stepped back. What had happened to the old man they knew? The weariness had gone, he stood before them tall and commanding.

'We . . . we couldn't . . . find her, find Rhiannon,' Tom found himself stuttering, aware that his heart was beating erratically. Glancing sideways he could see Michael's strained white face. He looked scared.

Gabe smiled and the spell broke. 'Rhiannon's safe,' he said calmly. 'We'll find her soon but in the meantime there's work to be done.'

Michael smiled back, the tension leaving his face.

'What do you want us to do?'

Gabe bent down and picked up a long wooden staff lying at his feet.

'I want one of you to take this from me, by force.'

Michael turned towards Tom, trying to keep the smile from his face. This was embarrassing. Gabe was twice his age. Tom grimaced back. 'You or me?'

Michael shrugged. 'OK, me.'

He turned confidently towards Gabe.

'You just want me to take the staff from you?'

Gabe nodded.

Michael measured the few feet separating them, then took off, racing towards Gabe. As he reached him, his outstretched hand met thin air. Michael pulled up, bewildered. Gabe had disappeared. Suddenly he sensed someone behind him just as his feet were swept from under him. He hit the ground with a thump and looked up to see Gabe standing over him.

'You've forgotten everything I ever taught you.' Gabe's expression was stern.

Tom peered uncertainly through the fading light.

'What happened, Michael? Did you trip?'

228

Michael staggered to his feet, breathing heavily.

'No,' he said slowly. 'He just disappeared.'

Tom laughed out loud. 'Yeah, right. I'll show you how it's done.'

Gabe's stern expression relaxed. 'OK, Tom. Let's see if you can do any better.'

Tom took several deep breaths then exploded into action. Seconds before he reached him, Gabe raised his right hand, palm outwards. Tom hurtled backwards and landed, winded, on the ground.

Michael ran over and hauled Tom to his feet. Tom rubbed his chest gingerly.

'How did he do that? I feel like I ran into a brick wall.'

Michael glanced back at Gabe. 'I think . . . it's something he used to teach us. Some kind of martial art?'

'Mastery of energy!' Gabe was suddenly beside them. 'You were my best students, though you wouldn't think it to see you today.' Then he laughed and clapped them both on the shoulder. 'Tonight we'll go through the theory, see how much you can remember. Then tomorrow – you practice.'

Michael grinned. 'Rhiannon would love this. Have you ever seen her karate moves?' As Tom shook his head, the smile faded from Michael's face. He turned aside and looked up at the darkening sky. A single bright star hung low over the horizon and as he watched the light grew stronger and more brilliant. A half-forgotten childhood memory floated into his mind, something about wishing on a star. Michael wished with all his might, *Please keep Rhiannon safe*.

51

Show flat, Imperial Wharf, London

'Why am I here?' Rhiannon asked when she had finally been given a glass of water.

Kayden shrugged. He was staring into the vast American-style fridge, which had one solitary loaf of white sliced bread, a tub of margarine, half a pint of semi-skimmed milk and six eggs – Xan's attempt at shopping.

'You can't keep me here for ever you know,' she tried again.

Kayden turned round, raised his eyebrows.

'We can do what we fuckin' like,' he said, laconically, slamming the fridge door shut in disgust.

She saw him eyeing her up and down, as if he was noticing her for the first time. And his dull, stupid expression suddenly slid into a dangerous leer.

Rhiannon turned quickly away. *No, she thought, please, no.* She wouldn't stand a chance.

Kayden moved over to the enormous plasma screen mounted on the wall and began to fiddle with the remote control. The screen sprang to life and he began to surf through the channels, finally coming to rest on an early evening chat show. An ex-footballer and two giggling, shrieking, French-manicured blondes capered about as if they were on speed.

Kayden put his fat finger on the screen. 'I like her,' he said, his finger lovingly tracing the blonde to the right of picture.

Rhiannon turned away in disgust and went to look out of the window at the panoramic view south across the river. It was dusk, gloomy and overcast, the city lights not yet on, and Rhiannon felt suddenly very alone. Kayden was like a huge, moronic child one minute, then nobody's fool the next. He scared her and she wished the other man would come back. But then she remembered his chilling stare, and thought perhaps she was better off with the thug. She couldn't believe this was happening to her. Would the others find her? They would know this was Brandon Crowe's work of course, but would Lily be able to see her? She thought of Jude. He'd said he would always help her, but he wouldn't know where she was any more than the others. Anyway, she'd rather die than ask that bastard. Crowe must want her as a hostage, to persuade Lily to reveal the whereabouts of the crystal. But Lily didn't know where it was. And nor did Maya.

She felt the tears prick behind her eyes and angrily wiped them away. She would not give that thug the satisfaction of seeing her cry. She turned from the window and jumped in fright. The other man, Xan, the cold-eyed one, was standing only a foot behind her. She had no idea how he'd got there, she'd heard nothing. She moved to avoid him but he blocked her way.

'Has Kayden been looking after you?' he asked.

Rhiannon glared at him contemptuously. 'Like you care.'

Xan stepped back to allow her to pass.

'On the contrary, I care a great deal. It is my job to make sure you come to no harm.' His tone was careful, formal. 'I have my orders.'

'From Brandon Crowe. Yeah, I know.'

Kayden shifted uncomfortably, eyeing Xan warily.

'What's going to happen to me now?' Rhiannon demanded angrily. She loved her anger, it made her feel strong, and kept the pathetic tears at bay.

Xan didn't bother to reply. He turned to his employee. 'Have you given her something to eat?'

Kayden shook his head.

'Well, do it. I'll be back in the morning. Make sure everything's secure. Lock her into the bedroom before you go to sleep.'

'I asked you a question,' Rhiannon grabbed Xan's arm, her voice rising in panic at the thought of being left alone with the thug overnight. 'What the fuck is going to happen to me now?'

Xan shook her off. 'I'll be back tomorrow.' He addressed Kayden again. 'And remember what I said.'

'Yes, sir,' Kayden replied meekly.

Evening: Lily and Gabe's farmhouse, Wiltshire

Maya tucked her feet under her and leaned back against the soft cushions, pulling Lily's shawl more tightly around her. She wasn't cold – the wood fire crackling in the hearth warmed the whole room and the soft candlelight was comforting – but after everything that had happened in the last few hours she felt like a lost child. She breathed deeply and her racing heart began to calm down. She glanced at Tom sitting beside her on the sofa. He felt her eyes on him and smiled. As she smiled back, a thought took hold. *I am not alone.* Her gaze travelled on to Michael stretched out in front of the fire between Gabe and Lily in their armchairs. *I am not alone. This is my family. I have finally come home.*

As she examined these surprising new thoughts a word caught her attention and she tuned back into the conversation going on around her. Tom was talking about the crystal, asking what Merkaba meant.

Lily leaned forward. 'The Merkaba was the most powerful crystal in Atlantis. It was a gift from the star people, our ancestors.' Maya found that she was unconsciously cupping her hands together and Lily caught the movement. 'Go on, Maya.'

Maya studied her hands for a moment, then looked up.

'It's clear crystal quartz, a three-dimensional Star of David. The original and greatest of all the Merkabas because it holds at its heart the twin flames.'

Lily nodded, pleased, and continued, 'It embodies the perfect balance between masculine and feminine energies – that's why we called it the Heartstone. But this was before the fall of Atlantis. The balance was destroyed then and has never been restored.' She leaned back in her chair and stared sadly at the fire, lost in thought.

'But why is that so important?' Tom asked.

Lily merely shook her head so Gabe took over.

'Our continuing existence on this planet depends on reconciling opposing energies – yin and yang, light and dark, man and woman. Masculine energy is in the ascendant now otherwise Brandon would never have achieved such dangerous power. If we can find the crystal in time it can help us restore the balance, even raise us to a higher level of consciousness, as the Mayan calendar foretold.'

Tom frowned. 'But what does that mean? Where does the Mayan calendar come into it?'

Gabe's smile was a little weary. 'You're asking me to condense countless years of history . . . OK. There were survivors from Atlantis. They took their skills and wisdom to many parts of the earth: our masons helped the Egyptian people to build the Pyramids, astronomers taught the Mayans their knowledge of the stars. The calendar records all the movements of the stars and planets over thousands of years and highlights key moments when human consciousness is accelerated. All these cycles are like wheels within wheels and the greatest and longest cycle of all comes to an end on the winter solstice. The Mayans were warning us that we stand on the brink of an incredible breakthrough, or . . . annihilation.'

Michael looked up. 'It's hard for any of us believe that the world could come to an end just like that.'

Gabe agreed. 'But even now you must feel how unstable the earth has become – mostly Brandon's work – and if the energy streaming from the Galactic centre on the winter solstice hits the weakened portal then the world will surely end.'

Michael was shaking his head. 'But how? What will happen?'

Gabe looked calmly at the anxious faces around him.

'You have to understand that this cosmic energy is immeasurably powerful and it's focused directly on Stonehenge. The portal here is the only remaining gateway to the underground grid that circles the earth, and once the energy breaks through, the grid will be overwhelmed. All the other portals are sealed and the only way back out is through Stonehenge. It will explode with the force of a million nuclear bombs.'

Silence fell as they tried to imagine the unimaginable.

Then Michael leaned forward eagerly. 'But we still have a chance. And if we succeed, then these cosmic energies won't be destructive?'

'On the contrary. The planet has been ready to rise to a higher level for a long time. Only the human race is lagging behind and this could be the boost we need. A whole new level of understanding would become possible.'

'That's what Rafaella was trying to tell us,' Tom whispered to Maya.

'But if we fail,' Michael continued, 'doesn't Brandon realise that he will die along with everyone else?'

'Brandon is a gambler. Everything he's been doing is a calculated risk. He probably thinks that possession of the crystal will neutralise the danger and bring him ultimate power.'

Lily rose gracefully to her feet. 'Brandon has no interest in the fate of the human race. That, in the end, may be his downfall. Now you should all rest. Tomorrow, Gabe will show you how to access the Merkaba energy field. That should help you face the dangers ahead of you.'

'And help us keep intruders out,' Gabe added grimly.

They all filed silently out of the room looking slightly stunned, leaving Gabe and Lily alone.

'There's so little time, Gabe. How can they possibly learn all they need to know? And what about Jude, what if –'

Gabe placed his finger gently on her lips, 'Relax, Lilith. They've already come a long way. As for Jude, you just have to trust me.'

52

Lily stepped out into the cold morning air and shivered. The sky was still dark and tattered ribbons of mist drifted aimlessly a few inches above the frozen earth. She scanned the eastern horizon but only a dull orange glow heralded the rising sun. She waited patiently and the monochrome landscape gradually took on definition. In the distance she could make out three shadowy figures raising their arms in celebration as the pale winter sun broke through the clouds.

Alone, she mirrored their movements, then brought her hands together in prayer. Slowly she placed her left palm over her right, rotated them one way then the other, then stretched her arms out sideways, right palm to the sky, left palm to the earth. She turned three times then brought her hands back to the prayer position.

'You're sealing the energy.' The voice in her ear brought her back to earth with a jolt. She hadn't heard Maya join her. She looked thoughtfully at the girl. Maya looked focused, intent, her eyes on the three men in the distance. They were working their way through a series of breathing exercises, led by Gabe.

'Merkaba Meditation,' said Maya quietly.

'So you remember your training.' Lily tried to keep the surprise from her voice.

'Of course. And look, they remember too.'

Both women stared at the distant figures and could see a faint luminous outline beginning to form around them.

'Their energy field is quite strong for beginners.' Lily was impressed despite herself.

'You should join them.'

Maya slowly shook her head. 'It doesn't feel right to use the energy for . . . for fighting.'

Lily shrugged. Tom was following instructions from Gabe, launching himself on Michael, who suddenly vanished and reappeared behind them. Michael's shout of triumph echoed through the still air.

'Yang energy is as valuable as yin as long as they are both used with integrity. And you will need all your strength and courage to protect the crystal. Remember, Rhiannon will need to learn this too and she's more likely to listen to you.'

Maya grinned. 'You're right.' And started off towards Gabe.

'Maya!'

Maya turned back.

'Remember the earth star.' Lily looked gravely at her, then suddenly winked.

Confused, Maya walked on. Did Lily just wink at her? Then it clicked.

When Maya reached them, Gabe was demonstrating how to repel attacks by energy and intent. Tom and Michael were hot, sweaty and exhilarated as their technique became more and more focused. They greeted Maya with boisterous good humour, eager to show off their new skills.

'Wait,' Gabe ordered, 'Maya has something to show you.'

Tom and Michael smothered their amusement as Maya stood stock still in front of them. Silently she concentrated on the earth star beneath her feet and, to her secret delight, she felt the connection. She nodded to Gabe.

'Which of you,' he began, 'thinks he is strong enough to lift Maya off the ground?'

Michael shook his head, remembering last night's experience. This was too easy – Maya was as light and delicate as a feather. But Tom rushed forward, grabbed her round the waist and . . . failed completely to lift her even a fraction of a centimetre. She was as rooted to the earth as Mount Everest. He stepped back, puzzled, and made a concentrated effort to remember Gabe's teachings. Then with a shout, he tried again with all his strength. Maya smiled into his eyes, as he struggled and strained then suddenly released her connection to the earth. Tom toppled backwards and Maya soared into the air then landed nimbly beside him. He glared up at her, torn between anger and amusement, as she pulled him to his feet.

'I can see I still have a lot to learn,' he said ruefully as Michael swung Maya high in the air, though he was fully aware that it was only because she allowed him to.

Gabe called them to order. 'We'll break for breakfast. You obviously need to build your strength up. Then more practice – every minute is precious and you'll be leaving here very soon.'

53

Rhiannon opened her eyes slowly, disorientated. Where was she? The shock of realisation set her heart beating wildly. She looked around the darkened room, saw broad daylight through the chink in the curtains. But she couldn't move. She felt drunk almost, her body heavy and listless, her tongue stuck to the roof of her mouth – as if she had the world's worst hangover. She forced her numb brain to go over the events of the night before. Cold-eyes leaving, the thug making her toast, which she ate despite herself. Tea . . . he'd put loads of sugar in, and she didn't take sugar, so it tasted vile. But she didn't care and hadn't said anything. She couldn't bear to talk to the moron. Then nothing. She didn't remember anything after the tea; the bastards had drugged her.

Anger gave her strength. Despite lethargy and a pounding head, Rhiannon forced herself out of bed and stood up straight.

Do it, she told herself, dragging up every ounce of willpower she had. Taking a deep breath, she raised her arms in the opening moves of the salute to the sun kata, ignoring the ache in her shoulder. As her movements became more fluid, she shot one leg straight out at right angles to her body, the opposite hand meeting it above the ankle. She felt pain shoot through her stiff limbs. Then the other leg. Again. She leapt, punching the air in front of her, her fists lethal weapons, right–left–right–left. She repeated this routine silently until her body responded. Then, breathing fast, she stopped and rolled her head around, first one way, then the other, loosened her shoulders, hands, legs, shook out each foot. *Fuck you*, she whispered silently to herself as her head cleared and her heart beat with a strong, healthy rhythm again. *Fuck you*.

She pulled the curtains back and waited on the bed. Just waited. He would come eventually, he'd have to. She could hear him in the other room, his bare feet thudding on the stripped pine. She cringed at the thought of him.

It was a while. She heard the lock turning and she was ready. Kayden's pasty face appeared around the door. He saw her standing very still beside the bed and looked surprised. But before he had time to react, Rhiannon went into action. She stepped within range, then turned quickly side-on to the thug and dropping one arm to the floor for support, swung both legs off the floor, bent up close to her body then punched them out with as much force as she could muster, directly at Kayden's crutch. Bingo! She felt her feet crunching into his flesh and saw the shock register on his heavy features. He yelled in pain as his huge body doubled over, staggered, almost fell. By the time he'd gained his balance, Rhiannon was up close. She smashed hard into his sternum, feeling the power flowing through her body to her fists, left–right–left–right, and met steel. But the blows winded him. He coughed, spat, then she felt his paw close over her face, forcing her head back. Blinded, she sliced the edge of her hand hard across his bull neck, and his grip loosened momentarily, but long enough for her to dart past the slow-moving giant. She was free! She rushed headlong out of the bedroom, her heart bursting with elation, and slammed straight into Cold-Eyes. Xan only took one minute to twist her in his grasp until her arm was rammed agonisingly behind her back, her knees buckled beneath her with the pain.

'For fuck's sake,' he cursed his henchman. 'You're more of a bloody girl than she is.' He handed Rhiannon over, and she felt Kayden's fist tighten round her arm like a vice. The thug picked her up bodily and flung her hard onto the bed. The door slammed.

54

Lily sat alone in her workroom. She felt low, lacking in energy. Her young guests were a challenge but they were not the problem. With a shock of insight she realised the problem was Gabe. She had spent so long holding him together and now, when she had expected the brutal killing of Atlas to floor him completely, he had been galvanised into action. *So what's wrong with that?* She asked herself irritably. *It's what you've been wanting for ever.* But now she didn't have to support him, encourage him, summon up belief for them both, she felt curiously deflated and worn out.

She pulled herself together and turned her thoughts to Brandon. There had been no word from him in the twenty-four hours since they'd taken Rhiannon. So it wasn't her he wanted. And if it wasn't her, it could only be Jude. Brandon must know, somehow, what the girl meant to Jude. He must be using her to get to Jude. Because there is no way Jude would even speak to his brother unless there was serious provocation.

Would Jude buckle? Gabe said no – he said Jude was solid. But blood can be thicker than water . . . And what if Jude *was* seduced, and the two brothers joined forces? It would be curtains for the ceremony, for this last chance to put things right. She heard a soft knock on the door, and reluctantly responded.

'Maya . . . thanks for coming.'

The girl entered hesitantly, as if she sensed, despite the summons, Lily's reluctance.

'We haven't much time,' Lily made an effort to be strong. 'Let's see if we can get closer to the crystal.'

Maya immediately looked distressed.

'But what if I can't? What if it's my fault that we never find it?'

Lily smiled gently. 'We work as a group, but your anxiety won't help. Try to relax, allow the flow of memories, of knowledge.'

Maya nodded and sat down.

'Close your eyes. Remember the places you have been. Tell me about them.'

'In this . . . lifetime?'

Lily sighed. 'Any lifetime, Maya, you have had many, but they are all only one.'

Maya still looked worried.

'Relax . . . close your eyes . . . focus on the crystal . . . its beauty. Remember holding it. It feels cool, smooth . . . but vibrant with energy and light that transports you. It is an extension of yourself, but also your teacher . . . it lights your aura, makes you better than yourself . . . with it you have astonishing power . . .'

She watched as the girl began to feel what Lily was feeling. She visibly relaxed.

'Now, where have you been where you felt that power, even to the smallest extent?'

'South America, about an hour south of Machu Picchu was my first dig. We travelled to the ruins and I thought it was the most magical place in the world. The clouds hovered beneath us, down in the valley . . . it was our world.'

'Good . . . then . . .'

Maya told Lily about Nepal, Egypt, Uluru. She was working her way through the main energy portals, and in every one she knew she had felt something, but there was none that stood out. Lily beckoned the girl over to her table.

'Sit.'

'I'm not doing well, am I?' Maya stated. 'All these places were so magical . . . so extraordinary, particularly for someone like me who is fascinated by the ancient world. But . . .' she shrugged.

'It can't be Stonehenge,' Lily was talking to herself. 'You were there when Jude built it, but that was much later. The crystal must have been re-formed and secured at the time of Atlantis. Uluru, Angkor Wat . . . Machu Picchu, Nepal . . . Sedona.' She sighed. Such a vast canvas, she wasn't sure the girl was up to it. Not yet, not without more training. But there wasn't time for that.

Lily stood behind her and began to smooth her hands over the girl, a few inches from her body, starting at the top of her head and ending at her feet. After each stroke Lily shook her hands to remove Maya's disruptive energy. She also cleansed the table and blew out all but seven candles, which she placed around the edge of the wooden surface. Maya seemed calmer now.

Lily laid an ancient map on the table in front of her. It was basic, short on detail, but the energy portals were heavily marked.

She handed her a pendant crystal she had carefully selected from the shelves.

'Hold this in both hands. Imprint your own energy.'

Maya did as she was told.

'Now, hold it lightly at the end of the chain.' The pendant swung gently back and forth in Maya's fingers. 'Clear your mind . . . breathe . . . slow breaths . . . in to the count of four . . . out to the count of seven. Think only of the Heartstone.'

After a few minutes, Maya settled into a rhythm with her breathing. The crystal just circled lazily. The only sound in the room was the gentle exhalation of Maya's breath.

Without being prompted, Maya began to move the pendant over each of the portals in turn. She started with Machu Picchu. The pendant began to swing with more purpose now, gathering momentum in an anti-clockwise direction until it was circling smoothly. Maya moved on. Each one had the same result, a firm but sedate swing anti-clockwise. Until Sedona, the last one she tried. Lily had begun to lose heart. This time the crystal pendulum hesitated, swung initially anti-clockwise, then changed to clockwise, circling more and more purposefully until it was swinging wildly round and round over the marked Sedona portal.

Maya looked up joyfully.

'This is it! It must be in Sedona.'

242

There was loud knocking on the door, and Gabe's face appeared through the candlelight.

'Come in, come in,' Lily beckoned him.

Gabe was followed by Michael and Tom. They had been in the orchard, where Gabe was continuing their master classes in energy control.

'Maya's found it. The crystal. It's in Sedona.'

After the initial rejoicing, Tom, who knew Sedona well, spoke up: 'But where in Sedona exactly? It's a big place.'

Lily shook her head irritably.

'I never said I'd solved the problem entirely. But this is an important start. You will have to go there. You will know what to do.'

Michael laughed. 'What . . . we just wander about blindly till we feel the Force?' He was angry with Lily for not doing more to find Rhiannon. Angry with himself. He didn't know what Lily could have done, but doing nothing seemed so pathetic.

Lily shot him an irritated glance and went on, 'Of course you can't do any of this without Rhiannon. Each of you represents an essential component in the search.'

'And how are we to do that? Find Rhiannon I mean.' Maya asked softly.

55

Kayden's hot, stale breath on her cheek woke Rhiannon. She froze in the solid darkness, hoping Kayden was just checking on her and would go away. She felt sick, her stomach knotted, her heart pounding as if it were trying to burst from her chest.

But Kayden wasn't going anywhere. His thick, stubby finger began to trace circles round first her lips, then her cheek, just as he had on the screen image of the television presenter. Rhiannon shrank back in revulsion, then took a huge breath and screamed with all her might, flailing her arms against his hovering, sweaty face in the darkness. Kayden jumped back. Rhiannon tried to struggle from the bed, only to find the man's huge fist pinning her down, his grip tight around her neck, his bulk pinning her body to the mattress. She fought in silence now, trying to get some leverage, to scratch his face, his eyes, anything. She was powerless against his incredible strength. And as his grip tightened she found she could barely breathe, let alone scream. She tried another tactic and stopped moving altogether.

For a moment nothing happened, and then she felt the thug's grip slackening. She waited, trying to control her breathing. The rank, unwashed smell that came off his skin made her want to vomit.

'You ain't my type you know,' Kayden whispered into her ear. 'Too scrawny, too tall.' She heard his breath coming faster now, hot and thick over her face. 'But I like a bit of spirit . . . you owe me one.'

Rhiannon whimpered in the darkness. *No . . . please . . . no . . . NO.* As she felt Kayden's hand press down inside her jeans,

244

his fingers ripping at her clothes in a frenzy of lust, she found herself doing the one thing she had vowed she would never do. It wasn't a rational decision, just pure gut instinct. She called out for Jude – a heart-felt, desperate, totally silent scream. She knew it was ridiculous. Jude couldn't know where she was, nor help her even if he had; it was too late. But the cry came from the depths of her soul, channelling past the horror there on the bed and out into the universe to the man who had broken her heart, the man who had promised always to help her.

For a moment nothing changed in the horrible darkness. Then a ball of glowing red energy suddenly materialised in the room and slammed into Kayden's head.

'Fuck!' He leapt off the bed as if it were on fire. 'Fuck . . . what the fuck was that?'

The overhead light came on suddenly. Kayden was standing by the door, blinking and dazed, holding his hand to his head, his eyes wide with shock.

'What the fuck was that?' he repeated, staring bewildered round the room and then at Rhiannon, who leapt off the bed and stood against the wall, as far from the thug as she could get.

'How did you do that, bitch? You hit me? You couldn't have –' Kayden sounded whiney and peeved, suddenly unsure of himself, the rampant beast from the darkness totally vanished.

'Get out. Get out of this room,' she shouted. Kayden didn't move, still in shock.

'Do you hear me?' Rhiannon yelled at the thug. 'Get the fuck out right now! And tomorrow I'll tell your cold-eyed boss exactly what you've done.'

Kayden, at the mention of Xan, came to and shook his head nervously. Then without a word, he shuffled his bulk out of the room, leaving the door open.

Rhiannon collapsed on the bed. Her body was suddenly freezing, trembling, her muscles without strength to move at all. *Jude . . . Jude . . . Jude . . .* She kept repeating his name, as bewildered as Kayden had been. She had no idea what had happened either, but she knew without a shadow of doubt that Jude was responsible, somehow. He had promised, and he had been true to his word. Without his intervention . . . Rhiannon couldn't even think about what might have happened.

'Thank you,' she whispered into the empty room.

Rhiannon didn't know how long she sat there. It could have been minutes or hours but it was beginning to get light when she came to. There was no sound from the other room. Eventually she felt strong enough to face Kayden again. She edged into the living area of the flat to find the thug stretched out full-length on the white sofa, one arm behind his head, the other dangling off the side of the sofa, fast asleep and snoring softly. On the cube-shaped Perspex coffee table next to him were the contents of his pocket: half a packet of chewing gum, a worn Swiss army knife, a scrunched up ten-pound note sitting next to some loose change, an old receipt, his Oyster card, mobile phone – and the keys to the show flat that Xan had given him.

She stood for a long time watching Kayden's sleeping face, screwing her courage up to approach the table. The events of the night were so fresh in her mind that the sight of him made her stomach knot with disgust and humiliation. She took a deep breath, crept a step closer. *Get on with it, you wimp*, she chided herself. *The other one will be here soon. Go . . . go.*

Kayden slept on. Rhiannon silently lifted the ring from the table, holding her breath. The keys jangled against each other for a second, and the thug stirred, rubbed his dribbling mouth with the back of his huge hand, then rolled over away from her, his face buried in the cushions at the back of the sofa.

Rhiannon let her breath out very slowly as she inched away towards the front door – and freedom. She checked the lock: Yale. She checked the bunch in her hand. There were two Yale keys, but both looked the same. There was also what looked like a mortise lock at the top and the bottom of the door, but she couldn't see a corresponding key. If the door was double-locked then she was lost. Casting a look back at her jailer, she selected the first of the Yale keys and very slowly pressed it into the lock. The key turned soundlessly to the left. Rhiannon paused, took a deep breath, and felt the door give. *Yes!* She began to pull the door open, praying it wouldn't creak. When it was wide enough for her to slide through, she gave one final look back, then stepped out into the dusty, unfinished corridor. And came face to face with Xan.

Rhiannon screamed in fright. Xan said nothing. He pushed her firmly back inside the flat, slamming the door and waking Kayden.

'Boss?' Kayden didn't know yet that anything was wrong. He stumbled to his feet and stood looking bleary-eyed.

Rhiannon, unable to stop the tears of rage and disappointment, wrenched her arm from Xan's pincer-like grasp and threw herself onto the white leather armchair on the far side of the room by the glass doors.

Xan stood for a minute, glaring at his henchman.

'Out. Get out.' His voice was icy.

Kayden raised his eyebrows.

'Boss?'

'Get your stuff and fuck off,' Xan repeated.

'What's up, boss?' Kayden said nervously, gathering his things from the coffee table and cramming them into his pockets. 'We finished here?'

'*You* are,' Xan said tersely.

'But . . . I did what you said. I –'

'Yeah, sure you did,' Xan interrupted. 'That's why the girl had your keys and was making off down the corridor while you caught up on your fucking beauty sleep.'

Kayden looked puzzled.

'She couldn't've . . .' Kayden looked at Rhiannon.

Xan didn't bother to answer, just opened the front door.

'What d'you want me to do now, boss?' the thug asked.

'Wait for me by the car,' Xan snapped.

◎◎

Rhiannon breathed a sigh of relief once the door was closed on Kayden.

'He tried to rape me,' she stood and confronted Xan.

Xan stared at her, unblinking. He seemed to be assessing her, perhaps wondering how she had managed to fend Kayden off a second time.

'I'll deal with him,' he said after a minute.

'I won't stay here with him,' she declared fiercely.

'I said, I will deal with him.'

'You can't keep me here. That brute assaulted me. He's a fucking criminal. You can't do this, it's illegal. Tell me, tell me what the fuck is going on.' Rhiannon heard her voice rising, the hysteria hard to control.

Xan just turned away. As he closed the front door behind him she heard the clunk of the mortise lock.

56

Brandon Crowe drove through the security gate of the underground car park and parked beside the lift. As he locked the car the overhead lights flickered then went out, leaving him in darkness. Brandon smiled triumphantly.

'What kept you, Jude?'

Silence. Brandon peered into the gloom but could see and hear nothing, only the distant roar of traffic. Suddenly the lights came back on and Jude was standing there beside him. Brandon's smile faded as he saw the cold fury in Jude's eyes.

'Get in.' Jude gestured at the car and Brandon slid behind the wheel. Jude sat in the passenger seat and swiftly programmed the satnav.

'Drive.'

Brandon shrugged. He didn't like being told what to do by his brother but decided to humour him – after all, he held all the winning cards.

The precise female voice of the satnav directed them east then north, finally announcing 'destination ahead'.

Brandon parked and looked at Jude, but he was already getting out of the car. Brandon followed him, increasing his pace to keep up. They were approaching the entrance to Primrose Hill. Jude strode on up the hill then paused, placing his hand on the frosty grass. He appeared to listen for a moment then strode on, angrily. Finally they reached the summit and London spread out before them as far as the eye could see, landmarks poking through the morning mist like beacons: the BT Tower, the London Eye, the distant towers of Canary Wharf.

Brandon had had enough of the silent treatment.

'Come on Jude. Cut to the chase. I've got something you want and you've got something I want. Let's make a deal.'

Jude looked at him thoughtfully. 'Something tells me the price would be too high.'

'Get off your high horse. You're hardly the one to take the high moral ground.'

The anger in Jude's eyes was replaced by sadness.

'You just don't get it, do you? Can't you see the damage you're doing? Earthquakes, volcanoes, floods, hurricanes. Millions of people dead or homeless, food rationing, fuel shortages, the financial markets in free fall. You're bringing the world to its knees. Any minute now you'll reach the tipping point. Once the balance is lost, you can never bring it back.'

Brandon couldn't keep the sneer from his face.

'Yeah, yeah, yeah. That old story. Respect the natural rhythms of mother earth, live in harmony, blah, blah, blah. You always were a romantic, and look where it's got you.'

'That's why I've got to put it right. Once you would have understood that.'

Brandon saw an opportunity and grabbed it.

'But we can put it right – together. Only not the way you're planning to do it. I agree the world is in deep shit but that's not all my doing. Greed, war, religious strife, waste of precious natural resources . . . mankind was doing this long before I came along.' Jude turned away and Brandon grabbed his arm.

'Jude, you can help me, we can help each other. If I can access S-3 we will have a clean, safe, unlimited source of energy and solve all the problems you're so concerned about.'

Jude shook his brother off roughly.

'And you will be the most powerful man on the planet.'

'Better me than governments or cartels fighting for the monopoly. Look at the way they're manoeuvring over oil in the Arctic, look what's happening in the Middle East and North Africa. That's the way to World War III. So much damage has been done. It's time for a new beginning.'

Jude looked at him curiously.

'You feel it too, a new beginning?'

'I do, and you can be an equal part of it, my conscience, if you like. I know what you think of me but you are my brother. If we work together, we could save the world.'

Jude looked quizzically into his brother's eyes as if trying to see into his very soul, but remained silent.

Brandon pressed on. 'I need the crystal and I need you to unlock the portal at Stonehenge. You do that for me and in return you can have Rhiannon.'

A gasp of pain escaped Jude's tightly folded lips.

'I can't have her.'

'Why not? Because Lilith says so? Bullshit! Rhiannon could work with you – you could bring S-3 to earth together.'

Brandon sensed Jude was weakening.

'Just think about it. If Lilith's crackpot plan works then we lose forever the chance of using S-3. In twenty years' time all the remaining sources of energy will have been exhausted. Millions will die and the survivors will fight each other to the death for food and shelter. That's not the world I want to live in.'

Jude sighed. 'And if I do as you say, you'll release Rhiannon?'

Brandon nodded.

'And what about the others?'

'I need them to lead me to the crystal. Once I have it they're free to go wherever they wish.'

'And do you really think Lily will just give up?'

'What else can she do? Without the crystal she's powerless.'

Jude reached a decision. 'First, release Rhiannon. Once I know she's safe, then we'll talk further.'

Brandon seized his brother's hand and shook it.

'I knew you'd see sense. You've made the right decision, trust me.'

'Oh, I trust you, Brandon,' said Jude with a wry smile, 'I trust you just about as much as you trust me.'

57

Lily and Gabe's farmhouse, Wiltshire

'What if Crowe doesn't let Rhiannon go? What if he harms her?' Michael paced about Lily's room, his whole body wired with frustration and worry. 'Do you know for sure she's OK? I mean really know? You seem so bloody calm, but shouldn't we be doing more than we are?'

Lily could hear the hysteria in his voice, and sympathised. She wasn't calm. It wasn't just Rhiannon who was in danger, it was all of them, including herself. But Brandon had a single focus. The crystal. She believed he would hold off from doing any of them harm until he had secured the prize. If she was wrong . . .

Lily shook off her dark thoughts and moved to her seer stone.

'I checked an hour ago. She's all right, I promise you, but I still can't see where she is. Brandon's obviously blocked the area they're holding her in. I'll look again.'

Michael stood behind her and they both waited while the crystal came to life. At first there was nothing, just the static fuzz of a broken TV. But Lily worked on it; Michael could feel the concentration coming off her in waves. And sudden the crystal cleared. He watched as the bright, clean images showed Rhiannon leaving the show flat, going down in the lift, getting into the back of Xan's car with Xan. She looked fine; angry, pulling away from Xan's touch, shooting him disdainful glances, but obviously as tough and feisty as ever.

Michael laughed.

'Even kidnapping can't dent her spirit,' he said with awe.

There was a knock on the door and Gabe and Tom came in.

'They're letting Rhiannon go I think. I can finally see her clearly,' Lily told them. 'That's Jude,' Lily pointed to a shadowy figure hovering against the wall of the underground car park.

Gabe peered over her shoulder.

'So it is.'

They looked at each other, then the screen went dark.

'What does it mean?' Tom asked. 'If she's being released and Jude is there too?'

Lily shook her head.

'Is he in league with Brandon?' Michael chimed in.

'We haven't got time to speculate. Whatever has gone on, you need to get going. If she's being released she'll go back home I imagine. I'll keep trying to get her location, but I couldn't keep the channel open any longer.'

Michael nodded at Tom.

'We should tell Maya and leave straight away.'

'When you find her,' Lily continued, 'bring her back here. She's strong but she's been through a terrible ordeal. She'll need all our love and support to recover.'

When the others had gone, Gabe sat down with his wife.

'So . . . Jude.'

Lily nodded.

'Would his feelings for Rhiannon in this lifetime make him betray us?'

Gabe sighed. 'I stick to my guns. Jude is on the side of the angels. Brandon will be trying to use him, of course. We know that. But he's not a traitor.'

'He hasn't contacted us, Gabe. He'll know what we are trying to do. If he were really on our side, wouldn't he have been in touch before now? Wouldn't he have been here, helping us? Why is he avoiding us, yet meeting up with Brandon so quickly? I don't like it.'

'I don't "like" any of it. But we have to assume he is onside. What else can we do?'

He looked at his wife and was surprised to see tears in her eyes. Lily never cried.

'What is it?'

Lily shook her head fiercely.

'The young ones . . . we've brought them so far. And they're good. They struggle with it all, who wouldn't? But they are trying really hard to understand. What if all this is for nothing?' She looked at Gabe. 'You and I aren't so attached to this life. When all this is over, we can let go. But the others?'

Gabe rose and put his arms around her.

'Don't lose your belief, Lily. Not now. We can do this, you and I.'

58

Rhiannon was in a daze as they drove through London. She sat as far as she could from her cold-eyed minder, neither of them uttering a word. Rhiannon was terrified he would change his mind and take her back to the penthouse. She had no idea why she was suddenly being released. The car drew to a stop and she realised with overwhelming relief that she was in her own street. The man who was driving turned to Xan.

'Here?'

Xan nodded and leant over Rhiannon to open her door. She sat there in the blast of cold evening air, suddenly too weak to move.

'You are free to go,' his said, his voice stony. Although he was glad to see the back of her, he felt her release was something of a humiliation for him. She had treated him like dirt.

Rhiannon began to shuffle out of the car, helped by a vicious push from Xan.

She stood, wobbly, in the street next to the parked cars as Xan reached for the door to shut it.

'You have Jude to thank for your freedom,' he said, looking her straight in the eye.

'Jude?' Rhiannon questioned. 'What do you mean?' But the door slammed and the car was already halfway down the street.

Xan smiled in the darkness. The boss's plan was working perfectly. United we stand, divided – they fall.

She glanced around her flat in wonder. It seemed so familiar, so untouched by the nightmare events of the last few days. She did nothing except drink two large glasses of water, then stagger to her bedroom where she collapsed on the bed. She was home. But even under the comforting duvet, she found she was cold, shaking and scared to death. She no longer felt safe, even in her own bed. The slightest sound made her jump and begin to sweat.

As she lay there unable to relax, all she could think of was Jude. Had he made a pact with the devil to save her? She began to cry, long, desperate sobs of despair. She had felt so vulnerable in that horrible flat, so alone. It hurt her to think there was no one in her life who'd missed her, no one who would bother to rescue her, except the one man she really couldn't trust. Her life had been one long struggle never to be vulnerable. But now she badly needed a friend.

A sudden series of loud bangs shocked her to her feet and she raced to the window to see shards of light exploding in all directions. Was the world ending ahead of schedule? She suddenly realised that tonight was Bonfire Night but found it impossible to calm her shattered nerves. Slowly she returned to her bed and wrapped herself in the duvet.

Jude, she whispered into the darkness. *Jude . . . where are you?*

59

Christina backed out of the boss's office breathing a sigh of relief. Crowe had been grilling her for hours about where Sam had gone. She said she didn't know, which was mostly true, although he had mentioned a project in Finland. But Finland was a big place. She thought she'd convinced him that she knew nothing, but Crowe was not a man to countenance disloyalty among his employees. She turned the coffee machine on and made herself a strong cappuccino.

Who was that man with the boss? she wondered, as she sipped the hot, reviving caffeine. *Drop-dead gorgeous, with the same piercing blue-green eyes as the boss. Sort of scary the way he stared though, as if he was looking straight into your soul.*

Christina looked at her watch – nearly eight o'clock, time to call it a day. There'd been a bad atmosphere around the office since the incident with Sam and that other guy – the boss had become a nightmare. Sometimes she was scared of him. She realised she wasn't comfortable here any more. Perhaps it was time to move on, find another job.

Jude leant over his brother's shoulder as Brandon accessed the files of the prototype of his manufactured crystal.

'Look Jude, it's identical to the Merkaba. I've had each tiny specification checked. This is a work of genius. I only employ the best.'

'But it doesn't work?' a smile that his brother couldn't see played round Jude's mouth.

'Of course it works . . . just not well enough. S-3 is being drawn down OK, but the flow is sporadic . . . explosive at times. We just can't control it properly.' Brandon paused, clicking through the specifications on the screen absent-mindedly. 'This has cost me ten years and over six million pounds,' he muttered, almost proudly.

'So you need the real one.'

Jude found his brother so unchanged, so totally, selfishly single-minded, that it freaked him out. But seeing him again, although a shock, had been a pleasure of sorts – they had loved each other once. And Brandon reminded him of their father, also single-minded and strong.

Brandon looked up at him, a calculating look in his eye.

'First we find the crystal. Then if you clear the 'Henge as you promised, we can be up and running within a year.'

Jude looked at him curiously. 'Does it never cross your mind that you've already gone too far? That the world might not be able to recover, even with the crystal?' He pointed to the screens showing breaking news from across the world: streams of refugees desperately trying to find shelter from the latest tsunami, a nuclear power station going into meltdown after an earthquake.

Brandon's confidence was unshakeable.

'It's healthy to cut away dead wood. All those out-dated structures, religious fanaticism, rival ideologies are sabotaging any real progress. I'm not the one selling arms so dictators can annihilate their opponents. What the world needs is one strong leader who can unite and control all the factions.'

'Like Atlantis did?' Jude interrupted.

Brandon's face darkened.

'I'm not the one responsible for what happened to Atlantis,' he said pointedly.

Jude turned away and Brandon felt an unfamiliar emotion – could it be regret? – for rubbing salt in his wounds.

'Jude,' he said persuasively, 'we're on the same side. None of this is random. It's designed to reshape a system that no longer works. I've got some amazing plans . . . I'll show you what we could achieve together.'

Jude shrugged. 'You know I can't do anything about Stonehenge until the solstice.'

'Why?' Brandon's suspicious eyes scanned his brother's unresponsive face, then his expression suddenly cleared.

'Oh, yeah. I get it. The sun in a position of power, all that astrological mumbo-jumbo Gabriel taught you.'

Jude nodded briefly. 'He taught you too. Maybe you should have paid more attention.' He was still reeling from the knowledge of how far his brother would go. He couldn't stop thinking about Rhiannon, how frightened she must have been, alone, unprotected. He took a deep breath and tried to forget her, but it was as if Brandon had read his thoughts.

'And the girl . . . then the girl will be yours. She's a catch. Beautiful, brave . . .'

Mine, Jude thought. *Rhiannon . . . mine.* For a moment he allowed himself to indulge in fantasy. He and Rhiannon could work together; the bond they shared was more than enough to activate the crystal and together they would have the power to hold Brandon in check. Perhaps there was a way . . .

'You'll help me, won't you?' Brandon's insistent voice broke into his reverie. 'Jude? You'll help me find the crystal?'

60

6 November 2012: Lily and Gabe's farmhouse, Wiltshire

Rhiannon woke with a start and cautiously opened her eyes. A thin strip of pale November sunlight poked through a chink in the curtains revealing a small room with low beams. Not her bedroom then, nor that hateful apartment where Brandon had kept her prisoner. Rhiannon stretched and tried to remember the last few hours. Fragments came back to her. Michael collecting her from her flat; the late-night drive from London; arriving at the farmhouse; Lily and Maya leading her upstairs to a candlelit room and settling her in bed.

And Lily's voice, quiet and intent, talking to Maya. 'The orange vibration. Concentrate on orange. We must treat the shock first.'

Then a pleasant feeling of warmth, an awareness that hands were moving close to her body but not touching.

'The left side?' That was Maya.

'The left. That's where the incarnational star tries to escape when the physical body is under extreme stress.'

The soothing voices faded and Rhiannon slept.

Now she felt wide awake and sat up in bed to see Maya drawing the curtains.

'How are you feeling?' Maya turned to her friend with an anxious smile.

'I'm fine.'

'Good, because we have work to do.' Lily strode into the room and handed Rhiannon a cup of steaming liquid.

Rhiannon sniffed it suspiciously.

'It's only camomile. It'll do you good.'

'And you always know what's good for me,' Rhiannon's tone was hostile.

Lily was unfazed. 'I understand why you're angry.'

'Too right I'm angry. If you can't have him, no one can. Is there no end to your egotism?'

'Rhiannon!' Maya sounded shocked.

'No, she's right,' Lily said calmly. 'You go and join the others Maya. It's time Rhiannon and I talked.'

Rhiannon put the cup down and swung her legs over the side of the bed. If she was going to take on the High Priestess of Atlantis she wanted to be on her feet. To her surprise, Lily sat down and gestured to her to continue.

Rhiannon took a deep breath.

'OK. This is 2012. We're not in Atlantis now and you have no right to interfere in my private life.'

Lily's eyebrows rose but she remained silent.

'You kept Jude dangling in Atlantis because it flattered your ego and look what happened. Now, when he could have been happy with me you warned him away.'

'I did,' Lily agreed, 'but you don't know why.'

'I can think of plenty of reasons,' Rhiannon began tartly but Lily ignored her.

'You remember what happened in Atlantis, during the ceremony?'

'Jude showed me. He was trying to save you!'

'And by doing so, broke the circle and unleashed a power we couldn't control.'

'That wasn't his fault,' Rhiannon burst out passionately.

To her surprise, Lily nodded.

'You're right. It was my fault. If I'd discouraged his infatuation he would never have forgotten his training. I allowed my own feelings to override my responsibilities as High Priestess, which is why I can no longer lead the ceremony.'

'What!' Rhiannon felt sick. 'Jude said something about not falling in love with the High Priestess. No! Tell me he wasn't talking about me!'

Lily's silence was the confirmation she feared.

'I won't do it. This is all crazy.'

Rhiannon paced up and down the room, then stopped as a new thought struck her.

'If I were the new High Priestess then why couldn't Jude be High Priest? You know there's an incredible connection between us.'

Lily shook her head compassionately. 'I believe there is, but it wouldn't work. He's not your true soulmate.'

'So you just know that, do you, like you know everything else.'

'There'll come a time when you'll know it too, I promise you.'

Lily rose to her feet with an air of finality.

'Your friends are waiting for you downstairs. You've got some catching up to do.'

'Wait,' Rhiannon said abruptly. 'Who is my soulmate then?'

Lily opened the door and looked back over her shoulder.

'I think in your heart you already know the answer to that.'

61

'Christina!'

A young PA opened the door nervously. 'Christina's not here, Mr Crowe. She's still on sick leave.'

Brandon frowned. 'Well, you, what's your name?'

'Sophy, Mr Crowe.'

'Get me the latest projections from the third floor, Sophy.'

The girl almost tripped in her anxiety to leave the office.

Brandon turned to Jude who was leafing through a thick report.

'What's her problem?'

'I think,' said Jude, 'that she's afraid of you.'

Brandon shrugged. 'Stupid bitch.'

Sophy rushed back in and put a sheaf of printouts on Brandon's desk. Brandon waved her away with a dismissive hand and flicked through the reports.

'That's good. I didn't trust them to keep well away from Stonehenge after the last fiasco but it seems they've got the message. Though,' he added thoughtfully, 'if I could guarantee precision, I'd send a small hurricane to shake up Gabriel and Lilith.'

He glanced up at Jude. 'They've gone suspiciously quiet. Any idea what's going on?'

'None whatsoever,' replied Jude.

'Hmm,' Brandon scrutinised Jude's expressionless face with narrowed eyes. 'Well, I'll know the moment they do make a move.'

Jude tapped the report he was holding.

'There are some brilliant ideas in here – that Eco Foundation of yours wasn't just a front.'

Brandon looked almost offended.

'Of course not. Some of these schemes will come in very useful when we start restructuring. That can be your department.'

'I'll look forward to it,' Jude said with a smile. 'But seriously, I don't see why you have to go to such extremes. You could have done so much to help the world. Now the fossil fuels are running out, and you've made sure that the nuclear option is completely discredited –'

'Surely you don't support nuclear energy,' Brandon interrupted in surprise.

'S-3 is infinitely more dangerous,' Jude replied.

'Not if we have the crystal,' Brandon glared at him. 'That's why you have no alternative but to help me.'

He swivelled his chair towards the PA's office.

'Christina! Get me a coffee!'

62

4 December 2012: Lily and Gabe's farmhouse orchard, Wiltshire

'Nothing wrong with her energy levels now.'

Lily sat down on an old wooden bench beside her husband and together they watched as Rhiannon and the rest of the group worked through the energy control exercises.

'She's very strong,' Gabe agreed, 'but she's driven by anger. If she can't rebalance her chakras correctly, she'll never reach the level of mastery we require.'

Lily shrugged.

'We both know that the major imbalance is the heart chakra. Maybe it's time you talked to her, Gabe.'

The sun was setting as she rose and walked slowly away. Gabe looked back towards the group – something had changed. Rhiannon was standing hands on hips, Tom had his arm round Maya's shoulders while Michael stood with his back to the others.

'Look, I didn't mean to upset Maya,' Rhiannon's voice sounded defensive. 'I just can't understand why you left her father to face Xan and Kayden alone.'

'We had no choice,' Maya began tremulously then stopped as Michael swung round to face them.

'Cut the crap, Rhiannon,' he snapped. 'We all know what this is about. You're saying I'm not worthy to be your partner – I couldn't even defend an old man. Well, you know what? I'm sick of your negative attitude. I didn't choose this fate any more than you did. Do you think I enjoy the thought of being shackled to a woman who treats me with such contempt?'

'Michael . . .' Rhiannon was shocked to the core at the vehemence of Michael's feelings. 'That's not the way I see you . . .'

Michael ignored her, ploughing straight on.

'When I look at you, all I see is anger and resentment. Stop behaving as if you don't have a choice. If you can't do this, then walk away. If you can, then you have to make a commitment, a hundred-per-cent commitment. You owe that to us, and most of all you owe it to yourself. Anything less is pointless.'

With that, Michael stalked away leaving the others open-mouthed.

'I think Gabe wants to speak to you,' Tom muttered, pointing to where Gabe sat.

◎◎

Rhiannon walked over to Gabe and looked at him defiantly. Nevertheless, she was relieved when Gabe smiled and gestured her to sit down beside him. She had a lot of respect for the old man and he had saved her life in the flood. As she looked at him sitting beneath the bare branches of the trees amid the dead and dying autumn foliage she was uneasily aware of the years slipping away for him. Her heart twisted with compassion but when she met his eyes he looked full of life.

'I know, I know,' she began. 'I'm being unfair to Michael and none of it's his fault.'

Gabe smiled. 'Lily told me about your . . . frank discussion. But she understands how you feel.'

'Does she? That's more than I do.'

Rhiannon looked into his kind blue eyes and felt an over-whelming urge to confide in him.

'You see,' she continued, 'it's Jude I feel the connection with. And he feels it too. He was the one who helped me when I was being attacked. I called for him and he saved me.'

Gabe looked at her and gently shook his head. 'That wasn't Jude. That was Michael.'

'Michael! No, I don't believe it.'

'I saw him. The ball of energy he conjured up demolished half a fence before he got it under control.' He suppressed a smile when he saw how upset Rhiannon looked.

'I thought you'd understand,' she began, 'I mean, how would you feel if someone had told you that Lily wasn't your soulmate and you had to be with someone else.' She took a deep breath, 'Like my mother, for instance.'

Gabe went very still.

'I'm assuming,' Rhiannon continued, getting into her stride, 'that you dumped my mother when you met Lily, your true soulmate.'

Gabe was staring into the distance, then stirred as if dragging himself back to the present.

'When did you find out?'

'That you were my father? Only a few days before the fall of Atlantis. I never had the chance to ask why my mother let me go, why you didn't acknowledge me as your daughter.'

Gabe said nothing.

'Tell me. Why?' Rhiannon said fiercely. Suddenly it seemed vitally important to know.

Gabe raised his eyebrows, exhaled softly.

'I thought I was protecting you. Your safety was the most important thing. It still is.'

She didn't return his smile.

'When I was a young man, long before there was any chance that I would become High Priest, I travelled to the Western Isles to study with a Celtic master. Like you, I loved to travel.'

Rhiannon nodded reluctantly.

'While I was there I met your mother, a Celtic princess. We fell in love the first moment we saw each other. I have never forgotten her. That's why you were named after her.'

'Her name was Rhiannon?'

'Yes, and the name of a Celtic goddess seemed appropriate for our beautiful daughter.'

'So what happened if you were so in love?'

Gabe looked away sadly.

'She died a few days after you were born. There was nothing we could do to save her, but she did hold you in her arms before she died.'

267

Rhiannon's eyes filled with tears.

'I thought she'd let me go. That I didn't mean anything to her.'

Gabe put his arm round her shoulders.

'I didn't want to leave you so I brought you back to Atlantis with me. Maybe I was being selfish.'

'So why didn't you acknowledge me as your daughter? Did Lily stop you?'

'No, it was nothing to do with Lily. When I got back, the previous High Priest had died unexpectedly and the city was in turmoil. I was approached as the only candidate who could unite the warring factions and I had to make a choice between family and duty.'

'You couldn't do both?' Rhiannon was not impressed.

'No, but I could keep you near to me and watch over you.'

The sky was almost completely dark, and Rhiannon shivered as a sharp evening breeze sprang up. Above them the moon began her nightly journey across the heavens.

'You're cold,' Gabe said. 'We'd better go in.'

'But what about Lily?' Rhiannon was determined to know everything. 'If you loved my mother, how could Lily be your soulmate?'

'I had a soul connection with your mother, as you have with Jude, but my destiny lay with Lily. We were brought together for a purpose greater than our personal happiness, though of course we have been very happy together.'

Rhiannon stood up abruptly. 'I could have been very happy with Jude. I don't see how I'm ever going to feel that about Michael.'

'I understand, but you must be careful not to confuse the past with the present. The past has made us the people we are today, but we are not the same as we were in Atlantis. Michael is no longer an awkward boy and Jude . . . well Jude is no longer the ardent young hero you used to know. Too much has happened to all of us since then.

He looked searchingly into her eyes. 'Perhaps Jude is your

soulmate but the crystal requires more than a soul connection – it needs the union of two equals. You have to ask yourself if you truly have that with Jude.'

Rhiannon sighed. *None of it makes any sense.* But she was grateful to Gabe for easing at least one heartache. They walked arm in arm through the darkness towards the welcoming lights of the farmhouse.

'Give it time, Rhiannon,' Gabe said softly, 'trust your heart, it will find the way.'

63

They were sitting around the table, their attention focused on the small TV on the kitchen counter when Lily and Gabe joined them.

'It's unbelievable,' Tom said. 'Over ten thousand people dead or missing.'

'And thousands more will die of disease or exposure,' added Michael. 'It's worse than anything I saw in my war reporting days.'

'Another earthquake in Chile,' said Maya to Lily. 'It really feels like time's running out.'

The kitchen lights flickered as if to prove her point. Power shortages were becoming more and more common.

Gabe sat down beside them. 'That's why we've decided that you're ready to go. If you're meant to find the crystal, it will reveal itself to you in Sedona.'

'We may have problems getting there,' said Michael. 'The fuel shortages are affecting flights now.'

'I'll get on to it,' Tom jumped up, eager to get going.

'And once we're there,' asked Rhiannon, 'what then?'

'We've taught you all we can in this limited time, and Maya's powers are well developed. She'll be able to sense the presence of the crystal, and the crystal will recognise her as its keeper.'

Lily's tone was reassuring, but Maya looked less than confident. Rhiannon squeezed her arm, whispering, 'It will drop into your hand, just like that.'

'But a word of warning,' Gabe looked unusually serious. 'All the energy work you've been doing will make you more visible to anyone with Atlantean heritage. That's what happened in Byron Bay. The man who attacked Maya was responding to some ancient programming he wasn't aware of. Atlanteans are drawn to places of power and there are likely to be people in Sedona who will recognise you on some unconscious level. And once you find the crystal they will feel its energy and be drawn to it. They may be friends but just as easily enemies. The destruction of Atlantis left a violent imprint on our supporters and Brandon's supporters alike. They won't understand their reaction, but if their allegiance was to Brandon they will try to take the crystal from you. Try your best to shield your own energy and trust no one.'

'Phew!' Michael ran his hands through his hair. 'Maybe you should be coming with us. It sounds like we'll need all the help we can get.'

Gabe shook his head. 'You don't need us. You can do it, all of you, and we have preparations to make here. Just make sure you're back before the solstice.'

Part III

64

'They're on the move, boss.' Xan looked up from the email that had just pinged into his in box. 'Four tickets booked to Phoenix next Monday.'

'At last!' Brandon felt more animated, more alive, than he had in months. The thrill of being so tantalisingly close to his goal was making him almost shake with excitement.

Xan was less thrilled. It was down to him to get the crystal. He wasn't leaving anything to chance this time.

'Heading for Sedona, no doubt. Do whatever you have to do.' Brandon never concerned himself with the details. 'Just bring me the crystal. Now send Arun up to me. I'm thinking of scaling down the weather operation.'

'Scaling down?' Xan couldn't believe what he was hearing.

'Yes,' Brandon said slowly. 'I think Jude may have a point. The crystal will be of no use to us if we take things too far.'

Xan kept his expression neutral but he was seething inside. *Fucking Jude again.* 'Whatever you say, boss,' he said curtly. 'I have to go.'

Brandon held his hand up.

'Hold on a minute. I haven't finished.'

Xan waited impatiently while his boss chewed the side of his thumb.

'Obviously as soon as you have the crystal, the group can be eliminated.'

Xan nodded. He knew that.

'And if you need any extra ground support you can probably round up some foot soldiers. Bound to be some in a place like Sedona. Remember Xan, we're dealing with Atlanteans, same as us. Do NOT underestimate them. Are you listening? Good, because these people are just as fucking smart as we are.'

Xan doubted that, but he said nothing, remembering that Rhiannon had somehow managed to fight off a man four times her size without any apparent help.

'But the two at the farmhouse, Lilith and Gabriel. They're expendable. You can dispense with them now.' Brandon turned away. 'Deal with it before you go.'

65

The meal had been served, but Rhiannon hadn't touched it. Maya nibbled on the cheese and biscuits, picked at the chilly fruit salad, but Rhiannon just slumped in her seat. Her legs were too long, even in the aisle seat. She hated flying, it made her claustrophobic.

Tom and Michael were five rows forward. Maya could see the two heads, one very blond, one dark.

'How long is the drive to Sedona?' Rhiannon asked.

'Only a couple of hours or so, but Tom has a pilot friend. He's taking us up in his single-engine Piper. Says he can put down where we like.'

Rhiannon nodded approval. 'I suppose landing off-piste might confuse them for a while.' She turned and looked at her friend. 'What are we *doing* Maya?'

Both girls shook their head.

'Best not to ask,' Maya said. 'If we start to analyse why, we'll go mad.'

'But you seem to believe in the truth of it, the overall truth.'

Maya nodded. 'Sure, yes, I do. And if it isn't true, then it's been an experience.'

Rhiannon raised her eyebrows.

'That's very sanguine. And say we get killed in the process?'

Maya suddenly looked tired.

'I don't know Rhi . . . I don't know. All I can say is that I feel compelled to do it. It's not rational but I trust my gut instinct.'

The flight attendant came past collecting the unfinished trays. Rhiannon pulled her thin airline blanket out of its plastic packet and wrapped it round her body. She was always cold these days.

'And this bloody ceremony. The crystal is one thing, but even if we find it, do you really think Lily and Gabe can set up a ceremony with me and Michael as the High Priest and Priestess? I misjudged Michael, I even feel close to him after all we've been through but . . . it's not this cosmic connection Gabe and Lily are talking about.'

'And that's what you felt for Jude?' Maya ventured. She needed to know.

Rhiannon didn't answer at first. Maya could feel her friend's stubborn resistance.

'I can't explain . . . it was as if we were one. I've never had that strength of feeling for anyone, ever.'

'And you don't think it had something to do with the Atlantean thing. Like we have all known each other before?'

Rhiannon shrugged.

'That's what Gabe said, but it went further Maya, so much further. Until Lily . . .'

She sighed.

'How would you feel if Michael walked off with someone else?'

'He wouldn't . . . would he?' Rhiannon thought uneasily of her apology after the argument at the farmhouse and Michael's cool acceptance.

'See what happens, Rhi. Just wait. If it doesn't come right, then it doesn't. But Lily's no fool, she must think it's possible.'

Rhiannon just sighed and turned away from Maya, dragging the inadequate blanket over her ears and trying, unsuccessfully, to find a position where her long legs would fit. It reminded her of being cramped in the boot of that airless car. Despite herself, she couldn't help her thoughts returning to Jude.

Five rows ahead of them Tom gazed in concern at his friend's drawn face.

'Don't give up, mate. I thought you two were getting on much better now.'

Michael forced a smile.

'We are. But there's a big difference between good mates and soulmates. I can't force her to see me as anything more than a friend.'

Tom nodded sympathetically.

'Does she really mean that much to you?'

'Of course,' Michael looked surprised. 'I can't explain it, even to myself, but I know we're meant to be together. Even if all this Atlantis stuff hadn't happened, she'd still be the one, but I don't want her making any sacrifices. I'd rather let her go. She has to want me too.'

'Give it time, mate, that's all you can do. She'll get over this Jude guy.'

Michael slammed his fist against the arm rest in frustration, 'Time is the one thing we don't have.'

66

10 December 2012: Lily and Gabe's farmhouse, Wiltshire

The black car drew up silently onto the verge outside the farmhouse. Gary had driven for the last hundred yards without the lights. But the lights were on in the farmhouse, and a bright bulb lit the porch.

'We better wait, looks like they's still up,' Cal whispered in the darkness beside him.

Gary looked at his mate askance.

'Gone soft have ya?'

'Nah, but it's easier when they's asleep.'

'We're talking about an old man and a middle-aged woman. How hard can it be for fuck's sake?'

Cal said nothing.

'They don't even have a bleedin' dog. Kay saw to that.'

'I don't believe in hurting animals,' Cal mumbled.

'But humans is fine?' Gary cast a cynical look at his mate. Cal wasn't like Kayden. Kay was a fucking psycho. But he'd seen the way Callum set about that techie who'd upset the boss. Fast, efficient and deadly. The poor bugger didn't know what hit him.

The two men got out of the car. Gary opened the boot and pulled back the tartan rug. He handed Callum the older semi-automatic and took the newer one for himself. He loved guns. He'd got this Springfield for peanuts off an Albanian bastard he'd met in the pub. Fifteen rounds, 9 mm ammo. Beautiful. For a moment he cradled the black frame, ran his finger over the polished steel slide.

'Loaded is it?' Cal asked, waving his gun about.

'Nah, don't believe in killing folks with fucking bullets. That's why I gave you a fucking gun, cretin.'

Callum sniggered.

'You crack me up, Gaz.'

∞

They peered at the farmhouse through the border hedge, then forced their way through.

'Fuck!' Callum grabbed his shoulder, wincing in pain. 'Something hit me!'

Gary looked at him in disgust.

'Shut it, you moron. It's just a fucking hedge.'

Callum looked around suspiciously then followed Gary across the grass, avoiding the gravel in the drive. The curtains in the first room were only partially drawn. The room was empty, lit only by a single candle. Moving on past the front door, Gary flattened himself against the stone wall of the farmhouse beside the open window and gingerly moved his head until he could see into the lighted room. The old man sat alone at the kitchen table. He held his head in his hands. Gary thought he looked gutted. Must be the dog.

He turned and beckoned to Cal.

'Problem. I can't see the woman,' he whispered, as they hid around the side of the farmhouse.

'We gonna wait then?'

'Dunno. The old guy's easy, he's sitting like he's waiting for us to shoot him. Window's even open. But we can't risk the woman hearing and calling the Old Bill on us.'

'Are we going in?' Cal asked.

'We'll have to if the woman doesn't show.'

For a moment they hesitated, then they heard talking. Gary gave the thumbs-up sign and they both moved into position, standing in the shadows behind a line of shrubs, around four feet from the kitchen window.

Gary was nervous, pumped up now. He was a good shot, he practised every weekend at the range near his Essex flat. This was almost too easy. Two sitting ducks. The plan was to fire together, just to be sure. He was to take out the woman, Cal the old man.

He lifted his gun and lined it up. She stood with her hand on the man's shoulder, facing the window, talking softly. Such a perfect target, both of them blissfully unaware that they were about to die. He smiled to himself, then silently cocked the gun and checked quickly on his mate. Cal's usually dumb expression had sharpened into the killing machine he was. He looked focused, alert, his gun levelled plumb at the target. They couldn't miss.

Gary held up his left hand, his index finger poised. On the signal they both fired. The noise echoed explosively in the empty countryside, glass shattered. Both men fired repeatedly at the targets. Then the world seemed to pause for Gary.

Unable to believe the evidence of his own eyes he saw the bullets travelling in slow motion towards a shimmering wall of light which swallowed them up then suddenly exploded into a ball of fire. He closed his eyes against the dazzling light and felt something whistle past his ear. Then he heard a soft thud beside him. Callum was lying on the wet grass, clutching his chest.

'What the fuck . . . ?'

Gary looked into the kitchen, there was no one there, no bodies, no blood, nothing. He bent to his partner.

'Cal . . . Cal . . . what's up mate?'

'I think I've been shot . . . help me . . . someone fucking shot me . . .'

Bemused, Gary looked back at the farmhouse. The only evidence that someone had fired a shot was the shards of glass glittering across the kitchen tiles. His own blood ran cold. He looked quickly around him, but the front door was still closed, there was no sign of life at all, no sound to disturb the night. Panicking, he grabbed Callum's gun from his hand and stuffed it into the back of his jeans, then began to haul his friend upright.

'Come on mate, come on, get up,' he urged. They'd sure as hell have called the police by now.

Callum was groaning, a deadweight. Gary put his arm under his partner's, wrapped it round his body, dragged him across the gravel. He no longer cared who heard. This place was downright spooky, he could feel it. How had they escaped? He couldn't have missed, he never missed . . . And what had hit Cal?

When they got to the car he stuffed Callum onto the back seat, then got into the car himself and locked it. He snapped on the headlights, full beam, and noticed his hands were shaking. Taking one last look behind him at the peaceful farmhouse, he cursed and drove off down the lane like a bat out of hell. He couldn't get away fast enough.

'I was wrong,' Lily muttered, as they heard the car drive off. 'I thought Brandon would wait till he got the crystal.'

Gabe shrugged. They were back in the kitchen. He collected the broom from the corner and began to clear up the glass.

'Obviously he thinks we're expendable.'

Lily smiled. 'Brandon never sees the wider picture. It's a flaw. He misses things.'

'Lucky we took precautions,' Gabe muttered.

'Yes, it's good to know we haven't lost our magic,' Lily commented. She felt elated. The endless waiting, endless worry and planning were almost over. Things were moving now, she was sure of it.

67

Sedona airport, Arizona

Maya peered eagerly through the window as the small plane circled and made its final approach. Night had fallen and all she could make out was a bare, desert landscape punctuated by fantastic shapes carved from the red rock by countless aeons of exposure to the elements. The lights of the town were stretched like garlands of Christmas lights – a reminder that time was running out, only eleven days to the solstice.

The engine roared as the plane bounced, then touched down and bumped along the runway. She followed Michael and Rhiannon out of the plane, the cold, crisp night air a welcome relief from the stuffy cabin. The tiny airport occupied a space as flat as a table top, high above the valley floor. As soon as her feet touched the ground she could feel the energy, the power surging through the rocks. She knew that Sedona had at least four major vortices – finding the crystal would be like looking for a needle in a haystack.

Tom stood by the cockpit talking to Joel, the pilot. As the others watched, Joel handed Tom two sets of keys.

'Help yourselves to whatever you can find in the fridge. It'll just be beer and frozen pizza, I'm afraid. I won't be back for a fortnight. And put the snow chains on the truck. There's a snow storm heading this way so you've got a couple of days at most if you're thinking of doing some climbing.'

'We should be out of here by then.' Tom shook his friend's hand. 'I owe you, man.'

'It's not a problem. But, hey, you can show me round London next year.'

'You bet!' Tom replied, hoping that London would still exist by then.

◎◎

The house, a low, sprawling bungalow, was set back from the road leading down from the airport. Inside felt cold and unlived in and they moved around quickly switching on lights, lighting the gas fire, examining the contents of the fridge. Soon the spacious living room seemed more welcoming and Maya turned to the huge plate-glass windows. Pushing aside the sliding door, she stepped out on to wide terrace. The lights of the town spread for miles, and beyond she could make out the shadowy outlines of the mountains. Her eye was drawn to a pale glimmer behind the rocks and slowly the winter moon rose into the sky. Without conscious thought, Maya bowed her head then moved smoothly through the salutation to the moon. As she drew her hands back to her heart she became aware of a figure beside her, following her movements. Rhiannon turned to her, tears streaming down her face.

'It's all so beautiful, Maya, but how can I be part of it? I don't belong.'

Maya shook her head, baffled by Rhiannon's inability to recognise her own spirit.

'But you do. You just have to open your heart to it –' Maya stopped, not wanting to upset her friend further.

She saw Rhiannon take a deep breath and begin to pull herself together.

'It all seems so . . . so alien to the way I've lived. But, hey,' she grinned with some of her old feistiness, 'I suppose I've come this far. Don't expect miracles,' she added, when she saw Maya's face lighten.

'What would be a miracle is if either of those two men can cook. I'm starving!'

◎◎

They sat in front of the fire sharing the three beers from the fridge while Tom heated up a frozen pizza.

'We must be on the lookout,' Michael warned. 'Xan and his thugs can't be far behind us, and we may have trouble with the people Gabe warned us about.'

Rhiannon raised her eyebrows. 'Would people really do that? Fight and kill without knowing why they're doing it?'

There was silence for a moment.

'We saw it . . . in Byron,' Tom said quietly. 'Erik would have killed me. He tried very hard.'

'It doesn't really matter how or why. We just have to be vigilant,' Michael repeated, and was relieved that Rhiannon didn't argue.

68

11 December 2012: Sedona, Arizona

The house was quiet, the others still asleep as Rhiannon grabbed a cup of coffee and opened the sliding door on to the terrace. *Let's see what this place looks like in daylight.*

The panoramic view before her took her breath away. Pure white snow glistened on the mountain peaks but lower down the slopes the red rocks glowed with fiery intensity. She felt shaken to the core by the beauty and majesty of the place.

'Quite a sight, isn't it?' Tom leaned on the railing beside her, sipping a cup of coffee.

'It's amazing, the colour of the rocks, the fantastic shapes . . . I've never seen anything like it.'

Tom pointed across the valley. 'That's Coffee Pot Rock.'

Rhiannon peered in the direction he was pointing and sure enough, the tall thin rock appeared to have a spout on one side and a handle on the other.

'Do they all have names like that?'

'Well, some do. Camel Head, Steamboat . . . Snoopy.'

'Snoopy? Like the dog?'

'Yeah, it looks like Snoopy lying on his back on his kennel, nose in the air.'

Rhiannon laughed. 'I'd like to see that.'

'That's the plan. I thought we'd drive round, see if Maya gets a feel for any one place.'

Hours later, Maya was in despair. She slithered the last remaining feet to the base of Bell Rock and looked at the hopeful faces of her friends.

'It's not here. It's the same as Cathedral Rock – incredibly powerful energy but not what we're looking for.'

Rhiannon was reassuring. 'At least you can feel the energy. You'll know when it's right.'

'Will I? I hope so.'

Tom looked at Maya's anxious face.

'Time for a break. We've been searching for hours. You're tired and cold.'

He hustled them back into the truck and drove to the main street of uptown Sedona. The town was busy, the store fronts bright and welcoming. Rhiannon glanced into the windows as they passed. *Crystals everywhere*, she thought, *but we're no closer to finding the Heartstone.*

Tom led them into a coffee shop and Michael ordered while the others settled into a table by the window. Outside the winter sun was sinking fast, adding a luminous fiery glow to the red rocks. Flakes of snow drifted slowly by. Maya turned anxiously to Tom.

'We've got to find it before the weather breaks.'

'We're good for another day or two.' Tom was happy to be back on his home ground. He knew how the place worked, he could feel his confidence growing. 'Once we've got the location, I'll get us there. No probs.'

Michael was waiting patiently at the counter for their coffees. Suddenly Rhiannon nudged Maya.

'Look. That girl over there. She's watching Michael.'

Maya glanced over and saw a slender redhead edging towards Michael, never once taking her eyes off his face.

'She's trouble,' Rhiannon hissed. 'I can feel it.'

She began to rise from her seat but Maya pulled her back.

'I don't think she's a threat,' Maya said with a grin. 'At least, not in the way you mean.'

Over at the counter the girl was writing on a piece of paper and handing it to Michael with a shy smile. Michael smiled back at her and, blushing, the girl headed for the door,.

As Michael put their coffees on the table, Rhiannon glared at him accusingly.

288

'What was all that about?'

Michael shrugged. 'She said she's a fan of my work. She gave me her number.'

'Oh.' Rhiannon looked furious and glared towards the doorway but the girl had gone.

'Rhi,' Maya whispered, 'relax. She just fancied him. That's not a problem is it?'

'No, no. Of course not.' Rhiannon was feeling embarrassed now and more than a little confused. *Where did that streak of possessiveness come from?*

Looking up, she met Michael's puzzled eyes and looked away quickly.

Tom looked around the table, suddenly aware of the tension.

'OK, guys,' he said briskly. 'Let's call it a day. We're bound to find it tomorrow.'

◎◎

Twenty-four hours later Tom thumped the dashboard in frustration. Hours of driving through steep and winding canyons had brought them no closer to finding the crystal.

'Are you sure you didn't pick anything up, Maya?' he asked yet again. 'We've only got eight days left. Sorry,' he added as Maya shook her head wearily.

'I'm sure it's here,' she said distractedly, 'but it's like listening to a radio playing several stations at once. I just can't tune everything else out. There's so much going on here.' Her voice trailed away.

'What we really need is some specialised local knowledge,' Tom was looking thoughtful.

Rhiannon laughed. 'Yeah, right. Excuse me, nice local person, can you help? We're looking for the fabled Merkaba crystal of Atlantis and we thought you might know where it is.'

Tom ignored her sarcasm.

'There is someone I think might help us. The only problem is finding him.'

69

Tom parked the truck and walked into yet another New Age shop. Since he'd left the house that morning he must have visited at least a dozen. Crystals sparkled on the shelves and the smell of incense drifted through the air. Wind chimes harmonised with the laid-back New Age music. Tom headed for the notice board and scanned the various cards – reiki, yoga, hot stone massage, meditation, aura soma, crystal healing, but the name he was looking for wasn't there. Maybe Hari was still in India.

As he was leaving, he bumped into a plump dark-haired girl, bundled up against the cold.

'Hey Tom! Long time no see. How's Australia?'

'Great, great, just back for a visit. Catching up with old friends.'

'There's a magic dance party tomorrow night. We'll all be there.'

'Sounds good. Any word on Hari?'

'Yeah, he got back a few weeks ago. He's living in a trailer out by Oak Creek.'

Tom grinned with relief.

'I might go look him up.'

'Just past Indian Gardens; if you reach Slide Rock you've gone too far.'

The girl looked at him in surprise as he gave her a hug.

'Just glad to be back in the red rocks.'

She smiled understandingly. 'Everyone feels that. See ya.'

Tom climbed back in the truck and set off for the house. Instinct told him that Hari could help them. And his instinct better be right – he didn't have a Plan B.

◎◎

Maya moved gracefully through the grounding exercise Gabe had shown them, painfully aware of Rhiannon fuming beside her. Michael lounged by the fire, reading up on Sedona.

Finally Rhiannon stamped her foot in frustration.

'I just can't feel it today, and it doesn't help having Michael watching every mistake I make.'

Michael rose unhurriedly to his feet and headed for the door. Maya caught his arm as he passed and he smiled down at her.

'Don't worry Maya. It's cool.'

As he closed the door quietly behind him, Rhiannon muttered, 'I wish he wouldn't be so fucking understanding.'

Maya grinned. 'Yes, it's so irritating. If only he'd be as rude to you as you are to him.'

Against her will Rhiannon burst out laughing.

'I really am sorry. I'm still not sure if he's forgiven me for that argument we had at Gabe and Lily's.'

Maya stared at her friend in bewilderment.

'What's going on, Rhi? You've been in a strange mood ever since we got here.'

Rhiannon rubbed her eyes and sighed.

'There's just something I can't work out. You know when I was locked up and that thug attacked me . . .'

Maya nodded. Rhiannon hadn't told them much more than the bare facts.

'I couldn't fight him off, I thought he was going rape me. I was so desperate I called to Jude to help me. And something happened. A blast of energy appeared from nowhere and knocked him flying.'

'Jude did that? He saved you?'

'That's what I thought. I wanted it to be Jude but Gabe told me it was Michael.'

'And that's a problem?'

'Oh, I don't know what to think. I'm so confused. I've been pushing the thought away but maybe Michael is more on my wavelength than I thought and now all I seem to do is antagonise him.'

'And you didn't like it when that girl chatted him up.'

Rhiannon's look of dismay was almost comical.

'There's no pleasing some people,' Maya teased her. 'Two gorgeous men coming to your rescue and you're still not happy.'

'I know, I know. But the more I think about it, the more awkward I feel around Michael.'

'Then don't think about it,' said Maya. 'Concentrate on the grounding exercise. It might even help.'

This time Rhiannon began to feel a flow to her movements as the tension left her body. It reminded her of her karate training, but something was different: there was an element she hadn't felt before. She couldn't quite pinpoint it but to her surprise she suspected it might be joy.

Tom burst through the door as they were eating lunch.

'I've found him!'

The others looked enquiringly at him.

'His name's Hari. He lived here for years before he went to India – following the path of the seeker. Anyway, he knows everything about Sedona, its history, the Native American traditions, the sacred places.'

'If they're sacred places, would he tell us about them?' Maya looked doubtful.

'I don't know. But we can try.'

Oak Creek, Indian Gardens

Tom drove cautiously along the highway leading north out of Sedona. The road was icy and although the snow hadn't settled yet, flurries drifted down from the pine trees clinging to the precipitous cliffs to their left. On the other side they could see Oak Creek racing down the valley.

'Must be somewhere near here,' Tom muttered as he passed the trading post at Indian Gardens. He slowed, then suddenly turned on to a rough track that led through pine trees and bushes festooned with a dusting of snow and glittering icicles. The track ended at a clearing close to the water. A single dilapidated trailer stood next to an old station wagon.

'You two stay here,' Tom said to Michael and Rhiannon. 'I've got a feeling it's Maya he'll talk to.'

'If he talks to anyone,' Rhiannon muttered. She wasn't happy being left in the truck with Michael, sidelined again. *Still,* she reasoned to herself, *this is more Maya's territory than mine.*

'Maya's into all this stuff, Rhiannon. There'll be plenty for you to do later.' Michael's quietly spoken words mirrored her thoughts so closely that she turned to him with a delighted grin. Michael smiled back, a little warily, and Rhiannon turned away abruptly, apparently absorbed in the landscape.

Tom and Maya walked towards the trailer. The air was icy but so pure and clean they felt almost light-headed. The trailer looked deserted apart from thin wisps of smoke drifting through the half open window. Tom sniffed the air.

'Incense . . . and weed. This may not be a good time to disturb him.'

He tiptoed to the window and peered in. He could just make out a figure sitting cross-legged in front of a low table covered with candles.

'Is he meditating?' Maya whispered.

'Yeah. That or stoned.'

As they stood uncertain what to do next, they heard the skitter of paws on the rocky ground and a large shaggy creature ran purposefully towards them. Maya shrank back in alarm. *Did they have wolves here?* Then relaxed and held out her hand. The large, unkempt husky bounded up to her and licked her fingers.

'I think we've come to the right place,' said Maya as the dog barked loudly towards the trailer. After a moment, the door opened and a tall, thin figure appeared, dressed only in T-shirt and jeans, despite the cold.

'Hari, hey man. Long time no see.'

Hari swept his tangled black hair away from his face and smiled, his eyes icy blue against his dark tan, and gestured them to come in. He seemed unsurprised by their arrival.

'This is Maya,' Tom introduced her and for a moment they stood awkwardly in the cramped, dark space. There was very little furniture – a mattress on the floor covered with an Indian blanket, a low table, a few posters and wall hangings.

'Can we talk, Hari? We need your help.'

Hari shrugged, nodding slowly as Tom settled himself on a floor cushion. Maya found herself drawn to a collection of crystals arranged on the table. Her hand hovered over a beautiful moonstone, then drew back.

'You can hold it.' Hari smiled as Maya held the stone reverently between her hands, then turned to Tom.

'You got here just in time guys. A few more days and I'll be riding the rays to Sirius.'

Maya sat down beside them.

'The solstice?'

Hari raised his eyebrows. 'When else?'

Tom and Maya exchanged glances. *You or me?*

Maya took a deep breath and leaned forward, still holding the moonstone in her hands.

'There's something we need to do. Urgently. Before the solstice. Something we have to find.'

Hari looked pleased. 'A quest. I like it!'

'But . . .' Maya didn't know how to go on.

Hari scratched his head thoughtfully.

'I can see that you serve the goddess, the divine feminine.'

Maya nodded uncertainly.

'And you need to reclaim the power of knowing.'

Neither Tom nor Maya knew how to answer this.

Hari looked away from her towards the candle flame flickering between them. He stared into the light, his gaze suddenly blank. He seemed to withdraw from them. After what seemed a long time, he looked up. His crystal-blue eyes focused on Maya as he began to speak in a soft voice.

'In the winter, the bear enters the cave – the place where in dreams we find the answers to the questions that trouble our reality.'

Tom looked blank, but Maya leaned forward eagerly.

'A place where answers are found, sacred to the feminine?'

Hari bowed his head gravely.

Maya's eyes lit up. 'Tom, is there a Bear Mountain here?'

Tom leapt to his feet excitedly.

'Hari, you're a genius! Both of you are. Come on, we have to go. Thank you . . . thank you.'

Hari nodded, pressed Tom's outstretched hand. He seemed as unsurprised by their departure as their arrival.

'See you on the other side, cosmic travellers. And here,' he handed Maya the moonstone.

Maya backed away.

'No, no, it's yours. I couldn't possibly take it.'

Hari shook his head.

'Not up to me. Crystals decide where they go, not us. But then you already know that.'

He waved them off. '*Hasta la vista* . . . till the other side . . .'

West Sedona shopping centre

Tom eased the truck into a parking space and turned off the ignition.

'So, we're all agreed? First thing tomorrow we tackle Bear Mountain.'

'We could check it out now,' Michael suggested. 'Give Maya a chance to see if it's the right place.' He was reluctant to waste any more time.

'It is the right place, I'm sure of that,' Maya said confidently, 'but it'll be dark soon.'

'And way too dangerous,' Tom added. 'It's a straightforward climb in summer, but there's snow on the upper slopes now. We need to plan this carefully and take supplies in case it takes longer than we expect.'

Rhiannon's stomach turned over. She hated heights at the best of times. A tricky climb in midwinter filled her with dread.

The supermarket was busy and Christmas songs played quietly in the background. Rhiannon felt a twinge of regret. How pleasant it would be to belong here, choosing food for dinner, going home to her soulmate. Her heart ached and Maya hugged her briefly with instinctive sympathy.

As they stood at the checkout, Rhiannon suddenly felt uneasy. Glancing round she saw a heavily built man with short cropped hair staring directly at her.

'Maya,' she hissed, 'trouble,' she indicated behind her with a turn of her head. Maya instantly began packing their shopping at top speed.

'Let's go!' Behind them, the man took out a mobile and punched in a number.

They raced towards the truck, forcing the unwieldy trolley over the frozen, bumpy ground. Michael, coming to help them, stopped short.

'What's up?'

'There was a man watching us. I think he's one of them,' Maya gasped as they unloaded the shopping and leapt into the truck. Tom took off, tyres squealing as he headed for the highway.

'It may be nothing,' Michael said hopefully, but they all knew that wasn't true.

70

'Isn't this great!' Tom stood beside the truck and spread his arms wide, embracing the crisp morning air, the red rocks, the clear azure sky. 'I can't wait to get started. We'll find the crystal this morning, be on a plane tonight and still have a few days to prepare for the solstice.'

Rhiannon smiled politely, trying to hide her trepidation about mountains and heights in general.

He put the last of their bags in the back of the pickup and pulled the tarpaulin tight.

'I used to climb around here a lot when I was younger. Bear Mountain's more a hike than a climb, just one or two tricky bits near the top. It'll be a walk in the park.'

Rhiannon envied his enthusiasm. Last night Tom and Michael had exercised for hours, moving more and more quickly until some of their moments became a blur. Time was she would have joined them, enjoying the pace, the swirling interplay of yin and yang energies. Instead, she had joined Maya, attempting the Merkaba mediation and making little headway.

Michael and Maya emerged from the house, locking the door behind them.

'Got everything?' Michael asked. 'We may not have time to come back here once we've found the crystal.'

The truck, with Tom driving, set off down the steep, twisting road leading to the highway. Michael and Rhiannon, together in the back, kept checking the rear window for anyone following them, but there was very little traffic so early in the morning. By the time they turned into Dry Creek Road they were the only car on the road. As the truck crunched over icy patches of snow,

Tom glanced up at the sky.

'Those clouds are moving fast. I reckon we've only got a couple of hours.'

'Just as well it's only a walk in the park then,' muttered Rhiannon.

As they turned into Boynton Pass Road, Maya sat up sharply.

'The energy's suddenly very strong here, we must be getting close.'

'It says here,' said Rhiannon, looking up from the trail guide she was holding, 'that the energy of Boynton Canyon recalls past lives! Got to be a good sign.'

'Bear Mountain's this way,' said Tom. 'Whoa! They've paved the road since the last time I was here. Used to take ages bumping over the potholes.'

Maya wasn't listening, her eyes fixed excitedly on the mountain range to her right. The crystal was up there, she was sure of it.

Tom parked the pickup and they set off across a flat meadow, the yucca and juniper bushes sparkling with a fine dusting of snow. Ahead they could see the trail zigzagging across the lower slopes of the mountain.

That doesn't look too bad, thought Rhiannon.

The first stages were as easy as Tom had promised. After twenty minutes the switchback trail opened out onto a plateau and they rested briefly. Far below they could see the truck, but apart from that the vast landscape was deserted.

'We have to cross a canyon, then up to another plateau like this one,' Tom told them. 'After that it gets a bit more tricky. Ready?'

Tom set off again at a brisk pace followed by Maya then Rhiannon and Michael. Rhiannon plodded steadily upwards, averting her eyes from the view, until they reached the second plateau. There, the views were spectacular, the whole panorama of the red rocks stretching out in front of them and beyond to the vast, empty plain. Rhiannon shrank back, astonished at how high they had already climbed. Michael caught her eye but she forced a bright smile, *I'm fine!*

298

Tom was leaning over the edge, checking the car park.

'No one's following us that I can see,' he told them.

Maya was itching to get going again but after a few minutes the trail stopped at a steep rock face with only a narrow ledge going on round the corner. Tom edged carefully along the ledge and disappeared from view.

'It's this way,' he called back, 'take it slowly.'

As Maya edged carefully around the rock face and out of sight, Michael turned to Rhiannon. Her face was white. *I can't do this,* she thought, then realised Michael was watching her. Gritting her teeth she edged around the rock face and stopped, horrified. Ahead she could see Tom and Maya sidestepping along a ledge no more than six inches wide. To one side, sheer rock, to the other a drop of hundreds of feet. She felt her head spin, her legs turn to jelly. *I'm going to fall.*

'Rhiannon.'

Rhiannon heard Michael's concerned voice behind her but she couldn't move. She closed her eyes and felt her heart pumping as if it would burst from her chest. *I'm going to be sick . . . I'm going to fall . . . I'm going to die.*

'Rhiannon.' Michael's voice was close and calm in her ear.

'Listen to me, just listen. Did Maya tell you about the earth star?'

Rhiannon couldn't speak, she just shook her head very slightly, still clinging to the rock for dear life. *Save the New Age baloney,* she thought angrily.

'Listen to what I tell you,' Michael's quiet voice continued calmly, 'I can't do it for you but you can do it for yourself. You can.'

Rhiannon tried to get her breathing under control.

'Remember your connection to the earth. A few inches beneath you is your earth star. Concentrate on the energy flowing down through your body . . . through all the chakras . . . down, down and into rocks and the earth beneath.'

Rhiannon gulped back a sob and tried to do what Michael said. *You've been in worse situations than this, girl,* she told

299

herself sternly, seeing a flash of Kayden's leering face. She forced herself to concentrate, to marshal her energy. Gradually, all other sounds ceased except the in-out-in-out of her own breathing. Her heart began to slow as she felt the breath building, coursing through her body, strong and pure, flowing downwards towards the earth.

She gasped with astonishment.

'It's working?' Michael asked anxiously.

Torn between tears and laughter, Rhiannon nodded. 'There's a problem though. I daren't move . . . the connection might break.'

'It won't. Just move slowly and focus,' Michael reassured her.

Rhiannon took one step, then another. The vertigo had gone. She felt amazingly at one with the elements and had to fight an impulse to skip along the rest of the ledge.

'Thank you,' she whispered.

'You did it yourself,' he replied. 'I only reminded you of something you already know.'

Rhiannon continued along the ledge to find Tom and Maya standing in a small open space. Ahead of them was sheer rock. Tom looked puzzled.

'It's a dead end. I must have gone wrong somewhere.'

Maya shook her head. 'This is right, I'm sure of it.'

Michael noticed a small round opening a foot or so above his head.

'Is that a cave?'

Maya started scrambling up towards it and the men helped her reach the opening. She looked back down.

'I'm going in.'

Tom and Michael helped Rhiannon climb up and squeeze through the opening. It wasn't a cave at all, more a window leading to a small flat platform surrounded on four sides by rock but open to the sky.

Maya looked at her with shining eyes. 'It's here . . . I know it . . . it's right here.'

Michael and Tom dropped down to join them.

'Where?' Rhiannon glanced around the space doubtfully. 'There's nothing here but solid rock.'

Maya ignored her. She walked slowly across to the farthest wall and stood silently before it. Tentatively she raised her hand and passed it back and forth across the hard surface. Rhiannon felt so tense she could hardly breathe. Then Maya placed her left hand firmly on the rock and bowed her head.

Rhiannon stifled a gasp of surprise. 'Look!' She could see a very faint glowing outline appearing beneath Maya's hand. Gradually the outline resolved itself into the shape of the Star of David as tiny sparks of light exploded from the rock.

There was absolute silence for a moment, no one dared to speak, no one noticed the small flakes of snow that had begun to fall.

The Heartstone. Rhiannon could hardly believe it. Had they really found it?

Maya brought her hands together in one fluid movement and began chanting a single low note which gradually grew in intensity, drawing in higher and higher tones and reverberating around the stone walls in a sinuous unearthly melody. The outline of the crystal grew stronger as the rock surrounding it began to vibrate and shimmer like water, then suddenly drew back to reveal the crystal hanging suspended in mid-air. A blinding light dazzled them momentarily and their vision cleared just as the crystal dropped neatly into Maya's outstretched hands.

'Yes!' Tom shouted with joy and pulled Maya towards him into a tight hug.

Rhiannon turned to Michael and to her surprise, and his, kissed him passionately on the lips. Just as abruptly, she sprang away from him, trying to make sense of the myriad emotions flooding her body. Was this just the effect of the crystal? Then her mind cleared.

Michael had given her an incredible gift. He wasn't her protector like Jude had been. He had shown her she could protect herself. With Jude, she would always depend on his strength and wisdom. With Michael she could stand beside him as an equal.

Michael stood watching her, more than a little confused. They both joined Maya rather self-consciously to admire the crystal. It was the most amazing stone they had ever seen. One upright triangle of purest crystal quartz fused into a second inverted triangle to produce eight glittering points. Looking closely they could see a suggestion of a red glowing heart. But even as they watched, the light began to fade, leaving the crystal an unremarkable lump of quartz.

'What's happened?' Tom looked anxiously at Maya. 'The light's gone. Is it still working?'

Maya still cradled the stone lovingly in both her hands.

'Nothing's wrong. We should get it back to Lily as soon as possible. She'll know what to do next.'

Rhiannon groaned at the thought of the journey back down the mountain but her new-found equilibrium brought her safely along the ledge and they had reached the lower plateau before they stopped for a rest.

Tom looked dubiously at the sky. The snow was beginning in earnest now, with thick black clouds sweeping in from the north. They would have to hurry if they were to stay ahead of the storm. As they began the final descent they suddenly heard heavy footsteps thundering down the trail above them. Out of nowhere a figure rounded the corner and bounded towards them. A woman wearing a cowboy hat, heavy boots and climbing gear swerved towards them, a broad smile on her face. Startled, they began to smile back, but the woman kept on coming towards them, hurling herself directly at Maya.

Tom moved to stop her, but she was too fast. She lunged at Maya's backpack, where the crystal was hidden, but Maya was quicker. She sidestepped neatly, just eluding the woman's outstretched hand.

With a snarl of rage, the woman lost her balance and hurtled over the edge of the rock.

They looked at each other in horrified silence. Michael rushed to the edge and peered down, expecting to see her body broken on the rocks below. Instead he watched her continuing down the steep slope with sure-footed speed.

'Weird.'

Maya clutched her backpack tightly to her.

'She was definitely after the crystal. She came straight for me.'

Far below they heard the revving of a car engine.

'She's probably gone for reinforcements,' Michael said. 'Is there any other road out of here?'

'There is,' Tom replied, 'but it takes us away from Sedona.'

'We can't go back there anyway now. Let's go.'

They reached the car park in minutes and jumped into the truck. As they sped off, the snow began to fall in earnest.

71

Red Canyon Road, Highway 89A, Sedona

'Stop! Stop now!'

Tom slammed on the brakes and the truck skidded uncontrollably on the icy road before coming to a halt. Rhiannon leaned forward urgently from the back seat.

'Look! At the junction.'

Tom peered through the whirling gusts of snow. The storm had broken and visibility was down to a few yards. Rhiannon's sharper eyes had seen what he hadn't: two square, black jeeps blocking the turn on to the highway.

'Traffic accident?' asked Maya.

Tom shook his head. 'I don't think so. That woman targeted you on the mountain. These must be the reinforcements.'

Maya shuddered. 'The look in her eyes was just like Erik.'

Tom glanced at Michael and Rhiannon. 'She probably didn't know what she was doing, any more than Erik did.'

'That's not a big help,' Rhiannon broke in. 'They're still lethal.'

Tom considered the options. 'We can't go back. Even if they haven't blocked the other exit yet, the road will soon be impassable. We've got to get onto the highway somehow.'

Michael shrugged. 'Then we force our way out. Think the truck can take it?'

Tom punched the air. 'Sure. Hold tight everyone, we're going through.'

He slammed the truck into gear and stood on the accelerator, trusting the chains to keep them on the road. In the back, Maya clutched the bag containing the crystal. She would never let it go.

As they picked up speed, they saw the two jeeps start to move and turn towards them, travelling side by side and completely blocking the road.

'Shit,' Tom shouted. 'They're trying to force us off the road.'

'They're going to ram us,' Michael yelled back as the black jeeps accelerated towards them like sharks scenting their prey.

The gap between them closed and Tom looked desperately through the driving snow for a way past. Almost blinded by the oncoming headlights, he took a split-second decision and wrenched the wheel to the right, bouncing off the road and avoiding a collision by inches. The jeeps roared past, then screeched to a halt.

Tom revved the engine, the chains grabbed and they were almost back on the road when the truck lurched to the side and the engine stalled.

'It's stuck,' Tom shouted. 'Must be a pothole.' He tried desperately to restart the engine.

'They're stopping,' Rhiannon gasped. 'They're reversing back this way.'

Tom frantically turned the key in the ignition.

Behind them two men leapt out of one of the jeeps and started running towards them. The truck's engine spluttered, stalled, then finally caught, the wheels spinning uselessly. Just as the men came alongside, the truck juddered then freed itself, and they hurtled off towards the highway.

'Way to go, Tom!' Michael clapped his friend on the shoulder.

'Shit!' Rhiannon was staring out of the rear window. One of the men had jumped onto the back of the truck and was clawing his way along the tarpaulin. She caught a glimpse of ice-cold eyes filled with hatred, as the man struggled to his feet and raised a tyre iron.

'Look behind, one of them's on the truck . . . Tom . . .'

Tom steered violently from side to side sending the truck into a fishtail, but still the man clung on. Desperate, Tom stamped on the brakes and as the truck came to a juddering stop the man overbalanced and topped over the side.

'Where is he?' Tom yelled.

'Lying in the road. I can see headlights, they're stopping.' Rhiannon turned back, 'They can sense the crystal.' Maya's face was white with fear. 'Don't stop. Go, go!'

'Are they still there?' Michael asked.

Rhiannon watched the sinister black jeeps gaining ground through the snow and fading light.

'Right behind us.'

Tom put his foot down.

'Any ideas guys?'

Michael frowned, 'We can't outrun them. Not in this weather.'

Tom slapped his hand on the steering wheel.

'I've got an idea. It's worth a try.'

The road began to climb and the engine whined in protest. The windscreen wipers were fighting a losing battle against the blizzard outside.

'There's an old mining town, up ahead,' Tom yelled above the noise of the storm. 'It's almost deserted, just empty buildings. The streets double back on each other like a maze. We may be able to get off the main road and lose them there.'

Ahead of them they glimpsed old wooden houses clinging precariously to the sides of a steep canyon. Tom drove dangerously fast up the narrow main street following a hairpin bend down and to the right.

What is this place? Rhiannon didn't think she was over-sensitive to atmosphere but this place was spooky. It felt abandoned, haunted.

Tom suddenly took a sharp turn into an alley barely wider than the truck.

'There should be a cut through – oh fuck!' He slammed on the brakes. Ahead of them a rickety old building had collapsed, completely blocking the narrow road. There was no way through.

Behind them they heard cars pull in to the entrance to the alley. Tom switched off the engine and they sat in silence in the sinister half-light as the snow swirled around them. For a

306

moment they could see nothing, then two sets of headlights on full beam lit up the road behind them.

'How many do you think there are?' Tom asked quietly.

'Not sure,' Michael replied. 'Six? Maybe seven? We could take them.'

He glanced at Rhiannon. 'Stay with Maya. The crystal's our priority.'

Rhiannon opened her mouth to argue then thought better of it. He was right.

Tom and Michael got out and scanned the dark alley. Seven figures were walking silently towards them, a terrifying phalanx of muscle and silent fury. Michael stood close to Tom and tried desperately to remember everything Gabe had taught them.

'We can do it,' he heard Tom hiss.

Suddenly the group of men began to sprint towards them. Their silence was more disturbing than battle cries. Michael and Tom adopted defensive positions, preparing themselves for the onslaught. But their opponents acted as one, an overwhelming fighting machine. Michael and Tom landed blow after blow, twisting and turning their bodies like quicksilver, their limbs slicing like blades at the oncoming hulks. Gabe would have been proud of them. But the enemy was relentless and possessed the same fighting skills. Tom disappeared under the weight of attackers, feeling the icy stone beneath his back, the blows raining down on his face, his chest, his gut. He was trapped. He knew it was over. Michael couldn't help him. He fell to one knee, winded by a vicious blow to his kidneys, searching desperately for some purchase on the slippery ground.

Suddenly the freezing air was split by a blood-curdling scream. The sound reverberated across the narrow alley, bounced off the stone walls, building to an ear-splitting crescendo before finally dying away. Their attackers fell back, momentarily stunned, and one man clapped his hands to his nose as blood ran down his face. Rhiannon raced to Michael's side and pulled him to his feet.

'How did you do that?' he gasped. His ears were still ringing.

'Kiai-jutsu, the hero shout. I've never managed it before but I saw you in trouble and it just happened.' She stood proudly beside him, a war-like glint in her eyes.

'Help me with Tom,' Maya yelled, starting to drag Tom's inert body towards the truck. At the far end of the alley, the enemy had regrouped and was beginning to advance towards them again. Rhiannon and Michael smiled into each other's eyes. *This may be the end, but we're together.*

At the far end of the alley, Xan leaned against his car, arms folded, watching the action. This was better than he'd expected. Let the peasants do the dirty work. He punched in Brandon's number and when he answered held his smartphone towards the scene unfolding in the alley.

72

'Check this out, boss! Another few minutes and we'll have the crystal.'

Brandon scrutinised the murky image on his phone. What the hell was going on?

He could just make out Rhiannon and her friends at bay. He didn't recognise any of the men attacking them. Must be local muscle.

'Just make sure none of them gets out alive,' he snapped at Xan.

Jude turned from his computer screen, a look of horror on his face. He seized the phone and took in instantly what was happening.

'Call them off! You have to stop them now!'

Brandon angrily shook his head at his brother.

'Do anything to save the girl, eh?'

Jude threw the phone back to him.

'I said stop them. I thought you understood. The crystal is just another lump of rock until it's activated . . . by . . . them.' Jude hesitated on the word 'them'.

Brandon blanched, then shouted into the phone.

'We need them alive, Xan. Do you hear? Alive. All of them. Do whatever it takes. They die, you die.'

The screen went black.

Brandon turned slowly to Jude. 'Anything else you haven't told me?'

Mining town near Sedona

'Look,' Rhiannon turned to Michael, fear in her eyes, 'Xan and Kayden.'

Unspoken thoughts passed between them. *It's all over.*

They watched mesmerised as Xan moved swiftly towards them, followed by the hulking figure of Kayden. As he strode closer, Xan casually grabbed the nearest man and snapped his neck like a twig. The other men swung round in surprise, as Kayden waded in, fists flying. Within seconds, four men lay silently on the ground while the others cowered against a wall.

This makes no sense. They've saved us. Rhiannon stood rooted to the spot until Michael grabbed her hand and bundled her into the truck.

'What'll we do now?' Rhiannon asked. She glanced back anxiously at Tom, who was lying doubled up in the foetal position, groaning softly. Maya sat beside him, his head in her lap.

'We can't get out,' Michael stated flatly, looking at the two menacing black shapes parked tight up at the head of the alley. The snowstorm had blown itself out and they could both see clearly there was hardly a foot between the jeeps.

As they waited, paralysed by the horrific, yet unreal scene in front of them, Xan casually dispatched the last man standing with a sharp chop to the side of his neck.

Even at this distance Rhiannon could see the cold, blank eyes of Crowe's front man. She shivered.

'What's going on? I thought they were on the same side.'

'If they were,' Michael replied, 'they're expendable now. I don't –'

He stopped mid-sentence and watched in amazement. Xan was signalling to the jeeps blocking the alley. Within seconds, whoever was inside had begun to back the vehicles out of the restricted space.

Michael looked at Rhiannon.

'They're letting us go?' she whispered incredulously.

Xan turned to their pickup in the fading light, stood aside and, with a contemptuous bow, made a gesture ushering them towards the exit.

Rhiannon looked at Kayden, who was glaring at her, murder in his eyes.

'Go,' she hissed, 'go, go, before they change their mind.'

Michael didn't need encouragement. He gunned the pickup and reversed down the narrow street like a bat out of hell, the chains on the tyres clanking and shifting until they found purchase on the frozen snow.

As he shot recklessly down the winding hill none of them spoke. Now that the storm had passed they could see the reassuring lights of Sedona across the plain, but Michael didn't slow down until they reached the highway.

'Did that really happen?' Rhiannon asked quietly. The previous two hours seemed totally unreal, like a nightmare from which she would wake.

Tom stirred and sat up, rubbing his head.

'What happened?'

'Xan and Kayden . . . they killed them . . . the men who attacked you . . . at least I think they killed them.' Rhiannon was shaking now the adrenalin had worn off. 'Then they let us go . . . bowed us out. We can't work out why.'

'Must be orders from on high,' Tom muttered, then groaned. 'God, I feel like shit. My head's splitting.'

'But why?' Maya, who'd been silent since they'd left the alleyway, spoke so softly that the others barely heard her.

Rhiannon turned to check that her friend was all right, but saw that Maya looked calm and in control. More so than Rhiannon felt.

'Whatever his reason, it doesn't matter,' Michael chipped in. 'We're safe, thank God, and we still have the crystal. Now we need the fastest way home. What's the best way to Phoenix, Tom?'

73

Lily and Gabe's farmhouse, Wiltshire

Lily moved away from the seer stone, white with shock, and Gabe looked at her with concern.

'I thought we'd lost them. The hypnotic effect of the crystal was even stronger than I feared. They must have been Atlanteans to react like that, prepared to kill to get it back. Then Brandon's men turned up. They saved them. Why?'

'It's got to be something to do with Jude. He must have told Brandon that the crystal can only be activated by us.'

Lily frowned. 'What else has Jude told him?'

'Only enough to save their lives.' Gabe looked so sure that Lily kept her doubts to herself. At least they were safe for now. She changed the subject.

'Michael and Rhiannon. They've got to reach a level together that only we have known. The union of the twin souls. I'm not sure they can do it.'

Gabe smiled at her. 'Maybe not our level, but they're doing OK. And they have found the crystal. We need time to prepare for the solstice but they should be back in a couple of days.'

Lily remained silent. Something was not right.

Uptown Sedona

'Don't get it, boss,' Kayden was grumpy. He'd had a bit of fun with those zombie types, but what he wanted was the girl. He'd been promised the girl. 'What was we here for if it wasn't to, like, slot the girl and those jessies she hangs out with?'

He heard Xan sigh.

'We're not to hurt them. Seems this fucking crystal they found doesn't work if they're dead.'

'Huh? Don't get it.'

'You and me both, Kayden.'

'So what we gonna do now?'

'We have to follow them. Make sure they don't disappear with the crystal.'

Kayden harrumphed and slid down the car seat, crossing his huge arms across his chest.

'Fuckin' mental.'

'Go and get yourself something to eat,' Xan told him. He wanted to be alone to think and this moron was driving him nuts. What a waste of bloody time and organisation. A waste of resources. He could have monitored them easily without going to all this fucking trouble. The boss had lost it. Clearly the brother was in charge now.

The thug brightened. 'Yeah . . . OK . . . get you somefing?'

Xan shook his head, still angry. He'd have his day in court on this fiasco, he'd make sure of that.

Phoenix Airport, Arizona

Leaving the battered truck in the car park, Michael followed the others through the heaving crowds. They'd have to square the damage with Joel later. If there was a later. The atmosphere was hectic, far more people than he would have expected, even with Christmas so close. They forced their way into the International terminal and stood amazed at the sheer volume of people. Huge queues snaked around the building, passengers looked bewildered and frantic, clustering round airport staff, questioning and shouting. The noise was deafening.

Rhiannon glanced up at the departures board.

'What? Look, guys: "All flights to Europe cancelled".'

They turned to a TV screen above them. A rolling news channel showed endless shots of a volcano spewing fire and ashes into the air. The Icelandic volcano, Eyjafjallajökull, that had caused so much trouble to air travel in 2010, had erupted again and Britain and northern Europe were cut off from the rest of the world by a cloud of toxic ash.

313

'Fuck.'

'What are we going to do now?'

Tom sank to the floor, clutching his head.

'Can't believe this. We've come all this way, done the impossible, and now we're fucked by a stupid volcano.'

Michael nodded. 'Does seem a bit harsh.'

'And it's only six days till the solstice,' Maya added anxiously.

'It can't take us six days to get home,' Rhiannon said. But as they stood watching the chaos, the terminal echoing with the high-pitched demands of the hundreds of stranded passengers, she added softly, 'Or can it?'

74

Brandon's office, west London

Jude leaned his forehead against the cool surface of the plate-glass window and breathed deeply as his racing heartbeat returned to normal. *Rhiannon was safe – at least for now.* The night sky was dark, overcast, but the lights of the city stretched to the far horizon and the busy roads pulsed with energy. Human beings going about their business with no idea that existence hung on a thread.

He suddenly became aware of his brother's reflection, pacing restlessly back and forth behind him. Slowly he tuned in to Brandon's angry voice.

'. . . and what else haven't you told me? Can I even believe what you *have* told me?'

Jude turned and faced him. 'Only the Seven can activate the crystal. That is the truth.'

Brandon looked searchingly into his eyes. 'And the solstice? Why do we have to wait till then? Or were you just buying time?'

Jude sighed wearily. 'That also is true. I know astrology bores you but the solstice is the only time when we can access the energy needed to release the power of the crystal.'

Brandon nodded. Instinct told him that this much, at least, was true. 'So,' he continued, 'there's no point in rounding them up now and forcing them –'

'No!' Jude turned back to the window.

'OK, OK, just thinking aloud.' Brandon moved to stand beside his brother. 'But there's still something you're not telling me.'

Jude looked at their shadowy reflections with a pained smile. *So alike and so different. The light and the dark. But which was which?*

315

Brandon picked up this new sense of doubt. *Jude was weakening. Go for his Achilles heel.*

'I don't understand your problem with Rhiannon. As far as I remember, she was just a novice. Gabriel and Lilith did the sacred union of the male and female crap –'

Brandon stopped short as it hit him. 'Of course! The twin cores. That's why the replica wouldn't work. There's a second stage of activation, isn't there? Isn't there!'

Jude stood rigidly silent but Brandon knew he was right.

He moved away, leaving Jude to his thoughts. As he reached his desk, his mobile rang.

'Xan, where are you?' He listened intently. 'OK . . . Don't follow them . . . No need . . . Just get back here as fast as you can.' He sat back in his chair, suppressing his impatience to end the call. 'No . . . that's not your problem. If they're as resourceful as I think they are they'll be back by the solstice . . . Yes, yes I'll explain everything when you get here. Yes . . . everything's going according to plan.'

There was silence in the office for a moment, while Brandon mulled over what Jude had said. He'd always assumed it would be Lilith and Gabe who'd attempt the ceremony. But perhaps not.

'Got it,' he waved his hands triumphantly at his brother. 'Got it. It's Rhiannon, isn't it. Your Rhiannon's taking over as High Priestess.' Brandon couldn't hide his amusement.

Jude said nothing, turning away from Brandon's sneering.

'You wanted Lilith, couldn't have her. And now Rhiannon. So who's the lucky man? Tom Page?'

Brandon thought for a moment, then quickly dismissed the idea. 'No, it's the other one, the dark guy on the motorbike, always hanging around the girl.'

Brandon glanced at his brother's agonised face and saw an opening.

'Jude, this is crazy. You're giving up the woman you love for what? Something that happened thousands of years ago?'

'It's my fault it all went wrong in the first place,' Jude snapped back, 'so my happiness isn't important. Putting that mistake right, keeping the earth safe, is all that matters.'

Brandon sensed the divided loyalties in his brother's heart.

'If you let this go ahead, Rhiannon is lost to you forever. And what does *she* want? Don't her feelings count?'

Jude flashed back to their first meeting – the inevitable coming together of soulmates, Rhiannon's broken-hearted look of reproach as he turned her away – and he buried his head in his hands.

Brandon delicately put his arm around Jude's shoulders.

'Jude, we can find a way around this if we work together. I can help you get what you want. And you can save the planet too.'

Jude smiled sadly. 'You really believe that, don't you? Maybe you're right. Maybe there is another way.'

75

Phoenix Airport, Arizona

'So nobody knows anything!' Michael turned away from the harassed ground staff and rejoined the group, shaking his head. All around them was hysteria, pushing and shoving, tears, shouting, with groups of dispirited travellers slumped on their luggage. It looked hopeless. The four moved off to get some coffee and sat in silence as they sipped from cardboard takeaway cups. Rhiannon seemed deep in thought, but suddenly Michael noticed a light in her eyes.

'I've got an idea.' She dug out her mobile and moved off to stand against the wall, away from the noise and crowds. They watched as she embarked on a long and animated conversation.

'Maybe she's got a mate with a Learjet,' Tom said hopefully.

'A cruise ship'd be better,' Michael muttered.

'No sea,' Tom replied.

'OK, it's complicated,' Rhiannon said when she eventually got back to them. 'I called my friend Diane, who works for Trailfinders. She's checked it out and says our best bet is to fly to JFK, then to Portugal – which is south enough to be clear of the cloud – then trains to Paris and the Eurostar to London.'

'How long will it take?' Maya asked.

'That's the bad news. If we make all the connections it could still take four days.'

'So we could be back by Tuesday or Wednesday at the latest.' Maya chewed her lip, wondering if that would give them enough time to prepare for the solstice on Friday, and then turned to Tom, anxiety clouding her blue eyes.

'Will you be OK to travel?'

'I'll be fine,' he answered cheerfully though the nasty welt across the left side of his face looked raised and angry. 'Can your friend organise it, Rhi?'

'I told her to go ahead. Hope that's OK?'

They all nodded, relieved.

'The tickets should be through here within half an hour. But she says we can't get on a flight to JFK till the morning now.'

'At least that will give Tom time to rest,' said Maya, determined to look on the bright side.

Airport hotel, later that evening

'Why did Brandon's thugs let us go?' Michael mused as he lay sprawled on the hotel room bed. 'They must have known we had the crystal. Why didn't they just take it off us?'

Tom slumped wearily in the uncomfortable armchair, delicately probing the angry graze on his face.

'Because they knew it wouldn't work without our activation?'

'But why did they suddenly know that?' Michael lay back on the bed, exhausted.

'You mean if they knew that all along, why did they chase us in the first place?'

Michael nodded.

'It's got to be Jude. Crowe didn't know. He can't have. Jude must have told him at the last minute – in time to call the dogs off.'

Neither spoke for a while.

'My head hurts,' Tom got up and gazed at his battered reflection in the mirror. 'I need a hot shower.'

'So does this mean they aren't after us now?' Michael persisted as his friend disappeared into the tiny hotel bathroom. 'Are we safe until the ceremony? It'd be good to know.'

Tom poked his head around the bathroom door.

'Look, I don't understand zip about any of this crazy business. I'm just doing what I'm told. Ring Lily, ask her.'

'It's the middle of the night in England,' Michael told him. 'Anyway, she'll have seen it all already.'

76

16 December 2012: Stonehenge

There were only two other cars in the visitors' centre car park. *Not surprising*, Gabe thought, as he watched the horrific weather beating against the windscreen of his car. Although it was barely ten in the morning the sky was dark as night, the pitch-black clouds lowering close to the earth as if they were threatening to engulf it. They looked like snow clouds, but it was rain that poured down in torrents, the wind catching it and blowing it around in sheets, like a demented dance. Gabe struggled out of the car, managing to close the door before it was blown off its hinges.

The stones stood proud and solid, seemingly unaffected by the maelstrom crashing around them. No one was there. For a moment he stood, absorbing the energy from the stones. They always calmed him, centred him, reminded him from whence he came. He looked around. There was no sign of extra security for the winter solstice. The druids would be there in force no doubt, and the hippies. It wasn't as popular as the summer event, but this was 2012 after all.

What worried Gabe was how the Seven were going to slip unseen past Brandon's thugs. The stones were fenced off; the only way into the inner circle was via the tunnel from the visitors' centre. It was after the second stage of activation when they'd be vulnerable. Brandon would be waiting to pounce and snatch the all-powerful crystal, making absolutely sure they had no chance of completing the ceremony. But fighting off the thugs and completing the ceremony at the same time – he really didn't see how it was to be done. He gazed up into the heavens. Behind the clouds, that's where Sirius lay: his spiritual home. Would he and Lily ever see it again?

Barely able to stand against the wind and rain, Gabe battled his way back to his car. This reminded him of the last days of Atlantis. He could almost feel the planet shaking on its axis. If it was like this in five days' time, there would be no ceremony. And that was assuming the others made it back in time. Still, they were crossing the Atlantic now. There was hope.

Lily and Gabe's farmhouse, Wiltshire

'The roads are getting really bad,' he told Lily. 'I only just made it back. If it doesn't stop raining soon, we'll have trouble even getting to the 'Henge.'

'If bad weather was his aim, Brandon certainly gets a gold star.'

'This isn't just Brandon, Lily. It's way beyond his powers. This is the planet hanging on for dear life. It's so destabilised it can barely function. And yes, Brandon hasn't helped.'

Lily threw her hands up in the air.

'The roads, the sun, the guards round the stones . . . none of this will matter if the others don't get here.' She looked at Gabe. 'And then there's . . .'

Gabe sighed. 'He'll come,' he assured her.

77

17 December 2012: Valladolid, northern Spain

'Now what?' Tom groaned as the train slowly reversed away from the station and came to rest in a siding. They were all exhausted by the endless journey – the flight from Phoenix to New York, the long hours on standby waiting for seats on the flight to Oporto. Then the scuffle for places on the overcrowded train and they were still hundreds of miles from home. Now, when yet another day was coming to a close, the train had stopped.

Michael listened attentively to the staccato burst of Spanish coming from the tannoy.

'The service has been terminated,' he translated, 'because of an incident . . . something nuclear . . . in Marseilles.'

He turned to the others. 'They're refusing to cross the French border. We all have to get off.'

Wearily they picked up their bags and left the stuffy compartment which suddenly seemed the height of luxury. The evening stars appeared above them as cold pinpricks of light and a sharp wind whistled along the crowded platform.

Tom and Maya huddled together and Michael looked at them with concern.

'Can you find somewhere for them to rest?' he asked Rhiannon. 'I'll go and sort out some transport.'

Rhiannon nodded. 'I'll call you when I've found somewhere.'

They smiled briefly at each other and Michael disappeared into the milling crowd.

Three hours later he joined them in a small hotel which was overflowing with stranded travellers.

'I paid over the odds but I think it'll get us home.'

They looked out of the window at the ancient black Jeep

Cherokee parked outside and Rhiannon raised her eyebrows.

'We'll be back in two days max,' Michael said confidently. 'Now everyone get some sleep. We'll leave first thing in the morning.'

18 December 2012

Michael drove the first lap, and Rhiannon monitored the satnav on his phone. They'd been on the road over six hours already. Traffic was heavy and now darkness was closing in. They had stopped once, outside San Sebastián, but Michael refused to allow anyone else to drive. Maya and Tom were asleep in the back now, and the world seemed only to consist of Rhiannon and Michael together in the front of the jeep, the headlights lighting their way north.

'OK,' Rhiannon spoke up in the darkness. 'You have to stop at the next service station, before Bordeaux. Not only do we need petrol urgently, but I'm going to drive.'

Michael cast a quick glance at her.

'I'm fine,' he said.

'Sure you are. What? Are you scared of being driven by a mere woman?' Rhiannon teased.

'Not scared, but we have no time to waste.'

'And me, being a woman, will drive at a piddling, girly speed which ensures we miss the solstice you mean?' Rhiannon laughed. She thought how angry his remarks would have made her a few weeks ago but now she just shook her head.

'You're a good map reader,' Michael conceded with a grin.

Rhiannon ignored his remark.

'Just stop the car at the next service station. You've been driving on empty for the last twenty minutes.'

Signs to Bordeaux flashed up.

'It says take the exit toward Paris/Toulouse/Bordeaux/Talence. Here . . . here . . . slow down,' Rhiannon gesticulated at the next exit.

'We're not going to Bordeaux,' Michael complained, but obediently pulled right just in time.

'Just do it,' Rhiannon held his iPhone tightly in her hand. It seemed to symbolise their only contact with the real world. She felt if she could follow its instructions to the letter, order would be restored; they would get back in time. They would do what had to be done.

Michael drove into the silent, almost deserted service station, its neon lights casting a ghostly hue on the few huddled occupants, and pulled up at the pumps.

'I don't believe this,' he muttered, jumping out of the car and running towards the café.

'What's up?' Maya asked sleepily from the back seat.

Rhiannon pointed at the roughly scrawled notice draped across the pumps.

'No petrol.'

Michael opened the door and peered in.

'There's a problem with the deliveries. Something to do with the explosion in Marseilles. There's a tanker on its way.'

'When?' Rhiannon exploded in frustration.

Michael shrugged.

'OK,' Rhiannon pulled herself together. 'Let's get something to eat. Assuming they haven't run out of food and drink as well.'

Four hours later Rhiannon shifted uncomfortably in her seat and looked out of the car window for the hundredth time, hoping to see the petrol tanker arriving. Behind her Tom and Maya slept huddled together under a blanket, and Michael dozed beside her. She found herself watching his sleeping face, the laughter lines around his eyes, the few streaks of silver in his dark hair, then suddenly blushed as if she'd been caught out in something embarrassing. She felt she was seeing him clearly for the first time and realised with a shock just how important he was to her. Her heart started to hammer in her chest and Michael, as if aware of her scrutiny, opened his eyes and smiled.

'Rhiannon?' he whispered.

'Yes, what?' she whispered back, as headlights suddenly swept across them and a giant tanker rolled to a stop at the petrol pumps.

'Tell you later,' he said, putting the car into gear and joining the rapidly forming queue at the pumps.

'OK,' she said. 'But I'm driving.'

19 December 2012

The car responded well to Rhiannon's touch. She loved driving, always had.

'Fuck,' Michael swore softly as she narrowly missed a giant Norbert Dentressangle HGV, which suddenly skewed in front of them just outside Poitiers. 'Take it easy.'

Rhiannon didn't reply. She was enjoying herself. Enjoying having Michael beside her, admiring and fearing her driving skill. She almost forgot why they were there, in the middle of France in the middle of the night. Almost.

This journey was just the beginning, she realised. If everything went right in this lunatic venture, she and Michael would be standing together on Friday morning in the centre of Stonehenge. Could she do it? Could she share her heart with this man here beside her?

'What'll we do when we get to Le Havre?' she heard Michael ask.

'Get a ferry?'

Michael snorted in exasperation.

'Well, obviously. I meant what'll we do if there are massive queues?'

'No idea. The Chunnel'd be way quicker obviously, but you say it's closed.'

'Yup, snow in the engines or something; wrong sort of leaves, you know the thing. Same deal as 2009 or whenever it was.'

'It doesn't feel cold enough for snow.'

'It doesn't. But there's been loads further north apparently.'

Rhiannon groaned. 'That's all we need . . . bloody snow.

What day is it?'

'Morning of 19 December.' The car clock said it was 5.30 a.m., but it was still pitch-dark outside and would be for at least another two and a half hours.

Suddenly, in the chilly pre-dawn darkness, there was an almighty crash. All of them jumped. The heavens lit up in a terrifying crackling and thundering light show, then almost instantaneously rain engulfed the car in a torrential cascade. Rhiannon couldn't see a thing out of the windscreen, even with the wipers on the highest speed. This reminded her of that night at Stonehenge.

'Fuck – pull over,' Michael shouted.

'Can't do that,' Rhiannon shouted back. 'We'd be a sitting duck on the hard shoulder.'

'You can't drive in this,' he said.

'I don't have much choice.'

'What's happening?' Tom mumbled from the back.

'Not a lot . . . just the world coming to an end,' was Rhiannon's terse reply.

The road ahead was already awash, the water sliding across the tarmac in waves. Then almost as suddenly as the rain had begun, it stopped. The blazing lights in the sky dimmed to a threatening radiance on the horizon, and hail stones the size of golf balls began pounding on the roof of the car like grenades.

They huddled inside the car, shocked, the jeep crawling along the icy road in convoy with the few other cars out at that time of the morning on the almost deserted autoroute.

But the storm hadn't finished. Snow quickly replaced the hail. Huge, perfectly formed snowflakes began crowding the windscreen, coming at them like daggers, then melting away against the heat of the glass.

'I can't see a bloody thing,' Rhiannon muttered.

'Pull over,' Michael repeated. 'I said, you can't drive in this.'

Rhiannon didn't bother to reply. She wasn't about to die in a sodding French snowdrift.

There was a tense silence as Rhiannon inched the jeep forward blindly, their world suddenly reduced to the interior of the car itself. Nothing else could be seen, nothing heard, as the snow muffled all sound like a heavy blanket. Outside the storm grew in intensity, the wind howling, the temperature dropping viciously.

'We'll freeze to death,' Tom said cheerfully, dragging Maya against his side when he noticed she was shivering violently.

'Reminds me of . . . back then . . . Atlantis,' Maya whispered into his shoulder, her words barely audible above the storm. No one responded. No one wanted to hear.

'They won't run the boats in this,' Tom said.

'We won't *get* to the bloody boats in this,' Rhiannon replied.

'How far are we from Le Havre?' Maya asked.

Michael consulted his mobile, typed in a distance request.

'We've just passed Le Mans. In normal weather we're just over two hours away.'

There was a tense silence in the car. Rhiannon clutched on to the wheel like grim death, her eyes, already tired and scratchy from lack of sleep, wide and fixed on what she could see of the road ahead. As the storm let up a little, some drivers began to ignore the conditions, impatiently picking up speed in the fast lane, sliding from side to side as they went.

'Stupid bastards,' Rhiannon swore under her breath.

'Maybe it'll stop people turning up at the ferry,' Michael suggested hopefully.

Tom grunted. 'Yeah, maybe. But they'd be the sensible ones if there aren't any boats.'

Michael clicked the keys of his phone.

'The ferry doesn't leave till 5 p.m. Gets in at 9.30 p.m. We should make it.'

After what seemed like hours, the frustration at their slow crawl palpable from everyone in the car, Rhiannon peered out of the windscreen, looking up at the blank, snow-choked sky.

'Don't hold your breath, but I think it's passing.'

Michael glanced up from his phone.

'Yeah, looks promising.'

'OK, guys,' Rhiannon flexed her shoulders, shifted in the

seat, took a huge breath. 'Hang on to your hats.' She gripped the wheel and pressed her foot hard down on the accelerator. The ancient jeep responded satisfactorily, bounding forward as if it had just been released from captivity.

Until the lights of Le Havre came into view, the only sound in the car was Michael's clipped directions to Rhiannon.

Lily and Gabe's farmhouse, Wiltshire

Lily had sat at the seer stone through most of the night. Gabe dozed in the armchair, got up to make them tea occasionally, or joined her at the table. They had watched the four as the car made its way slowly through Spain, then north through France into the snowstorm, towards the ferry terminal. They saw the growing intimacy between Michael and Rhiannon. At one point Lily looked up at Gabe, and despite her tiredness there was a smile on her face.

'They seem to be closer.'

Gabe, also watching, nodded.

'Will they make it in time?' he asked, for the hundredth time. It wasn't really a question; he knew Lily couldn't answer him.

Lily shrugged.

'At least it will all be over, one way or another, in the next twenty-four hours. We've given it our best shot.'

She felt Gabe's hand on her shoulder, squeezing it gently.

'I'm beginning to get excited,' he whispered. 'We've waited so long it hardly seems possible that we're nearly there.'

78

Jude squatted against the back wall of the squash court and towelled away the sweat trickling down his face. They'd been playing all out for over an hour and Jude knew Brandon wouldn't give up until he'd won. He glanced across the court. Brandon was ten years older but in great shape, quick and ruthless. Jude rubbed the bruise forming on his shoulder where Brandon's racquet had whacked him. Brandon caught the gesture and grinned.

'We can stop any time you want, Jude. Just admit defeat.'

Jude leapt to his feet. 'Your serve!'

'We're two of a kind, Jude, you know that.' Brandon stood ready to serve then lowered his racquet. 'You really think your plan will work?'

Jude nodded.

'OK. Go to the farmhouse tomorrow night. But I want a guarantee that I can trust you.'

Jude raised his eyebrows. 'Such as?'

'Remember the unbreakable oath? When we were boys?'

'"May I die in torment if I betray you",' Jude quoted. He looked steadily into his brother's eyes. 'If that's what it takes.'

'It is, and now . . .'

Brandon served with lightning speed hoping to catch Jude at a disadvantage, but Jude was ready for him.

Xan, watching impatiently from the gallery, was forced to admire their skill as they fought to return impossible shots, but he wished they'd get on with it. He needed to speak with Brandon urgently. His narrowed eyes followed Jude around the court as he thwarted Brandon's every move. *Patience*, he reminded himself, *he's in favour now but my time will come.*

And then, payback.

His thoughts were interrupted by an angry shout from the court below.

'It was NOT out!'

'Out by a mile, Brandon. Game and match to me!'

Brandon looked furious but at least the game was finally over. Xan headed down to the door opening into the court where he could hear the argument continuing. As he stepped onto the court, Brandon picked up the ball and served viciously. The ball ricocheted off the wall and headed straight for Xan who ducked awkwardly to avoid it. Seething inside, he straightened up to see Jude standing next to Brandon whose good humour had been miraculously restored.

'Xan! You're back. Just in time to witness a historic event. My brother beat me at squash.' He turned to Jude, smiling. 'Make the most of it. It'll never happen again.'

Jude returned the smile and despite their outward dissimilarity the brothers looked almost like twins. At that moment Xan wasn't sure which brother he hated the most.

79

19 December 2012: Le Havre, France

They crossed the Normandy Bridge and arrived to find the Terminal de Grande Bretagne white and sparkling in the snow. The port was huge, stretching miles to the east, the acres of colourful container terminals – now uniformly white – flanked by the high white gantry cranes lining the quays. But the ferries had been disrupted because of the storm the night before.

'*Mais il n'y avait pas ferries la nuit dernière. Le temps en Angleterre est très mauvaise. Nous ne savons pas si le ferry arrivera aujourd'hui.*' A thin, harassed official muttered to Michael.

'He says the incoming ferry has been trapped in England because of the appalling weather.'

'*Quand allez-vous savoir si ça vient?*' Michael pointed to the sky and grinned, '*Il fait beau maintenant, non?*'

The man shrugged in true Gallic fashion.

'*Oui, oui . . . mais je n'ai aucune idée.*'

'He says he hasn't a clue when it'll come.'

'Very helpful,' Rhiannon commented.

So they had waited, tense and tired, one of them accosting a different port official every half an hour and getting the same negative response. Then at around six o'clock that evening – when they'd all but given up getting back to the farmhouse that night and were sunk in silent despair – the welcome lights of the ferry hove into view.

The storm erupted again when they were within sight of land.

'Is this how it will end?' Maya whispered fearfully to Rhiannon

331

as they huddled on plastic seats inside the smelly interior of the boat, gazing out of the misted windows. Even the solid cross-channel vessel had begun to hurl itself left and right as the sea was whipped up by the storm.

'Don't think like that,' Rhiannon told her. 'It's not over yet. As soon as we complete the ceremony then . . . things'll get better, won't they?'

Maya nodded.

'That's what Lily says. The balance restored. But there is so much to do and the solstice is the day after tomorrow.'

Rhiannon thought Maya was on the edge of tears, and she put her arm protectively round her thin shoulders.

'You're tired. We'll be there soon. You'll see, Lily will know what to do.'

Road to the farmhouse, Wiltshire

Tom took over the driving when they disembarked from the ferry at Portsmouth.

As they struggled down the lanes leading to Gabe and Lily's farmhouse, the weather ripping into the car and skewing it off-course, wind howling like a banshee, freezing sleet slashing the windscreen, Rhiannon sat beside Michael in the back of the car. They were both exhausted by their marathon drive, but the tiredness was like a drug, making them light-headed, almost euphoric. Rhiannon was intensely aware of him beside her in the dark. They weren't touching, they weren't even looking at each other, but she felt as if they were. Her barriers were down, she was too tired to be defensive, and she realised that all she wanted to do was lean into him and feel his arms around her. She did not dare look at him.

'Left . . . next left,' Maya shouted above the mayhem.

'This one?' Tom leaned forward, trying to make out the road ahead. He yanked the wheel to the left, almost clipping one of the stone pillars that flanked the entrance to the farmhouse.

◎◎

Gabe threw open the door and ushered the four tired and frozen travellers inside. There was intense relief as they realised they were finally at the end of their journey and were together again. Michael hugged Lily close.

'I wasn't sure we'd make it,' he said.

Lily laughed.

'I was sure you would,' she said proudly.

Maya collapsed on a kitchen chair and carefully let go of the backpack she'd been nursing for the last week, barely letting it out of her arms. She unzipped the black canvas and took out a bundle of grey sweatshirt and placed it tenderly on the wooden table. Everyone was silent with anticipation, Lily particularly. It was thousands of years since she had set eyes on the Heartstone, and she could feel her heart quicken.

Maya drew back the edges of the sweatshirt to reveal what looked disappointingly like a lump of dull brown rock. But Lily knew what to expect. She leaned forward and let her fingers run gently, almost lovingly over the rough surface. Within seconds of her touch, the crystal began to lighten.

'Wow,' Tom exclaimed. Like the others he looked shattered. But the weal on his face was beginning to heal and the swelling had gone down.

'But first,' Gabe ordered, 'you must eat. Get your strength back.'

The four were ravenous and for a while they ate in appreciative silence, the Heartstone sitting there between them, a potent reminder of why they were all there.

The clock chimed 2 a.m. Rhiannon looked at Lily. For a moment their eyes met. There was challenge there from the younger woman, met with confident authority from the older one.

'What happens next?' Michael asked.

'We have to complete the first stage of activation of the Heartstone,' Gabe replied.

'But we can't, can we?' Maya said, 'Without . . . without the Seven.' She cast an anxious look at Rhiannon as she spoke, unwilling to name Jude.

'We will be Seven,' said Lily with authority, 'by this time tomorrow. Now you must rest.'

80

Rhiannon knelt by the grave Gabe had dug for Atlas and brushed away the dead leaves covering the tombstone. Her fingers traced the circle and crescent that were now so familiar to her and she struggled to contain her sadness for the dog that had died trying to save her and her anger at the casual brutality of the man who had destroyed him. *One day, Kayden, you will pay for this.*

'Rhiannon.' Michael's voice broke into her thoughts and she jumped to her feet in confusion. They hadn't had a chance to speak since that moment on the journey when she had felt they were on the brink of some kind of breakthrough.

'Don't worry,' he said gently. 'I just wanted to tell you that I understand that it may be difficult for you this evening . . . if Jude turns up.'

'Of course he'll turn up,' she replied tersely, then immediately felt sorry for the hurt she saw in his eyes.

'Whatever,' he hesitated, suddenly looking boyish and awkward. 'Maybe this isn't the time, but I wanted to say something, before it all kicks off.'

She waited.

'I wanted you to know that I love you, not because I have to, just because I do. I think you're the most incredible woman I've ever set eyes on.'

'Oh, Michael.' Rhiannon felt her heart would break. She so desperately wanted to tell him that she loved him too, but something was holding her back.

He lifted his hand and laid it gently against her cheek. She didn't pull back, but wrapped her arms around him and they stood motionless as the sun sank beneath the horizon and the evening star shone down on them.

Michael was the first to stir.

'Come on,' he said. 'Lily's waiting for us.'

Lily's workroom, Wiltshire

The room was lit with row upon row of fat beeswax candles, the atmosphere hot and flickering with reflections from hundreds of crystals.

There were already seven chairs placed around the honeywood table. Lily moved her seer stone and replaced it in the middle of the table with the Heartstone. It was now no longer rough brown, but a soft, glassy yellow, the myriad facets catching the light from the candles and creating an intense, hypnotic radiance which drew everyone's gaze.

'Sit,' Lily ordered.

Tom obediently moved forward and sat in the chair nearest him. He wasn't sure what was about to happen, but he was without thought, on automatic pilot, just doing what instinct told him to do.

Maya sat to his left. She was the only one of the four who was perfectly in tune, confident at last in her ancient role as Keeper of the Crystal. Being so physically close to the crystal since they had left Bear Mountain had softened her twenty-first-century self, taken her back to her Atlantis soul. As a result, she, of all of them, had found the journey across continents in the real world the most traumatic.

Michael hovered, then settled one away from Maya. Like Tom, he had instinctively given himself over to the moment. Gabe put himself between Maya and Michael. Rhiannon held back, reluctant to sit down, to finally commit to this terrifying enterprise where she would hold such a vital role. In the end she sat down beside Michael. She looked at the one remaining seat shimmering in the candlelight – still empty. For a moment she hoped he wouldn't come so she wouldn't have to face him, then pushed the thought away. Far greater things were at stake. The silence stretched and Michael stared challengingly at Lily.

So where is he then, your golden boy?

Suddenly the candles all flickered then dimmed, leaving the room in darkness for a second.

'Welcome!' Lily's joyful voice pierced the gloom and the candles flared into a brilliance that revealed Jude sitting in the empty chair.

'So glad you could join us,' Michael said, his arms crossed tight over his chest. Tom looked bewildered, Maya relieved.

Jude said nothing. Rhiannon found herself staring at his handsome face, so heartbreakingly familiar. His sea-green eyes held hers and she saw a terrible sadness there. As if he were saying goodbye. And in that moment, she knew Jude was letting her go. The ache that she'd carried since that foggy night in Scotland, the longing to be with him, be part of him, to never to let him go, was slipping away. She felt quiet, at peace.

Gabe's voice pierced her consciousness, stern and in command.

'It's time,' he said, nodding at Lily.

81

'I can't believe you let him go!'

Xan glared at his boss, unable to understand why Jude had been allowed to leave alone.

Brandon stepped closer, arrogantly invading Xan's space.

'How dare you question my decisions.'

Xan quailed inwardly at the fury in those cold blue eyes but stood his ground.

'I don't trust him. And I've seen the others in action. It's not going to be easy to take the crystal from them.'

'Losing your nerve, Xan?' Brandon taunted. 'If you're not up to it, maybe you'd better just fuck off.'

Xan took a deep breath. He'd invested too much in this to walk away now.

'Boss, I've stuck with you on this through thick and thin . . . been with you since the beginning. You've got to listen to me. At least you owe me that.'

Brandon nodded grudgingly. 'Go on.'

'I think we should forget the crystal and concentrate on the replica. We know a lot more about the twin cores now and,' Xan paused, 'and even without your brother's help we can probably make the replica work. I know we can. It might take longer, but we aren't risking so much.'

Brandon's expression was stony.

'You've forgotten one thing. If they activate the crystal, then go on to seal the portal, S-3 is lost to us forever. A replica would be utterly pointless.'

Xan ploughed on.

'But that's the thing. I'm saying stop them before they have the chance to activate the crystal. Go to the farmhouse now – they're bound to be there. Destroy them. Destroy the crystal before they seal the portal. The timing's impossible if we allow them to activate it. And once the portal's sealed we can never reverse it.'

Brandon relaxed slightly. 'I hear what you're saying. You're right about the danger and the split-second timing, but you've forgotten something. We have a secret weapon: Jude.'

Xan exploded. 'You're crazy to trust him. Look what happened last time.'

'Enough!' Brandon's tolerance was at an end and Xan flinched as if he'd been struck.

'Now, you listen to me. We need to be in position at Stonehenge well before sunrise. If the roads are still impassable, organise the helicopter. Understood?'

Xan stared back impassively then bowed his head.

'Understood, boss.'

82

Lily's room, Wiltshire

Into the silence Lily closed her eyes and began to chant – a low note deep within herself, unused for aeons, yet still profoundly familiar. She felt the energy of the vibration rise strong through her body, touching each chakra as it went, lighting the path towards the Heartstone. She heard Gabe take up the note, hold it, guide it through his own sacred centres. She felt his ecstasy as their souls came together within the vibration and a pure, illuminating light began to build around them, enveloping them all in its powerful aura. It both flowed from the Heartstone, and flowed towards it. The crystal was all the time becoming brighter, more translucent. Maya took up the chant, reaching her hand to rest against the crystal's surface. Tom followed suit, his voice deep and pure. The sound was breathtaking, more a living presence than a note, which swept around and through the seated figures, blending with the rays now emanating from the pulsating Heartstone. Red, orange, yellow, green, blue, indigo and violet, the rainbow rays began to split into seven distinct paths of light which enveloped each of the Seven in turn. Jude joined the chant. Only Rhiannon and Michael remained. As if by common consent, they both touched their fingers to the smooth, cool stone at the same moment. As they did so, the seven rays came together, joined above the Heartstone in the twin flame that represented the balance of male and female energy, the harmony of the planet. As they watched, the flame was drawn down, absorbed into the crystal itself, lighting it from within, creating the most extraordinary, almost blinding luminosity. Each face was bathed for a moment in the unearthly radiance, before it died to a steady, silver-white glow.

The first stage was done.

'I had forgotten its power,' Gabe's voice was low and reverent.

Lily smiled at him almost teasingly, 'How could you? It's what we were born for, you and I.'

For a moment no one else in the circle existed. It was just her and the man who had loved her, believed in her, followed her so faithfully through the ages.

'We have to plan,' Jude interrupted them softly.

Lily covered the crystal, wrapping it in soft purple velvet. The silver glow was still visible through the cloth. The group, dazed by the power of the Heartstone, moved like sleepwalkers away from the table.

Gabe herded them through to the warmth and normality of the farmhouse kitchen. Rhiannon noticed the clock on the wall said 4 a.m. For a moment she felt sick with apprehension.

'We have to leave for the 'Henge as soon as possible,' Gabe announced. 'Brandon will ensure the stones are cordoned off by his bodyguards – our only way in is through the visitors' centre tunnel, and they will be expecting us. He will know to wait till we've completed the second stage of activation, when the crystal is touched by the rays of the solstice sun – if we get any sun, of course. So the problem is carrying out the ceremony under the eyes of Brandon and his thugs.'

'How are we going to do that?' Tom asked.

There was a blank silence from the Seven.

'We need an element of surprise . . . to throw him off the scent somehow,' Lily sounded exhausted.

'He certainly ain't going to let us just go ahead with the ceremony. That would be the end of his dream of world domination,' Michael said, looking pointedly at Jude. 'He'll just snatch the crystal and kill us all.'

'We don't have time to worry about all this,' Gabe snapped. 'We get there, we do what needs to be done to be in position for the solstice, which is in less than three hours.'

'But we'll be walking into a trap,' Michael protested. 'How will we fight off Brandon's forces without weapons, or help?

We have no idea how many men he'll have there.' He thought of Arizona and the brutish, insensate thugs who had attacked them in the alley. How many more would there be this time? His blood ran cold.

'We do what we have always done,' Gabe's voice was calm. 'We use our powers, as I taught you.'

'What about the roads?' Rhiannon interrupted. 'They were partially flooded when we came up from Portsmouth and now it's snowing hard. Suppose we can't even get close to Stonehenge?'

'That's why we have to leave now,' Gabe insisted doggedly.

Jude, always the outsider, leaned against the far wall, away from the table and the others.

'It won't work, Gabe.'

They all stared at him.

'What choice do we have?' Gabe's eyes flashed angrily at Jude.

'There is another way. I don't know if it's possible, but I believe it's our only chance.'

They waited.

'When we built Stonehenge, we also built an underground tunnel, from the inner circle to Avebury.'

'Is it still there?' Tom asked.

'Yes. Although in what state of repair I don't know. We built it for just such an eventuality, knowing we needed to keep the link between the energy portals open in the face of possible opposition.'

'Avebury's really close,' Maya commented.

'Close to us, yes,' Gabe said, 'but twenty miles from Stonehenge. How can we walk twenty miles in three hours? In an underground tunnel which may well be blocked and fallen in.' He shook his head, 'Which may well not even exist any more.'

'We put two entrances along the tunnel,' Jude stated. 'One was just outside Alton, the other at Woodhenge, which is only two miles from Stonehenge.'

'And you know where this entrance is?'

Jude nodded. 'I know it exactly.'

'And we'll be able to get into the tunnel?' Michael asked.

Jude nodded again. 'And the exit is inside the inner circle of the stones.'

'Why hasn't someone dug it up if it's so accessible?' Rhiannon asked. She found she could look Jude in the face now, without pain.

'Trust me,' Jude said quietly.

Michael snorted angrily, and received a reproving look from Lily.

'Well, sorry,' Michael said, 'but here we are, all happily entrusting the planet's future to a man who up until now has hardly demonstrated any loyalty to us.' He flung his arms in the air in frustration. 'Why doesn't anyone else see it?' He pointed accusingly at Jude. 'How do we know you aren't working for your brother? You conveniently pitch up here in time to activate the crystal, then you persuade us into some dodgy tunnel. It's a trick. We'll never see the light of day again, let alone the solstice.'

There was a dangerous silence in the room.

Jude shrugged.

'If I'm working for my brother, then surely I need the second stage of activation complete,' he replied softly. 'Wouldn't you agree?' he challenged Michael, who said nothing, just stared him out.

Lily saw the fierce competition between the two men, and knew Rhiannon was the cause. She looked at Gabe for help.

'We go with Jude,' Gabe stated. He looked sympathetically at Michael. 'If we can arrive in the centre of the stones without Brandon spotting us, we stand a chance.'

83

*21 December 2012, the winter solstice: Woodhenge,
two miles from Stonehenge*

The snow was coming down thick and fast. There was no accompanying storm, like the one they'd experienced near Le Mans, no wind, just a silent, relentless emptying of the sky onto the earth below. It had already begun to pile up as they drove in convoy towards Woodhenge, skirting the roads that Gabe knew might still be under water, or even frozen by now, taking a wide eastern arc to catch the main road south and then west again. It was slow going. Lily and Gabe went with Jude. The other four travelled together again in the beat-up jeep with the Spanish number plates. Michael drove. Jude was at the wheel of his anonymous Volvo. There was silence in both cars. It was as if the Seven were holding their breath. They met no one. The muffled world appeared to be uninhabited except for themselves. And the snow.

The three in the Volvo pulled up first at Woodhenge and waited for the jeep to catch them up.

'Are you sure you know where the entrance is?' Gabe broke the silence.

Jude nodded but didn't explain.

'Even in the dark? In the snow?'

'Yes, even in my dreams,' Jude replied with a smile.

They parked on the A345 and the Seven crunched across the snow in the freezing night air to the gate which led to the ancient site. They were wrapped in scarves, shawls, hats and parkas that Gabe had produced.

'We look like a gang of homeless people on a raid,' Rhiannon muttered through her scarf.

'But we'll fit in just fine at the solstice,' Tom replied. 'We'll be identical to every other New Age person there.'

It was still pitch dark, except for the wavering beams of the four torches they'd brought which lit up the glittering snow, lying like a pristine blanket over the field. Jude led the way. Michael, carrying a spade, followed closely behind, unwilling to lose sight of the other man. The beam caught the tops of the concrete posts that substituted the original wooden ones. Over a hundred of them peeked above the snow in six concentric circles.

At the southernmost point, Jude stopped. He shone the torch on the nearest post, then moved the beam to the one immediately to the right. He paused, then drew a light triangle joining the two posts to a point almost at his feet. Rhiannon saw him sigh with relief.

'This could take forever,' Michael grumbled softly to Tom, jumping up and down in an attempt to get the circulation going in his frozen feet. 'Suppose we dig and it's the wrong place. It'll be Christmas before we find the sodding tunnel.'

Tom grinned. 'Can you be doubting the mighty Jude?'

Jude began to position himself over the tip of the triangle he had sketched in the snow. He stood on the spot in his black, heavy-duty parka, hood up, his booted feet slightly apart, his hands hanging loose by his side. Then he went very, very still.

'What's he doing?' Tom whispered to Maya.

'He's driving his energy into the earth – seeking the entrance.'

'OK, better than digging up the whole field I guess.'

Lily glared at him, and he fell silent.

Maya, unlike the other three, could see Jude's aura, glowing first a pale green, then gradually changing into a fiery, vigorous red.

After a short while, Rhiannon noticed the snow beneath Jude's feet beginning to melt. A perfectly circular patch of bare earth revealed itself. Jude began sweeping the wet mud with the toe of his climbing boot. He glanced at Lily, who smiled in response. Stone lay beneath the mud. As Jude scraped away, Michael's torch picked out a smooth, round slab.

'How do we open it?'

Maya shuddered. Like Rhiannon, she hated being enclosed. And she was so cold now she could hardly breathe. The thought of spending two hours or more in an icy, subterranean hell which hadn't been used in thousands of years made her feel physically sick.

Rhiannon, Michael and Tom stood beside Jude, looking down dubiously at the stone slab. Lily and Gabe kept their distance; they seemed in another world, standing close together, silent and calm.

Jude caught Rhiannon's eye, looked away.

'Well?' Michael snapped impatiently at Jude. 'How do we open it?'

Jude stepped once more on to the stone and leant his full weight on the right-hand side. Nothing happened. He shifted his feet slightly and suddenly the slab began to move, rotating very slowly to the right, inch by inch, the stone grinding loud in the still night air. It took less than five minutes for the entrance to the tunnel to be fully open. A smell of dank mustiness filled the air, as if the tunnel had belched. Jude took Michael's torch and shone it down into the darkness.

'Looks OK,' Tom commented, jumping down through the stone aperture. It was damp but not flooded, with very little debris, only narrow bare mud walls held up by blackened timber supports. The ceiling was high for a tunnel, the mud roof at least four or five inches above Tom's head, but the walls were barely wider than a single person.

Jude jumped down behind him.

'Which way – south isn't it?' Tom let the beam wander over the walls.

Gabe was next down and helped Lily negotiate the stone ledge. Then Michael handed Maya down. The girl was shivering so violently now that she could barely stand. He held his hand out to Rhiannon.

'I'm OK,' she said, almost out of habit. But despite her words, she took his warm hand in her own and held it for a second before climbing over the edge.

The underground space, although cold, musty and airless, was at least sheltered from the biting wind that had got up since the snow had stopped. The Seven began their journey south along the ancient tunnel in single file, the torch beams bobbing and dancing across the dark close walls. Jude led, then Lily, Maya, Tom and Michael, Rhiannon, with Gabe bringing up the rear. It was very silent underground. Nobody spoke. They were all praying there would be a clear run to Stonehenge. And the going was steady, with nothing underfoot, no sign of a collapse in the well-made structure, although Michael feared that their presence alone could destabilise it, like triggering an avalanche.

'Keep the noise to a minimum; tread softly,' he whispered to Tom.

Tom passed the message up the line. He found he was enjoying the adventure, now they were on the move and had a final goal in sight.

Maya was just trying to keep it together, carefully putting one foot in front of the other, one . . . two . . . one . . . two . . . making it into a meditation, and keeping her eye fixed on Lily's reassuring back.

Rhiannon felt the comforting presence of Gabe close behind her. He had rescued her before: he would surely keep her safe this time too.

'Can you see the time?' Rhiannon heard Gabe's voice when they had been trudging at a consistent speed for a while.

She ran her torch over her wrist.

'Ten to seven.'

'How far do you think we've come?' he asked.

'We started a bit before six . . . Jude says as the crow flies it's slightly less than two miles . . . it shouldn't take us more than an hour and a half at this pace,' Rhiannon calculated, 'so we must be over half way.' She felt clammy and hot now, the airlessness and the crushing darkness beginning to suffocate her. She tore off her scarf and hat and refused to allow herself to think of the miles of narrow tunnel in front of and behind them, the long way to the exit. Maya was softly chanting through her claustrophobia, Rhiannon wasn't going to give in to her own.

Suddenly Rhiannon felt Gabe's hand on her shoulder.

'Did you hear that?' he whispered.

Rhiannon listened, but heard nothing beyond the tramp of the others up ahead.

'Water,' he said.

'Water . . . where?' She felt her heart pumping wildly with dread. *No . . . please.*

'Get them to stop,' the old man said urgently.

Rhiannon called softly ahead and the line came to a halt.

Jude appeared beside her, his worried face half lit by his torch beam.

'What is it?'

'Water,' Gabe repeated. 'Up above, I can hear it.'

Jude cocked his head, shushed the others to complete silence. And then they could all hear it. It was a rushing sound almost above their heads.

'How can that be?' Michael asked. 'We're no more than fifteen feet underground, there can't be any water between us and the surface . . . can there?'

'Wouldn't it be frozen?' Rhiannon asked.

'Not this far below ground,' Jude told her. 'We *are* near the river . . .'

Gabe squeezed past the others along the tunnel to the front of the group, playing his light along the roof as he went. Rhiannon could sense his anxiety. She saw him reach up, and his hand came away wet.

'OK,' his voice was low but commanding. 'Move, all of you, move. Now.'

But Tom, first in line, suddenly stumbled and came to a halt.

'It's blocked . . . there's . . . rubble, earth . . . must be a partial collapse.'

The light from all their torches concentrated on the spot.

'Fuck,' Michael swore softly as he viewed the solid bank of debris. Rhiannon felt his hand reach back for hers and she held on to it for dear life.

'Can you move it, get through?' Gabe asked, still holding his hand up to the roof. They heard Tom grunting as he attempted to haul the debris out of their path.

'Give me some room,' Jude urged, grabbing the lumps of stone, earth and wood that Tom was scrabbling from the blockage. The noise from the water was becoming louder by the second. Maya whimpered involuntarily, flashes of the waters of Atlantis closing over her head horribly vivid.

'How's it going?' Gabe's voice was increasingly urgent. 'Because we have only minutes.'

'There's just about enough space to climb through now . . . come on,' Tom shouted.

Jude reached behind for Maya, hauling the paralysed girl past him and pushing her bodily towards Tom and the small gap he had opened out near the roof.

But the roof was buckling – Rhiannon could see it beneath Gabe's upstretched arms. They were all going to drown, she was certain of it now, and an odd calm came over her as she clung to Michael's hand. Clearly this was her fate, in that life and in this.

'Go . . . go . . .' Gabe urged her, flattening himself as best he could against the tunnel side as he continued to hold up the roof timbers. The water was pouring down the wall behind him, turning into a river of mud at his feet.

Michael pulled her towards the rubble. His torch had gone out and the only light was from the other side of the hole. Lily was through, so were Tom and Maya. Jude followed. Rhiannon yanked her hand away.

'No, I'm not leaving you,' she cried desperately to Gabe.

Gabe's face was contorted with the effort he was making to keep the roof up.

'Go, Rhiannon . . . please. Make her Michael.'

Michael didn't hesitate. He grabbed her round the waist and lifted her off the ground, hoisting her with all his might towards Jude's outstretched hand on the far side of the blockage. She screamed as she felt Jude's strong grasp locking around her shoulders. The rocks were rough, the gap small. She felt her clothes

349

tear, her body bruise as she arrived in a heap on the other side.

'Gabe . . . Gabe . . .' she heard herself crying.

But Michael had no intention of leaving the old man to his fate. He dragged a heavy blackwood post from the heap on the wet ground and rammed it tight under the support that Gabe was holding up.

'Let go . . . let it go . . .' Gabe didn't budge, he couldn't, or wouldn't. Michael didn't argue, he just yanked Gabe's arms free and dragged the resisting old man towards the hole. 'Get on with it,' he shouted, looking back at the cracking, buckling roof.

As he heaved his own body clear of the stones, they heard an almighty crash behind them. The tunnel had given way and some deviant tributary of the nearby river plunged into the underground space.

'Close call,' Tom muttered to himself.

'Go . . . go . . . let's go,' Jude shouted above the din.

But the blockage held. The tunnel was coming up towards Stonehenge by now and the water flowed harmlessly downhill, back the way they had come.

Gabe was soaked and shivering, but his bright blue eyes twinkled in the torchlight.

'Life in the old dog yet,' he smiled serenely at Lily, who shook her head gently at him in loving reproof.

Rhiannon reached up and kissed Michael on the cheek.

'Thank you,' she said softly. 'Thank you, thank you.'

Gabe, watching, noticed Jude wince and turn away. As they set off down the remaining yards of the tunnel, he pulled Jude back. Shining his torch into the younger man's face, his voice was very low.

'I trust you. I have always trusted you. When it comes to it, I know you will do the right thing.'

'Then you know more than I do.'

Jude held Gabe's steady gaze for a brief moment before turning abruptly and striding off down the dark tunnel. Behind him Gabe just shrugged.

'Time?' he called ahead.

'7.45,' Rhiannon replied. 'We've only got fifteen minutes till sunrise.'

The end of the tunnel had been fashioned into a small, stone-walled chamber. Steps also in stone, led upwards to a circular slab trapdoor, similar to the one at Woodhenge. This one had a heavy iron handle which spanned the surface. Damp, cold and pitch dark like the rest of the tunnel, it was nonetheless more spacious than the claustrophobic passageway. Maya breathed a sigh of relief as she sat down against the wall, knowing that in a minute they would be breathing the fresh dawn air of Stonehenge.

Jude was already up the steps and pulling on the metal hinge when they all heard Lily's low command: 'Stop . . . not yet.'

Jude turned to her in surprise.

'The sun will rise in a moment; we have to position ourselves.'

Lily shook her head.

'Not yet, I said. Not yet.'

84

Above ground, Stonehenge

Xan and Brandon had been hovering in and around the stone circle since the helicopter had dropped them at five thirty that morning. They took it in turns to walk the perimeter, check the inner circle every ten minutes, retreating from the freezing night to the car Kayden had driven down before the storms. But there was nothing to see, nothing except snow.

'They won't be here yet,' Brandon said as they both stood leaning against the black Audi. He was bone-cold, even in his heavy down jacket, but Xan, who had little more than a leather jacket against the wind, seemed not to feel the icy temperature.

'Do they really think we won't spot them?' Xan's voice was contemptuous.

'They're clever. I keep telling you that.'

'Yeah, I get it, boss, but this isn't exactly a big place. And it's enclosed. How hard can it be to spot seven people doing a ceremony with a crystal?' he laughed to himself.

Brandon sprang off the car and rounded on his henchman, grabbing the collars of his jacket and pulling Xan's face to within an inch of his own. Their frozen breath rose into the dawn air.

'You see that's the problem with you, Xan. Too bloody pleased with yourself. I'm going to say it one more time: Do not underestimate these people.' Brandon relaxed his hold on Xan's coat and smoothed the leather down in a mock solicitous fashion. Xan had not moved a muscle. 'We have one chance. ONE CHANCE,' Crowe shouted in the other man's face, spittle spraying the air. 'Fuck this up and you . . . are . . . dead.'

He moved off, stamping his feet on the icy ground, breathing hard through his rage.

The visitors' car park, Stonehenge

Kayden and his team were holed up, dozing inside two people carriers, the engines running softly to prevent them freezing to death. He waited impatiently to be summoned to the stones, looking forward to dealing with the girl. He'd told his team she was his, and only his. And he would make her suffer for fucking with him in that flat. Really suffer. He looked at his watch. The boss had said six, but you never knew with Mr Crowe.

85

Underground chamber, Stonehenge

'There's something we haven't told you.'

Gabe put a protective arm around Lily's shoulders as the others stared in bewilderment, their strained faces white in the flickering torchlight. Michael, Rhiannon, Maya and Tom moved instinctively closer together while Jude stood alone as usual, an unreadable expression in his eyes.

'What? What is it?' Rhiannon spoke in a whisper but her eyes were fierce. 'Tell us. We haven't got time to hang around.'

Gabe and Lily exchanged glances then Lily spoke decisively.

'Gabe has already explained to you that this is our last chance to complete the ceremony.'

'And?' Michael muttered impatiently.

'What we haven't told you is that the light of the sun alone is not enough.'

'Not enough!' Tom exclaimed. 'Then what are we doing here?'

Jude looked up sharply. 'I should have guessed. The path to the underworld.'

Rhiannon grabbed Gabe's arm.

'What's he talking about? What path?'

'He's talking about the alignment of planets that will power the crystal,' Gabe replied. 'The ancients called it the path to the underworld. We know it as a portal to another world, the world Lily and I are waiting to return to.'

Maya jumped to her feet. 'You're leaving? No! You can't go! We need you.'

Rhiannon looked around angrily at her friend. 'We haven't got time for this. It's almost sunrise, we're running out of time.'

Jude's deep voice sounded almost amused. 'It's OK, you

can relax. We've got at least three hours. The sun lines up with the centre of the Milky Way at, if I remember correctly, eleven minutes past eleven exactly. That creates the energy we need to close the portal here on earth. It also creates the energy Gabe and Lily need to return to their home in the stars.'

Lily turned to Maya who was holding back tears.

'This is our last chance. All of you have many lifetimes ahead of you but for Gabe and me this is the end of the road. We have tried so many times to fulfil our sacred contract. Now, at last, we have a good chance of succeeding. And then we are free to leave.'

Michael's loud exclamation echoed round the stone chamber.

'Right. Simple. We activate the crystal at exactly 11 minutes past 11. We dodge Brandon and his men while we do it. We seal the Stonehenge portal. We wave goodbye to Gabe and Lily. Should be a doddle. What could possibly go wrong?'

'We can do it, I know we can,' Maya's eyes were sparkling with tears but she spoke with conviction. 'I just wish you didn't have to go.'

Tom hugged her. 'Don't think about that now,' he whispered. He didn't understand how Lily and Gabe could leave for another planet, but he had become used to accepting the impossible. Maya trembled in his arms and he realised how much she meant to him. How much they all meant to him.

'Just one thing, Gabe,' said Michael thoughtfully. 'Why have you kept this new timetable from us? Were you worried that Brandon might find out?'

He looked hard at Jude, who shrugged and said, 'Not from me. I've only just remembered it myself.'

'You all have our complete trust,' Gabe replied firmly. 'But Lily and I decided long ago that it was safer for everyone if only we knew the final plan.'

Michael looked unconvinced and turned to Rhiannon who smiled back at him. Jude's heart ached. Seeing her with Michael was unbearable, yet the thought that Gabe or Lily might not trust him cut him to the quick. He prayed he would have the strength to do what he had to do.

86

Stonehenge

Brandon scanned the eastern horizon. The sky was still dark and cloudy, the wind bitterly cold and the thick covering of snow radiated an icy glitter in the light of the setting winter moon. Behind him in the stone circle a large group of hippies and New Agers took up a solemn chant, led by a tall Druid dressed in white. Brandon started forward. Could that be Gabe? Surely not. Just an old man in a white sheet. The chanting grew stronger as the darkness began to lift and a faint glow crept over the horizon. Despite himself Brandon smiled. They must believe they're encouraging the sun to rise. Well, he had no problem with that. He was so close to his moment of triumph that even help from a bunch of hippies was welcome.

Xan returned to his side.

'No sign of your brother.' He succeeded in keeping his voice neutral but inside he was gloating.

'Kayden's men are still checking out the crowd.'

Brandon looked at him coldly.

'Jude said he'd see me at Stonehenge. Your job is to find them.'

Xan moved away silently. He was looking forward to finding them, especially Jude.

Brandon turned back towards the east. The golden glow tinged with red was intensifying as the dark clouds melted away. For once the sun would be visible on the winter solstice. Everything was going his way. He moved swiftly towards the centre of the stone circle pushing his way through the expectant crowd. Ahead of him he saw a tall broad shouldered figure. Jude! The stranger turned as Brandon touched his shoulder, smiled uncertainly, then turned back as the winter sun rose steadily then suddenly blazed with brilliant intensity through the framing archway of the stone pillars.

The crowd reacted as one, smiles of joy on their faces as they cheered, hugged and clasped hands. Brandon looked around in disbelief. All his plans, all his power directed to this one moment and now – nothing. No Jude. No crystal.

He fought down his fury and forced himself to think calmly. There could be many reasons why Jude had failed him. Maybe the others were on to him. Maybe they'd kept him prisoner. He dismissed this notion, knowing, even though his knowledge of the inner circle was sketchy, that they needed all seven for the ceremony. So maybe there was another site that Jude didn't know about in time to tell him. Or maybe . . . Or maybe his brother had betrayed him. Impossible! Brandon breathed deeply, and smiled to himself. Jude knew that he'd be sacrificing his own life if he reneged on their deal; but whatever had happened, the Stonehenge portal was still open. There was still a chance.

Xan materialised beside him.

'They're definitely not here, boss. What do you want to do?'

Brandon's mind raced through the possibilities. He knew there were other sacred sites in the area. He reached a decision.

'Send the men to the farmhouse and check out Avebury, Silbury Hill and Woodhenge.'

Xan was tapping the locations into his phone as Brandon reeled them off.

'That's a pretty big area, boss. And some of the roads are blocked.'

Brandon ignored him.

'And leave someone here to keep watch.'

He headed for the car park.

'What's nearest?'

Xan looked at his phone.

'Woodhenge.'

87

Tunnel beneath Stonehenge

Tom stretched his cramped legs and groaned.

'Why couldn't we have waited at the farmhouse? It's freezing down here.'

'You know why,' answered Maya tolerantly, 'that's one of the first places Brandon will look when he realises we haven't appeared.'

'I just want to get on with it.'

'Me too,' Maya agreed, then glanced over to Michael and Rhiannon who were deep in conversation with Gabe and Lily.

Tom jerked his head and raised his eyebrows questioningly.

'Think they can do it?'

Maya nodded. 'I think so. As long as . . .'

As one, they looked towards Jude, who sat on his heels against the stone wall, his gaze fixed unwaveringly on Rhiannon.

Lily was also aware of Jude's intense concentration. She could feel the pain coming from him in waves. She tuned back into the conversation. Gabe had been explaining how he and Lily had once embodied the harmonious union of male and female energy.

'If you and Michael can achieve this now, Rhiannon, we can put right the damage caused in Atlantis and help raise the vibration of the planet.'

'You mean like the dawning of the Age of Aquarius?'

Rhiannon was joking but Gabe nodded seriously.

'That's exactly what I do mean. Whatever happens, this is the end of one age and the beginning of another.'

Michael breathed out. 'Whoa . . . sounds momentous.'

He and Rhiannon exchanged self-conscious glances.

Michael wondered what she truly felt about him. Was it enough for this huge task Gabe was setting them?

Rhiannon moved closer to Lily.

'When you first met Gabe,' she whispered, 'did you love him or . . .'

She stopped, uncertain how to go on.

Lily looked into the girl's eyes and read the doubt and anxiety.

'You're thinking about destiny versus choice.' Her imperious eyes suddenly softened. 'They can be the same thing. It was my destiny to be united with Gabe. It was my choice to love him. I loved him then, but only a fraction of how much I love him now. We are soulmates. You and Michael can be soulmates too. Only you two share the energy that will power the crystal. Allow what you have to grow and you can be happy together.'

Rhiannon hugged her impulsively.

'I do love Michael. I just don't know if it's enough after . . .'

The eyes of the two women met.

'He wasn't your destiny,' Lily looked sadly at Jude, 'nor mine.'

Woodhenge, tunnel entrance

Xan squatted on his heels and looked down into the dark entrance of the tunnel. The cold and damp rose up like a physical entity and far below he could hear running water. He straightened up and looked at Brandon.

'Someone opened this recently. This must be the way they went.'

As he spoke the earth shuddered for a moment beneath their feet.

'Might have overdone it with the earthquakes, boss.'

Brandon suppressed his rage at the other man's flippancy. He needed him on board right now.

'That's not us. The pressure's building under Stonehenge. That's why we need Jude to open the portal completely before it explodes.'

'Or seal it completely,' Xan suggested, a taunting note in his voice.

As Brandon stepped angrily towards his henchman, his phone rang.

'What? When? . . . OK, get everyone back, we're leaving now. Wait for us . . . no, you can't do anything on your own.'

He turned to Xan.

'That was Tyson, at Stonehenge. He was talking to one of the hippies. Some of them are still hanging round and he wondered why. We're fools. There's a major cosmic event at eleven minutes past eleven – all that end-of-the-world Mayan calendar bollocks I don't believe in. So it wasn't sunrise they needed after all.'

As Xan drove dangerously fast towards Stonehenge, Brandon sat back in his seat feeling strangely calm. Somehow it seemed entirely appropriate that the planets were converging to mark his moment of triumph.

88

Stonehenge

Stone ground against stone as the heavy slab guarding the entrance to the tunnel slowly slid open for the first time in thousands of years. Jude looked out cautiously.

'OK . . . can't see anyone.'

One by one, seven people emerged from the darkness and stood, cold and stiff, blinking at the sunlight reflected on the snow covered ground.

Jude looked around at the stone circle he had created so long ago in atonement for his fatal mistake and in hope that harmony could be restored. The stones had endured well, he thought ruefully, better than he had. What had karma in store for him this time? Was redemption too much to hope for?

Suddenly he became aware of the tremors beneath his feet. The portal was beginning to give way and Stonehenge was buckling under the strain. Time was running out, for him and for the planet.

He looked up to see Michael and Tom returning from a scouting trip around the perimeter.

'No sign of Brandon,' Tom reported breathlessly, 'apart from one man in a four-wheel drive over there. Could be one of his.'

'And quite a few people beyond the fence,' added Michael. 'The entrance is closed now but they must be waiting to see what happens in,' he checked his watch, 'the next five minutes.'

Jude moved close to Rhiannon and whispered urgently in her ear.

'Rhiannon, you must believe I never meant to hurt you. I was trying to do the right thing. Can you forgive me? You have to tell me.'

As Rhiannon stared at him, unable to speak, Gabe strode up and led her to join Michael in the centre of the inner circle while Lily showed Maya and Tom where to stand. Jude silently took his place, completing the five-pointed star Lily and Gabe were creating around Rhiannon and Michael.

'Remember,' said Lily urgently, 'we have to hold the energy within the circle and focus on Michael and Rhiannon. No one must break the circle.' She nodded to Maya who carefully unwrapped the crystal and held it out to Rhiannon.

For a second Rhiannon hesitated. Lily was the High Priestess. Could she do this? Lily caught her eye, then slowly bowed her head to her successor. Gabe watched her proudly – she could still surprise him after all this time.

Rhiannon took a deep breath and took the crystal from Maya. Instantly she could feel its power and her heart lifted.

'Rhiannon and Michael,' Lily continued, 'you must hold the crystal together so that it catches the light from the sun. Focus your hearts and minds on oneness. Only if you are in perfect unity will the twin flames at the heart of the crystal ignite. When that happens,' she continued confidently, 'you must stand back as Michael and Rhiannon must lock the crystal into the energy stream flowing from the stargate,' she pointed upwards to a distant glow in the sky, 'and direct it to seal the portal.'

She turned to Jude. 'The portal is here, at the altar stone?'

'Yes,' Jude confirmed gravely.

'And then?' asked Maya.

'Once we are certain the portal is sealed,' Gabe replied, 'Lily and I will step into the stream of light and it will carry us home. Do you all know what you have to do?'

They all nodded silently.

'Thirty seconds to go.'

Suddenly Gabe turned to Lily.

'As soon as the stargate is open, you must leave.'

Lily's eyes flashed. 'No. We go together or not at all.'

Gabe shrugged. He just wanted her to be safe.

As the final seconds counted down, Michael placed his hand

next to Rhiannon's, supporting the crystal.

'Now!' commanded Lily.

A blinding explosion of light forced Rhiannon to close her eyes and she flashed back to her vision on the summer solstice six months before. That had been a vision of disaster in the past, in Atlantis. Did they have the power to change the future? Suddenly she could feel the thoughts and feelings of all her companions. There was hope and joy and strength and sadness. And greatest of all, love. She opened her eyes and could see the powerful auras surrounding each and every one of the group, flashes of gold and red, brilliant blues, greens and yellows. For a moment she could feel the power and authority they had known in Atlantis and her body shook with awe.

Michael turned to her and the love in his eyes was reflected in her own. Together they raised the crystal towards the sun. The light caught its myriad facets. It began to glow and pulse with energy.

High above, glittering particles began streaming towards them from the heavens. Waves of amethyst and green light surrounded them, filling the sky. The crystal jerked in their hands and filaments of light emerged from its depths, rotating clockwise then anti-clockwise in the air around them, then expanding to enclose the whole group. Deep within the crystal a red flame began to take shape. It flickered, split in two then came together, gaining in strength.

Suddenly the flame wavered and dimmed. Rhiannon looked frantically around the circle. *Jude! Help me. I can't do this!*

Jude's eyes met hers. *My love. I wish there was some other way but the balance can never be restored if we are together.*

With infinite sadness, Rhiannon bowed her head. *You'll always be in my heart.*

As you will be in mine, Rhiannon. Now you must fulfil your destiny.

Rhiannon dragged her mind back to Michael and was grateful for the love and understanding in his eyes. Her hand tightened on his as the flame flickered, then blazed into life with increasing power, spiralling in intricate patterns until, with a final explosion of glowing light, it came to rest at the heart of the crystal.

It's done. Finally, it is done.

The unspoken thought flashed around the circle and the particles of light streaming from above coalesced into a single, powerful beam connecting the sky to the earth and the stone circle.

'Congratulations, dear brother.'

Brandon's sneering voice broke the spell binding them. Shocked they looked round to see Brandon, Xan and five of his men standing at the edge of the circle.

As one, Gabe, Michael and Tom moved to confront them. Brandon dismissed them with one contemptuous glance, all his attention on Jude.

'Give me the crystal, Jude. The girl is yours, as we agreed.'

Rhiannon gasped with shock and Jude turned to her, his eyes begging her to believe him. *It's not true.*

He turned back to Brandon, his expression blank, masking his pain.

'Brandon, I can't let you do this. If I could have believed there was even half a chance that you would use the crystal for good, then we might have been able to work together. But I know you too well. This is the only way.'

Brandon's face registered shock.

'Stop play-acting,' he snapped, unable to believe his brother wouldn't fall in line as he had always done. 'We had a deal. Just give me the crystal.'

As Brandon and Jude locked angry glances, Lily seized Rhiannon's arm.

'We have to close the portal. Align the crystal with the energy beam. Do it Rhiannon, now!'

Jude moved to shield Rhiannon as Gabe, Michael and Tom advanced to block Brandon's men.

'Accept you've lost, Brandon. Neither of us can have what we want. It's over.' His voice was low, but the words were clear-cut and unambiguous. He had finally let Rhiannon go.

As Brandon glared at his brother, his attention was caught by the girl's sudden movement. He stared for a moment, before realising what Rhiannon was doing. She was once again in the centre of the small circle of stones. She held the crystal aloft as it locked onto the immense forces streaming from the centre of the galaxy and juddered in her hands. Immediately Lily and Maya sprang to her side, using their energy to help her hold the crystal steady. Straining every muscle, Rhiannon directed the pulsating light, drawing it down very slowly, closer and closer to the altar stone.

'Stop her!'

Brandon's men leapt towards Rhiannon and found their way blocked. Gabe knew it could last only a few crucial seconds, but he brought every single atom of his failing strength to bear as he created a temporary shield round the women. The thugs crashed uselessly against the invisible barrier, their expressions bewildered and frightened as they regrouped.

Xan stood back, balancing a razor-sharp knife in his hands, waiting for an opening.

The men attacked again, knives drawn, against the bulk of Tom, Michael and Jude. One man went down with a blow to the head from Michael's boot and lay still on the frozen ground. Kayden grappled with Tom, his blade flashing inches from Tom's face, his rage at these insane people clear in his brutal slashes. Jude downed another, his quiet, effortless strength making the fight look ridiculously one-sided.

Suddenly Xan saw his chance and, drawing back his arm, threw the knife at Rhiannon's throat with deadly accuracy. Jude moved like lightning, leaving the man who was attacking him limp and lifeless in the snow. He plucked the knife out of the air and, turning with balletic grace, hurled it straight back at Xan.

Reacting with the same lightning reflexes, Xan did not hesitate. He grabbed his boss, who stood beside him watching the fray, and quickly yanked Brandon's body in front of his own. The knife found its target. Its lethal point sank deep into Crowe's chest, the hilt lost in the bulk of his down jacket.

'Sorry, boss,' Xan whispered contemptuously. He pushed Brandon off him and moved swiftly and silently away from the stones. Brandon seemed to hang immobilised in the air for a moment, then staggered, falling heavily onto his back, clasping his hands to the hilt of the knife. His agonised eyes searched for Jude's. But his brother had turned away, his gaze fixed on Rhiannon as she triumphantly brought the crystal in line with the altar stone. Energy sparked and crackled all around her then suddenly exploded in a flash of iridescent light, knocking Rhiannon off her feet. The ball of energy hovered in the air then suddenly passed right through the altar stone leaving it glowing but undamaged. As she lay there she felt a strange sensation. She could hear the grass grow, the rivers flow, the trees drawing nutrients from the soil, the flowers turning their faces to the morning sun. They were not separate, but flowing through her, inhabiting every cell of her body. She felt the tides pulled by the moon, the orbiting planets, the earth shuddering, then slowly settling. It was as if the planet was thanking her.

'You've done it. The portal is sealed.' Lily's voice was shaking with emotion as she pulled Rhiannon to her feet. Maya flung her arms round Rhiannon.

'Have I?' Rhiannon looked dazed. 'Has it really worked?'

'It's done. It's over,' Lily's breath was coming in gasps. 'I've waited so long for this moment. I can't believe, after all these lifetimes, we've finally completed our mission. Gabe and I –'

She stopped speaking and looked around, her dazed expression becoming anxious.

'We must leave now. We only have a short time before the stargate closes. Where's Gabe?'

In the centre of the melee she spotted Gabe fighting a hideous giant of a man. He had Gabe round the neck, his ham-like fists balled against the older man's throat. Gabe's face was livid purple. And as she watched in horror, she knew this was the man who had killed Atlas.

◎◎

'Gabe . . . help him someone, please help him,' Lily shouted. 'We have to go before it's too late.'

But Gabe's powers hadn't quite run out. With a supreme effort he loosened Kayden's fists around his throat and turning, sharply sliced the thug's temple with the side of his hand. Kayden fell like a stone. Gabe wasted no time. He ran towards Lily. Behind her, the beam of light leading to the stargate began to flicker and break up.

'Go Lily!' Gabe ordered as Lily positioned herself and the light enveloped her like a translucent veil.

'Gabe . . .' Lily's cry was despairing as she held out her hand to her beloved consort. He had almost reached her when a blood-stained figure crashed into him from behind and knocked him to the ground. Brandon.

Gabe struggled to his feet, but he was too late. The beam of light suddenly accelerated away from them, up into the clear blue sky. Lily was carried away with it. For a moment they could see her, an erect, majestic figure who seemed to dematerialise before their eyes. Then she was no longer of this world.

'No . . . Lily . . . NO!' Gabe stared hopelessly at the empty sky as the light veil disappeared as suddenly as if a switch had been thrown. He grabbed Brandon and shook him violently.

The dying man stared back at him, his face held in a vicious grimace.

'You were the one. You and Lilith. You destroyed my dream.' He began to choke on the blood filling his mouth but the hatred in his eyes was as strong as ever. 'It's a small revenge that you'll never see her again.'

Gabe slumped to the ground as Jude supported his brother's body.

'As for you,' Brandon forced the words out, only hatred keeping him alive as he gazed into his brother's eyes. 'I hope you're proud of what you've done.' He coughed violently. 'I'm your brother, your own flesh and blood. You swore never to betray me. Yet you chose them, and now you will die too. In torment.'

Jude saw the light fading in his brother's eyes and spoke softly.

'I was *living* in torment. Now I hope we both shall find peace.'

Brandon stared back in bewilderment then his head fell back. Jude looked in stunned silence at his brother's lifeless body. In that moment he felt the powerful strength of the blood tie Brandon had evoked. Yes, this *was* his brother. Yet it had always been a conflicted love they had felt for each other. And there was a strange freedom in knowing that the conflict between them was over. Never again would Jude have to choose. He laid Brandon gently on the ground and reached his hand over to close his brother's eyes for the last time.

Michael and Tom lifted Gabe to his feet, shocked by the utter desolation in his face.

'There's nothing I can do,' he said slowly. 'The stargate has closed. Lily and I are separated for all eternity.'

The old man continued to look skywards, even though it was hopeless, his face a mask of despair.

'All these lifetimes. All that we have been through together. It can't end like this can it?' He turned to Tom, who could think of nothing to say which might comfort his friend. Had she really gone? He wondered. Just gone, disappeared into the ether? He put his arm round the old man's shoulders, and for the first time felt how frail he was.

'We're here, all of us,' he muttered.

Rhiannon and Maya moved closer, wanting to comfort him too.

'Is there really nothing we can do?' Maya asked.

For a moment they all stood still, missing Lily, stunned too that she had gone forever. Like a death. No one was left but themselves in the stone circle. Brandon's men had all gone, scarpered when they saw that the boss was dead and Xan disappeared. The only one still there was Kayden, still unconscious from Gabe's blow, lying at the edge of the stones, his bulk suddenly soft and harmless in the snow.

Then a thought suddenly hit Rhiannon with such conviction she knew it had to work.

'Gabe and Lily had worked tirelessly for oneness,' she said to the others. 'Separation can't be their destiny, I don't believe it.' She grabbed Michael's arm. 'We've got to reactivate the crystal. It must hold their essence from all the times they worked with it. Surely it can reunite them now.'

Michael looked into her shining eyes and hoped she was right. Together, they raised the crystal towards the sun and focused their entire being on the light. At first nothing happened. Then gradually the red heart of the crystal glowed into life once more, the twin flames weaving their intricate patterns, separating and reuniting before burning with concentrated power. Rhiannon's arm began to shake with the strain of holding the pulsating crystal aloft and Michael put his other arm around her, holding her and supporting her. Suddenly a jagged streak of lightning split the sky, momentarily blinding them.

When their eyes adjusted, Lily was standing there in front of them in a halo of swirling light. They all stared at her in stunned silence. Gabe's face was illuminated with joy and disbelief.

Lily reached out and pulled Gabe to her, holding him tight in her arms.

'We go together or not at all. You know that.'

Gabe's joy encompassed them all as the light swirled around them like a vortex drawing them upwards; then all the others could see was a shooting star streaking towards the heavens.

Michael and Rhiannon lowered the crystal and clung together, exhausted but exultant. Rhiannon knew in that moment, beyond a shadow of a doubt, that this man beside her was the person she was meant to be with. Throughout all the preceding months, when there had been such pressure to be one with him, she had been equivocal, held back. She had always believed that men were never to be trusted. But this man she could trust. They could stand side by side as equals and have the same strength, the same bond, the same love as Gabe and Lily, the two people who had bequeathed them this honour. Rhiannon had no idea

369

what the future would hold, but she knew she would face it with Michael.

Maya dried her tears and carefully retrieved the crystal from Rhiannon's grasp. It seemed lighter than before, less substantial. And as she held it in the palm of her hand, it began to fade, almost as if it was losing its shape. She stared at it in wonder, and as she watched, the stone suddenly dematerialised into a thousand sparks of light, which cascaded into the air around her body, then vanished.

Tom looked on in amazement.

'What happened?'

Maya seemed unfazed.

'I think it's returned to a place where no one can ever find it.'

'Except us,' added Tom, irrepressibly.

While the attention of the others was concentrating on Gabe and Lily's ascension, Kayden came to. His head felt like a thousand hammers beating out of sync. His gaze was unfocused. He could make out the blurry figures of the others, but he couldn't understand who they were, or what had happened. All he knew was he needed to get out of there fast. He staggered to his feet and began to cross the circle. His one aim was to get away from these sinister, terrifying people. But one minute he was sliding across the snow, making his escape, the next he was plunged into freezing darkness.

Kayden wasn't alert enough to know what had happened. He just lay there, semi-conscious, every inch of his body screaming in pain. He heard voices faint above him, but he couldn't speak, his voice wouldn't work. And as he gazed up at the sky, the circle of light began to get smaller and smaller. He tried again to call out, but nothing happened, only a weak mewing sound he didn't recognise as his own. In his stunned state he thought it sounded like the dog, Atlas. Was it back to haunt him?

Then there was total, solid blackness.

How long he lay there he didn't know. But when he got

to his feet and began groping around the stone chamber, he began to panic. He, who tortured animals and killed without conscience, was afraid of the dark.

He found the tunnel, but although he crept along its length, he soon came to the blockage and could go no further. There was no way out.

As he found his voice, he began to shout. But even as he bellowed for help, he knew it was pointless. He knew he might never be found.

◎◎

Jude had not heard Kayden as he closed the tunnel entrance. He glanced down to where his brother was still lying on the snow. It was hard, even with the evidence, to believe he was dead.

'What do we do now?' Tom asked as they stood around, dazed and exhausted, but somehow unable to move on. The stones felt sacred, protective. They had offered their magic, and the universe had responded. It didn't feel safe to leave the inner circle.

'How will we know the planet has really been saved?' Michael asked.

'Perhaps the tsunamis, earthquakes and such will stop?' Rhiannon suggested.

'Trust that the planet is safe now. It may take some time to right itself, but already the balance is returning.' Jude spoke quietly but he spoke with authority and they turned to him with relief.

'So it's really over? The promise we made in Atlantis has been fulfilled?' Michael needed to be sure.

Jude nodded. 'It's really over. We're free now, all of us.' For a moment his eyes rested on Rhiannon.

'No more quests!' Tom looked jubilant.

Jude laughed. 'No more quests. But remember: the planet is safe and stands at the beginning of a new age but there will always be men like Brandon who want to control it.'

'Come with us,' Maya grabbed Jude's arm impulsively. 'Tell us what to do.'

'I can't,' Jude answered gently. 'I have to go now, but you'll know. Maybe you'll create the new Atlantis.'

For a moment the five stood together, the sun shining down on them, the light brilliant as it bounced off the snow. They did not touch, but each of them felt, for the last time, the powerful essence of the group, and silently acknowledged the closeness that had grown up between them. It seemed as if Lily and Gabe were there too, their presence as potent as if they actually stood among them.

'I wish you all every happiness,' Jude looked at each of them in turn. He felt peace. For many lifetimes he had wanted to be absolved from the guilt he carried. Now he knew he was forgiven. He'd done enough. He turned back to where Brandon lay as the others slowly began to leave the stone circle.

He knelt beside the body and closed his eyes. He wasn't praying, just thinking. When he looked at Brandon again, he thought the body had changed; it seemed to have lost definition. He focused, rubbed his eyes. He was tired, he knew that. But, like the crystal, the edges of his brother's body seemed to be less distinct. And as he watched, he saw the body break up – there was no other word to describe it. Break up and begin to disperse into tinier and tinier fragments, until there was nothing left. Only the patch on the ground where the snow had melted.

'Brandon,' he called softly. But there was no reply. Soon, he knew, he would follow his brother.

As he waited he raised his head, looked up into the sky. It was perfectly clear, blue and cloudless. He wished he could have gone with Lily and Gabe. And as he thought of them, a distant star suddenly appeared. It sparked and blazed with light. Jude smiled and the strain left his face. He could feel his body beginning to dematerialise and he waited peacefully for the moment when his spirit would be free.

Rhiannon paused for a moment as the group walked away from the stones. She looked back at Jude, knowing this would be the last time she would ever see him. She knew it had to be this way, but it was still hard to leave him. Then she realised that it was Jude who was leaving. As she gazed back at him, the strong, powerful body was beginning to lose its shape. It gradually took on a faint, insubstantial outline. In a flash she knew what was happening: he had honoured his soul contract for this life. He was ready to go.

Slowly he turned towards her. Already their telepathic bond was fading but the words were clear. *Rhiannon. This is not goodbye. We will meet again.*

Rhiannon concentrated all her energy on reaching him. *When the time is right.*

She watched him turn his face up to the heavens. Following his eyeline, she too saw the star. She knew immediately. It was Lily and Gabe. And as it pulsed for her too, she was overwhelmed with happiness and peace.

Watch over us, she whispered, blowing a kiss into the cold air, before turning to catch up with Michael.

The End

Subscribers

Unbound is a new kind of publishing house. Our books are funded directly by readers. This was a very popular idea during the late eighteenth and early nineteenth centuries. Now we have revived it for the internet age. It allows authors to write the books they really want to write and readers to support the writing they would most like to see published.

The names listed below are of readers who have pledged their support and made this book happen. If you'd like to join them, visit www.unbound.co.uk.

Tara Agace
Christena Appleyard
Simon Arthur
Andres Bastidas
Philip Bland
Karl Bovenizer
Alistair Boyd
Amanda Boyd
Clare Boyd
Don Boyd
Kate Boyd
Nic Brisbourne
Rebecca Buckle
Xander Cansell
Viv Carbines
Lillian Chandler
Joni Clark
Simon Clark

Tilda Clark
Geoff Deehan
Brian Docherty
Gemma Droughton
Jane Dyball
Jody Dyde
Charlie Finlay
Martin Firrell
Archie Foulds
Norma Fox
Isobel Frankish
Mandy Gage
Denise Gain
Lesley Gilroy
Ellen Goodman
Neil Graham
Kris James Harrison
Caitlin Harvey

Lori Heiss
Violet Herrick
Kirsty Holmes
Rob Holmes
Andy Horton
Wayne Jackman
Gail Jones
Brenda Knox
Nicola Kohut
Jimmy Leach
Peter Lilley
Pete Mackie
John Macmenemey
Susan Mills
John Mitchinson
Hilary Newiss
Margaret Nixon
Simon Nixon
Sean O'Connor
Jenny O'Gorman
Justin Pollard
Mari Roberts
Carolyn Robertson
Paul Robertson
Annie Roddam
Franc Roddam

Patrick Roddam
Alice Sandeman-Allen
Judie Sandeman-Allen
Christoph Sander
Andy Shields
Angie Shields
Ben Shields
Mavis Shields
Shenagh Shields
Steven Shields
Sarah Stacey
Peter Taaffe
Nicole Tibbels
Patricia Tibbels
Jill Tilling
Hayley Tolley
Dixie Turner
Beryl Vertue
Mike Wassall
Carmen Wheatley
Ben Whitehouse
Robin Wight
Felicity Wilkes
Dyllis Wolinski
Neil Wynne
Shuang Zou